The Decision

The Decision

Reuben Bibi

Library of Congress Control Number: 2006907948
ISBN: Hardcover   978-1-4257-3235-6
                   Softcover   978-1-4257-3234-9

The arguments and facts that are presented in the novel relating to religion are from actual Biblical and religious writings and lectures. The historical and scientific facts presented are also from sources that are believed to be true and accurate.

This book was printed in the United States of America.

To order additional copies of this book, contact:
Xlibris Corporation
1-888-795-4274
www.Xlibris.com
Orders@Xlibris.com
35454

1

It was 6:30 in the evening. I always loved coming home to get a hug from my wife, Susan, and little Jennie. Since three months ago, when my son, Eric, was born, I had an added reason to hurry. It was just a short subway ride home and the train was nearing my stop. There was a crowd of people, as usual, but, by now, the main rush hour had already passed. As the train slowed down, I excused myself, and edged toward the doors. A few moments after the doors had slid open, I stepped out onto the platform.

As I walked out of the station and up the steps, I bundled my coat tighter around my body, and redid the belt. I thought of how lucky I was to have met my wife, Susan, and to have been blessed with such beautiful children. This feeling was mixed, however, with an uneasiness. For all the good things that have come to me, I still felt uncomfortable, as if I had lost control.

I got to the top of the steps and looked around. The streets of Manhattan were a voyeur's paradise. There was always something new to notice. The pet store window was being eyed by a dark haired little girl, as the puppies that were behind the window propped up their front legs on the glass, aching to touch their admirer. A businessman, dressed in a stylish suit and tie, stood examining a jewelry store window while holding up his hand to imagine what the ring in the window would look like on his finger. The health club, with a clothing store on the first floor and exercise room on the second floor, was always a place to look at. You never knew when you would get a glimpse of some actor walking in, and you would try to remember whether he was in "Law and Order" or "The Practice". I'd been noticing things on the street more and more, as if, deep down, I was wondering if anyone else was going through what I was experiencing, and, if so, how they would be dealing with it.

As I entered the front glass door of my building, Tom, the doorman, greeted me with his usual cheer. "Good evening, Mr. Klein. It looks like we'll be getting our first snow soon." I smiled back, and said, "When December rolls around, I just feel good that I'll be going away on vacation soon, to a nice, warm beach." Tom was a real winter person. If there was snow in the park on his day off, you would find him pulling a sled loaded with kids, and you wondered if he wasn't really a kid himself.

I passed the sitting area in the lobby and walked up to the elevator. The doors were already open. I went in and pressed 7. The doors closed, and I felt the movement as the elevator was pulled upward. A low bell called out, the doors slid open and I stepped out of the elevator and walked to my door. I looked up to the right of the door at the painted over mezuzah, which I had inherited from the previous tenant, and stared for a moment before putting my key in the lock. With that sound, I heard an excited voice cry out, "Daddy's home!"

As I slowly swung the door open, the patter of little feet, more exhilarating than the finest symphony, wiped out any morose thoughts on my mind. My little Jennie then appeared in the hallway and jumped into my waiting arms to give me a big hug. "You have to see the picture I made! Come! Hurry!" I set her down and she pulled me by the hand to the living room, and pulled a sheet of paper off the coffee table. On it, she had drawn both myself, as well as Susan. I was the stick figure on the right, and behind me was a building with a Jewish star. On the left was Susan, and behind her was a building with a cross. "See", Jennie said excitedly, "I can have the Holidays from both the buildings, and the other children only get to choose from one!"

2

Susan and I met about 6 years ago, on a vacation to Club Med, in Haiti. I guess it was a vacation not so much to meet someone, but to get away from having to meet someone. Every time I would see one of my aunts, I would be greeted with one word. "So?" Never did a single word carry so much meaning behind it, especially when accompanied by raised eyebrows, a tilt of the head, and a pair of open hands. It isn't easy being raised in a Jewish family.

When I was in my early twenties, there was no pressure with dating. You meet someone, and go out just to have a good time. As time went on and I grew a little older, dating was not so easy. But where some of my friends would complain of having a horrible time on a lot of their dates, I never really went through that. I had figured out an angle that made dating a little easier.

I used to love to read up in New York Magazine on different places to go to. It could be a comedy club, an off Broadway play (and sometimes, off-off Broadway), or a restaurant. I would love to go bike riding on Saturday and Sunday, and I would make it a point, after my ride, to pass by any place that seemed interesting but was a place I had never been to before. With that information under my belt, I ended up with a whole list of places that I wanted to go to. That was my angle. When I asked a girl on a date, even if the girl turned out to be horrible company, I at least did what I enjoyed, so that it was still worthwhile.

Even though I got to sample so many different events in the city, my social life was not on a par. Too many girls had the attitude that whatever you did for them was expected. If you were to hold open a car door until they got in, or tipped the maitre' d for a better table, or waited until the end of a play (in an off Broadway production) in order to meet the actors, there was never a 'Thank You'. Nothing was ever good enough.

My vacations were a much needed break. I used to enjoy the different Club Meds because the atmosphere was very relaxing. You weren't going there with the hope of meeting someone to have a long term relationship. People went there from all over the United States, and sometimes from other countries, so the odds of meeting someone who lived nearby were slight.

The first few days would be days to just vegetate. I needed time to blank out from New York and get into "vacation mode". This was a great place to do it. You just sit by the pool or on the beach and hang out during the day. I would never even try to meet anyone at that point. At meal time in the evening, they put you on round tables that seat eight, and you can't help but meet other people. After a few days, you tend to gravitate towards personalities that are most like you. Besides being able to meet during the evenings, there are also opportunities to meet during the activities that take place throughout the day. Those activities also make for a great icebreaker. As long as you are not overly shy, it isn't really hard at all to meet other people, as everyone has a very open attitude.

It was on the third day that I went on a small sailboat they called a Caravelle. The boat was big enough for 6 people, and, that morning, we had a full vessel. It was fun to be taught the basics of how a sailboat works, and everyone was pitching in. That was when I introduced myself to Susan, who happened to also book that trip. I had seen her the day before, and thought to myself how she had a sparkle about her that made it easy to notice her. You could see that she was refined, but she could have fun at the same time.

I can't say that it was love at first sight, although Susan is a very attractive girl. I just felt very comfortable talking to her. It wasn't that she was such a special person, which she was, but it was that she made me feel special when I was just being me.

When the boat finally docked, I was wondering if I should push the relationship, and maybe tell her that I would meet her later. As we climbed out of the boat and started walking on the beach which was right next to the dock, there was an attraction that I felt when I was next to her, and from which I didn't want to break away from. As we walked on the sand, we came across a couple of lounges under a palm tree and stayed there for the rest of the afternoon. It felt like we were speaking together for only a few seconds, but in the meantime, we had skipped lunch, missed several calls to play volleyball in the pool, and didn't even notice how time was passing until we saw the orange glow slowly develop in the sky as the sun started to set.

We ended up meeting by the dinner area and sat together at one of the dinner tables. We just talked to each other, and pretty much shut out the rest of the people on the table. I really hadn't taken in how pretty she was until that evening. She was on the tall side, thin, with long dark hair, and large brown eyes. She definitely had a sparkle about her.

When we had introduced ourselves on the boat, we had only given our first names. I knew her as Susan, and she knew me as Michael. Maybe that's what made it so easy to be ourselves.

It wasn't until the next day that I found out that she was Susan D'Angelo, and she found out that I was Michael Klein. We made a joke about how crazy a match like that would be, but when I was with her, it didn't seem crazy at all, and I could tell she felt the same.

During the rest of the vacation, we stayed pretty much together. Even though I knew, or should I say, thought that I knew that we would not end up with each other, there was an unmistakable feeling that there couldn't be someone more perfect for me. The more each of us thought of each other as forbidden fruit, the less we wanted to let go.

When we both returned to New York we kept on seeing each other. Whatever I was doing with her, even if it was something I had done several times before, felt like a new experience, because I was now doing it with Susan. The differences in our background didn't matter to me so much, because, though my background was Jewish, all I knew about my religion was that on Rosh Hashanah and Yom Kippur, you didn't go to work.

3

Even though I was raised to know that I was Jewish by birth, the ritual part of the religion was absent. Religious prohibitions were meant for a different time and were thought to be archaic. Those Jews who still practiced the religion were thought of as relics, out of touch with today's world. I went to public school and then Baruch College. My only encounter with learning anything to do with Judaism was during my Bar Mitzvah lessons. I could never even understand why I was being Bar Mitzvahed. The Rabbi taught us that the Bible was inspired by God, though it was written by Moses and that the stories in the Bible were created to teach us things, and they were just that, only stories. Being kosher was considered no longer necessary since the kosher laws were really for health reasons. We now understood that you had to cook meat properly, and you had to be careful of tainted food. Our medications nullified the effects of any food that was originally considered to have been not kosher and which may not have been good for us. Sabbath laws were to force us to relax, as people use to have to work for seven days. Now we only have a five day work week and we have both Saturday and Sunday to relax. All in all, my upbringing revealed Judaism to be a religion that couldn't keep up with the times.

Both of my parents and all of my grandparents were born in the United States. My family came here around 1880. I guess there was a general feeling by many immigrant families that to be an American, you had to blend in with the people that were already here. America was always thought of as being the great melting pot. Despite the fact that we were told to blend in with society, we were reminded that we still had to be good Jews. What was a good Jew? A Jew was measured by his character. A Jew showed kindness to others and led by example. In this way, the Jew's actions were a light unto the world.

My parents, Jonathan and Margaret, were raised with this way of thinking and raised me with the same type of ideas. The idea of everyone being equal, with the Jew personifying a higher level of kindness, became confusing to me when I found Susan to be kinder and to have more fine qualities than most Jews. In a sense, she became the epitome of what I should look for in a Jewish girl.

Even though this twisted logic made sense to me, my parents were still under the impression that only a Jewish girl could correctly "act Jewish". The only way I could convince them that Susan was a perfect wife for me was for them to see that she had all those qualities that they always told me to look for.

My opportunity came very quickly. My younger brother, Steven, was graduating college, and my parents were making a small party for him. I decided that that would be a good time for me to introduce Susan, as I would be able to cut the night short if anyone asked anything which was more than a superficial question, like, for example, what was her last name. Before that time, I hadn't even told anyone in my family that I was dating anyone.

My parents decided to take Steven out to an Italian restaurant in Bay Ridge, Brooklyn, as my father loved Italian food. I told my parents ahead of time that I would not be able to stay long, but I would be bringing a friend. My mother caught on as to what I meant.

I was very lucky that night. One of Steven's teachers had come to the restaurant so that when I came in, I was almost a non-event except to my mother. But from the corner of my eye, I could see her examining Susan; from the way she dressed (that night, she had what you could call a "preppie" look), to the way she smiled, to her posture, and how she spoke. When I saw a slight smile form on my mother's lips, I knew that Susan got my mother's seal of approval. Once she learned of Susan's background, she would not be so happy, but how much could she object when she was everything a Jewish boy could want?

After what I considered to be a very successful hour, I made my excuses and we left the restaurant. Neither of us was really comfortable because it was as though we were playing a game of deception. I convinced first myself, and then Susan, that this would be the best way. First, let them get to see her, and then, the objections would not be as great.

The next day, first thing in the morning, my mother called me at the office just to see how I was doing, and to tell me that she felt bad that I couldn't stay. She asked me if the family would be seeing Susan again, and how Susan seemed like a very nice girl. I evaded a direct answer, with a reply like, "It's just the beginning stages, but she happens to be someone very special. We'll just see what develops."

I would have liked it if things went on like that, with our relationship shrouded in mystery, with my hopeful parents, who had no idea of the truth, pushing me on.

I wasn't even thinking of the meeting that I would be having with Susan's parents. It was a lot more blunt and it happened a lot sooner than I was ready for.

4

Normally, when I went out with Susan, I would pick her up from an apartment that she shared in the city with two of her friends. The day after my brother's party, Susan asked if I could pick her up at the end of the week, on Friday night, from her parents' house in Brooklyn, as she had wanted to bring some things from there to her apartment in the city. On Friday morning, she called me at the office and said that when she mentioned to her parents that I would be stopping by, they asked if they could meet me.

I couldn't tell her no, especially after I had brought Susan to meet my parents in the way that I did. I began to wonder if her parents would be as upset as I knew my parents were going to be. Images of her father standing over me with a baseball bat, while threatening me to be good to his daughter or else, kept coming into my mind.

The reality was that she came from a well to do, respectable family. Her father was a real estate lawyer, and did fairly well, both as a lawyer and an investor. Being that my father and I owned a sizable amount of real estate, I hoped that our common business would be a starting point for a conversation. All during that day, though, my mind was pre-occupied with how this night would turn out.

When Friday night came and I drove out to Susan, I was still very nervous. The apprehension I felt when I brought Susan to my own parents was still lingering in me, and truthfully, I was feeling a little drained from the mental pressure I was putting myself under. I had no idea what to expect, but I did know that they were aware that I was Jewish. According to Susan, they were not really thrilled with the idea. Her mother had always pictured having a Catholic wedding for her daughter. She didn't know how the different religions would affect her daughter's future life. Her father was more reserved in his reaction, and he ultimately said that it was important for her to be happy.

Susan's parents live in Bay Ridge, not far from the Verrazano Bridge. I found a parking spot down the block from the corner where their house is. As I walked down the block while looking for the correct house number, I noticed that the homes were all very nice and well kept. The sun had just set and the sky had an orange glow in the distance, which gave a very soft appearance to the area. I found the house and I noticed that you could see part of the Bridge from their corner and the view was like a picture postcard. I tried to take in the serenity of the view to keep me calm, like a Yoga master repeating the word "Ohm" again and again, to push out all of my nervous thoughts. It didn't work.

I went up the walkway to the door, and pressed the bell. The outside of the house was very nicely tended. The colors of the flowers around the house all had an orange cast in some areas because of the setting sun, but the yellows and reds of the flowers on either side of the walkway were apparent from the soft glow of the lights that were arranged on each side of the concrete path. This gave the front of the house a very country feeling.

I rang the bell, and to my relief, Susan answered the door. I knew I should not have been so edgy, but I so much wanted to make the right first impression. Having Susan greet me and bring me into the house, with her radiant smile, relaxed me more than a dozen sunsets could.

The house had been decorated years before, but still had a nice look. It was very contemporary and plush. Once inside, I noticed that the sofa was oversized and a light color, with dark throw cushions neatly arranged against the sofa back. To the side of that room was the dining room with silver leaf chairs and a sleek looking table and breakfront. When my parents had redone their house several years ago, I had gone with them to look at some of the things they were ordering. I recognized some of this furniture as being similar to things my parents had in their house. It was another example of common ground that I could bring out.

Susan's father came out from the kitchen area first, followed by her mother. Her mother looked very much like Susan with that same type of glow. Her father was very dignified and well dressed. He smiled and reached out for my hand as he approached me. He said, "Susan has been speaking a lot about you. It's nice to finally meet you." I complimented them on their taste in the house, and mentioned that my parents had similar pieces in their home. Basic light conversation. I figured I would just have an easy time of it as I did with my own parents earlier in the week.

Susan's father then turned to me and said, "Michael, let's sit in the den for a few minutes. The girls have something to do in the kitchen." Although a sense of dread came over me, I kept up my outward display of calm. As

Susan got up with her mother and went to the kitchen, I felt like I was in for it, but I realized I may as well plunge in and deal with it.

Before we even sat down, Susan's father continued. "I always believe in being direct. There's no use in dancing around a subject you want to discuss. I don't want to make this too heavy, but I have to bring out certain concerns that my wife and I have with your relationship with our daughter."

He was now in total control of the conversation. I became totally unaware of what the room looked like or whether I sat on a chair or a sofa. I just became very aware of everything about Susan's father, from the tailored collar on his pale blue shirt and solid colored silk tie to the way he parted his graying hair, to his deep but gentle voice.

"I'm wondering how much you and Susan have discussed the future of your relationship. She happens to like you very much, and it appears that you feel the same for her. What concerns me is not that you'll be kind to her. I know that my daughter has an excellent sense of character, and would only choose to be with someone who is kind and caring. My concern is for what happens in the future, when, hopefully, you would start a family. With you being Jewish, and we being Catholic, how would the children be raised?"

I answered almost by reflex, as that question was something I knew that my parents would ask. I had reviewed over and over how I could answer. I felt the reply would not be totally satisfying, but it came from my heart. With all of the confidence I could muster, I told him "I really love your daughter and I know she feels the same for me. We could try to focus on the morality of our religions and try to impress that on our children. I have to admit that I was never raised to do all of the acts that Orthodox Jews do, because what really matters is how you treat people. That's the essence of the religion."

"So you think that the acts associated with different religions no longer have any meaning?"

I thought of something that I had heard in a sermon by our Rabbi during the high holidays a few years ago. I continued, "About two thousand years ago, there was a great Rabbi, who was asked by a foreigner if the Rabbi could teach him the whole Bible while the foreigner stood on one foot. Although other Rabbis had dismissed this person, this particular Rabbi agreed. He told him "Do not do unto others what you do not want done to yourself. The rest of the Bible is just commentary to this. Go and learn it." [1] So if that's the essence, then it boils down to how each person treats the other, not whether or not you went to synagogue or to mass every week."

He smiled at this reply. He seemed to enjoy this back and forth debate.

"So", he answered, "you want to focus on the morality that the Bible teaches. You must be well read in the Bible to be able to separate the acts that we're commanded to do and to just go straight to the moral teaching."

I was a little puzzled by his answer. "I don't follow you", I said.

"Very often in life, we go through situations and we seek guidance as to the proper thing that we should do. If we want to be charitable, for example, is it proper to give half of our money to causes? We know from the Bible, your Old Testament, in fact, that the Lord wants us to give ten percent. We are required to be kind to the poor, or the orphaned, and that is what tells us what is morally right and wrong. In fact, many of the laws in this country are based on Biblical laws that were established when the colonists first came to this country, since the laws of the Bible determined what the law of the land should be."

"But", I replied, "People know in their hearts what's right and what's wrong. The Bible gave us a guideline to how we should live, but it doesn't always apply to our everyday laws in our time. After all, that's what the separation of Church and State in this country is all about."

"Yes", he countered, "this country is famous for its doctrine of the separation of Church and State. But the problem with the standards of morality of the State, are when those standards veer too far from those of the Church."

He paused for a moment to collect his thoughts, but then continued speaking. "I can understand your way of thinking. After all, the Constitution of the United States makes no mention of G-d. Thomas Jefferson, who wrote the Constitution, was considered an atheist in his time. In fact, the entire graduating class of Yale University of 1796 did not believe in G-d save for one graduate.[2]

"In both Europe and America, the late eighteenth century and early nineteenth century were famous as the era of the Industrial Revolution. Science became the religion of the day, and the cracks in the foundations of religion were already being laid. Erasmus Darwin, the grandfather of Charles, was already formulating his own theory of evolution, as it pertained to plant life. He was part of a group of men who would meet once a month, at the height of the full moon, to discuss scientific theory, and they were known as the lunar men. Besides Darwin, you had men like James Watt, of steam engine fame; Josiah Wedgewood, who founded Wedgewood China; Mathew Boulton, who merged both science and commerce, as well as others.[3]

"They never strayed too far from religion because their morality was still rooted deeply in the religious morals of their day. They still read the Bible and were aware of its lessons. In fact, when I asked you if you read the Bible to study its moral teachings, I was thinking of Thomas Jefferson who did just that. He put together what is known as the Jefferson Bible, which is the Bible with the episodes of miraculous events literally crossed out. He humanized Jesus and the Disciples. But he maintained that the morality of the Bible could not be discarded.[4]"

"From what you're saying about Thomas Jefferson," I said, "it seems like you agree with me that the morality of the Bible can be separated from those acts the Bible says we should perform."

"Not really", he continued. "Once you start to choose which parts of the Bible should be followed and which should not, you're putting yourselves over G-d. You're letting your personal views cloud what's right and wrong. That could set you upon a dangerous path, which could ultimately lead subsequent generations to disaster.

"You say that you know what's right because you follow your heart. Let's look at others who followed their hearts. Those who are part of the Mafia exhibit a great deal of respect for their parents, and yet have no mercy when it comes to killing. They've accepted upon themselves the commandment to honor their parents, but have somehow justified their disregard of the commandment of not killing. On the other extreme, even certain people who appear to follow the outward signs of these symbolic acts, sometimes lose sight of the fact that these acts are to teach them to do the right thing. I often see people who appear to be pious get caught breaking the law in business matters, when, in their religious life, they try to be pure. It's because each of these groups pick and choose what they want to follow, instead of accepting all of what G-d has told them to do as holy.

"All of those acts that we do, whether it's celebrating Christmas by giving gifts, or going to mass, or going to confession, makes it easier for us to realize that we are subservient to a higher authority.

"People learn by example. When you want to take away those acts that you feel are unimportant, you take away the physical symbols that remind us, on a daily basis, that there is someone over us. Your personal bias in deciding what to keep and what to discard has to come into play. Teaching and performing these religious symbolic acts in their entirety must be coupled with the knowledge that the purpose is for us to have more fulfilling lives. At a certain point, we have to follow what was laid down by G-d, or by our religious leaders in G-d's name. It will only lead to our benefit."

He again paused to allow his words to sink in before proceeding. "My point is that this is especially true when it comes to children. When a child sees his parents helping others, he wants to emulate them. When a child sees his parents praying to G-d, and doing those acts that G-d wants us to do, he more readily accepts that there is a higher authority that must be followed. By accepting the Bible as our moral compass, we remove our personal definitions of morality. Our own biases no longer cloud our understanding of right and wrong and our children are taught the same thing.

"The symbols of your religion are different from mine. My symbols say that your religion does not have to be followed because a new world has come as a result of Jesus' suffering, while your symbols point to no change in the world order. They are not compatible with each other. You can't give a child both, because there will come a day when that child has to choose which symbols he'll follow, and if he can't make a choice because each is ingrained in him from childhood as holy, then he may choose neither of these and turn to science as his G-d.

"You quoted a story about a Rabbi from two thousand years ago. It sounds like you look up to him for what he said. Did you consider examining if he also decided to discard the symbolic acts of his religion and just believe in the moral teachings of the Bible exclusively? I'm not familiar with who he is or what he did, but I can be certain that he coupled his understanding of the purpose of his religious acts, with the religious acts themselves.

"In my business, an hour spent anticipating and preparing to avoid a potential problem up ahead can save weeks and even months of agony in the future. I'm not going to tell you not to continue seeing my daughter, but there's a problem up ahead that you have to prepare yourself for. To preserve the true sense of right and wrong in future generations, religion with its symbols must be preserved. Ultimately, children can be either Catholic or Jewish, but they can't be both, and if the two of you understand that from now, maybe you can decide how you'll handle this problem in the future.

"I've already spoken to Susan about how I feel. Now it's up to the two of you to discuss it."

We both got up, and he smiled and patted me on the back, I guess to give me encouragement. He felt that he had gotten his point across, but I felt that Susan and I could overcome the difficulties that he foresaw ahead of us.

We stayed a little while longer for some coffee. About five minutes into the drive away from her house back to the city, I noticed some people with skullcaps on, who were walking away from a synagogue. I realized it was Friday night, and after sundown. The Sabbath had started. My mind went back to the conversation with Susan's father, and I wondered, but then I pushed those thoughts out of my mind.

5

I didn't like having any doubts as to how right my marriage to Susan would be. I simply refused to consider the possibility of a conflict that the two of us could not work out. It's like they say in fairy tales: true love conquers all.

The thought that this marriage would be anything less than perfect made me push harder to get everyone to just accept it as a fait acomplis[5]. I fortified my resolve to fully commit to this relationship, and I decided to confront my mom and dad and just tell them what I decided.

The next morning, on Saturday, I called my parents, and spoke to my mom. I told her that I wanted to pass by on Sunday and talk to her and dad. She was still totally unaware of the bombshell that I would be dropping.

I knew that it was better that I go without Susan, in case they said something in the surprise of the moment that may hurt her. When I got to the house, my mother looked like she had been preparing for hours, and was trying to hide the excitement that she felt would come with my announcement. My father was being nonchalant and had Friday's newspaper on the table, which he was feigning to read.

"I've got something to tell you, which I think is good news, and I hope you'll take it that way. It has to do with the girl that I've been seeing; you know, Susan, who I brought to Steven's party last week?

"The truth is we feel very strongly about each other and we'll be getting engaged soon."

With that my mother got up and started to give me a hug, while saying, "I knew it. From the moment I saw her, I could see that she was someone we would want in our family." My father also rose, with a smile that betrayed his often repressed emotions.

"Who is her family? What's their name? Where do they live?" My mother began to throw questions at me like an out of order pitching machine in a batting cage.

"I think you should sit down for this one, Mom. Her full name is Susan D'Angelo."

My mother's hug loosened. There was dead silence for several seconds, which I didn't want to break. I wasn't sure how to proceed and was waiting for my parents' reaction first. With my mother being so close to me, in the middle of a hug, I was doubly uncomfortable, to say the least.

My father appeared dumbstruck, and he suddenly turned stone like, and stared at me. My mother wasn't as much at a loss for words as my father. She slowly pushed away from me and I could see that the realization of what I said sank in. Within just a few seconds she gained her composure, and, like an angry prosecuting attorney, started peppering me with questions and statements again, but with a belligerency that I wasn't prepared for. She started with, "What did you say? You couldn't have! Why are you doing this? This can't be happening. It must be a dream." In between her remarks, I kept telling her that it was true, and that I loved Susan and we could work out whatever differences we had. She stopped suddenly, and stared at me, with a burning intensity, and said, "Why are you doing this to us? Why are you doing this?"

My father walked to my mother and held her and told her, very softly, to sit down. He looked at me and said, "You're coming to us now, and after you're experiencing what you think is love. I should have spoken to you about what you were doing, and who you were with. I felt that once you grew up, you would use whatever we taught you to know right and wrong. But it isn't too late. This is wrong, and I want you to see that."

"All of my life you taught me to find a good person", I calmly answered. "I don't understand what it is that you could be objecting to. Here is a girl that is good and that until this morning, you yourselves felt would be a great match for me. The quality of the person is more important than anything else. What changed from yesterday to today? She's still the same person you would have accepted with open arms. She's still the person that you yourself said was someone who you would be proud to have in this family. Think about it. I don't know what this whole religion thing is all about and why you're just now getting all upset. It was never important to you before."

"We raised you to be a good Jewish boy." My father said these words very slowly. "It's true that the laws don't have meaning anymore. We taught you that. But Jews have to remain Jews. A Jewish boy marries a Jewish girl. That's the way it is."

"Dad, you're not making sense. If you look at a Jewish girl as someone that has good values, and is kind, and would make a good wife and mother, why can't I choose someone that I love that has those qualities? Why does it have to be a Jewish girl who has cornered the market on goodness and kindness? Don't you think that I tried going out with Jewish girls? All I found were girls who were spoiled and selfish. They wanted to know what I could do for them, and never the other way around. That's why this girl is different. She cares about what I feel, and what I say. She likes to be with me for me, and it doesn't matter if I take her to a fancy restaurant or to a simple bagel shop. It makes her just as happy when I bring her a single flower for her hair, as when I surprise her with an expensive leather handbag. She appreciates what I do. Isn't that what I'm supposed to look for, to be with someone who would make me happy?"

I could see that my mother's hardness was softening. She understood from my words the pain of dating, and she understood my happiness at finding someone who I could make a life with. My father, on the other hand, seemed to be holding back. It was as though there was some other argument that he wanted to throw at me, but felt he couldn't.

My mother wanted me to consider again some of the girls, the Jewish girls, that I had gone out with in the past. In response, I lay bare my emotions and started to list out those girls, and described their character which I know my parents would never have approved of, and which I could not have lived with. My mother was breaking down fast.

"Mom, Dad, I'm going to be bringing Susan here one night this week. Look at her again as a person, and don't look to see how she prays. All I'm asking is that you take the time to see again what you saw last week, and what I see in her every time I'm with her. Please."

With that, I got my hug from my mother, along with some leftover tears on her cheek. From my father, there was the silence of defeat.

6

Needless to say, we survived parental scrutiny, with a lot more episodes of conflict than I care to recount. Our wedding had both a priest and a rabbi officiating, and Susan and I agreed to respect each other's religions in the house. We celebrated Xmas with a tree, and I called it a Hanukah Bush[6]. We set up an electric menorah[7], something I must admit I don't ever remember doing in my house as we grew up, but we kept it lit with all eight lights throughout the holidays. The truth is, I didn't know what day Hanukah started and on what day it ended, and it was just easier for me to keep all of the bulbs lit all of the time. On Xmas we gave each other gifts, and I went to her family's house for their get-together.

For Passover, Susan bought a box of matzahs[8] for me, and I would have the matzah instead of bread with my meals. Occasionally we would go out to Denny's or some other restaurant during the holiday, and Susan made sure that they never brought bread to the table, so as not to tempt me.

Easter and Xmas, and the days leading up to them, were always a time when Susan would go to Church. I guess they were like her High Holidays[9]. I would go with her, and we would sit side by side in the pews. She would participate in the hymns while I would look around at all of the statues and stained glass, all the while marveling at the workmanship. The sermons would hit home, and in a way, they sounded very similar to the sermons that I heard in my synagogue when I went on Rosh Hashana and Yom Kippur. There were stories about honesty, kindness, and examples from the Bible of how certain people exemplified those desirable qualities that we should all emulate.

As a result of Susan's prodding, I became a regular in the synagogue during my High Holidays. I really hadn't always gone in the past, as it was enough that I stayed home from work. Susan, though, didn't want me to feel short changed in respecting only her religion, so she made sure that I attended synagogue. On Yom Kippur, though, I had always broken the fast in the early afternoon, and I never stopped that habit. Better some fasting than nothing.

Jennie was born a little over a year after our marriage. It was only a few months after that when Susan's father had a mild heart attack and had to be hospitalized. If there is one sure effect of a heart attack, it is that the family's ties to religion increase exponentially.

On one of our visits to the hospital, the priest of Susan's church also happened to be visiting my father in law. Although I had never taken the time to remain in the church to speak to the Father, I guess he knew who I was, since I was the only Klein attending services. My name had made me an instant celebrity.

The priest, Father Nicholas Baldino, knew my wife's family well, and greeted me kindly in the hospital. "Perhaps", he said to me, "you could come to services this Sunday and stay for a little while? It may be good for you to understand a little more about the religion that your wife's family follows." My wife, who was standing next to me, looked at me, waiting to see what I would say. She never wanted to push me to speak to any of the clergy, but I could feel that she wanted me to learn more about the things she felt so strongly about. Almost like a marionette being directed by strings attached to the different parts of its body, I felt my lips mouthing an affirmative reply in response to an invisible force emanating from my wife's beseeching eyes.

Before this time, I had never accompanied my wife to Sunday services unless it was a special holiday. Even though I agreed to go, I couldn't push myself that next Sunday to do so. My thoughts that I would be going to Church for myself and not because I was going with Susan, bothered my Jewish sensibilities. It wasn't until the second Sunday after my short conversation with the priest that I ended up going. By delaying my trip to the Church by a week, I felt like I was exhibiting some sort of control over my life. I guess it was a mental justification that I wasn't being swept up by something beyond what I could handle.

That second Sunday morning came, and I reluctantly got out of bed to get dressed. Susan hadn't spoken to me about my decision, but I knew that her religion was very important to her. Despite our initial agreement regarding each other's religious beliefs, she still felt I was missing out by not following the teachings of the Church. I could sense her willing my shirt buttons to close by themselves faster than I was doing it, and the thought of her turning into one of the X-men and using her powers on me to make me get dressed faster made me laugh.

I was very much in robot mode when I left the house with Susan. In what seemed like the blink of an eye, we left the house, got to the Church, and were walking through the entrance doors. We walked directly to a set of seats without hesitation, then sat and waited.

Father Baldino came out after hymns, to give his Sunday sermon, and slowly eyed the crowd. He briefly surveyed the congregants, and hesitated a moment as his eyes caught mine. I could see a trace of a smile come to his face, just as my face turned slightly red.

My eyes moved away from his and they jumped to the perimeter of the room. I became acutely aware of the multitude of statues arranged, like a permanent audience, all around us. Every ten feet or so stood another statue that was so lifelike you could sense the emotions etched into each face. I always wondered what could occupy students for hours a day over several years in religious schools. As I counted the number of statues I had a thought that it would probably keep those kids busy just trying to memorize the names on all of the statues in this room.

"Each of us", he began, with his arms outstretched and his palms opened wide, "has concerns which are unique, concerns which sometimes evolve into problems, sometimes into difficulties and sometimes into crises. It is that very uniqueness of our concerns that make us feel alone. We feel as if there is no one that we could reach out to. That there is no one who could fully understand what it is that we are feeling.

"King Solomon said that there is nothing new under the sun[10]. As unique as our problems feel, they, as well as the problems of everyone else in the world, all have a common element. All of "the slings and arrows of outrageous fortune"[11] are sent to try and shake our faith. We can succumb to our feelings of despondency, or we can turn these feelings into a resolve that will strengthen us.

"No man was ever subjected to more difficult trials than Job[12]. He lost his wealth, and that alone can shatter the self-esteem of most men. He then lost his children, but it didn't end there. He lost his wife and was now alone in the world. But his test was not complete. He was afflicted with illness and was forced to be a beggar. The Lord wanted to show the world what true faith was, and Job was given an inner strength, but how much can a man bear? His faith seemed to waiver, but he remained strong in his belief in the judgment of G-d. The Lord looked down on him, and returned his blessings at the end of his life. Job married again, had more children, and regained his lost wealth. He actually gained so much more. He passed his test of faith in the Lord. We read of his rewards in this world, but he was also rewarded beyond our comprehension in the world of the spirit. He confronted Satan and was victorious for the Lord.

"When we read of the apostle Paul, we always think of him as the primary proponent of the teachings of Jesus. But we forget that he, too, was tested. He began his life as Saul of Tarsys, a Jew who rejected Jesus. He was so possessed by Satan that he was a persecutor of those who followed the teachings of Jesus. He hunted down his fellow Jews, and even put many of them to death. He gradually came to realize the truth, however, and became the most ardent supporter of our Lord. He turned away from sin and led many of his fellow Jews on the proper path. He had a greater calling however, and he reached out to those outside of the Jewish faith, and spread the word of the Gospel to the world.

"Jesus said, "Behold, I stand at the door and knock. If any man will open the door, I will come in." You see, he asks permission of you to enter. He does not force his way into your life. He asks, can I come in to help you with your life, with your marriage, with teaching your children the right path to choose? He offers his love and waits patiently for our reply. By accepting him we allow him to come into our lives so that we can be saved. We must remember his mission on this earth, from his words, "I have come that you may have life."[13]

"Every day, we are faced with temptations which are meant to turn us away from the Lord. Every day, we must gird ourselves for battle with sin. We cannot rest on what we have already accomplished. Yesterday's manna will not suffice for tomorrow. We must look at each day of our lives, and at each occurrence throughout the day, as the Lord's test, which will allow us to rise to ever-greater spiritual heights once we pass it. As long as we embrace Jesus, he will accompany us on these tests, and help us to overcome the influence of Satan so that we may achieve the rewards that G-d wants us to have."

There was a silence that enveloped the room as the Father completed his remarks. The clicking of his shoes on the floor, as he stepped off the dais, was clear and sharp. A slowly rising sound came from the congregants, as each of them began saying the word, Amen. The statues, too, now seemingly imbued with a soul of their own, appeared to join the affirmation of the chorus that rose up from the center of the room. The mournful expressions and sorrowful eyes of those stone figures were beseeching anyone who looked at them to repent.

I wondered, as I rose, as to whether he chose that sermon for my benefit, especially when he referenced Saul as a Jew who was saved by believing in Jesus. It was as though the sermon was being directed to me. Before I could collect my thoughts, he came down and walked directly to myself and to Susan. He asked if we enjoyed the sermon, and, to me, he asked if there were any questions that I had. He could sit with us a few minutes if we would like. I hesitated, but Susan didn't want to pass up this chance, and said how we would like to sit with him.

I had no sense of what was right and what was wrong. I just decided to clear my mind and listen. The validity of the messages were comforting in one sense, but a small doll like image of myself, which stood at the corner of my eye, still kept repeating, "but you're a Jew". The image, though, was becoming smaller and smaller.

We went with the Father to his private quarters, passing several more statues, which now appeared to be guards who would stand over the exits and prevent my escape. With the Father leading, Susan following and me in tow and holding Susan's hand, we proceeded down a hallway with an arched Gothic ceiling. Each door that we passed was about nine feet high, and rounded at the top. They each had recessed panels and all the woodwork had a soft sheen, as if they were slowly aged to perfection. We came across a door with a gold nameplate, on which was written Father Baldino, and we entered.

The room was all done with wood wall paneling in the same type of wood as the doors in the hall. An open bookcase stood to one side, filled with books on theology. To the back of the room was a large desk, with a tall leather tufted chair behind it. In front of the desk was a large area that was delineated by a deeply hued oriental carpet, with a series of chairs over it to seat about a half dozen people. The Father sat in one of those chairs and motioned for us to sit as well.

He only had a few minutes, and, as I didn't have questions, he said, "In the sermon today, I only touched on the forgiveness aspect of Christianity. When we focus on Jesus, we tend to first think of him dying for us on the cross, to make amends for our sins. But we forget that there is another part of our belief, which is embodied in the resurrection. Once we are able to atone for our actions, we are ready to live a life of purity, and that's what a resurrection must lead to. You see, the resurrection goes beyond the resurrection of Jesus alone. When the blind man is cured, when the lame man is able to walk, we are witnessing the rebirth of these people. In the same way, each of us undergoes a resurrection after we accept the Lord, and we can only grow from our efforts to delve into truth.

"The most confusing thing for us when we first discover the Lord, is to determine the type of behavior the Lord wants us to follow. What do we do after we accept the Lord and confess to the sins of our past actions?

"People have a misconception when they read of the people mentioned in the Bible. We tend to look at those people as exceptions. It is superhuman for a Moses to speak to G-d. It is superhuman for a Queen Esther to risk her life and stand before King Ahasverosh, it is superhuman for a King David to suffer so many losses in his life and still maintain a strong faith in G-d. These people are not exceptions, however. They are examples. They show how we are to act and we must learn from them and try to emulate their qualities.

"Michael, it's difficult for me to encapsulate the whole religion in a single sentence, but the religion is one of love of the Lord for all of his creatures. Through that love, we can rise to unlimited heights.

"There are so many other things that we can touch on. Anytime you would like to come and sit in on a class, we would be happy to explain more to you. It's best to learn a little bit each time, so that you can digest it all. Michael, I thank you for coming and for giving us the chance to explain to you what Susan has found so much happiness with."

With that, we all rose, and both Susan and I shook the Father's hand. As we left to go back to the apartment, Susan was holding my arm close to her and seemed to be very content. I was content to have her there, but there was a tiny image, that kept trying to attract my attention, that I could still see out of the corner of my eye.

7

Over the next several years I made it a practice to go to Father Baldino's classes. I learned more about the stories in the Old Testament during that time than during my entire adolescence. There was so much that should have been a part of my education, but was just skipped over. It's odd that it took a Catholic priest to give me lessons on my own Bible.

Along with the Old Testament, I was taught about the New. Some of the lessons he gave were probably given for my benefit, as they covered prophecy from the holy books written pre Jesus, which foretold of a Messiah, and how the coming of Jesus satisfied these prophecies. I became familiar to some extent with a who's who of the men and women referred to in the New Testament, which made it easier for me to understand what was being discussed during the sermons and classes.

For the Church, there was sanctity to the words of the Bible that wasn't present in the Judaism I grew up with. The words of the Bible were believed to come from G-d. The belief in a divine figure, actively taking part in the lives of the general populace was part of the core foundation of Christianity. The practices that Moses required of the nation were from G-d's mouth, and were valid at the time that he gave them. According to Christianity, once Jesus came, a Messianic period began which did away with many of those practices. That made more sense than my Rabbi saying that we just outgrew those laws one day.

The Reform Judaism in which I was raised, proposed a hidden G-d, who was more interested in guiding the ignorant people of the past. Because of the advances in science in the last few hundred years, these practices had now become unnecessary. We have outgrown all of the decrees imposed on the Jewish people. Jews were to be separate from the rest of the people of the world, but, as far as I could see, we didn't do anything to keep us separate in this day and age, except remember certain High Holy Days. Those days in synagogue, though, were without the fear and desire to repent which I saw in Christianity. Everyone in synagogue just kept wondering how quickly the services would be over so they could carry on with their lives.

When I studied for my Bar Mitzvah, I was taught that G-d declared that the Jews were to follow certain laws. I had always wondered why G-d's laws and decrees would not be eternal. My Rabbi explained that the five books of Moses were just that; a set of laws based on that time period, prefaced with stories of the ancestors of the Jewish people. The way I learned it, Moses recorded that information through divine inspiration. Many of the laws also came from the ancient laws of Hammurabi.[14] Those were in practice over five hundred years before the time of Moses, and were well entrenched even by the time Abraham was born. Moses expanded on those laws and they became the basis of the Jewish religion.

On my Bar Mitzvah, I wore my Tefillin[15], only to pack them up afterward so they would never see the light of day again. Recognition of my becoming a man was composed of my giving a speech about being accepted into the Jewish community, with thanks to my parents, grandparents and relatives. This was followed by a circus themed party where we all danced to the disco music and ended with each member of my family lighting one of the candles of my cake. The next day, other than being tired and being allowed to sleep late, I felt no different than before, nor did I do anything different from before.

I never really thought much about religion until I started going to Father Baldino's classes. My wife's religion was so appealing that I honestly would have converted at that point in my life, but there were two things that stopped me. The first was my father. I worked with him, and judging from my parents' reaction to my marriage and their efforts to dissuade me, I knew my father would have completely lost it if I left Judaism. The second thing was Susan's father. No, it's not what you would first think. You see, I found out that after Jennie was born, my father-in-law told Susan that she now had a family, and whatever children we have should be raised with a religious foundation. Being that I was oblivious to my own religion, her father felt that Susan should focus on teaching the children Christianity. I guess I should have seen it coming, especially after the talk we had when we first met, but my Jewish survival instincts were put into play, and I didn't want my Jewishness to just evaporate into nothing.

From all of this, I was becoming one very confused person. I didn't want to give up my Jewish heritage, but I felt my Jewish identity really had no meaning. Susan's Christianity was so much more fulfilling, but thoughts of my Jewish identity dying with me were still very unsettling. Hitler tried to destroy the Jews and failed, but here I was allowing my Jewish identity to die in a different way. I was losing no matter which way I turned.

8

The years have a way of passing quickly. My attendance at the Father's classes became a regular part of my life. After each day when I went to work and saw my father, and reflected on his feelings, it made me want to hold on to Judaism. I had a recurring nightmare that I was driving down a highway while the car was directly over the center of the solid white line between the lanes. A police officer up ahead, that happened to look like my father in law, was telling me that I had to choose one lane only. I must get to the right or the left, and I had to make the decision now. I would always wake up in a sweat.

Jennie was now about four and a half years old. It was just last night that she gave me the drawing of myself and Susan that showed my wife's Church in her background and a synagogue in mine. She was proud to have both religions in her life. I was condemning her to ride the same road in the future as I now ride in my dreams. I knew that one day she would have to make a choice. Which lane should she take? Unfortunately, her father, unlike my own, had no strong Jewish feelings to impart. To her, the choice would be no dilemma at all. When I considered that, I felt I lost her already, and feelings of defeat would compound the confusion that had been building up in me all of these years.

I arose that morning, and got ready. I looked out of the window and saw that it was still a little dark outside. It was winter, and the sun hadn't risen yet. My inner gloom was matched by the view outside my window. It was not quite day, but not quite night, as if the heavens had not yet decided whether or not the day would even be arriving.

My doorman, Tom, gave his usual cheery greeting, and I wondered what kind of problems he faced each day. I tried to absorb his positive attitude. As I walked to the subway, the rays of the sun were starting to peak through the buildings and I walked in their path to feel the warmth of their glow.

My short subway ride exposed me to smiling faces and glimpses of conversations that centered on gifts that had been bought, and requests for suggestions for gifts that were not bought yet. During the walk to my office, bright red and green lights adorned the buildings, while store windows were filled with Xmas symbols on which crystals of fake snow were sprinkled. In the corner of most windows was a menorah with its unlit red bulbs. It was as though the menorah was telling me that in the midst of all of this excitement and the competition from all the colored lights throughout the city, don't forget my lights. They may not be the brightest, or the most obvious, but the light will reach into my heart. Thoughts of my own electric menorah in my house, with all eight bulbs already lit for several weeks now, appeared in my mind. All of a sudden, a desire to understand what the lights meant began to take hold of my heart.

My office was on the third floor of one of the buildings that we owned. It was still a little early and the employees were just coming in. My father was to be out today, as he had a meeting in the office of the bank that we used regarding a property that we were in the process of buying. Within a half hour, the office was full, and the hum of printers working, coupled with the sound of the voices of people speaking into their phones and to each other, filled the air.

After lunch, one of our employees, David Greenblatt, came up to me. "Tonight is the first night of Hanukah", he said. He would usually ask my father if he could leave a little earlier to light his candles for the holiday, a request which my father always granted. As my father was out, he wanted to clear it with me. I couldn't pass up this chance to find out more about what these days were all about and I asked him.

"It's a time of year for miracles" he began. He knew that I really had no background at all to start from. I could also tell that he hesitated as he spoke to me, as though he wanted to explain, but didn't want to go out of his way to proselytize, as he didn't want to upset my father by putting religious ideas in his son's head.

"There was a great miracle which happened then. About 2,300 years ago, the Greeks had defiled the Temple in Jerusalem, and the Jews, though few in number, fought back. The Greeks of that time period were a world power, and it was considered suicide to attempt to fight them. The high priest of that time period, Matisyahu, along with his sons, organized the people to rebel. They were known as the Macabees. Though they were vastly outnumbered, the Jews, under the leadership of the high priest, slowly pushed back the invaders, expelling them."

I asked him, "If the whole point of the holiday was the fighting against the Greeks and the expulsion of their armies from Israel, then what does the menorah have to do with the holiday? Why don't we use a symbol of the power of the army instead of the lights of a menorah?"

"That question was raised by certain of our Rabbis many years ago." David seemed to be suddenly energized. "In our prayers, we don't mention the miracle of the oil. Our prayers speak of the battle of the few, referring to the Jews, against the many, referring to the Greeks. The military victory is the only thing that's mentioned. The prayers declare that the many were routed by the few; that those wishing to perform evil were defeated by those acting righteously. In short, then, it's the military might of our battles during that time period which is stressed. If that's the case, then a question arises. There were other military victories that we had won in the past, against overwhelming odds, and yet we don't celebrate those. What is it about this military victory that must be remembered, and what is the tie in to the Menorah?

"The Maharal of Prague[16], who lived in the early 1600's, and was known as one of the greatest Rabbis of his generation, wrote[17] that he was in agreement with the idea that the military victory and Jewish independence from the Greeks were the real reasons for the holiday. The problem is that military victories, even against overwhelming odds, can still be satisfactorily explained according to the natural order of things.

"This is where the miracle of the oil in the Menorah comes in. The act of lighting the oil in the menorah was something that was a gift from G-d, given to the high priest to perform for the merit of the Jewish nation and began shortly after the Exodus of the Jews from Egypt, about a thousand years before the time of the Hanukah miracle, which was before even the Holy Temple in Jerusalem was built.

"After the Macabees expelled the Greeks from the Temple area, the family of Matisyahu returned to the Temple to purge it of the idolatry that was placed there. Upon restoring the Temple to its pure state, they found only one sealed jar of properly prepared, pure oil for the Menorah. The one jar would only last for one day. It would take a week to prepare oil in the proper way to continue the lighting, so that after lighting the Menorah with the oil they found, they would have to discontinue the lighting for a week until they could process more oil. To fight so hard to resume the sacred act of lighting, only to realize they must interrupt the act for a full seven days was difficult for them to accept, but they had no choice.

"A miracle occurred, however, and the oil which should have lasted for one day, remained burning for a whole week. A military victory against great odds, which could have been explained by natural means, was now given a different meaning. The miracle of the lights of the Menorah, which now burned for eight days instead of one, became direct physical evidence that, by right, the Macabees, and their Jewish followers, should have lost the war. It was only because of the hand of G-d that the Jews were victorious. Ever since the miracle which took place that year, we acknowledge, through the lighting of the candles, our recognition of the hand of G-d in all that we do, both the miracles that he performed for us then, as well as now."

It was now a little after 2 o'clock, but I didn't want him to stop. There were other things that I had to ask. "What do you mean by miracles then and now? The miracle of Hanukah and the lights occurred thousands of years ago, and this act that we do now is only a remembrance."

David continued. "I earlier referred to the special prayer that we say during these eight days. It's known as Al Hanisim, which means "regarding the miracles". There is a very unusual sentence in it that really shouldn't be there. That first section includes all the great deeds that were done by G-d for our forefathers before us during their days, and the prayer ends with the words "in our time period".

"The words, "in our time period", cause a problem. This section should have us giving thanks for what G-d had done for us during the time of the initial miracle, not in our current time period. What we learn is that the holiday of Hanukah is one when miracles can happen for us each and every year. We may not realize it, but the Lord is doing great things for us. We only have to open up our eyes to see them."

"But" I said, "I don't hear of any great miracles that happened in December. I don't know of anything that could have happened that affects me that could be attributed to this holiday."

David smiled, looked at his watch, and said that he was really taking too much of my time. We were still standing in one corner of the office, and I could see he was getting a little embarrassed that he was speaking to me on this topic so long in front of the other employees. I asked him to step into my office, as this was something I had to understand. He agreed, and he stepped in, and took a chair. After I also sat, he continued.

"There are many miracles which happen on different levels when we light the menorah this holiday. They may be events that affect only an individual or they may be events that could even affect nations."

"What kind of miracles?" I asked.

David thought for a second, and then answered, "My family is originally from Russia. There's a story that my father told me which happened many years ago in his home country and it's regarding the Lubavitch Rebbe of that time period. One of the Rebbe's congregants had come to him on one of the Hanukah nights for a blessing. The Rebbe, who was blessed with what we call Ruach Hakodesh, a holy inspiration that allows him to sense possible future events, told him that the congregants' work might force him to spend the night away from his home. The Rebbe instructed him to carry a set of candles and matches to prepare for such a possibility. As it turned out, this congregant was in the woods a day later, and a brief snowstorm forced him to be delayed in returning home. As luck would have it, a band of thieves came across him in the forest and demanded his money. He tried to avoid giving them all he had, but when they threatened to kill him, he revealed a sizable amount of money hidden at the top of one his socks. After he turned the money over, the thieves realized that to leave this Jew alive would mean that their identities would be revealed and the local landowner would have them arrested and possibly killed. They decided, despite the pleadings of this Jew, that death to the Jew was their only alternative.

"With tears in his eyes, the Jew asked that he be allowed to perform one last mitzvah, or holy deed. He remembered what the Rebbe had told him and he asked that he be allowed to light the candles of Hanukah one last time. They agreed, since a few more minutes of life for this Jew would do them no harm. He took out his candles and lined them up on a bank of freshly fallen snow, while packing the snow tightly around their bases. He then took out his matches and slowly said the blessing and proceeded to light the candles with intense prayers one at a time.

"At last they were all lit, and he now rose up to face his future killers. They surrounded him and held him down, while the leader began to approach him with a knife. From several directions, they heard the beating of horses. The landowner and his entourage, who came in time to prevent the killing, quickly surrounded the thieves. The landowner had gone out hunting, and his men had seen flickering lights where there should have been none. They quickly followed the light and came across the scene before harm could be done to the Jew.

"The Jew's performance of the lighting of candles for what he thought would be his last time, ended up saving his life."

I was impressed with the story, but still there was something I wasn't connecting to. "You explained how it saved that Jew in Russia. How does this holiday affect me, here, today? In fact, you said that nations could be affected by this holiday. Can you give one example to show me?"

"We live here in America, these United States. You take it for granted that there is a country like this, in which you have freedom. Do you believe that G-d did not have a hand in it?"

I was skeptical. "Are you implying that this country would not be here were it not for Hanukah?" I asked. I was almost defying him to come up with a proof for that one.

David lowered his voice. He stared at me, directly into my eyes. I immediately calmed down. I told him to please continue.

"You wonder how this holiday affects you, and from what I just said, how it would affect everyone in this country. Do you know your history of the United States, Mr. Klein, and, in particular, the Revolutionary War?" I nodded and said, "Even though I have studied it, I'm not aware with what it has to do with Hanukah. Please go on."

David continued, and seemed to be looking past me when he spoke. "[18]When the battles first began, in 1775, the armed forces of the rebels were pushing back the British. George Washington was pulled out of retirement to lead the cause of the rebels against the British, and he became commander in chief of its army. By 1776, a month after the signing of the Declaration of Independence, the British brought in a large force to Staten Island, and proceeded to force Washington's troops out of Brooklyn and into Manhattan. By the end of September, Washington was forced out of New York State altogether.

"As October and November came and went, Washington encountered the British in several battles and faced crushing defeats. The Battle of White Plains, and the Battle of Fort Lee forced Washington to retreat further inland to prevent the loss of his army. As the army kept pushing back, supplies became scarce. Munitions were running low, and food was rationed to the point that the troops were barely able to stay alive. The winter of that year was extremely brutal, and the threadbare clothes of the troops were a pitiful sight.

"It was in December of 1776, that the army was camped in Pennsylvania. As the men proceeded to retire for the night, there was a Jew in the camp, by the name of Isadore Solomon, who had one more thing to do before he retired.[19] He pulled out of his bag a group of candles and arranged them very neatly on the ground in front of him. He pulled out a book, said some prayers, and proceeded to light each candle without stopping until all were aflame. He had been so intense in the act of lighting, that he didn't notice the hurried footsteps of someone who quickly walked up to him.

"What are you doing? Is this some sort of signal you're sending? Are you a spy?" Isadore looked up at the giant of a man standing over him, and realized that none other than his General, General George Washington was before him. Isadore stammered a reply and said, "No, no, general. Please. I'm a loyal soldier. These are candles I'm lighting for my holiday, the holiday of Hanukah. You see, I'm Jewish and this lighting is a commandment that we Jews obey."

"General Washington saw the sincerity in the man before him, and then leaned down on one knee. "What is this Hanukah? What type of commandment do these lights signify?" he asked. Isadore then proudly replied. "Over two thousand years ago, there was a war that we Jews were fighting which was very similar to this war we are fighting now. The Jews then were fighting for the cause of truth and justice. During that time, despite being heavily outnumbered, we were victors, because G-d was with us." The General was listening eagerly now. Isadore went on. "General, we will win tomorrow, sir. G-d will help you now, just as he helped the Jews then, because we are fighting for truth and justice. Tomorrow, sir, I know we will win."

"There were a few moments of silence. The General then said. "You're a Jew. The Jews are known as a nation of prophets. I will take what you have said to me as a true prophecy. Light your candles in peace." General Washington shook Isadore's hand, asked him his name and where he was from, then rose and saluted, and continued to review the troops.

"Very shortly afterwards, Washington led the troops across the Delaware in a surprise attack against the British in Trenton, on December 25, Xmas day. He was victorious. That victory led to others, and put new hope in the fledgling country, enough hope to allow them to continue and establish this fine country that we live in.

"The story doesn't end there. It picks up several years later, in the home of Isadore Solomon, in Boston, Massachusetts. One evening, in the early 1790's, there was a knock at the door. Isadore went to answer it and a group of distinguished looking gentlemen asked if he was, indeed, Isadore Solomon, who served under General Washington in Valley Forge. He replied in the affirmative. A tall man in the back stepped forward, and a familiar voice said "Hello, Isadore." Isadore stepped back, and when he realized that he was standing in front of none other than President Washington, he requested that all of the men come in to his home. After Isadore introduced the President to his wife and children, he asked why his house was graced with someone such as his current guest. Although Isadore fought bravely, he knew he was not a war hero, and he couldn't understand why the President had come to his home.

"President Washington pulled out a box from his chest pocket and said, "Isadore, we are here to present you with this." Isadore was stunned, and the President had to place the box in Isadore's hands. Inside the box was a coin, on which a menorah was embossed, with the inscription "With admiration, General George Washington."

"The President looked at Isadore, and said, "That night that I saw you in Valley Forge, I couldn't sleep. I was very disheartened by the sight of the men who were serving under me so valiantly, and yet were suffering so tremendously. I felt there was no chance of our winning this war. As I walked among the men, I made up my mind to surrender in the morning.

"Isadore, your lights and your prophecy changed that. If not for my chance meeting with you and seeing your menorah, there would not have been a United States of America."

David sat there, and I was frozen. Because of a Jew's faith in adhering to his commandments, the world was indeed changed. As unbelievable a tale as it seemed, this story was verified by Isadore Solomon's descendants, with the coin now in a museum as proof.

David then looked at his watch, and said he didn't realize how the time had passed. It was now 4 o'clock, and it would be time for him to leave soon. He excused himself and left the office, while I pondered the miracles that I may have been missing.

9

It was now about 5:30 PM. I would be leaving the office myself in about another half hour. It had already gotten dark, and my mind had shifted to the paperwork that I had put off doing during the day, and which I now had to hurriedly deal with.

I heard the chiming of the first few notes of Beethoven's "Fur Elise". They were the notes from my cell phone. I pulled it out and looked at the number of the caller before answering it, and saw the call was from Susan, at home. I quickly clicked on the "talk" button.

"Hi, what's up?" I said, expecting her to ask me to pick something up for the house on the way home. There was concern in her voice, however, and she told me that she was worried about Eric. She was still breast-feeding him, and, after this morning, he just refused to eat. I told her that it was probably nothing and that I would be leaving momentarily and should be home soon.

I decided to set aside the rest of my work for tomorrow morning, and left the office a few minutes later. On the way to the subway, I again passed the store windows, each with their Xmas lights and decorations, and each with a single menorah in the corner. My eye immediately went to the menorahs. All of the menorahs now gave off the light of a solitary light bulb. So this was the start of Hanukah. It was the first night. This was the time of miracles, I thought. I brushed off the possibility of anything being wrong with my son. Only good could come from this week.

As I entered my building, I remembered that from the first days when I set up my apartment with Susan, she was insistent on only getting "healthy" food. No junk food was allowed, only natural, pure foods. She was a firm believer in always stocking up on fruits and vegetables. When Jennie was growing up, Susan would prepare only home made baby food, using only fresh vegetables. She would use a minimum of salt, and absolutely no processed sugar. Out of necessity, I acquired a taste for fresh honey, as it was the only sweetener that was allowed into the house.

Susan insisted on breast-feeding Jennie until Jennie was 6 months old, and Susan intended to do the same with Eric. She always felt the children would be much healthier. Besides, in the parental books and magazines that she read about raising children, there were many more psychological benefits for the baby when it was fed this way.

After the way Susan watched over Eric from when he was born, it was no wonder that the prior checkups of Eric by our pediatrician always showed that Eric was developing normally. There was no sign of anything wrong. The sudden onset of his refusal to eat had to be something that was minor, and that would prove to be temporary.

When I rang the doorbell, Susan answered it. I developed the habit of ringing the doorbell instead of using my key because Jennie wanted to be the one to open the door for me. This time, Susan was anxiously waiting for me and she ran from Eric's room and opened the door just moments after I released the ringer. "Michael, come on in and take a look at him." She turned to go to Eric even before I entered into the doorway, expecting me to hurry behind her, which I did. "He seems uncomfortable, and tired, but he isn't crying. I can't really imagine what's wrong, but something is definitely wrong."

I had to reassure her, even though I hadn't yet reached Eric's room. "I'm sure it's something temporary. He'll probably be fine in the morning." When I saw him, he was sleeping soundly, and I would never have imagined that there was a problem.

We decided to let him sleep, and to see how he was in the morning. All during the evening before I got home, Jennie was a perfect mother's helper. With Jennie standing next to her mother, Susan told me that she was very proud of Jennie for helping her take care of Eric. You could see Jennie beam with delight when Susan said that she was such a good girl. I had to lean down and give Jennie a hug myself, and tell her that I was proud of her, too.

After a few minutes, with me being there for moral support, Susan's demeanor became much more relaxed. She apologized for getting so nervous, but she couldn't help being overprotective. Eric was such a precious little bundle, that just the thought of anything being wrong, no matter how minor, bothered her tremendously.

After dinner, we put Jennie to bed, and I walked into the living room just to sit and relax a little. I noticed the Xmas tree in the center of the room, and the fully lit menorah on the windowsill. I decided to get up and I wet my fingers and started to unscrew the bulbs of the menorah to turn out the lights. Because the bulbs were too hot, I just pulled out the plug, and let all the lights cool down.

After a few minutes, I unscrewed each bulb a little, so that they wouldn't turn on when I reinserted the plug. After the bulbs cooled I reinserted the plug into the socket. I reached for the first bulb to turn it on, and I wondered if I should start with the bulb on the right or the left. Since Hebrew is written backwards, from right to left, I decided to turn on the first bulb on the right. As I reached for the bulb, I stopped.

I stood up, and left the room. Going into Eric's room, I reached down into his crib and lifted up his now sleeping body. I cradled him in my arm, and just stared at his little features, and played with his tiny hand with my index finger.

I slowly walked with him to the living room, and then straight to the window. As I slid across the room, Susan looked up at me and said, "What are you doing?" I told her, "Eric and I are going to light our Hanukah menorah. We're going to see a lot of miracles from our son, and I want him to have his first Hanukah."

With that, I reached over to the menorah with Eric cradled in my left arm. As my right hand approached the bulb, I was silently composing a prayer for my son's well being, and I prayed that everything would turn out all right. My fingers touched on the bulb, which was now only slightly warm, and I began to turn it in a clockwise direction. The first solitary bulb now shone brightly.

Susan asked, "Aren't you going to light the rest?" "No", I told her. "This year, we're going to light one day at a time."

10

Susan tried to feed Eric at about two in the morning, to no avail. Since we couldn't do anything until the morning anyway, we decided that we would call the doctor by then if there was no change. I was out of the house before seven, and went directly to the office to catch up on my work. I was feeling good that I had lit the first Hanukah light with my son. It was as though a special protective force had suddenly enveloped me.

The morning quickly passed. It was at 10:30 that I received the call from my wife. "There's no change with Eric. I know that something is wrong. I already called the doctor, but he's at the hospital this morning, and can't see me until 2:30." "I'll leave the office about then and meet you there" I said. I started to get worried myself, and I hoped that my protective force would remain intact. "There's something else", she continued, "he seems to be a little floppy, as though he's tired and doesn't have the energy to move his arms and legs."[20]

The afternoon didn't come quickly enough. Although the doctor's receptionist tried to assure us that the doctor would see Eric as his first patient, we were both very shaken. As it turned out, the two of us arrived at the doctor about the same time, at two o'clock.

I rationalized Eric's weakness by the fact that he wasn't taking any milk. I told Susan that his body was weak, and his limpness was a natural result of that. Eric still was aware of us, and partway through the wait, he fell asleep again. I knew that we really should not be getting so worrisome, but when you're faced with an unknown, your mind tends to imagine all possibilities.

It wasn't until 2:45 that the doctor came in, but because both Susan and I were waiting together, it made the wait more bearable. During the examination, the doctor said it would be okay if the two of us were in the examining room together with him. The exam didn't show up anything unusual. Unfortunately, he said, it would now be necessary to do some tests, and they would best be done in the hospital. We pressed him for an idea of what he thought was the problem, and he said that until certain tests were done, he didn't want to speculate. He did say that the droopiness of Eric's limbs was more distressing to him than Eric's refusal to eat. He would make arrangements for Eric to be admitted immediately, as he didn't want the added complication of Eric being dehydrated, and he wanted to address that as soon as possible.

We went back to the waiting room. It was now 3:30. I was holding Eric in my left arm, and reached with my right hand to cradle Susan's trembling palm. It wasn't until then that I realized that my own hand was trembling as well. The two of us sat there, waiting. As I stared at Susan, I could see tears well up in her eyes. I squeezed her hand tighter, and continued to look alternately at both Susan and Eric. Neither of us could speak.

At 4:05, the nurse asked us to go in to the doctor again. With the calm manner of the old time doctors from TV shows of the 1950's, the doctor sat us down, while he sat at the edge of his desk. He began, "Eric has always tested as healthy, and you've always been very caring parents for both of your children. Just consider this as part of what a parent deals with, and, hopefully, this will all be over soon, and you'll be able to take your son home and continue to give him all the love that you've been giving." He told us that he had placed all the necessary calls and we could take Eric directly to Mount Zion Children's Hospital, which was downtown Manhattan. Fifteen minutes later we were in a taxi and were on our way to the hospital. Susan realized that Jennie had already gotten home, and she placed a call to our day worker that we would be late coming home and we needed her to stay a while and watch Jennie.

The taxi crawled through traffic. We were driving at the beginning of rush hour. The ride took over half an hour because of traffic. The silence that had taken over us while in the doctor's office continued as we rode in the cab, but it was broken up by the sounds of the street noise of horns honking, distant sirens flaring, and the voices of angry drivers. I think we both welcomed those distractions, because as much as we both wanted to get to our destination, we both wanted to delay, because, what if the tests showed something serious? As much as we wanted to know what was wrong, we didn't want to know.

At a few minutes after 5:00, we arrived at the hospital. The entrance was at street level, and could have been mistaken for a large office lobby with an information desk. Susan was holding Eric as we went up to the front desk. Once we gave our name, Susan and Eric were ushered through. Even though the doctor had set up our admission, I still had to go through the process of filling out forms and signing releases.

After I was done, I was directed to an elevator down the hall. There was something antiseptic about hospitals that always made me feel uncomfortable. As I walked the halls, the stark whiteness of everything around me, from the linoleum floors to the walls, to the uniforms of the nurses and doctors, all contributed to a feeling that I was in a place removed from reality. I stepped into the elevator, amidst a group of people who were visiting a woman who had just given birth. Their laughter seemed to be in stark contrast to my own feelings. They got out and the elevator continued on to the sixth floor. It was my turn to get off. It was now twenty minutes past five.

I was now told to go to an area to the right of the elevators, and I spotted Susan up ahead. I followed her into another large, open room where Eric was being wheeled towards a group of infants, all under six months old, who were tethered to various machines that were set up on the periphery of the room. Susan and I watched helplessly as the nurses attached clear plastic tubes into Eric's little body, as well. He was positioned in front of a set of machines that kept track of his vital signs and displayed the information on the type of monitors used on personal computers in the early 1980's. Although I knew that this was for his benefit, to watch him like that from a distance made it feel as though part of my soul was being ripped from my body. Eric was now isolated from us and we were asked to step out of the room and view our child from behind a glass window.

The doctor in charge saw us standing in front of our son. "Mr. and Mrs. Klein?" he asked. He was holding a freshly written chart that turned out to be Eric's. "I just got off the phone with your family doctor. We'll be giving some tests to your son, but there are certain questions we have that I'd like to review with you. In fact, a specialist in neurological diseases will be examining your son tomorrow just to check on certain possibilities." "Neurological?" Susan and I both repeated at the same time. "Why are you saying neurological? We brought our son in to be examined because he hasn't been eating."

"There's a remote possibility of a problem and we'll be checking that out. But let's go into my office, and we could review different things that we'll be examining." As he finished speaking, he started to turn and lead us, but Susan blurted out, "Is there a problem or not? Just tell us." I took Susan's hand, and told her that we should just follow the doctor and let him explain it to us.

I held Susan close to me as we followed the doctor. He seemed to be just a little older than me. He was about average height, and he appeared trim. His hair was dark, but you could see that it was thinning at the front. He wore a knitted skullcap that was clipped to his hair with a bobby pin. The sight of his skullcap dominated my mind like a lighthouse beacon, as we followed him. I was hoping that this was somehow a sign that the protective shield I had envisioned around Eric this morning because of Hanukah would now reappear. An image of the menorah then began to occupy my mind and I lost track of where we turned and how we got there, but we were suddenly at his office. We both slipped inside behind the doctor and sat down on two available chairs in front of a desk, while he sat in the chair behind it. A brass name tag over his pocket spelling out the name "Dr. Birnbaum" stood out from the stark whiteness of his hospital smock.

"Now why is it that you have to check out my son with a neurological specialist?" I asked again. He began, "In medicine, as much as we like to believe we can just listen to a person's chest or check his tongue to determine what illness a person has, it's never like that. We have to be detectives. You take symptoms and any other information that may seem at first to be relevant and maybe not so relevant and put it all together to get some idea of illnesses that have that result. In many cases, it's very difficult to determine the illness of an adult, despite all of our tests.

"When you're dealing with an infant, the difficulty increases exponentially. We can't ask questions of the child to see what he feels, or when he felt it. We can't ask if it hurts if an area of his body is touched, or if his hand or leg is moved in a certain way. The only way that we can determine an illness is by carefully examining the symptoms and the conditions that existed when those clues were first observed. We're sitting down right now, not so much for me to tell you what is affecting your child, but for you to give us whatever information you can about your son, at the time just before and just after he began showing the symptoms that we're all seeing now."

His logic was calming. Susan squeezed my hand and we looked at each other. I nodded for her to speak. "Yesterday morning, Eric was fine. I breast-feed my son, and we usually have a morning feeding, which was fine. He seemed alert and healthy. After I put him to bed for a nap, he woke up in the early afternoon, and he wasn't hungry. This continued into the night, and I told this to my husband when he came home." I picked up the conversation. "That's right. My wife actually felt that something was wrong at that point, since he always has his feedings at a certain time of day. This morning I went to work early, but my wife called me to let me know that Eric still hadn't eaten, and that he seemed a little limp."

"Is there anything else that you missed?" he asked. "Anything at all, even if it seems trivial?" We were both at a loss as to what we could have forgotten. "That's it. There's really nothing more that we could tell you. You said earlier that a neurologist was going to examine Eric. Is there something about his limpness that means something?"

"When I spoke to your doctor, we reviewed something that fits with what your son is going through. I'm not an expert in that field, but when you spoke about your son becoming limp, it made me consider a certain disease known as SMA or spinal muscular atrophy. Limpness of the muscles is a symptom. Part of the reason for the tests we will be giving your son is to check on this and to hopefully rule out this possibility.

"We'll be doing some DNA testing on your child in order to determine the next step that we should be taking in dealing with this. Again, in all likelihood, there's only a slim chance that this is what is affecting your son. I would like to complete our tests, so that we can rule this out.

"Because your son is being breast-fed, I would also like to have some blood and urine samples from you, Mrs. Klein. There may be a similar problem currently affecting you, but because of your adult immune system, no symptoms are showing up. It's a long shot, but we want to check every possibility.

"Also, from my conversation with your family doctor, I understand that you have a daughter, age between four and five. I'd like to have her tested as well, but, if it's easier, you can bring her in to your pediatrician and he can take some blood samples at his office tomorrow and then have them sent here for analysis."

It was good that Susan and I were sitting down. I had thought that we were drained before, but now I felt like I had been hit with a sledgehammer. I didn't know what questions to ask or what to do. I looked at Susan and realized that she seemed to take the news even harder than me. I asked the doctor if we could just have a few minutes to take this whole thing in. The doctor immediately rose and said that we should take as much time as we needed.

We sat there for about fifteen minutes. Susan was struggling to control her emotions and I knew I had to be her strength. I told her, in a low voice, we had to be positive, and for now, we had to leave everything up to the doctors. We got up and hugged each other then left the room. We had a busy night ahead of us and we had to get going.

We walked out of the room. It was now 6:00 PM. I put together in my mind what we had to do. My cell phone rang. It was my father calling to see how my son was. I quickly briefed him, adding that the tests were routine. There was no sense in my parents carrying a burden which we all hoped would turn out to be nothing. I told Susan that for tonight, it would be best if she stayed home with Jennie, while I stayed in the hospital until the morning. I had her call her mother to see if she could stay in the apartment with Susan for the night. Thank G-d for parents. Susan's mother would be leaving her house immediately, and she berated Susan for not calling earlier.

We went down to a sitting area, where we each got a cup of coffee. We began reminiscing of the day Eric was born. I had been elated that I had a son. The time in the hospital, with so many visitors looking at how adorable little Eric was, was hectic, but happy. It was a pleasure to bring him home, and to show Jennie her new brother. Jennie took to caring for him so readily, like he was her private little doll. Just remembering the feeling of joy that Eric brought into our lives overshadowed the events of the past few hours.

Susan's mother got to the hospital at just past 7:30. She wanted to come up to see the area where Eric was and to speak to the doctor herself. When she was resigned to the fact that nothing could be determined tonight, she left with Susan to our apartment. I promised Susan I would call in case I got any news, but I knew that Susan would call me at any rate.

I was now alone. I decided to search out Dr. Birnbaum again. Now that I had my bearings, I realized that I didn't know anything about the disease that they suspected was affecting Eric. I went to the information desk on the floor, and asked them if they could page the doctor for me. One of the nurses said that he was in his office, and she guided me there.

I knocked on the door even though it was open. "Dr. Birnbaum?" I called his name to get his attention and he looked up. Upon recognizing who I was, he rose and asked me to come in. I hadn't realized earlier, but the office was very small and it just barely fit the furnishings that were inside.

"If you have a couple of minutes, I have some questions that I'd like to ask about the conversation we had earlier regarding my son", I said. He put down a pen which he had been using to write out some notes on a pad that was on top of his desk. "Please, by all means, take a seat", he replied.

I continued, "You had mentioned that you were going to be testing for something called spinal . . .". I hesitated, as I had forgotten the complete name. "Spinal muscular atrophy", he broke in. "Yes, exactly," I said. "My question is, what is it? If it turns out that my son has this, what are the chances of his being alright?"

The doctor looked up at me and said, "It's not really necessary to go over the details. As I had mentioned, the disease itself is relatively rare, and we are trying to rule it out. That's why we have a specialist who will be on duty tomorrow, and who will be examining your son."

I could tell that he really wanted to avoid the explanation, but at this point, if that was the only direction the doctors were looking at, I wanted to know more and I told him my feelings. "I really could just look it up on the internet, but I'd rather get the explanation from you directly."

"That internet. Sometimes it's a blessing, but sometimes it gives people a little knowledge, and it makes them think they're experts. In a way, though, I appreciate that you would rather get your information from me, but you just have to accept right now that, even though we have no other direction at this point, that doesn't mean that we won't rule this out." After I insisted again, but more strongly, he pulled out one of the medical books that were on a shelf behind him. He slowly turned the pages, and quickly scanned one of the entries. He then looked up, took a breath, and continued.

"The nerves of the body are, in a sense, what connects the brain to the muscles. When the brain signals for your hand to grasp a glass, or pick up a pen, for example, your muscles respond to your brain because the nerves transmit the command. The nerves are the link. In a case when someone gets nerve damage from an accident, for example, that cord that links the brain to the muscle is affected. Christopher Reeve, for example, suffered from an extreme case of just such an injury, and his nerves no longer transmitted the signals from his brain. Spinal muscular atrophy is a disease that weakens all of the nerves, not just the ones from the neck down.

"The disease, which I must repeat is rare in its infantile form, is an inherited disease in which the nerves that control the muscles mysteriously degenerate and disappear. In its adult form, it's also known as amyotrophic lateral sclerosis. Neither form is fully understood as to the causes.

"In the childhood form, in the first few months of life, the child becomes progressively weaker. There are initial problems with feeding, coupled with difficulty on the part of the child in controlling his limbs. This fits in with what your child is currently going through. The progression of the disease in your child's case is much more rapid than past cases on record. A child's future that actually has this disease? At this point, very bleak. There is no known cure, and not even a way to slow down the accelerated weakening which a child undergoes. We don't know the underlying reason of what is actually occurring. In short, Mr. Klein, all we could do is try and make the child as comfortable as possible over the short amount of life which remains.

"The floppiness which your wife, your doctor, and which our own examination has confirmed, is in line with a symptom of this disease. The thing that causes doubt in the case of your son is that the disease usually begins at an earlier age, but because of the rarity of this disease among children, I must say, that we don't really know. That's the reason for the tests, and the need to have your son examined by a specialist tomorrow.

"We as doctors, are doing all that we can. I must admit that we often believe that symptoms appear to lead us one way, and it turns out to be something minor. We all must believe that this will happen in this instance as well."

I looked up at the doctor and said, "I feel helpless without being able to do something for him. Just watching my son and only being able to wait is very difficult. I feel like I have all of this power in my body that's just waiting to be used, but I have to just keep it restrained."

"Whenever a parent must do something, and they don't know what, they usually turn to prayer. That's really the best thing that you can do right now. Mr. Klein, I understand that you'll be in the hospital overnight. We have a chapel downstairs and if you'd like, I can walk you down there myself. I know from past experience that it will give you comfort."

I thought of that protective shield again, and I told him that maybe his idea was a good one. As we went to the chapel which was on the second floor, the doctor was filling the time with small talk just to keep my mind busy on things other than our discussion. When we exited the elevator, I glanced at my watch and noticed that it was already 8:45. This day seemed to have no end in sight. We finally reached the chapel, which turned out to be the size of a very small school classroom.

Dr. Birnbaum was now leading the way, and he stopped at a door, turned the knob and began to enter. As soon as he was fully in the room, I heard a voice inside call out "Sam!". The doctor then replied, "Isaac, I didn't know you were still in the hospital. I thought you already went home." "I did go home to take care of a couple of things, but I had to come back", Isaac said. "Even though my daughter is being released tomorrow, Karen and I didn't feel right leaving her alone in the hospital."

I was now standing almost next to the doctor, as he faced Isaac. Dr. Birnbaum smiled, and said, "Excuse me, Mr. Klein. This is a friend of mine, Isaac Cohen. He and I have been very good friends since high school. His daughter is in the hospital also, and should be released tomorrow." He then addressed Isaac. "I was just dropping Mr. Klein off to the chapel, and I have to go back up to my floor. If you're going to be here for a few minutes, maybe you could keep Mr. Klein company? His son was just admitted, and Mr. Klein will be spending the night as well."

Isaac smiled and said, "It would be my pleasure. I was going to be staying here for a little while longer anyway. Is that okay with you, Mr. Klein?" I smiled back, and said "Please, call me Michael; and yes, I would appreciate the company right now." Dr. Birnbaum said goodnight to both of us, adding to let him know if we needed anything, and left.

Isaac had the greatest praises for Dr. Birnbaum. "My daughter, Grace, is just two months old. Since I have a grandson who's a year old, you can say that Grace was a very pleasant surprise to my wife and me. Yesterday, my wife felt that something was wrong with my daughter, and brought her in to our family doctor. It turned out that Grace's heartbeat was 220. Her temperature was normal and her color was good so my doctor had her admitted to the hospital to see what could be causing her high heart rate."[21]

"Wait", I broke in. "I didn't know that a pulse rate could go that high, especially for a child."

"I was surprised, too", he said, "but apparently, a baby's resting heart beat is over 100 and they could deal with an abnormally high heart rate, but for not more than a few days. Fortunately, women have this intuition and they can just sense that something is wrong. If it was left untreated for any length of time, Grace would not have made it."

"My wife also felt that there was something wrong with my son and pushed to have him checked. I sort of held her back, but she was right. So what happened when you brought her into the hospital?"

Isaac continued, "At first, they thought there was something wrong with my daughter's liver, because they said it was enlarged. When the liver showed up as functioning okay after an ultrasound exam, they thought that it could be a viral infection."

"It's the most difficult thing when they just don't know," I said, while thinking of my own predicament.

"It was then that I decided to contact Sam. I knew that Sam was a cardiac specialist and treated children. After I spoke to Sam last night, he made a special trip back to the hospital even though he had already gone home after a 12 hour day. Just a few moments into the exam, Sam realized that she had what he called SVT. I wish doctors had an easier way of referring to those diseases than with acronyms of the cryptic Latin names that they always use."

"I know what you're talking about," I said. I thought to myself about the SMA that they said Eric may have. Isaac began fumbling for a paper in his pocket as I spoke and he pulled it out when I finished speaking with him.

"I ended up writing down what the letters stood for. Here's the paper. Let's see. It's called supraventricular tachycardia. It means that the natural pacemaker in her heart wasn't controlling her heartbeat correctly. He tried a number of different treatments, but he got her heart down to normal. She's going to have to be monitored for a while, and may have to take certain medications until they're sure the problem won't recur, but she'll be fine. I have the utmost confidence in Sam. Whatever your child is here for, I just want you to know that this is an excellent hospital and Dr. Birnbaum is top rate."

"They don't know what the problem is with my son, yet. Hopefully, we'll find out tomorrow after a specialist examines him and checks results of some tests that he'll be taking," I answered him. I was a little dejected that Dr. Birnbaum was able to figure out the problem with Isaac's daughter within seconds, and yet, here I was, still in the dark.

Isaac glanced at the front of the chapel. "This is not what I expected when I was told there was a chapel. I always pictured it as being much larger. I guess it's like comparing those half gallon containers of milk to the small milk cartons they serve kids in school lunchrooms. You could call this room individual size." He pointed to a corner in the front. There was a menorah with two of the bulbs lit. "They won't allow candles to be lit here because it would be a fire hazard, so they put up the electric one. That's why I had to go home this afternoon. I needed to light the candles for tonight in the menorah at my home. When I was in the chapel earlier in the day, I had found a book, translated into English, called the Book of Maccabees.[22] It's a history of the time period when the events of the holiday first took place. I wanted to come back to the chapel this evening to go through it again, being that this week is Hanukah."

The fact that there was such a book surprised me and it showed. "I never realized that a history of this holiday was ever written. I guess I never thought there would be a need for it. The story seems so straightforward. It's just a story of the Jews fighting off their Greek oppressors, so they could worship in their Temple."

"It really isn't as simple as that. In fact, we should have learned from that event, but our mistakes kept on getting repeated throughout history. Most people have the same misconception of the actual story of Hanukah that you have. In truth, though the battles were with the Greeks, the main battle was Jew against Jew."

"This is news to me. So you're saying that this was also a civil war?"

"Most definitely," he said. "You have to understand that in those times, the Jews were an anomaly. All of the nations around the known world believed that a pantheon of specific gods ruled each specific country. If one country were to defeat another country, then the defeated country would accept the gods of the victor. It was only logical. After all, they believed that the battle was not between one group of people and another, but between the gods of one country in a battle with the gods of another country. The gods of the conquering country proved that they were stronger than the gods of the vanquished, so it would be prudent of the vanquished to add the gods of the victors to their collection of gods to worship.

"Jews did not subscribe to this world view. If they were defeated, they told the conquering army that there was only one god, and it was the one G-d almighty who caused the defeat of Israel because of transgressions of the Jews. No other gods existed.

"When the Greeks defeated Israel, it was only natural for the Greek armies to set up temples to the Greek gods throughout the country and expect the Jews to worship them. What followed, though, was not only the introduction of the Greek gods, but the introduction by the Greeks of their way of life.

"Now the Greeks then were a world power. Subjugated people tend to look up to world powers and want to attach themselves to their ways. When the Greeks began to set up the symbols of their culture within Israel, namely, the architecture, the theatres, and the sports competitions leading up to their Olympic games, it was only natural that certain Jews wanted to ingratiate themselves with their masters, and also participate. Though only a few followed the Greek ways at first, more and more began to follow the Greek behavior, and gradually, Jews began to emulate their idolatrous practices, as well.

"It was really human nature for the Jews to want to emulate the Greeks. Try to imagine spectators to modern baseball who see a certain team they had always been ambivalent about, suddenly winning the World Series. Because of all the excitement, those spectators would morph into ardent fans. In the same way, certain Jews looked at the might of the Greeks and their string of victories throughout the known world, and began to long to be their equal by following the Greek way of life.

"The physical pleasures introduced by the Greeks took hold of those Jews whose desire for the glamour of the Greek culture was greater than their desire to follow the laws of the Bible. As more people turned to the Greek way of life, more and more Jews were induced to follow. In the book of Maccabees, it goes so far as to explain that the Jews who followed the Greeks actually outnumbered the Jews who held on to their traditional ideals.

"The start of the rebellion by Matityahu,[23] who was the high priest of the Jews, began[24] when the Greeks requested that a sacrifice of a pig be made in the Temple. Now a pig is unclean for our religious purposes and to use them as sacrificial animals was blasphemous. Up stepped a Jew, who volunteered to perform the sacrificial rites, and it was then that Matityahu took out a sword and killed the Jew. A battle ensued, and the Greek soldiers and their Jewish backers who were present were killed. Matityahu and his followers had to escape from both the Greeks, and the Jews who were Greek sympathizers. It was a battle for the traditional way of life according to the Torah given to us by G-d.

"The outcome of the battles and the miracles that were shown to us should have opened our eyes to the fact that our safety and well being is dependent on our following the laws of G-d as handed down to us in our Torah. It is only when we remove ourselves from performing these laws that we see punishment meted out to the Jewish people."

Isaac paused for a moment. If it weren't for the fact that this information was in a book written shortly after that period in history, I would have dismissed Isaac's story as a fairy tale. The existence of the Book of Macabees forced me to accept it, even though it made me uncomfortable for reasons that would strike me later. "You're putting a whole new slant on this holiday, but now I'm confused. According to what you're saying, what's the point of this holiday? What do you mean when you say that we should have learned from this? Do you mean to say that every time a catastrophe happens to the Jews, it's because of something we've done?"

"Let's look at a general concept. If someone was a thief, and gets caught, they have certain restrictions placed on them as a punishment. They're forced to go through a process to make them realize that what they have done was wrong. Now, how does society know that the thief has been reformed? It's when he has an opportunity to easily steal again and he's able to control his urge. He holds himself back from stealing again.

"That's the basic pattern that also governs our existence as Jews. We become complacent in our religious beliefs and turn away from what we're supposed to follow. We're then forced to go through a process to make us realize we were wrong. Then comes the test, to see if we now will do the right thing under difficult conditions.

"Before our military loss to the Greeks, we, as a nation, were not following the commandments as we were obligated to. As a punishment, the Greeks were permitted to defeat us so that it would be more difficult for us to abide by the Biblical laws, but when we proved that there were still many Jews who would fight to follow the laws of the Bible, despite the difficulties imposed on us by our Greek masters, then we were given a sign through the miracle of the oil that G-d forgave us and would protect us again."

"I'm beginning to see what you're saying," I replied. "So you believe that when we don't follow the laws of the Bible, we're punished as a nation. I don't think that's always true, though. The Spanish Inquisition arose because there was an ongoing hatred of Jews throughout time, and it happened to reach a peak in 1492. There was nothing that we could have done to prevent it."

Isaac shook his head and said, "Here, again, you only are familiar with part of the story. The reasons for the Spanish Inquisition didn't begin that year, but you have to look over 30 years prior. The Spanish Inquisition happens to be an excellent example of the pattern I laid out.[25]

"In the mid to late 1400's, there were several events that were happening at the same time. There was a holy war against the Moors in the south of Spain, which had been going on for over 800 years. There was the Spanish Inquisition and, lastly, there was the voyage of Christopher Columbus.

"After the initial rise of Islam, Spain was almost completely taken over by the Moors. After hundreds of years of fighting, the Catholic kings gradually were able to push the Moors down into the south of Spain. By the early 1400's, the north of Spain was split into two regions, with each controlled by a different family. Ruling over Aragon, which is in the eastern portion of Spain, was the father of Ferdinand. Castile, in the west of Spain, was ruled by the family of Isabella. In 1469, the marriage of Ferdinand and Isabella united the separate kingdoms of northern Spain under one ruler.

"In the 1460's, there were about 500,000 Jews in Spain, many of them wealthy merchants. Because of the religious fervor of the war of the Christians against the followers of Islam, many Jews thought it would be to the advantage of their businesses for them to convert to Christianity. With some, the conversion was a pretense, but for others the conversions were real. By the time the year 1492 arrived, out of the population of 500,000 Jews, about 300,000 voluntarily converted."

"Ferdinand, in one of his first actions, had made a pact with Pope Sixtus IV which allowed his government to set up an Inquisition in 1478. The Pope allowed this in order to investigate the truthfulness of the Jewish conversions. The initial Inquisition, then, was directed only against the converts from Judaism.

"Wait," I said. "You mean to say that conversions took place before the Inquisition? I only read about the Marranos as being forced to either convert or leave the country penniless after the Inquisition took place." Even as I spoke, I began to realize that my knowledge of the events was proving to be sorely incomplete. I turned to Isaac with questioning eyes for him to supply me with a history lesson of my own people during a period of time of which every Jew knew of the effect, but very few of the cause.

"Yes, conversions took place on a grand scale prior to the Inquisition itself. I was saying that a number of events were taking place that set the stage for King Ferdinand to decree that the Jews be expelled from the country. If these events did not converge, the King would never have been able to go against the Jews on the level that he did.

"As I was saying, the Inquisition was initially targeting the 300,000 Jews who had converted to Christianity, and they were known as the conversos. The 200,000 Jews who stayed loyal were left alone. In 1483, Tomas de Torquemada, who happened to be from a converso family himself, rose to power, and was put in charge of the Inquisition. He pressed the King to go against not only the conversos, but the 200,000 Jews who remained loyal to their religion. The setting was prepared for the expulsion of the Jews from Spain. The King resisted, however, as the influence of this group of Jews in the commerce of the country was vast.

"More pressing to the King was dealing with the threat of the Moors. In December of 1491, after many years of battle, Boabdil, the leader of the Moors, surrendered to the armies of King Ferdinand and Queen Isabella. The final ceremony where Boabdil surrendered the keys of his remaining Spanish provinces to King Ferdinand, took place in January of 1492. Following this, Christopher Columbus approached the King and Queen of Spain to finance him in his search for a new route to the Orient. This was subsequently agreed to amidst great fanfare. With the great victory over the Moors complete, and with the possibility of Spain laying claim to the route to the Orient under Columbus, the King and Queen felt they had absolute power to do as they pleased. They succumbed to the persuasive words of Torquemada and decided the time was ripe to make full use of the unlimited powers written over to them by the Pope many years before. They now directed their energies against the rest of the Jewish population. The expulsion of the Jews was now a reality.

"The Jews of Spain, who as a group voluntarily left the religion to hold on to their money, were now faced with a choice. They could lose their much-cherished wealth and leave the country while cleaving to their Judaism, or they could remain in Spain and worship their wealth while turning their backs on their vows and the vows of their ancestors to never forsake their religion.

"You see, there's that pattern again. The Jews turned away from their obligations to G-d. They were punished. In order for them to prove that they realized that what they had done was wrong, G-d now presented them with a choice through the hands of the Spanish rulers. Those that chose to leave penniless while maintaining their attachment to their religion redeemed themselves in the eyes of G-d, just as those Jews during the time of Hanukah who fought against the Greek influences had done."

"Over the years, we, as a nation, again forgot the lessons we learned. The pattern, which was always prefaced with us casting off the laws that we are bound to, kept repeating itself. The 19th century brought the Reform movement, which led to the greatest disaster in our history, the Holocaust."

I interrupted him. "But, Isaac," I said, "the Holocaust was so horrible, I don't think it could be justified by any stretch of the imagination."

"You're right", he said, "but anytime a national tragedy befalls our people, we must look inwardly to see if we could improve our past actions and be worthy of G-d's protection in the future.

"There is a very interesting book which I read, called "Foiled, Hitler's Jewish Olympian". [26]Where the typical book on the Holocaust shows the savagery of the Germans while the Jews were stripped of their self respect, then their material possessions, and were finally brutally murdered, this book contains a history of German Jewry leading up to that period and continuing on until shortly after the war.

"Helene Mayer, the subject of the book, was one of the greatest fencers of all time. From the age of 15 her talent was well known throughout Germany. She became a national heroine in 1928 when she won the gold medal for fencing in the Olympics.

"The book is more interesting for the background of the Jews' struggles to be accepted into German life throughout the years. Although Helene was known as the Jewish fencer, she herself was not technically a Jew. Her father, from a prominent German Jewish family, had married a Christian. The book goes on to explain that by 1910, 13 percent of Jewish men, and 10 percent of Jewish women married partners out of their faith. [27] As time went on, the percentages worsened. In the 1936 Olympics in Germany in which Helene participated, the top three finalists were all half Jews. [28] Helene was a product of a mixed marriage from Germany; Ellen Preis was the half Jewish finalist from Austria; and Ilona Schacherer-Elek was the half Jewish fencer from Hungary. The problem of mixed marriages was not central to Germany, but it appears to have been a European epidemic.

"The ultimate tragedy of mixed marriages is that there is no coming back. The children are usually lost to Judaism, and if the father was Jewish, the children then carry a Jewish name, but are not recognized as Jewish according to our Orthodox tradition.

"Despite what we went through as a nation, losing one third of our people, we still haven't learned. In this generation in the United States, mixed marriages are again growing at an alarming rate, and there is no coming back for the offspring of those unions.

"That's why these lights of Hanukah are so important. They bring out what people call the pintele yid, the tiny flame that links Jews to their Jewishness, and brings us back to what we are supposed to do."

With his last words, my face began to grow flushed. The image of my father trying to tell me to only marry into my own religion began striking at me inside my brain. All of a sudden I wasn't feeling that well as questions about my life whirled in my head. My thoughts were broken by the sound of my cell phone ringing. It was Susan, probably calling to check on how Eric was doing.

"Excuse me for a second, Isaac, it's my wife", I said as I clicked on the talk button. "There's no change so far, and I've already sat with the head doctor again. They're monitoring Eric, but we really have no choice but to wait for a better answer tomorrow. How's Jennie?"

"Jennie was asleep by the time I got home with my mother. But my mom was really helpful. She ended up calling Father Baldino after she got our call, and asked him to say some prayers for Eric."

"That's nice," I said, while feeling a little guilty, especially after listening to Isaac just now. "All prayers are welcome right now."

"You know," she continued, "the Father really was concerned. He came to our apartment shortly after I got here with my mom, and gave us some moral support. He just left a few minutes ago."

Something about her tone made me uneasy. I could tell that there was something else that she meant to tell me. "And what did he say?" I asked her.

"Well, he thought, and me and my mom agreed with him, that maybe it would be the right thing if Eric were baptized. I mean, we agreed to a circumcision for Eric because it meant a lot to your father. A baptism would mean a lot to my parents. Eric could still decide how he wants to pray when he grows up, but maybe it's the right thing to do now. Maybe by doing this, it will give the extra push for him to be okay."

For some reason, I felt this coming. As the words left her mouth, I wasn't surprised at all. I felt as though everything that was happening was sort of a déjà vu, something that I already experienced a long time ago. All I could tell her was that we would discuss it in the morning. This was not something I wanted to deal with right now, and I knew that with her mother there, I wouldn't really be talking with Susan, but to my mother-in-law's influence over Susan. I told Susan I loved her, and that everything would be all right and clicked off the phone.

Isaac could tell something was bothering me. "Are you alright?" he asked. "There's something that I have to tell you," I answered as I took a deep breath. "My wife is a Christian."

11

Isaac froze and stared at me. It was hard for me to tell who was more shaken by my admission. Neither of us knew what to say next. He finally broke the silence with the words "I'm sorry."

"You didn't say anything wrong, Isaac. I think that, deep down, I wanted to talk to someone about this, and for a while I couldn't."

"The things I said to you, especially about intermarriage, must have hurt you deeply. I really feel bad. I should have been more careful in what I told you and maybe got to know you more, before I went on like that", he said apologetically.

"No," I told him. "I never heard anyone explain things about Judaism like you just did. I'd been hoping to come across someone who could help me to make sense of things that I didn't understand. I wouldn't have even told you about my wife unless I thought that you could help me make sense of my life."

"I really can't claim to have any answers for you but I should have known that you needed to talk, and get things off of your chest, just by virtue of the fact that your son is in the hospital. If you need someone that you could speak to, I'll be glad to be that person for you. Believe it or not, I can be a very good listener."

"Thanks," I said, "I appreciate that. I don't really know how to find the words to start." But find them, I did. All it took was a little prodding, and within a few moments a summary of my life began to unfold.

I proceeded to tell him, as briefly as I could, about my upbringing; my single life; how I met Susan; and how my parents fought against it, but then gave in. I told him about my meetings with Father Baldino, and how I felt that my wife's religion seemed to have so much more meaning than what I was taught of my own. A lot of the thoughts that I held inside of me were suddenly released. Though most of the pressures that had been building up inside of me remained, at least I was able to share my torment with someone else.

It had been 10 o'clock when I received the call from Susan, and I sat with Isaac until about 12:30 in the morning. It was so refreshing to be able to talk to someone who would just listen without judging me. Yes, he was right. Isaac was a good listener.

He had become more attentive when I told him of my conversation with David Greenblatt, and how I put my son on my knee as I turned on the light bulb of the menorah in my house. When I paused, he smiled and said, "That's the pintele yid that I spoke about before. There's still that Jewish spark which you won't allow to go out."

"In a way," I told him, "I can't help thinking that we were meant to meet tonight. When I saw Dr. Birnbaum's skullcap, I really began to hope that I would be having this conversation with him." I suddenly realized something. I looked up at Isaac and asked, "Now that I got to this point, where do I go from here?"

Isaac looked at me sadly. "If you mean to ask me what you should do about your marriage, I can't answer you. I can't advise you on something like that."

"You're right. I'm the only one that can decide what to do about my future, but maybe you could help me learn a little more about my religion? The only time I really learned anything was from Father Baldino, and I'm sure", I had to chuckle as I completed my thought, "that his agenda was not to endear me to the Jewish faith."

"I think I owe you that much", he said. "Maybe the two of us should take a walk up to the sixth floor and take a look at our kids, call it a night, and we could start fresh in the morning. I'm not really qualified as a teacher, but I'll try and answer whatever questions you have."

We both left the chapel and went up to the sixth floor. It was comforting to check on Eric with Isaac, knowing that Isaac had already passed through a crisis with his own child. It made me feel as though my son would pull through fine, as well.

I stared at Eric through that glass window for a good ten minutes, and waited for Isaac to finish checking on his own daughter. I couldn't hope for anything specific as I watched my little boy, other than for a second chance for me and my son.

Isaac returned, and the nurse brought us to an area with small rooms with sofas in each one that could be used as cots. This area was set up because it was common for parents to stay in the hospital overnight. The windowless room was a little claustrophobic, but I was exhausted. It was now 1:30 in the morning. The day was finally ending. It was a day that would be ingrained in my memory forever, but there was a lot more to come tomorrow.

12

I awoke with a start. I quickly looked at my watch, expecting it to be 3 or 4 o'clock in the morning. The darkness of the room made it difficult to gauge the time. I had to look again and focus to realize that it was 7:15 in the morning.

I still had a heavy head, and I closed my eyes and dropped back on the cushions of the sofa I had been sleeping on. I opened my eyes again, and pushed myself up. I was able to focus a little better, and after a few deep breaths, I rose and took a good long stretch.

Walking into the hall, I asked a nurse where the bathrooms were and she directed me to a door only twenty feet away. After freshening up, I looked to where Isaac had been, but he was already up and out.

At the front desk on that floor, there was a note from Isaac waiting for me. He had risen earlier to go to prayers, and would be back around 8:30. I decided to go straight to where they had been monitoring Eric, and found that everything was the same as last night.

I had to go back to the waiting room area to use my cell phone in order to place a call, but on the way, I went back to the front desk. I realized that I didn't even get the name of the doctor that would be examining Eric, nor what time he was expected to be here.

The nurse at the desk checked for me and said, "We're showing the name of the neurologist who will be examining your son as Dr. Chai, Dr. Steven Chai. According to our information, he should be seeing your son at about 10:00 AM."

As I walked away from the desk, I couldn't help thinking how much the doctor's name sounded like a form of tea. I started to picture tea leaves growing on the floor of the hospital. It's amazing how the mind wanders sometimes.

The waiting room was large enough to fit about twenty people. Sunlight was coming in through windows at the back. As I entered the waiting area, I heard voices but I quickly realized that they were coming from a television set that was on. The TV was affixed to a shelf which was elevated and angled downward so that the screen could be seen from anywhere in the room. A show was already in progress. It was one of those reality court TV shows. Divorce Court. I let out a silent moan. It's as though somebody up there was looking at the questions that were going on in my mind. I stopped for a second and looked up.

There were two podiums set up in front of the judge. Behind one was a woman, and behind the other was a man. The woman was angry; the man much calmer. It was the woman who was speaking to the judge when I walked in.

"Your honor, me and my husband separated because he just don't trust me. I can't go nowhere without him followin' me to see where I'm goin' and who I'm talkin' to. You can't live with a man like that. Just two days ago, he was waitin' outside of my apartment in the afternoon to spy on me"

"Is this true?" asked the judge while turning to the man at the podium on the right. "No, your honna, but I know that she's always talkin' to other men. If she thinks I'm watchin, she'll stay in line." The wife said to the judge, "He may not have been there, but he had his partner watchin'. They trade off watchin' 'cause they think I won't always catch that they're there. But I caught them that time."

The judge turned to the man and said, "And what's your answer to that? But first, what type of work do you do that you or your partner can be around in the afternoon? And tell me your version of getting caught."

"Well, your honna", he began, "I work as a bounty hunter. I wasn't in front of the buildin', but yeah, my partner was there." "Tell him where he was hidin'!" the wife cried out. The judge kept staring at the man and nodded for him to proceed.

"Well, your honna, as I said, me and my partner are bounty hunters. We always have to stake out places where someone may be hidin'. Well, my partner's car has a couple o' peep holes in the trunk and he was in the trunk of the car and was parked in front of my wife's buildin', 'cause we knew that she would be meetin' someone sooner or later."

"If your partner had such a good hiding place, how did your wife realize that he was there?"

"Well, like I said, my partner was in the trunk of the car. He was checkin' out the front door of the buildin' and just saw my wife coming out of the door, leavin' to meet with someone."

The judge was visibly a little frustrated. "So how is it that your partner got caught if he was concealed inside the trunk of a car with only some peep holes punched in it?"

"Well," the husband said, "when he saw my wife leaving the buildin' he was gonna call me on his cell phone so's I could let him out and we could follow my wife. But then . . . ."

"Keep going" said the judge.

"But then the repossessor man came." There was a gush of laughter from the audience on the show. "We couldn't get him out of the trunk until we paid to get the car out of the lot the next mornin'."

I had to laugh out loud myself. I guess all problems could seem bad, but it depends on how you're looking at them. The thought about problems made me think about last night's conversation with Susan, and the call I now had to make to her. There was no one in the room, so I picked up a remote control that was on a table near the TV, and turned off the set.

I pulled out my cell phone, hit the speed dial and called home. I heard a familiar voice say, "Hello?"

"Hi, Susan. It's Michael."

"Wow!," she said. "I was just walking over to the phone to call you. Any news about Eric?"

"I checked on him late last night, and again when I got up this morning. There's no real change. He's sleeping a lot, which they said, is normal."

"Your stay in the hospital last night must have been rough. How are you feeling this morning? Did they have a bed or a couch for you to sleep on last night?"

"They have sofa cots set up", I told her. "It really wasn't so bad, but I'm a little groggy this morning. I found out the name of the doctor that'll be examining Eric. His name is Dr. Steven Chai, and he's due in around 10:00 this morning."

"I'll be there before then. Once Jennie gets picked up for school, I'll be able to leave. Me and my mom will be coming in together." She hesitated for a few moments, while I temporarily froze at the mention of her mother. She asked, "Did you think about what I told you last night?"

"Yes, but, let's just focus right now on what the doctors are saying, and we can discuss it another time."

"Michael, I don't see why we can't do both. After all the time you spent with Father Baldino, I would think that you would understand the importance of a baptism, especially now. I know we can't go through a baptism while Eric is in the hospital, but we can at least accept it upon ourselves to have the ceremony once Eric is better. The Father offered to come down with me today, mostly to offer his support, but maybe to speak to you as well."

I knew I was going to be bombarded today, and I wasn't prepared for it. She was right that when I was going to Father Baldino's classes, he was able to influence me to the point that I was very close to giving myself over to his religion. There were so many questions that I now had, about both Christianity and Judaism, but I needed more time to think. Susan, right now, wasn't allowing me to have that time.

We were only on the phone another minute or so. Susan insisted that the decision for the baptism be made now. She mentioned things about the Kingdom of Heaven, and how only baptism prepared for that. The more she spoke, the more I was feeling pushed into a corner. I finally raised my voice in frustration. "If you want to come down with your mother and the Father to help, that's fine, but I have enough on my mind without these decisions about religion." I was aware that I raised my voice, and quickly looked around to see if anyone else had come into the room. I was alone. I then repeated again, in a calmer voice, "Susan, I'm sorry. We have enough on our plate to just deal with what's happening right now. Just come in as soon as you're able to. I'll be here."

I could tell she was hurt. Even though she was hanging up, she wasn't giving up. I just had to push this off. We never bumped heads about something like this before. Probably because I never really pushed my religion, and I was always open to her beliefs. It hit me that it was always me who had taken the effort to learn about her faith, not so much the other way around.

I walked back to Eric. No change. There was still no sign of Isaac. I needed a familiar face around me right now so I decided to see if Dr. Birnbaum was going to be in. It turned out he had other obligations today and a Dr. Fred Johnston was now on duty.

All I could do right now was sit and wait. It was just past 8:30 now. To fill the time, I started to watch the hospital personnel go about their daily duties.

A large cart was being wheeled past me by a middle aged man who wore a green, loose fitting smock. He had a head of thick hair cut short, but mostly gray. His short and stocky frame easily pushed the cart which I now saw was filled with fresh linens, and his slow and steady gait and blank forward gaze betrayed the monotony of his daily routine. An elderly nurse, with skin that was weathered by time, walked briskly in the opposite direction, with a smile that welcomed the day. At the desk, several nurses chatted among themselves while they peered into computer monitors, recording and checking the information that was submitted by the doctors from their last round of visiting each patient.

As I waited there, watching the goings on of those around me, I was aware of being watched as well. There were two people about 25 feet away from me who were obviously a husband and wife. The wife's eyes had briefly caught my own, but then turned away.

The two of them had to be in their early twenties, and it was apparent that even though the day was only starting, they were totally drained. They were both standing and seemed to be supported by a wall behind them. The man's head was propped against the wall and his eyes were closed. From his wrinkled shirt and pants, along with a beard that may have been two days old, it was easy to see that he underwent at least one all night vigil, and maybe two. His wife was not as haggard in her appearance. As she held his limp hand, she seemed to be scanning the room, with her gaze jumping from one object to another, but without really seeing what her eyes looked upon. When our eyes met, I felt the absence of hope that radiated from within her. After turning away from me, she continued to examine every facet of the hallway with the same hollow look, even as I began to stare at her with sympathy. The sight of the two of them made me momentarily forget my own troubles, and I made a silent prayer that their ordeal should turn out well.

Two doctors now approached the spot where I was sitting, and they were followed by a nurse whom I recognized as having been on duty when I passed by in the morning. They appeared to be deeply involved in a conversation. One doctor was holding a clipboard, and motioning with his free hand while the other seemingly focused his eyes on the air at waist level in front of him, as though doing that would help him to hear better.

As they got closer to me, I could hear the first doctor mention my last name, and then I jumped up, as I believed that they were speaking about Eric.

"Doctor?" I said. "Were you speaking about my son, Eric? My name is Michael Klein. I'm his father."

I noticed a brass nameplate on his white smock. The name "Dr. Johnston" was imprinted in black against the gold colored strip of metal. All three of them stopped and Dr. Johnston spoke.

"Oh! Mr. Klein! We were just discussing your son. This is Dr. Adams who's also looking into this case. The neurologist called to say he should be here very soon. He's actually running early. Dr. Adams asked me to brief him on a few cases, your son's among them. I haven't looked at your son myself yet, and I wanted to do that with Dr. Adams before the neurologist arrives."

"Thank you, and really, I have to say thanks to everyone in the hospital for the interest they've shown in helping my son. If there's anything you need to know, I'll be glad to help."

"It's a good idea for you to be with us," Dr. Johnston replied. "I've gotten a pretty good idea of the background on your son's case so far, but there may be some gaps that you could fill in."

We all walked over to where Eric was being monitored. The liquid that they were pumping into him through the tubes was only meant to rehydrate him, which was successful. The doctors spoke to me about Eric's limpness and they too, were concerned. Compared to his condition when he was first examined, Eric seemed to be getting worse.

As we were speaking, another doctor strode up to us. "Dr. Johnston?" he asked. Upon his noticing the nameplate on Dr. Johnston's lapel, he followed up by saying, "I'm Dr. Chai." A feeling of nervousness swept over me, as my heart started to pound audibly. All the tension I had been feeling while waiting for this doctor to arrive hit me all at once.

Doctor Chai must have been around sixty years old, and was a few inches shorter than me. He was a little on the heavy side, but still had a quick and easy stride. He had penetrating large brown eyes, and olive skin. He also seemed to have an easy going way about him, which was very comforting to me right now.

I introduced myself to the doctor with a shaky voice. He took my hand firmly and looked at me in the eye for a fraction of a second, but it was long enough for me to sense that he was letting me know that he was in control now.

I excused myself, and went to the front desk to ask if I could use my cell phone. No, I was told, but I was allowed to use one of the phones at the desk. I gave them Susan's cell phone number to dial and held the receiver up to my ear.

"Susan. The doctor got here early. They're examining Eric now. Where are you?"

"I'm about a block away, and I should be at the hospital in about a half a minute. I'll come right up", she said.

As I strode back to where they were examining Eric, I caught a four way conversation among the medical staff.

"This does have the symptoms of SMA, but I wouldn't make that diagnosis", said Dr. Chai, as he was completing a cursory exam of my son. I stayed in the background while they continued speaking. Dr. Chai continued, "According to the information from the pediatrician, this child was perfectly healthy a month ago. His parents reported that even last week, he showed no signs of any problems. You see, SMA shows itself a lot more gradually. One day the child is not moving as before, the next day, there's a little more sluggishness. The limpness appears after a week, and the child is admitted to the hospital, because he hasn't the strength to accept food on his own. This case is too sudden. No," the doctor paused, as if in thought, "even without seeing any test results, I would have to say that this is definitely not SMA."

That statement brought a wave of relief to my shattered nerves. I was too elated to focus on what they next said, but after a few moments, I caught myself and began listening in again.

Dr. Adams was now speaking. "I agree with what you're saying, but the symptoms look like the result of a poison that was ingested."

The nurse now joined in the conversation. "Poisoned by what? He's only been breast fed up to now. From the tests that came back on the mother, nothing is showing up. If he hasn't eaten anything that could have caused it, where could a poison have come from?"

Dr. Adams replied, "You have a point, but I would still go with the poison. There has to have been another way it was ingested."

Dr. Chai suddenly turned to Dr. Adams and raised his eyebrows. It appeared that there was something that seemed to make sense to him.

I spun around as I heard hurried footsteps behind me. Susan was just arriving. "What's happening?" she asked.

"They're trying to figure out what's causing his illness, but thank G-d, it looks like they're ruling out that disease that Dr. Birnbaum told us about yesterday."

"So that's good news, right?" she said. "He should be okay then."

The doctors hadn't realized that I was standing so close to them, and they turned when they heard Susan and I speaking.

"Oh! Mr. Klein! And I assume this is Mrs. Klein. I'm glad that the two of you are here", Dr. Chai said as he walked over to the two us. He introduced himself, and gave my wife that same firm handshake that he had given to me. After introducing the other doctors and the nurse he turned to my wife and said, "I'm almost 100% certain that we can rule out SMA. It's good that you're here because there are some questions that I have to ask. I'm sure that you've been asked all of these questions before, but, please, humor me."

We heard more steps from behind us. It was Susan's mom. I instinctively looked to see if anyone else was behind her, but she was alone. She had driven Susan to the hospital and dropped her off at the front before leaving her car in the parking lot. Susan introduced her mother to the doctors and asked Dr. Chai to continue.

13

Both Dr. Chai and Dr. Adams had stopped for a moment when they heard my mother in law's last name, but they quickly regained their composure. It seemed to me that they had made a mental assumption that Susan was also Jewish and her physical features made them not question it. Because all eyes were upon Dr. Chai, it made the brief hesitation noticeable. Luckily, Susan and I were used to it.

Dr. Chai then took up the dialogue again. "Mrs. Klein, I understand that you're very strict with the foods that you allow into your house."

"Why, yes", Susan answered. "I'm trying to train my children from now to stay away from the processed cakes, and to eat in a healthy way. If you start them out correctly, I think there's a greater chance that they'll continue to eat properly in the future."

"That's a very good way of thinking", Dr. Chai replied. "It would be good if all mothers followed your pattern." For the next moment or two he stood in thought, slightly nodding his head in approval of her actions. "The types of foods that you have in the house are from health food stores or just a regular supermarket?"

"I do go to a regular supermarket, but there are certain things that I get from a health food store. Why?"

"Can you tell me again when was the last time that Eric was breast fed?"

"Excuse me," said Susan. "I'm starting to lose track of time." She turned to me and asked, "It was yesterday that we brought Eric to the hospital?" Without waiting for my reply, she continued, "Yes, we brought him to the hospital yesterday, and his last feeding was the day before that, in the early morning."

"So," Dr. Chai then asked, "your routine in the morning is to feed Eric, then get your daughter ready for school."

"Yes. Exactly," she answered.

"Your daughter, what was her name?" "Jennie," Susan replied. "Your daughter, Jennie is up after Eric has completed his feeding?

"Yes. I get her ready for school and put Eric in a small playpen that I have in the kitchen. She gets dressed, has her breakfast, and sometimes plays a little with Eric until we take her down to be picked up for school."

"She gets along well with your son?"

Susan became more relaxed as she thought of how good Jennie was. "Yes", she said. "Jennie gets along extremely well with Eric. There's no jealousy as far as we could see. When you see the way that Jennie acts with her brother, you would think that she was the mother. There's that much affection and care."

"And what does Jennie have for breakfast?" he asked.

I was beginning to see the point of his questions. The last time we were all sure that Eric was fine was a few days ago, in the morning. If they were talking about Eric eating something, then the most opportune time for that to happen would have been at breakfast of that day.

"Jennie has oatmeal and milk."

"Any sugar?"

"We don't allow sugar in the house," she said quickly.

"So she eats the oatmeal plain, without any sweetening at all?"

"Well, no" she said, "we usually allow her to put a teaspoon of honey on top."

"That's it" said Dr. Chai as he turned to Dr. Adams. "I believe that the baby's got botulism. Let's get an electromyogram done immediately, but I think that we've found the problem."

While Eric was wheeled away for the tests, Dr. Chai gave us a scenario of what he believed were the chain of events of that morning. "It was the fact that this family uses health foods that made me realize what must have happened." He now turned to me and Susan. "More than likely, probably when you, Mrs. Klein had either turned away or walked out of the kitchen, Jennie was having her breakfast at the table. She then must have wanted to play act that she was feeding her own baby, which in this case was Eric. There could have been some honey on the spoon when she put it into the baby's mouth. When Jennie heard you returning to the kitchen, she could have gone back to her seat to finish eating. Your daughter probably would have said that she wasn't feeding Eric anything, because, in her eyes, there was no food on the spoon. That small amount of honey, though, ingested by the baby, would have been enough to cause the damage."

"But," I asked, "why would honey do that? And such a small amount?"

This time Susan's mother interrupted. "There are certain foods that you can't give to a baby because of the danger of an allergic reaction. We're told to be careful of foods like honey, and even strawberries."

"That's right", said Dr. Adams. "Normally, when you hear the term "natural" or "pure", you think it's better for you. Sometimes it is, and sometimes it isn't. In the case of honey it isn't. It's true that many people take honey instead of sugar for what they perceive are the health benefits. Unprocessed honey, though, often contains spores of a certain bacterium, called Clostridium botulinum, the bacterium that causes botulism. Even processed honey can contain those spores."

"Do people just get sick from botulism, or is it more dangerous?", I asked.

"In most adults and older children, the immune system destroys the toxins. In infants under a year old, exposure to the bacteria can be very harmful. Once the bacterium enters the bloodstream, it spreads the toxins which bind to peripheral motor nerves. Small amounts of honey could be enough to produce this effect. In cases where the diagnosis is made early enough, the proper treatment can be given to allow for the child's immune system to recover over time."

"So he's going to be fine," Susan said emphatically, almost with the idea that if she willed it, it would automatically happen.

Dr. Chai then took over the conversation, and explained that there would still be a long road to recovery. He explained that when the toxins bind to the receptors, they become permanently blocked. We now had to monitor the child and allow his body to fight the toxins on its own. Time would be on our side, however, as the toxins weaken with each passing day. As new receptors are produced by the child, they replace the blocked ones, and the child gets back his ability to control his muscles.

I couldn't tell if what the doctor explained was good or bad. I realized that I had to be positive, because at least, with help, Eric could fight this. The doctor was suddenly interrupted by a nurse and went to the phone. He spoke in a different language, and to my surprise, it sounded like Hebrew. When he put down the receiver, I walked over to where he was standing, and asked him if he indeed spoke Hebrew and if he was Jewish. "Why yes", he said. "Why do you ask?" "Your name doesn't sound like a Jewish name", I answered. "My name? It actually is Jewish. I got in the habit of pronouncing it the way others do, with the "ch" sounding like the word "choose". It's actually a sound more like the clearing of a person's throat, a sound that doesn't exist in English." "Does your name have a meaning?" I asked. "Yes", he said. "It's also a Hebrew word that means "life".

14

Each of the doctors and medical staff had disbanded to deal with the next patient crisis that they would be facing. Susan, her mother and I now had to wait for the results of the test that the doctor ordered. Because I was uncomfortable with the subject that I knew was on the back of Susan's mind, I tried to dominate the conversation by focusing on how lucky we were, and contrasting that to the plight of some others that I had seen. I didn't have to do this long, because the confirmation of the doctor's diagnosis came relatively quickly.

Dr. Chai had Eric put on a respirator, to assist in his breathing which had become very labored. Eric now had to be monitored and would be in the hospital under 24 hour surveillance for at least several weeks. Susan and I were told not to reprimand Jennie, as she had been trying to do the right thing. It would be of no use for her to feel she was responsible for Eric's condition. It would have to be explained to her in a different way of the importance of not putting anything into Eric's mouth.

Throughout the morning, although I was uncomfortable with having Susan's mother around, she was still a tremendous help. Before we were married, Susan had never been close to her mom because of a rebellious streak that was part of Susan's character, but Susan's mom always wanted a better mother daughter relationship.

My mother in law was very modern in her outward behavior. She regularly went to a gym, always watched what she ate and even now, wore the same size clothing as Susan. When she dressed, it was always with a very good sense of fashion. Inwardly, she had an innate sense of right and wrong. Religion had been a strong part of the life of Susan's maternal grandmother, which is part of the reason why my mother in law was named Mary. The name must have had some effect, because if Susan's mom had an opinion that was sourced in religion, she was able to back up her arguments with quotes from the Bible.

You could see that she had the same fire as Susan, but it was directed to other areas. Susan's two older brothers liked to ask their mother for advice, and when Susan began to consult and confide in her as well, it brought my mother in law's spirits up a few notches.

Because I now associated her with the recent religious request of my wife, which I viewed right now as a negative, I felt that, to be fair, I had to balance that aspect of her against all the positive things that her family meant to us. My in laws were definitely both loving grandparents, and showered Jennie with affection. They also tried not to get involved in decisions that we had to make, and this was really the first time that I could recall in which they had openly pushed Susan to follow their way of thinking.

How could I really blame them? These last few years in which I was exposed to their religious beliefs opened up a whole new world for me. They were sure of who they were and what they believed in. Seeing my indecision made them feel as though I needed some extra push in what they considered to be the right direction.

When I made a call to my father to update him on what was happening, I wondered what his father had taught him and why he felt strongly about Jews marrying Jews. He could be warm and talkative to others in a social atmosphere, but when it came down to talking to his children, he was always more aloof. It was as though he always had to be the strict disciplinarian and just tell us not to do something without ever explaining why.

When I was alone this morning, I had briefly wondered why all Jews could not worship in the same way. Why is it that the establishment of Reform Judaism, which really seemed logical to me, did not spread to all of Judaism? How could the Orthodox hold on to their beliefs that the words in the Bible were dictated to Moses directly by G-d when scientific fact didn't coincide with so many Biblical records?

All of these thoughts and more kept dancing in my head in between the conversations with the doctors and my family. The day was proceeding more quickly than yesterday, maybe because we at least knew what we were facing. When there was finally a quiet moment, my mother in law held my arm and told me that she could stay in the hospital with Susan. She suggested that I go home and get some rest since all we could do anyway was wait. After Susan insisted as well, I decided that they were right.

When I got down to the lobby, I started to walk to the glass entrance doors, but then stopped. My confusion was gnawing at me and it made me reflect on my conversation with Isaac from last night. It made me realize that I hadn't seen Isaac all day and I wondered why he hadn't tried to contact me.

I was fearful that there was a turn for the worse in his daughter's condition. My curiosity was mixed with concern and I reasoned that it would only take a few moments to find out what happened.

I went to the front desk and asked if Isaac Cohen's daughter, Grace, was still in the hospital. I said that I was a friend of the family and that I knew Isaac and Karen, the parents. The nurse advised me that they were still in the hospital, and that Grace was moved to the fifth floor.

I decided to go up to visit them before I left, and took the elevator to his floor. When I got out, I saw Isaac speaking to a nurse who was behind a desk, and I called his name.

He turned, and gave me a big smile. "I can't believe you're here! What are the chances of my bumping into you now?"

"You know what they say," I told him. "Chance is the fool's name for fate!"

He smiled and said, "I didn't know you were a fan of Fred Astaire and Ginger Rogers. I remember that line from one of their old movies[29]."

"You must be older than you look," I said. "My father used to love to watch movies from the early '30's."

"I sort of have a thing for old movies, myself. But what brings you to this floor?", he asked.

"Truthfully, I was on my way out of the hospital, and I decided to ask at the front desk if you had checked out. When I was told that you were still here, I thought that I would come up and see if everything was okay."

"I really appreciate that," he said. "My daughter is fine, but there's what the doctors were calling a minor blip which was easily corrected. As a result, though, they have to keep a tighter watch on her than I first anticipated, and they're now telling me we've got to keep Grace in the hospital for another week, if not two. What's happened with your son?"

I briefed him in just a few sentences on my son's situation. He told me I should be very thankful for how things have turned out and that everything that happened is for the best.

I decided to take advantage of my meeting with him. I told him that there were questions that I had after we had spoken last night, and I asked him if he wouldn't mind answering a question for me. "How do you know that what you read about in the Bible actually happened?"

He was surprised at my question. "That's not a simple thing to answer, but why are you asking that now?"

"Because of all that's been happening to me, I feel like I'm being torn between my desire to stay Jewish and my wife's desire for our kids to follow their mother's religion. The problem is that I don't know enough about why I should want to be Jewish. As a Reform Jew, I was taught that the Bible was man made, and that's why we believe it doesn't have to be followed anymore. I know that religious Jews and religious Christians differ with us and believe in the divine source of the Bible and I don't know why. What's more confusing is that even though they both believe the Bible is from G-d, they believe different things. I think I'm hoping that I can understand why Christians and Jews don't think the same way."

He looked at me with sympathetic eyes and I could see that he was searching for the right words to say. "I don't want you to think that I'll be able to give you an easy solution to what you're going through. I'll try to answer any questions that you have as best as I can, but I want you to understand that the ultimate decision of what you should do has to come from you."

I nodded my head in affirmation, which prompted him to continue. "There's a lot going on in the question that you're asking. I think I know how to answer you, but just wait a minute. I want to tell my wife Karen something, and then we could sit and talk down the hall."

He came out a few minutes later with Karen and introduced us to each other. She was a little heavy set, taller than average and very energized. You couldn't tell that she just went through a difficult episode with her daughter. She seemed to take things in stride as if all of this was an everyday experience.

When she left to go back to her daughter, Isaac explained that his wife had volunteered in the 1973 Arab Israeli War, and saw what real problems really were. Most things that shake us as we go through life are manageable, as long as you put them in the proper perspective. Isaac had a lot of pride when he spoke of Karen, and you could even see it in his eyes as she walked away from us to the area where their daughter was resting.

Isaac then turned to me and began. "It's a little obvious that your wife's request that you baptize your son has gotten you thinking. A lot of questions that you never even considered are going to be coming into your head right now. Let's try to break down your questions into manageable parts. The first thing that you have to understand is why Orthodox Jews believe in the truth of the Bible and that it came from G-d. The next area that has to be explored is a little more complicated. If the Orthodox Jews believe in the Bible as divine, and the Christians do as well, then what prevents the Jews from also believing in the Christian Bible, based on prophecy in the Old Testament?"

"I don't know if I would have said it that way, but I guess I was comparing the religions in the way you just put it." Isaac had verbalized my own questions better than I could do so myself.

"Let's approach this", he continued, "by playing Devil's advocate and assume the Reform Jews are correct. The way that I understand the position of the Reform Jews vis a vis the Bible is that the Bible was written by Moses with the purpose of showing the world the correct morality. Now, for argument's sake, say that you were going to write a book that you wanted the world to believe was divine. The last thing you would want to do would be to put specific facts in there that could easily be disputed. Your language would be cryptic so that you would avoid appearing wrong. When the ancient Greeks would ask questions of the Oracle at Delphi, for example, they received one word answers that could be taken to mean anything. The burden was on the questioner to interpret the answers correctly. In effect, the Oracle could never be proven wrong.

"Since the Reform Jews claim that the Bible was written by Moses, let's look at Moses, the man. Moses was born in Egypt, and though he traveled as far south as the Sudan in Africa, he really could not have been familiar with the animals that lived in the rest of the world. If you look in the book of Leviticus, in Chapter 11, the laws which designate which animals are considered kosher are introduced. As a rule, a kosher animal must both chew its cud and have split hooves. Presenting that information alone would not get a human writer into any trouble. A curious bit of information follows this. A complete list of all animals in existence which have either split hooves or chews its cud, but not both, is presented. Now, if Moses is the author of the Bible, and he only traveled within the immediate vicinity of Egypt, how could he make such a declaration? Not only that, but for the more than 3,300 years since the Bible was given to us, that list has never been proven to be false. It stands to reason that the Bible could only have been presented by a being who knows with absolute certainty what creatures exist not only in that area but everywhere else in the world."

"You really can't argue with that logic, but what about when the Bible talks of the sun stopping in the sky?" I asked. "Didn't the ancients believe that the earth was the center of the universe from those portions in the text?"

"The language of the Bible is written in such a way so that the information given is from the point of view of the person spoken about. An example of this is the portion in the Bible after Isaac was born.[30] Abraham and Sara are discussing what to do with Hagar, the servant of Sara, and what to do with Ishmael, Hagar's son that was fathered by Abraham. When Sara's feelings are discussed, Ishmael is referred to as the son of the handmaid. When Abraham's feelings are discussed, Ishmael is referred to as Abraham's proper son, because Abraham considered Ishmael to be a valid heir to his estate. When G-d speaks to Abraham, Ishmael is again referred to as the son of the handmaid, in effect telling Abraham that Sara was correct in her assessment that Isaac and not Ishmael was the rightful heir. Ishmael is the same person in all of these instances, and yet, because the differing descriptions are presented of him, we have a greater understanding of the inner feelings of those around him which relate to him.

"When the Bible refers to the sun stopping in the sky, it is describing the event from the vantage point of our position on the Earth. It's describing how the event appears to us. The scientific process of what occurred is not given to us in the text. For a greater scientific understanding we can refer to one of two areas. First we can examine the Talmud, which contains the additional information given to Moses to help understand what the written text was referring to. The next area we can review would be books like the Zohar and Kitvei Ari which contain information on the hidden meanings of the Bible. The Zohar was put into writing about two thousand years ago by a Rabbi named Rabbi Shimeon bar Yochai. Kitvei Ari are a series of books which record information taught by Rabbi Isaac Luria a little over four hundred years ago.

"I happen to have an article in my bag that was written recently by a Rabbi Eli Mansour, in which he quotes a portion of the Zohar.[31] Now remember that the author of the Zohar only lived in the immediate area of Israel and never traveled outside of it. All of his knowledge is from an in depth learning of the Bible and Talmud." Isaac excused himself and got up to where his wife had gone and returned less than a minute later with a magazine in his hand. As he walked, he turned the pages until he found what he was looking for.

"Here it is," he said as he approached the spot where I was sitting. "I'll let you read it, and you can decide whether it sheds light on your question."

I took the magazine from him and he pointed to the spot which he wanted me to read from. The quoted portion began: "The whole world and its inhabitants revolve like a ball. Some live at the bottom and some at its top, and each ethnic group living on a different part of the sphere differs from its neighbors in color, physiognomy and the like, due to climatic changes. All manage to stand on the Earth, however, just as their neighbors in other lands. As a result of the spherical shape of the Earth, some people benefit from sunlight at the very same time that others lie in darkness. There is even a place in the world which is almost continually sunlit, visited by night for only a brief time. (Zohar Vayikrah 10a)."

I had to read the passage again a second time. "If this Rabbi describes the Earth as a sphere in an age when people thought that the Earth was flat, it's amazing enough. That he describes the Earth as spinning means that he knew that it was not the sun that went around the Earth, but it was the spinning of the Earth that gave the impression that the sun rose and fell. This was written two thousand years ago?"

"Yes," he said. "When the Bible mentions the sun stopping in the sky, we know that a process that we don't yet understand had occurred. We do know that something happened to lengthen the days, because all the Jewish people who were present at the time of the writing bore testimony to that fact."

I now interrupted him. "I think I know what you're saying. I've always heard that G-d is not controlled by time. He can see things that happened, things that are happening, and things that will happen as if they're all current events. That never made sense until I studied the discoveries of Albert Einstein. Before Einstein, it was said that if you put all of the matter in the universe into a suitcase and someone asked what you had left, you would answer that there was space and time. After Einstein, it was proven that if all matter was in the suitcase, then time would be in the suitcase as well.[32] I still don't understand it, but you're saying that science has not yet caught up with the Bible."

"That's exactly what I'm saying. I wasn't sure if you would realize my point so quickly," he responded.

"Now we're back to my original question," I said. "How do we know, for example, that something back then really happened to lengthen the day? What kind of evidence do you have to support the claim that the day became longer?"

Isaac stopped for a second, deep in thought. Suddenly, as if a light bulb went on in his head, he resumed speaking. "There was an article in a recent issue of Natural History magazine about certain types of insects.[33] A portion of the article described a particular insect that eats the interior of a leaf and leaves behind a sugary residue that is referred to by the locals as manna. This insect's habitat is in dry areas, such as is found in the Middle East. The author then stated that it was this food that is referred to in the Bible, in Exodus, as the food that the Jews ate in the desert when they left Egypt. In effect, he states that the miracle of the manna never happened, but it was really a naturalistic event which, over time, morphed into the miracle as explained in the Bible.

"Let's assume that his theory was correct, and let's try to project what could have happened in history, based on that theory.[34] We start with a naturalistic process that occurred in the area of where the Jews settled in Israel, and we have to keep in mind that, according to the theory, the process is still occurring now. The naturalistic process, then, is the production of the sugary food by the insects. The insects were producing the food in the

Sinai Desert where the Jews had traveled through. We know that even today, these same types of insects continue to produce this sugary food which is referred to as manna. The whole episode in the Bible of the manna falling from heaven for six days a week; of it having dough like consistency; of any leftover food turning rancid by the next morning, except for food left over and eaten on the Sabbath; that was a story that, in his eyes, developed over time. The event according to the scientist is that the food obtained as a by product of the insects was what sustained the Jews for all those years. Now let's go back to your question and phrase it for this case. How do we prove that it was manna as related in the Bible and not manna from insects that was eaten in the time of the Bible?

"There was a lecture given by a Professor in Israel by the name of Rabbi Dovid Gottlieb in which this exact theory is elaborated on. He said that if, as many scientists believe, the Jews obtained their food through a natural process, when could the story as shown in the Bible have started? It could not have started a year or even ten years after they left the desert, because the event of eating the manna from the leaves would have been fresh in their memory. You couldn't consider changing the story until fifty to one hundred years after the death of the desert generation.

"Let's look at one such scenario after that time period. Two children are playing. One tells the other of manna that fell in the desert from stories that his grandfather told him. The other child runs home and tells his father about the manna, but the father turns to his son, and asks where he heard that fanciful story. When he finds out, he explains to his son that it's just a story from the imagination of the other boy's grandfather, and not to believe it. After all, the manna is still being produced by the insects in the desert. The children and grandchildren of those who experienced the travels in the desert know from their families that their food came from the insects. The question arises as to whether it's possible to change such a story even after hundreds of years?

"There were millions of people who moved through the desert during the time period of the Bible. Written records were the norm of that society. Although you may not have the physical evidence of the manna coming down, you do have what is called social evidence. At what point in time can you change the stories of an entire nation of over three million people who all witnessed and participated in the event that occurred every day, over the course of forty years, especially when that naturalistic event is happening close by today? The truth is, you can't. Given all that I've said, the events as told in the Bible are much more plausible than the theories espoused by the scientists."

Isaac made his point again. I had never thought of the idea of social evidence. When you coupled the information that was handed down from one generation to the next, which was corroborated by the written information from that time period, how could a whole nation suddenly start a story of food coming down from heaven with miraculous properties? When you add the fact that the real source of nourishment would have been nearby in the desert and still providing food, it was truly impossible for the story to be initiated if it wasn't true to begin with.

I had a question, though. "We have stories that were believed for generations about certain events that whole groups of people believed. For example, you have stories of knights fighting fire breathing dragons, which was a widely accepted belief. How do you separate those beliefs from the ones that are rational, without the benefit of hindsight?"

"Rabbi Gottlieb explained that very point. Let's look at the manna episode and let's see what's special about the witnesses to that event. First of all, they were in a state of relative calm. They got up in the morning and found their breakfast on the ground and picked it up. Next, the miracle repeated itself each day for forty years, so that they were sure of what they saw. Most important of all was that because the whole population of over three million people experienced it, the miracle could be corroborated by everyone there.

"The testimony of those who witnessed the manna now becomes very compelling. That scenario is very different from the story that you gave of the dragons. Who witnessed the event? You only have the knight coming in from the forest all beaten and bruised, and claiming that he encountered a dragon. What you don't have is a story of a fire breathing dragon entering London in the middle of the day, and destroying buildings with the flames from its breath, and finally being killed and falling into the Thames River.

"Even the giving of the Ten Commandments at Mount Sinai is an event which had to have happened. There were masses of people that witnessed the event. The accounts that they gave to each other and their descendants, along with the written records from the time, show that something beyond belief had to have happened. In an age before microphones and speaker systems, the fact that all three million people say that they heard a booming voice from the heavens, is a miracle that you can't reject.

"Judaism is the only religion that can claim that every single one of its members heard the word of G-d directly. No other religion can make such a claim.

"Just to make this pertinent to what you're going through with the request by your wife to baptize your son, consider this. The Christians believe that

G-d spoke to all the Jewish people to proclaim an eternal set of laws. They then say that Jesus, a Jew himself, was able to declare many of these laws null and void and changed others. For example, for his followers, the laws governing the Sabbath were changed, and baptism became a substitute for circumcision.

"Let's look at logic again, and ask yourself this. Since G-d went through the trouble of proclaiming his eternal law to all the Jewish people at Mount Sinai, don't you think that if these eternal laws are truly now irrelevant, G-d should call all the Jewish people back again and tell them it's all off?[35] Can a man who claims to be the Messiah and who comes in the name of G-d, cast off those eternal commandments decreed by G-d which he doesn't agree with? The Jewish religion does not have the provisions to accept such a thing.[36] Christianity, then, is a religion that has no connection to the Jewish religion and is based on a belief that is in opposition to what the Jewish people believe in."

My classes with Father Baldino made me now protest. "What about all the prophecy that was satisfied by the coming of Jesus? I understand from what you said that we shouldn't disregard the commandments given to all the Jews, but what stops the Jews from accepting Jesus as the Messiah?"

Isaac stopped and smiled. He now looked briefly at his watch. I could tell that he was done for right now. "If you'd like," he said, "and you could come to the hospital tomorrow afternoon, we can continue the discussion, but I would have to bring some things with me to better explain what I want to say."

I felt like I was watching an episode of "The Perils of Pauline"[37] and had to wait until next week to see how the heroine would be saved. I decided not to press Isaac more, since it suddenly hit me that my body was yearning for some rest in a decent bed. The two of us walked to Karen, where I bid her good luck. Isaac then walked me back to the elevator, and I thanked him and promised I would meet him the next day. As I left the hospital to go my apartment, my spirits were both uplifted from this new source of knowledge, and at the same time, they were broken by my confusion over where my life was heading.

15

When I arrived at my apartment, I was greeted by the day worker who was inside, waiting for Jennie to come home from school. Susan and I had forgotten to call her today, and I quickly let her know that everything was working out fine with Eric. I excused myself afterwards and told her that I would be taking a little nap. With all that had happened over the last few hours, I was afraid that sleep would elude me, but the exhaustion I felt easily enveloped my body and brought on a deep sleep.

I woke to the sound of Jennie's voice as she came running into my bedroom. I must have been asleep for about an hour and was a little woozy, but when Jennie jumped on my bed and gave me a little bear hug, my head quickly cleared.

Jennie was now telling me how much she missed me, and of how grandma and mommy had cuddled with her last night and the stories they told her of when mommy used to be little and she cuddled next to grandma.

We sat there talking for about fifteen minutes, then I told her I would take a shower, and that afterwards we could play.

The hot running water on my back did a great job at reviving me. As the water pelted my back in rhythmic bursts, the conversation that I had with Isaac began to replay in my head as though it were poetry being read to the tempo of the water. The words never formed a conclusion. They instead were transformed into the questions that were now plaguing me. I just closed my eyes and waited for the answers to start appearing, but nothing happened.

As I got dressed, I tried to focus on the joy I always felt from watching Jennie just be herself and I began to look forward to some quality time with only the two of us.

After dressing, I called Jennie into my bedroom and told her we were going to call grandma. I dialed my parents' house, and heard my mother pick up the phone. "How's the baby?" she asked. I briefed her again on what transpired since I spoke to her earlier and relayed the information from the doctors that it looked like all would be well. With more concern than before, she then asked, "How are you, Michael? I'm worried about you. You sound very tired." I assured her I was doing okay, and told her I was home with Jennie, who happened to be tugging on my arm for me to give her the phone. "In fact", I told her, "a little granddaughter of yours would like to say hello to you now."

Jennie happily took the phone and the two of them spoke to each other for a few minutes. I then heard my daughter saying "I love you grandma" followed by my mother's reply that could be heard faintly through the handset saying, "I love you too, Jennie."

I took the phone and told my mother I would be in the hospital tomorrow afternoon. She promised to go to the hospital with my father tonight to see how things were doing.

Jennie and I sat together for the next several hours. First we had some milk and cookies. Then we sat on the floor with a deck of cards and kept playing the game, 'go fish'. As I watched her sitting cross-legged, like an Indian, I reflected on how oversized the cards appeared as she held them up in her little hands. Her soft giggles as I kept making mistakes became the highlight of my day. When the giggles came, she would tilt her head back and say "Daddy", in a drawn out way. Each time it was her turn, she would raise her eyebrows and give me a broad smile as she slowly asked me if I had a card. Her cute large eyes became more pronounced when she did this and seemed to have an added sparkle. She never tired of playing the game and it was pure pleasure for me as well. After a while, we put the cards away and took out some of the books she was given in school. I sat on one side of the sofa and Jennie crawled on my lap. One of the oversized picture books from her bag was propped up on her outstretched legs. We shared reading the sentences until the book was completed, and by then, it was almost seven o'clock.

Susan called and said she would be coming home soon. Eric was still under observation, but the doctors were confident that he would pull through okay. Susan spoke to Jennie, and told her how much she missed her, and that she would be home in a little over half an hour.

The housekeeper had prepared some salad and some whole wheat spaghetti with olive oil, some herbs, and dried tomatoes. Jennie and I played house, set the table and tried to prepare everything for Susan's arrival.

When Susan walked in, Jennie ran to her and hugged her, just as Jennie had hugged me. She dragged Susan to the dining room to show her how we had set the table for the three of us.

It was at eight o'clock that we put Jennie to sleep. I was looking forward to a peaceful night. The last thing that I wanted was another confrontation, but when Susan told me that we would be having visitors tonight, I knew that a confrontation could not be avoided.

As we were putting away the dishes, Susan had her head turned away from me so that our eyes couldn't meet. In a very matter of fact way, in the same manner that she would tell me it was very sunny out today, she said, "My parents are going to pass by soon along with Father Baldino. They should be here at about nine o'clock." She knew this was a topic which I didn't want to enter into right now.

I stopped and turned to her. I was noticeably upset. "I don't know why you're pushing this thing with the baptism now. I was always open to your religion before, but now, I really don't want to discuss it."

She now looked deeply at me, with a hurt in her eyes that always made me break. "I never wanted to push you with anything to do with religion. This illness that happened to Eric, though, is really a wake up call for us. He should have been baptized when he was born, but he wasn't. I agreed to forego it and only have a circumcision but a circumcision is not enough. Just like you made the effort to understand Christianity from Father Baldino, you should at least try to understand why baptism is so important."

Even though Susan's words were spoken softly, I felt as though I was being pushed into a corner, so that I felt like I had to push back. "When Eric was born, you never spoke to me about baptizing him. I don't know if this is coming from you or from your parents." I could see that the way that I emphasized that last word struck a nerve.

It was very out of character for Susan to raise her voice at me, so it hit me all the more when she now did so and yelled out to me, "How could you be so heartless when it comes to our children?" We both suddenly froze, and my mind now started to race.

In that split second, the conversation I had with Susan's father when we first met came back to me. At the time I had pushed aside the words he spoke as if they were meaningless rhetoric. I hadn't realized how prescient those words would prove to be.

I remembered the first time I was in his house when he sat me down to make me aware of the difficulties I would be facing with my marriage to Susan. He said that he was most concerned with the fate of the children that we would be blessed with. Susan and I had to choose a religion for our household. Our children can be raised either Jewish or Catholic, but not both. The two religions were not compatible with each other. It took me all of these years to realize the truth of what he had said. Now I was faced with this battle against Susan, whom I still deeply loved. She was raised with a deep feeling for her faith, and I now felt that my beliefs were just now starting to rise up to the surface of my consciousness and I couldn't walk away from them now.

As much as his words forewarned me of my dilemma, there was another way of looking at them. When her father said that the children could choose Judaism or Catholicism, but not both, why did that have to mean that I had to accept that they would be Catholic? Instead of me going over to Susan's beliefs, as I had been doing these past couple of years, maybe I could convince her to go my way. Her background seemed so strong, though, that it was almost unimaginable that she would turn away from her upbringing, and embrace my religion, especially when I was only groping through it myself. My only chance was to go about it by not fighting her. Isaac was showing me things about my own faith through logic and history. Maybe that's what I had to do with Susan.

The thought of leaving Susan was beyond my imagination. I felt that she was a part of me, and I had to do whatever I could to get past this impasse. I decided to go along with her suggestion to meet with her family and their priest, but not to commit myself to any path just yet, until I was able to sort out what I should do.

I walked over to her and took her hand, which she pulled away. I reached out for her hand a second time, and said to her softly, "I love you Susan. If it means that much to you, we'll meet with the priest tonight and discuss it. Let's always remember, though, how much we care about each other. I only want to make you happy."

She didn't pull her hand away this time, but she kept her hand relaxed in my grip. She looked at me with indecision, as though she was trying to understand what could have prompted this change that came over me. She then smiled and held my hand tighter, and said, "I love you, too."

16

During the time that we had until our guests arrived, Susan and I purposely avoided all discussion of religion. While Susan cut up some fruit and put on some hot water for tea, I laid out some dishes and serving plates. We spoke of the hospital, the doctors and the newfound respect we now had toward the whole medical profession.

It was only 8:30 when the doorbell rang, which was a little earlier than I expected. Susan's parents had arrived. As they came in, I noticed that both of them were dressed impeccably, as usual. Her mother was wearing a long, black suede coat which was fully buttoned. There was a thick plush fur that began at the collar, and which continued in a narrow band down the front of the coat, and bordered the whole bottom. Her left hand held both her hat, and a pair of suede black gloves which matched her coat. She smiled as she strode confidently into the room with her head uplifted, and hugged her daughter. Following her in was my father in law. He wore a tan overcoat, and plaid scarf. He had started wearing ear muffs which wrapped around the back of his head so that the top of his head stayed neatly combed. His suit was visible at the area under his neck, and it was either a very dark blue or black, while his shirt was a pure white, with a solid pale blue tie. His hair had turned almost completely gray after his heart attack, but his features and build were those of a younger man.

My mother in law told Susan and I that we both looked drained. She told us that as soon as Eric got out of the hospital, she would take care of him and Jennie while Susan and I went away for at least a few days. We both thanked her and we led my in laws into the living room. My father in law told us that Father Baldino would be a little delayed, and that he could only stay for a few minutes as he had another engagement. "He feels very close to both you and Susan and to you especially, Michael. He said that you had a strong interest in the weekly Bible classes that he teaches. After all the time you've been coming to him, he feels that you're just as much a part of his congregation as any of us are."

My mother in law now took up the conversation. "We really don't want to stay too long. We know that you've had . . . , we've really all had, a very trying couple of days. There are just some things that we'd like to bring up for you to think about. Michael, you know that we never pushed our religious beliefs on you all the time that you've been married, but I think it would be good if I explained a little about what our religion means to us as a family."

My father in law now broke in. "I think what we're trying to say is that when you marry someone that's of a different faith, it's almost like you speak two different languages at times. What we're trying to do is help you to understand us better by explaining some of the background to the language that either myself, or any practicing Catholic uses. We meant to discuss this with Father Baldino here, but I guess we can start with some thoughts of our own."

We were all still standing when Susan broke in, saying, "Why don't we all sit down inside? I put up some tea and prepared some fruit. Dad, I bought some green tea for you. Mom, I got you some mint tea."

"Thank you, honey", my mother in law said, as she sat at one end of the sofa. "Maybe I'll try some of the green tea tonight. The cantaloupe looks good, too. Maybe I'll have some of that as well."

As Susan poured out the tea, we all proceeded to sit around the coffee table. Manhattan apartments are not known for their large size, so that we only had a sofa and a bergere chair around the coffee table. The sofa was big enough for three, so my in laws and Susan sat there. Susan's mother then took up the conversation again.

"I know that I have a tendency to be very direct and sometimes stubborn. That's just my nature, but I also picked it up from my own parents, who were very strict. My father was a very unforgiving man and anything less than near perfection was not acceptable. My belief in G-d ran along the same lines. I saw G-d as an extension of my own father. Life was either black or white. Either I was good and I would get rewarded or I wasn't, and punishment would follow. It was almost like Santa Claus asking the kids if they were naughty or nice. If nice, you would be rewarded, and if naughty, you would be herded into your room until your punishment was over.

"I didn't know that about grandma and grandpa. They never seemed strict at all", Susan said surprisingly.

"They were very different when they were younger. Times were also different then and they felt that they had to rule over the household to stop us from straying.

"When I grew up, I still had that need to be perfect in anything that I did. It wasn't until after I got married that I found that perfection was not a requirement. Your father helped me to see that I was special even if things didn't go well. Over time, I came to understand that G-d's love was unconditional. In return, I felt I should live my life according to the Church and do the best I can. Tolerance of my own shortcomings as well as that of others was something I pushed myself to gradually accept. Kindness naturally followed. It was a matter of really picking up the essence of the Bible before I could comprehend the individual words.

"Being a parent also helped me learn what unconditional love was. When you have a child, and you care for him or her, you know that whatever that child may do, it can never diminish that motherly feeling that will compel you to protect your child from any harm.

"When I realized that the love that the Lord had for me was an unconditional parental love, I made a promise that I would raise my children to always love Him and obey the laws of the Church. As much as Susan or my boys go out in the world, there is that core part of their souls that will always be linked to the Church. Even though Susan agreed to forego the rite of baptism when Eric was born, the awareness that she would eventually have him baptized was always inside of her, and it took this medical problem to trigger it."

My mother in law had never explained why she had such a strong feeling for the Church. Both Susan and I thought that it was just one of life's constants. As much as Susan and her mother had tried to be close in the past few years, the reasons behind my mother in law's love of the Church had never come out. My mother in law, who was sitting next to Susan on the sofa, was looking at her daughter and was now holding her hand. She continued, "My religious convictions are as much a part of me as the color of my hair, or the shape of my face. Whether or not Susan realizes it, subconsciously, it's also a part of her."

I felt that with the conversation beginning as it was, I was not going to like what was going to follow.

"Michael," my father in law now said, "all we want to do is follow the teachings that we've been following for generations. There are certain rites that are important to our family and baptism is one of them." The doorbell rang and interrupted him. As Susan got up to get the door, my father in law said, "That must be Father Baldino. I think he could better explain why Eric's baptism is a necessary act for those of our faith."

It was Father Baldino who was now entering. He greeted everyone in the room, and his calm voice, which I had grown accustomed to listening to because of all his classes that I attended, now spread its magic on everyone in the room. All of us, me included, turned to him in his role as our teacher, to shed more light on this act which Susan's family was pushing so hard for us to do.

"I'm sorry I couldn't get here earlier", he said, with his slight smile that was his trademark. Susan helped him off with his coat, which was actually a heavy raincoat that served double duty as a winter coat. His black suit and shirt stood in stark contrast to the white collar that framed the bottom of his neck.

"You couldn't have chosen a better time to come, Father", said my father in law. "We were just discussing the importance of baptism and really needed you to shed light on the background of the rites for Michael."

Susan now interrupted, and said, "Please Father, why don't you relax a few minutes first. It's cold outside and you should warm up a bit. Would you like something hot to drink?"

"Tea would be fine", he said. He now turned to both Susan and me. "How are the both of you? It's been a harrowing few days."

"We're holding up pretty well", I said.

I had gotten up and offered my bergere chair to the Father, while I pulled another chair in from the dining room. As Susan began to pour some tea, the Father sat and began to speak.

"A lot of people don't realize how important certain of the acts we perform really are. I was wondering, as I came here, how to explain, and a story came to mind.

"There was a young boy of about 10 years old. It was a snow filled winter that year, and the boy kept on dreaming of getting a certain sled that he had seen in a toy store. It was all he spoke about, and in time, the years passed, and the sled was forgotten.

"When he was in his early twenties, he got married. As a wedding gift, he received a sled from certain neighbors who wrote how they remembered that, years ago, he always wanted one. With shock and surprise he turned to his new bride and said, "When I was young, having this sled was the most important thing in the world to me, but doesn't my neighbor know that I grew up and realize that having a sled doesn't mean anything to me anymore?"

"You see, Michael, all of us in this world are the same as the child who longs for that sled. When we're on this earth, we are the child who longs for material things. It is only when we move on to heaven, when we have a greater awareness of what's important, that we know that the things that were important to us in the world of the flesh are not what counts when we rise to the world of the spirit. The material things that we once longed for actually have no meaning or worth at all. True worth is governed by a different set of values. Those acts that enhance our spirits are the ones we should have focused on, but by the time we have moved to heaven, it's too late.

"The Bible is the road map prepared by G-d to show us what's really important in this world. Everything boils down to finding the truth of the meaning of our existence. The Bible states in John, chapter 16[38] that the Holy Spirit will teach us all things. The Spirit of truth which goes out from the Father will convict the world of guilt in regard to sin and righteousness and judgment; it will guide us into truth. How do we know that the truth of Jesus is for Jew as well as Gentile? For that we look to your bible, in Jeremiah. Chapter 31[39] begins with the word of the Lord being delivered by Jeremiah. "The time is coming when I will make a new covenant with the house of Israel and with the house of Judah. It will not be like the covenant I made with their forefathers when I took them by the hand to lead them out of Egypt, because they broke my covenant, though I was a husband to them."

"There is a new covenant, as foretold by the Jews, and it was heralded by Jesus. Jesus declared baptism to be a basis of the new covenant. For the proof of my words, you need only look again into the Bible, which is the most perfect of all books.

"In John, chapter 3, it's written that Jesus said that no one can enter heaven unless he has been born again of water and the Holy Spirit.[40] This applies to children as well, as we see in Mathew, chapter 19[41]. "Let the children come to me, and do not hinder them; for to such belongs the kingdom of heaven."

"Baptism is a sacrament which accomplishes several things, first and foremost being the remission of both original sin and actual sin. In the case of children and infants, it removes only original sin, since they have not reached the age when they could be held accountable for actual sin. We also know that under the new covenant prophesied by Jeremiah, baptism has replaced circumcision, because Paul refers to baptism as "the circumcision of Christ" and the "circumcision made without hands".[42]

You would not be doing anything that's against the word of G-d when you accept the rite of baptism for your child. In fact, as a Jew, it is mandated even more strongly for you than for a Gentile. You will be doing G-d's will."

"We're not asking you for anything that's not right for Eric", Susan said. "When you think about what Father Baldino just explained, there really shouldn't be any objections at all." Susan was anxious for me to accept the Father's words, but that made my resistance increase.

Father Baldino paused and I now felt all eyes on me, waiting for my reaction. Because of my lack of knowledge of the Bible, I wasn't sure even how to respond but I had to say something.

"I see what you're saying, Father, but . . ."

"Is there something specific that you'd like to ask?" replied Father Baldino.

I wasn't sure how to answer him. The thought passed through my mind that maybe he was right. I was tired and it would be so easy not to have to resist everyone anymore. Almost my whole life was carried out without a connection to my Jewish heritage. I didn't even know what being Jewish was all about.

As I groped for an answer to give him, my eyes turned to the area to his right. The Xmas tree, all lit up and decorated was shining brightly, but just to the side of it, sat my menorah with its single bulb still glowing. I knew what I had to say.

"There's a lot of logic in what you're saying, but I don't really know what to even ask right now. Susan and I had always planned on allowing our children to decide how they wanted to worship in the future. I know that Susan now wants to move more towards Christianity in raising our kids. Because of that change in her feelings, I want to try and be open-minded. I want to do whatever I can to make her happy, but for us to take a step like this, I need some time to discuss pros and cons with Susan before we can agree on a mutual course of action.

"The way you explained the Biblical sources for your position makes everything you say very logical. I think the thing that makes it difficult for me to embrace Christianity right now is that for the thousands of years that Christianity has been in existence as a religion, Jews as a nation have never accepted the precepts of Christianity as their own. I want to be sure we're doing the right thing in making this decision for our children. I just need some time to digest all of this."

"No one is saying that you should drop your Jewish ties. You are a Jew and you have your own obligations as far as the Church is concerned." Father Baldino now grew very serious and sat on the edge of the bergere cushion. He stared at me and continued to speak as if warning me of a danger that I was not heeding. "Jews remain the Chosen people. You should know, though, that while the laws of the Old Testament bring the Jews closer to salvation, they are not sufficient for salvation. According to Peter,[43] the Jewish Patriarchs and all mankind had to wait for the Messiah before being admitted to heaven in what is termed the Limbo of the Fathers. By not accepting Him, you are condemning your soul and the souls of your children to an afterlife in which they will be barred from entering Heaven.

"I know you need time to absorb what I'm saying, but I only mean well for you." He now spoke very slowly. "There is no redemption without Jesus."

The strength of how he said that last sentence made me shudder. I had never quite understood how pogroms against the Jews could be undertaken. I never could imagine what type of justification could be used to force the Jews of ages past to accept Jesus but here it was. They would say that "we are doing this for your own good."

I knew that I had to avoid being confrontational. "Please Father, don't misunderstand me. I'm not saying no. I just need a little more time to sift through all of this."

Father Baldino looked at me for a second and you could tell he was wondering how much effect his words had on me. He leaned back, then broke into his smile again and said, "Okay, then. All we really wanted was for you to listen. I wouldn't expect that you would decide anything now. I'm sure that by tomorrow or the next day, there will be a whole set of questions that you'd like to ask. I'll be more than willing to sit with you another time." His eyes became serious again, as he said, "This is a very important time of your life, Michael. This difficulty that you're going through may have been for the sole purpose of prodding you to do the right thing for your family. Don't ignore it."

With that, he glanced at his watch, and rose, while saying his goodbyes to us, and apologizing that he couldn't stay longer. As I went to get his coat, my in laws also rose, and my father in law said to Susan, "I think we should be running along, too. This decision is really between you and your husband. Also, Susan", my father in law hesitated as he looked at his daughter while dropping his voice, "give this decision some time. Just as it's not easy for you, it's not easy for Michael. Just focus on taking one day at a time, and deal with Eric's recovery. Your husband cares for you a lot. Remember that."

I was within earshot of them and I think my father in law spoke loudly enough on purpose, in order to put me at ease. We always got along very well and he didn't want my resistance tonight to be the cause of a fight between me and his daughter. Susan and I were both on edge because of the pressure that we'd been under and he didn't want something said that could not be taken back. Susan, who had appeared frustrated as she watched me replying to Father Baldino's remarks, did calm down from the words of her father. He gave her a hug and kissed her on the forehead, then walked over to me to shake my hand. Susan's mother hugged her daughter and said goodbye to me while Father Baldino waited for the two of them at the front door.

When they left, I looked at Susan and said, "Upset?" while raising my eyebrows and lowering my head. She said, "Don't think I'm not going to stop working on you. I want this for Eric. I want it very badly, but" she now smiled, "I'll let my father protect you for tonight." She put her arm around my waist and said, "Come on. Let's take a look at Jennie and call the hospital one last time. Then we'll clear up in here and go to sleep."

Within a half hour we had cleared up again. I told Susan I wanted to check on the front door to make sure it was locked. As I was returning to the bedroom, I passed the Xmas tree, and then the menorah. I stopped and stared at it. Last night was the second day of Chanuka, and tonight was the third, I thought, as I slowly turned on two more of the red bulbs.

17

Although I was in bed by 10:00 PM, I had a very restless sleep. I experienced the beginning of the realization that I was in a lose-lose situation. When I thought back to consider what decision in my life was most pivotal, I always ended up at the point when Susan and I met. It was one of the happiest days of my life but, at the same time, it led me to my current predicament. I was perfectly happy to carry on with life as it had been when I was first married, but with the illness of my father in law several years ago, coupled with the current illness of my son, the necessity of choosing a religious lifestyle was thrust upon me. The religion question, which I always felt would be a non-issue, was now tearing me apart.

Adolescence is usually accompanied by a feeling of invincibility. A young man in his late teens and early twenties feels that no adversity can overtake him. Risks are something that affects other people, but not him. Every action he takes and any venture he embarks on has Lady Luck as a partner. His whole life is guided by the mistaken notion that he is in full control.

When I got married and I was warned to acknowledge that I might be faced with difficulties in the future, I felt that I would have the power to prevent them. I became that foolish youth who thought he could overcome the obstacles that hundreds of people before him could not. I closed my eyes to the fact that an interfaith marriage would be difficult. I chose to ignore reality. I chose to ignore my father in law's warnings. I chose to ignore the difficulties experienced by all of the people that went down that path before me.

As I lay in bed and reflected on my past, I lamented the fact that the majority of my Jewish education spanned only the last few days of my life. I had no childhood memories of Jewish holidays other than the forced attendance to synagogue on Rosh Hashana and Yom Kippur. I was labeled a Jew, but there was nothing behind that label that explained what the label signified. I would laugh at Jewish jokes, donate to certain Jewish charities and identify with the country of Israel when the world would gang up against it. My everyday actions, though, helped me to meld into the common society devoid of any ethnic label. I wanted to feel that my religion did not set me apart. I wanted to eat whatever foods I chose. I wanted to ignore all the restrictions in the Bible as irrelevant. I wanted to ignore the idea that a weekly Sabbath was decreed as holy.

Sometimes, when certain celebrities were interviewed, they mentioned their Jewish background. It was very often to fit in with a joke, like the comedian who mentioned that he was Jewish and had made a trip throughout Europe several years back[44]. Inevitably he would be welcomed to visit the memorials set up in almost every country for the Jews. The memorials, he found out, were always dedicated to the time when the Jews were kicked out of that country. You laughed, but the full impact of their remark, that it reflected an ongoing reality of history, did not sting until later. When the sting was felt, it would be pushed aside and replaced with the thought that "it can't happen to me."

The stillness of the night allowed me to further sift through my memory. I remembered a movie that won a number of awards a few years back, called Life is Beautiful. The movie was an Italian film and took place during the Holocaust. The fact that the characters spoke in Italian and German gave the film more realism. The main character in the story, a Jew, was married to an Italian Christian woman, and they had a child. The story traces how the Jew and his child were torn from the wife and placed in a concentration camp. It ends with the Jew allowing himself to be killed so that his son would live, and the son ends up reuniting with the Christian mother. The point of the story was that even though the father died, the next generation would live on. I now tried to imagine the future of that child, who was to be brought up by his Christian mother. Although the movie ends with the intention of supplying a happy ending, that the son survived, it really ended by showing how Hitler's wishes were fulfilled. The Jew died, and his Christian wife now raised his child as a Christian. The Jewish line of that man's family ended with him.

The last few years made me realize that what embarrassed me more than anything was how my wife's family held that the words of the Bible represented unshakable truth. That included both the Old Testament and the New. Contrast that to my family and community. While the Christians believed that the Bible was bestowed on the Jews directly by G-d, my Reform Jewish community taught that men wrote the Bible. The Christians had more faith in G-d as the supreme ruler of the world and as the source of all Biblical law, than I ever did.

My beliefs, or what you could really call my disbeliefs, were rooted in the fact that science had supposedly disproved the facts of the Bible. Father Baldino focused his support for the Bible as a divine document by contrasting the morality of the period before the Bible with the period after. The Judeo-Christian values that we accept in our modern society are not derived from the rational thought processes of man. As part of the weekly classes, the issue of slavery was discussed. A slave in the pre Biblical world was property that was to be used or abused as the master wished. The slave had no rights, and had the status of an animal. He or she could be beaten, killed or abused in whatever manner the master desired. The Old Testament laid down a contrary view.[45] Life was precious, and no one could abuse the slave that he owned. In fact, the slave in a Jewish household had to be treated as if he were a part of the family and sometimes more so.[46] If there was one blanket or pillow between the master and the slave, it had to go to the slave. A slave that was beaten could be given his freedom if the beating were in excess of what he deserved. A slave was a being that was created in G-d's image, and, as such, he or she had to be treated appropriately.

Even fruit bearing trees were given respect. The Old Testament would forbid a Jewish invading army from destroying those trees when they battled other nations.[47] Such an interest in life was unheard of in the ancient world.

The poor had a special place in the Jewish Bible as well. Every field had to have a corner of it that was not to be touched. Its produce would be for the poor.[48] As the wheat in the rest of the field would be cut and gathered, whatever stalks of wheat were dropped would be the property of the poor. The landowner would be prohibited from taking it. During holy days when Jews were required to go to Jerusalem and sacrifice in their Temple, the Jews of the city would open their homes to all. Every Jew was of equal stature and no one was turned away because he did not have the same amount of money as his neighbor. Again, this type of treatment of the poor was unheard of in the ancient world. The ancient world was a world where might was right. The poor were to be shunned by the aristocracy as a lower class and could never be their equals. There could never be a possibility of a poor man sitting at the same table, as an equal, with his more successful neighbor.

Father Baldino presented all this of the Old Testament to me. When I would hear my relatives speak of Jewish morality, we would discuss how Jews were kind, and gave charity, but I never knew the source. A Catholic priest had to open my eyes to the uniqueness of my faith.

He also raised many questions. Along with those classes were the prophecies that were the basis of the New Testament. They created the foundation for the declaration that Jesus was the Messiah, and that he was both the Son of G-d and somehow, even G-d himself. My problem with the New Testament was simple. If the prophecies were so cut and dry, and if Jesus performed the miracles that he did and proved to the world that he was the Messiah, why didn't the Jews of his own time believe in him? Even if they didn't believe in him when he was alive, why didn't they believe in him after his death? There had to be something that didn't make sense to them at the time period when Jesus lived; throughout the centuries since his death; and even today. I had to find out what it was.

As I rolled over to my side, I opened my eyes and watched the sleeping body of my wife. I always felt that I could be with her forever. With the birth of Jennie and now Eric, the bond that we had became all the greater. Our children were our future. There had to be a way to reconcile our religious feelings. There were many famous people that had intermarried, but of the cases I was aware of, the Judaism of the one parent didn't carry on into the children. In fact, the Judaism was lost. John Kerry is symbolic of those cases. He was the Presidential candidate in 2004 who later revealed that his grandparents were Jews who escaped from Europe. They changed their name to Kerry and changed their religion to free themselves from persecution. Their son married a woman out of his faith, and John Kerry, the grandson of Jews of Europe, was raised as a fully practicing Catholic. The result of a mixed marriage is that one of the religions must give in to the other. Almost always it ends with Judaism being pushed aside. The outcome: no more Jewish descendants.

If I no longer had feelings for my Jewish faith, it would be easy for me to just give in. On the other hand, I didn't want to fight against my wife anymore; I didn't want to fight against my in laws or Father Baldino. For all the talk that my family gave about their Judaism, the truth is that they knew nothing about it. The fact that they accepted me after I married a Christian wife was proof that their religion was secondary. Because of the last few days, however, I felt that I was meant to probe deeper into my heritage.

It was more than fortuitous that only three days ago my father happened to be out of the office and my employee, David Greenblatt, had to approach me instead to get permission to leave the office early. What followed was more like links in a chain than mere coincidences. My son took ill and his diagnosis was mistaken for something far more serious. That brought in Dr. Birnbaum, who introduced me to Isaac.

I now made up my mind to conduct a test. Isaac had said that he could explain why Jews didn't follow Christianity. If his answer held up, despite the prophecies from the Old Testament that Father Baldino had explained, then I would go on fighting. If he could not explain it, then I would acquiesce to the wishes of my wife and her family. This thought set me at ease. Once I put the burden of my choice on someone else's actions, the exhaustion that I was fighting off was able to overtake me, and I finally fell asleep.

18

I woke in the morning to the sound of my wife yelling frantically into the telephone She kept on repeating "But is he alright? Just tell me he's alright!" As she spoke, my heart began to sink, causing me to fear the worst. While the phone was still in her hand, I was able to hear a voice at the other end. Susan trembled and started to turn to me. She fumbled the phone and it dropped, and she just broke down in tears. I leaned over her and hurriedly picked up the receiver. I then started speaking to see if someone was still on the other line.

"Hello! Hello! Who's this?" I nervously asked. A calm man's voice replied "Is this Mr. Klein? This is Dr. Johnston at the hospital. I was trying to explain to your wife that there's been a change in your son's condition and we had to put him on a ventilator to help him with his breathing. This was not unexpected, as we weren't sure to what extent he was affected."

"But what do we do now? Is this something that he can recover from?" I asked this while leaning over and cradling my wife as she now began to whisper the words, "Please G-d".

"We've already consulted with Dr. Chai by phone, and he feels that Eric can get by, but not without help. He'll have to be connected to the ventilator and fed intravenously until he can get more strength. I'm sorry for having to call you with this information, but we have to advise you of any change in his condition. Please tell your wife that we're doing everything in our power to help your son. I'll be on duty all day, so as soon as you come in, I'll be able to better explain what's happening. At this point, please tell your wife that your son's condition is stable."

"We'll be there soon, doctor. Thank you" I said. I was still holding Susan as I told her that Eric was going to be alright. "The doctor said he was stable. We had to expect complications, but our son is a natural fighter."

Susan took a few deep breaths and regained her composure. She then slowly said, "If anything happens to him, I won't forgive myself. This is all my fault. I should have demanded, and I didn't. Even last night, I should have demanded."

I got Susan to calm down as best as I could but she kept on saying that she had to go through with it. This whole episode concerning the baptism was weighing very heavily on her. I told Susan that we should try to leave for the hospital as fast as we could. She took a deep breath, and then told me I was right. She then briefly closed her eyes before getting out of bed, as if hoping that when she opened them again, she would find that these last few minutes were a dream. We both took quick showers, and got dressed. Susan now began to ask me why I couldn't be more reasonable. Why did I have to risk our son's life? A feeling of anger now rose up from within her as she began to say that she would never forgive me if anything happened to Eric. I had so much doubt as to what was right. She appeared to have none. As she kept attacking my past actions, her anger grew, and I began to consider that her assertions were right. I was willing to do anything for Eric to be better, and if conceding to my wife's demand was going to do it, then so be it.

My nerves were still on edge from last night, and this was breaking me completely. When we woke Jennie, our minds were temporarily fixed on her reaction to all of this, and we focused on her.

Because we wanted to get to the hospital as quickly as possible, rather than wait for the housekeeper, we decided to take Jennie with us. Susan got her dressed. As Jennie was getting ready, I received a call on my cell phone from my father. He was expecting to calmly tell us that he and mom had been to the hospital last night and that everything was alright. I had to tell him that we had a call that Eric had been put on a ventilator and we were told to come in. I repeated what Dr. Johnston had told me: that Eric was now stable, but we still had to go in to speak to the doctor and review Eric's condition.

When my father asked me if he could help, I hesitated, and he quickly followed up his question by asking me what we were doing with Jennie. "We're taking her with us to the hospital. The housekeeper won't be here until later, and we can't wait here with Jennie until she gets picked up for school." He quickly answered, "I'm already on my way to the office. I'll meet you at the hospital. I'll call your mother to meet us, and we'll watch Jennie. I don't want you to go to the hospital alone." He spoke with such authority that I forgot for a second that I was a grown man, and I replied submissively as if I was ten years old again. "Okay Dad. I'll meet you there in a few minutes."

As we ushered Jennie out of the front door while telling her that we were going to visit her brother, Susan began to reproach me again. Her words were part request and part demand, almost like a schoolteacher who was reprimanding her class for an unforgivable prank. With a new found strength and conviction, she said that she should have been more insistent on the baptism when Eric was born. She had made a mistake, but it had to be corrected. There could be no alternative. What was happening to Eric was proof of it.

By the time we had gotten into the cab, it was almost eight o'clock and traffic was building up. Jennie sat between us, and I had my arm around her, while Susan was holding her hand. Susan would not let up, though, and kept on repeating that the baptism had to be done, and questioning me without allowing me time to respond as to why I didn't agree to it before.

It was difficult for me to defend my actions, because I didn't know how to. I had no logical reason for even raising a defense, other than the fact that I was Jewish. I couldn't use biblical arguments. Father Baldino had already used those against me. My head throbbed as I began to mentally agree with her until I finally blurted out, "We'll have him baptized."

My voice cracked as I said this, and I could see Jennie look up at me as I spoke. She had never seen her father get emotional and this surprised her. Susan also felt Jennie's reaction, and I could see that Susan held Jennie tighter. After this, she began speaking softly to Jennie, while I felt an over riding guilt over what I had committed to.

While I looked out of the cab window, I began to watch all of the people hurrying to get to wherever they were going. In my mind, I pictured a court room where each person was going to be questioned as to why they acted as they did. I was second to be tried. Before me was an emaciated man who was being tried for stealing food. A jury of twelve people began to take their seats and I couldn't help seeing that each of them had full bellies and wore comfortable clothes. They were now going to hear this next case of a man who had no food to eat and was forced to go out and steal some bread. They were doing so right after they had all eaten a full lunch at the expense of the court and were fully satiated.

As the emaciated man took the stand to plead his case, the empty stares of the members of the jury were directed to him. The prosecutor kept calling out, "Did you steal? Answer the question with a yes or no." "But", he said, "I had no food for my family. I saw the bread sitting there, and it was just before closing time at the bakery. He wasn't going to sell it anyway at that point, and it would just go stale. I needed food for my family."

"That wasn't the question!" thundered the prosecutor. "You were asked only this. Did you steal the bread? Reply by answering either yes or no." The emaciated man now cowered in his seat, and sheepishly replied, "Yes, but . . .". "Enough! You have confessed to your crime. Gentleman of the jury, I now present you with this thief!" He now turned to the jury who were all silently nodding in agreement. "This thief has confessed his crime. Is he guilty or not?"

As each of the jurors called out their verdict of guilty, the emaciated man slowly rose with his head lowered. With the guilty verdict pronounced by the last juror, the man was led out of the room in tears to make way for me. The injustice of having a man tried for stealing food, and being judged by a group of people to whom hunger was nothing more than a word, struck me deeply. When I walked up in front of the judge for the prosecutor to state the case against me, the judge announced that the jury would be replaced. The jurors all rose as one and left the room, to be replaced by a group of Rabbis who had only known the walls of the Hebrew school in which they taught and had never known temptation of the outside world. These were to be the ones that would pronounce a judgment on my actions. Just as the poor man before me was judged for stealing bread without anyone looking at what caused him to do so, I would be judged without anyone looking into my heart and examining the emptiness of my Jewish education, along with the influences from my wife and her family. I had no chance for acquittal.

"$14.60". The taxi driver called out the fare as we stopped in front of the hospital and I was pulled out of my daydream. Susan and Jennie got out while I paid the fare and followed them in.

We quickly went up to our floor and searched out Dr. Johnston. He came to us just a few minutes after we had him paged. By the way he quickly walked over to us, it was apparent that he had a number of things to deal with besides us. He came right to the point and told us that everything was still stable as before. Jennie looked up at the doctor with apprehension as she grasped Susan's hand. I leaned down to lift her up to give her comfort, and when I did so she put her arms around my neck and nestled her head on my shoulder. Jennie's actions must have had some humanizing effect on the doctor, because his demeanor was transformed. In the brief moment that he hesitated, my parents stepped out of the elevator and approached us. The doctor now spoke in a softer, slower manner and asked us if we would like to come to his office so that he could brief us on Eric's condition. To both Susan and myself, this was like a déjà vu experience, as it brought back memories of the tension which followed our similar meeting in Dr. Birnbaum's office when we were told of the possibility that Eric was stricken with SMA. We quickly replied in unison to Dr. Johnston that we wanted to know what was going on now and didn't want to wait until we got to his office.

The doctor and my parents were taken back by the brusqueness of our reply. Dr. Johnston maintained his softness as if he understood the anxiety we were feeling at the moment and said "That's alright", while looking at my parents, as if he was responding to their inner surprise at our reaction. He then nodded and led us about twenty feet away to the side of the hall. Luckily, at this hour, there were only a few hospital personnel and no visitors, so the area was relatively empty. He began by assuring us that the hospital was monitoring Eric on a 24 hour a day basis and that they were doing everything they could to insure his recovery. "Botulism, though, is very debilitating to an infant his age", he continued. "Since the bacterium affects the nerves and the nerves control the muscles, the limpness that you first noticed was a result. We were aware, though, that the affected muscles cover his entire body and not just his arms and legs. Overnight, when we saw that his breathing was becoming labored, we understood that those muscles were greatly weakened as well. We performed a blood gas analysis, and confirmed that he had to be intubated and put on a ventilator to assist him with his breathing. That's why he was transferred to the ICU."

My father then spoke up. "Isn't there some type of medication that you can give him to fight the botulism? There has to be something else that can be done besides putting tubes in him to let him breathe."

"Unfortunately" the doctor replied, "there is nothing else that we could do but allow his body to use its own resources to fight the bacteria. We're going to continue monitoring him, and we'll be doing all we can on our end. According to Dr. Chai, even though this is a setback, he should be able to come out of this alright."

"How long do you think it will take?" My father was the only one with the presence of mind to ask questions.

"We have to allow several weeks. Dr. Chai already checked on past cases. Even though botulism is rare in an infant, it does happen, and based on the recovery of other children, we feel that because your son is being treated at this early stage, he has a very good chance of recovery."

"And for now?" my father asked.

"Just be there for him" said the doctor, "and let's all hope for the best."

My mother had her arm around Susan, but the doctor's positive attitude gave all of us strength. The doctor then led us to where Eric now lay, and explained the function of each piece of equipment that was surrounding him. When we saw the precautions that were set in place for Eric's well being, we were more at ease. In addition, Jennie's presence made all of us reluctant to dwell on a bleaker picture. Susan now took Jennie from me and showed her how the doctors were taking care of her little brother. It was touching to see Jennie wave to her brother and tell him how she was going to take care of all of his toys for him until he came home.

We decided to wait there for a few more minutes and the doctor excused himself to go back to the main desk. As we stood there I thanked my parents while they both gave us words of encouragement. Susan then looked up at me with tired eyes and said harshly, "As soon as he's better!" As she finished, my face felt hot and I could feel my skin turn red. My father noticed it, but didn't say anything. He told my mother to take Susan inside the waiting area with Jennie so they could sit for a few minutes over a cup of coffee and relax. He then took my arm and asked me if I wouldn't mind going for a walk outside the building for some fresh air.

Although my father had always avoided showing his feelings, I was aware that he realized that there was a world of meaning in Susan's words. As we silently walked down the hospital corridor, the echo made by the clicking of our heels accentuated the emptiness of the halls. The rhythmic sound now marked the repetition of the thought that kept circulating in my brain. The burning that I had felt in my face had gone away, but I was now plagued by the knowledge of the guilt I felt because of what I had succumbed to, which would soon be revealed to my father. How could I tell him what was happening? How would he react to the news that his grandson was going to be baptized? I resolved not to say anything. In my mind he became one of the jurors from my daydream, and I feared that he would prepare to judge me while never being able to understand all that was influencing me to act as I did. My mother was a Jew, so how could my father put himself in my place? The truth is that he couldn't, so I knew that he would never understand.

We went downstairs and into the street where we took in the cold crisp winter air. Even though I never liked the cold, I felt refreshingly revived. The streets were filled now, as it was just before 9 o'clock and people were hurrying to work. The sidewalks were wide, but it was still difficult for me and my father to walk side by side because of the amount of people walking in each direction. Trees were rare in this part of the city, but in their place, there were metal posts which were topped by "No Parking" signs. A building was going up in the middle of the block, and the sound of heavy machinery, coupled with the normal New York City street sounds, made it impossible to carry on a conversation. My father motioned for me to go into a restaurant so that we would be able to sit down and talk in a more quiet atmosphere over some coffee.

Once inside, I tried to avoid discussing Susan by bringing up my discussion with David Greenblatt, and his request to leave early for the holiday. I started to open up to my father that I never really knew anything about this holiday or anything else about Judaism, and I felt that I was ignorant about things that should have been a part of my education.

At a certain point, both of us became quiet. I was uncomfortable because I knew that he would next ask me about Susan's remarks. He was quiet after my comments about Judaism which seemed to strike a nerve in him, but I didn't know why. He broke the silence by telling me that he knew that something else had happened that was really bothering me. He said that he never kept a dialogue open between the two of us, but he was here for me if there was something that I wanted to say to him. Even though I had wanted to avoid the subject earlier, a part of me still had to open up to him, especially when he said that he knew that there was more going on than what I was telling him. I finally did admit that there was a problem, but I still felt I couldn't tell him what it was.

"There is something bothering me, but I can handle it", I said.

"You can handle it?"

"Yes, it's difficult, but I'll figure it out."

"It's difficult?"

It hit me that he was using an old trick that was taught in a course I took in College, called Personnel Management. If you're faced with a disgruntled employee who won't tell you what's bothering him, you repeat the last few words of what he said. That compels him to elaborate more on what he's feeling until he finally tells you what's on his mind. In a way, I wanted him to draw this out of me. This was my father in front of me, and even though we had never spoken about inner feelings before, I didn't want to pass up the chance to speak to him now. I knew that if my father was willing to listen, I was willing to go on.

"Well, it has to do with my religion and her religion." I became nervous, because the words I wanted to say were now on the tip of my tongue, and I was afraid that once they left my lips, they could never be taken back.

"What type of religious problem?"

"Dad, you're not going to like it."

"Try me. I already have a feeling of what it's going to be, so don't be afraid of saying it to your father."

"Well, Susan . . . . , how can I say this? When Eric got sick, Susan started to press me to have Eric baptized and I kept on saying no. This morning, though, when we got the call from the hospital, Susan started carrying on that his illness was a warning sign to us that he had to be baptized, and it was necessary for his well being, and I gave in. Now that I'm saying it to you, I know it doesn't seem like I fought against it, but she felt so strongly about it and was pressing me for days, I just gave up. She even had her priest come to see me last night to convince me."

I stopped to see my father's reaction. He didn't move, but only looked down at the table top, and directed his eyes to the salt shaker. He then started tapping his forefinger slowly on the table. That tapping was something he did when he was faced with a situation and needed time to reply. I could not detect even the slightest hint of emotion on his face. He stopped tapping and looked up to me. A look of surrender began to appear on his face.

"There's something I have to tell you, but not now. There's something that I never told you. Don't feel any of this is your fault. It isn't."

"What do you mean that it's not my fault? How could this not be my fault?" I sat up straight and stared at my father, not understanding what he was trying to say to me.

He ignored my question and regained his composure. "What else happened with this priest?" my father asked. I then told him of the classes I had been taking from Father Baldino over the last few years. I even told him that I thought of converting, but something always held me back. As I spoke he sat there and listened while still withholding all traces of emotion.

I didn't go into too much detail as I spoke, but I only touched on generalities, so that the length of time that we spoke was brief. When I paused he called for the check and said we should get back to the hospital. He told me not to worry, but that we would get through this and set everything straight. He told me to let him be my strength. I hadn't told him about Isaac, but it was just as well.

We walked back to the hospital, and he appeared different to me. We had our first real dialogue that I could remember. I had always wanted to be close to him and this was a time that I especially needed his direction. The thing that bothered me, though, was why he was always so reluctant to talk about himself, and after this conversation, I wondered even more.

19

The more I thought about what my father said, the more unsettled I became. As a child, I would have welcomed my father's intervention. Now, though, I was an adult, and I couldn't allow him to deal with my problems for me.

There was something I read once, in a book by Leo Tolstoy. He said that everyone lives and acts partly according to one's own ideas, and partly according to the ideas of others.[49] The differences in people are accounted for by the shift in the balance between the two.

My father's personality fell heavily into the former category. He now wanted to be my guide, as he had been when I was a child. That was not only in a general fatherly way, but it was his nature. He was a self reliant person who seemed to answer to no one. He always seemed to know what he wanted for his family or for his business, and he went out and got it. Maybe that was a reason for his success.

His personality, though, also created a mood of subservience on those around him. You were to react according to his lead, because, to him and those around him, he was always right. My own decisions always took his possible reaction to them into consideration, as if nothing could be done by me without his approval. The first thing that I had done which I know he objected to, was marrying Susan. Although I expected his comments one way or another, nothing ever came. He just seemed to turn off and accept. After I was engaged, I always thought of what would have happened had he spoken up more vehemently against me. It was odd to me that this strongly opinionated man had suddenly removed himself from comment at that time. I accepted it as a confirmation of my adulthood. It was the start of me making decisions without my father. My decision to marry Susan wasn't only affirming my love for her, it was an affirmation that I was an adult, and no longer subject to the requests of my parents. The more I looked back on it the more I realize that a father must be a father forever. A child, no matter what the age, always wants the approval of his parents, and the strong objection by a parent that is respected could influence the path the child takes. Even if the child doesn't follow the path desired by the parent, he still needs to weigh his parents' feelings, the more so if the feelings are strong. My father's council was needed more in that part of my life than in any other.

His comments tonight, coupled with his atypical reaction at the time of my engagement, reinforced the enigma that personified him. There was always something that he knew which he took into consideration for his decisions, but to which no one else could be privy to. In his talk with me, I understood that this was the case here as well. But I also knew that the important thing now was not for me to understand my father. I was past the point of that. I had to take over my life and decide on my own actions. My marriage to Susan had resulted in a situation which appeared to have no happy ending, but the burden of making a decision as to what to do with the rest of my life and the life of my children had to be made by me. I couldn't just hand it off now to my father and rely on him to help me out. I now had to become the man who would make decisions based on information that I would search out for myself. I believe that that's the real measure of maturity. It wasn't even a matter of right or wrong. It's picking yourself up to get as much information as you can to make the best decision you can, and then living with your decision. In Tolstoy's words, I had to lean more heavily on the reliance of my own reason.

After we got back to Susan and my mother, Susan let us know that she would be taking Jennie out for the day. The explanations given to us by Dr. Johnston gave her assurance that Eric was getting the best treatment possible. She now didn't want Jennie to feel neglected and wanted the rest of the day to be devoted just for her. They would be going out for lunch, then to FAO Schwartz, and then maybe for an ice cream treat. We both thanked my parents, as they told us they would be in touch with the hospital during the day to check on Eric. I told my father that I would be coming into the office later, and would return to the hospital after work.

It's funny, but after the heavy reliance that I was placing on Isaac Cohen to supply me with the information I needed for me to begin to make my choices, it hit me that I didn't even have his cell phone number to reach him. I only knew in which part of the hospital his daughter was being treated. I decided to have the nurse on his floor leave a message for him to call me, and I left my cell phone number with her for him to call me back. I realized that when we mentioned to each other that we would meet today, we had never set a specific time or place. We had only said that we would meet sometime in the afternoon.

More than ever, I needed Isaac to help me resolve some of these new questions that were raised last night, and that begged for an answer. I tried to formulate precisely what I would be asking him, but I had so many questions, I decided I would bring up whatever would come to mind when we would meet. Until that time I would do two things. The first would be to pray for the well being of my son. The second would be to try to bring myself back to doing the everyday things I always did and carry on with my life. Right now, that meant going to my office.

20

It was at about 3:00 PM that the call from Isaac came in on my cell phone. He was at the hospital now, but would not be staying long. He asked if I could meet him at his office, which turned out to be near mine. Anytime after 5:30 PM was fine, and he could stay until about 7:00 PM.

I checked in with the hospital, and was told Eric was now stable. I called Susan to relay this information to her. She told me that she had called the hospital a half hour ago, and got the same report. She and Jennie were now roaming through FAO Schwartz. Susan wanted to take Jennie to her parents afterwards, to visit, and would meet me in the hospital at about 8:00 PM.

The rest of the day passed quickly. My father briefly came into my office to see how I was doing, as did some of the employees with whom I worked closely. I told them that everything seemed to be on track, and that I appreciated their concern. Before I knew it, it was about 4:00 PM, and I saw David Greenblatt leave the office. As I immersed myself into dealing with certain documents it seemed like just a few minutes had passed, but 5:00 PM had suddenly arrived.

Certain of the employees began to leave. I told my father that I would be leaving a little early today as well. He nodded, and said he would speak to me tonight. I told him that I would be meeting Susan at the hospital at 8:00, but I had to take care of some other things right now. Before I left, I called Isaac to let him know that I was on my way.

As I walked through the streets, my eyes kept fixing on the menorahs in the windows. Four bulbs were now lit. I had to remember that so that I would light another bulb on my own menorah in my apartment.

I found out that Isaac was an attorney. I immediately noticed a large mezuzah[50] placed on the frame of the carved wood entrance door. A secretary at the front announced my entry to Isaac, and he came out to greet and guide me to the conference room.

We each shared updates to our children's condition. His was a story of status quo, while mine was still of upheaval, but he also expressed his assurances of the exemplary care that was given at the hospital.

He asked if I was ready for the next topic, and that he wanted to go over more background on Judaism before explaining differences between it and Catholicism. "If you wouldn't mind," I told him, "there was something that was told to me last night that I don't understand. The priest came over to my house last night with my in laws, and quoted something from the Bible that really bothers me. He was giving his case for baptism and I didn't even know how to answer him."

At my mention of the word, priest, I could see the muscles over his eyes tighten. "Do you remember where the quote was supposed to have been from?" he asked.

"There were actually a number of quotes that he gave, but there was one in particular that bothered me."

"And were these quotes from the Jewish Bible, or were they from the Christian Bible?"

"I believe there was one from the Jewish, but the rest were from the Christian. I remember the Jewish one being from Jeremiah, and speaking about a new covenant. Then he used the various Christian quotes to describe what the new covenant was all about. The thing that bothered me was the quote from Jeremiah. If Jeremiah, who was an accepted Jewish prophet spoke about a new covenant, doesn't that allow for a change in the Jewish laws which Jesus proposed?"

"So, let's understand what you were being told" Isaac said, as if he was summarizing the testimony of a witness in a court trial. "You were presented with information from the Jewish Bible. The Jewish Bible is a general starting point as a background for Jewish belief. The priest then used that information which seemingly foretold of a different set of commandments that Jews would have to follow. From there, you were told to believe the quotes from the Christian Bible as an extension of the Jeremiah prophecy."

"Yes" I said. "But why did you say 'seemingly' foretold? According to the priest, the prediction was black and white."

"I see" he said. "So your problem is that if the words of Jeremiah are as the priest said, then it follows that the Christian Bible quotes are also true. But what if the words of the prophet are not as he said?"

"Then I guess it would follow that the New Testament quotes are questionable."

"So", Isaac began again, with a slight smile developing on his face, "let's look at the source, in Jeremiah, to see exactly what is being said."

Isaac chose one of the books that was on the table and sat down. He had me take the chair next to him. He leafed through the book until he came to the page that he wanted. I could see that there was Hebrew writing on the right hand side of the book and English on the left.

"This is a Hebrew-English Bible, which contains the 24 books of our Bible. It includes the 5 books of Moses, which everyone usually refers to as the Bible, and also other writings which are holy. The book of Jeremiah is among them. Now let's look at the passage that was referred to. We'll read the English. Sometimes the English translation doesn't show the proper meaning of the Hebrew text, but in this case, it's fairly close. Here it is. Chapter 31, and sentence 31. 'Behold, the days come, saith the LORD, that I will make a new covenant with the house of Israel, and with the house of Judah.' Is this the text that you believe he quoted?"

"Why, yes. I think it is."

"Let's continue reading, then. The next sentence states, 'Not according to the covenant that I made with their fathers in the day that I took them by the hand to bring them out of the land of Egypt; which my covenant they broke, although I was an husband unto them, saith the LORD.'"

"Yes" I told Isaac, "I'm sure that's the passage that he quoted. But this means that he was right." I was now getting a little uncomfortable in my chair. I was wondering how Isaac could possibly negate what Father Baldino had told me, especially since Isaac was now showing me that the text that the Father quoted was stating what the Father had said it did.

"Let's continue reading further" Isaac continued. He was not disturbed at all at what he was reading. His faint smile had developed closer to a grin.

"Here", he said as he pushed the book to me. "You can continue the reading."

I slowly accepted the book and now searched for the place. He pointed at the spot, which was now sentence 33. I quickly scanned the two prior sentences to make sure that I hadn't missed anything, but sure enough, they were as Isaac had read them. I began to read out loud. 'But this shall be the covenant that I will make with the house of Israel; After those days, saith the LORD, I will put my law in their inward parts, and write it in their hearts; and will be their God, and they shall be my people.' "Wait a minute" I said. "It doesn't have anything here about a new law. It says that G-d wants his people to follow the law. It looks like it's referring to a law that was already given."

"It seems that way to me. Just go through the next couple of sentences to see if there's anything else written that may support the priest's contention."

I looked down at the book and began again with sentence 34. 'And they shall teach no more every man his neighbor, and every man his brother, saying, Know the LORD: for they shall all know me, from the least of them unto the greatest of them, saith the LORD: for I will forgive their iniquity, and I will remember their sin no more. 35 Thus saith the LORD, which giveth the sun for a light by day, and the ordinances of the moon and of the stars for a light by night, which divideth the sea when the waves thereof roar; The LORD of hosts is his name: 36 If those ordinances depart from before me, saith the LORD, then the seed of Israel also shall cease from being a nation before me for ever.'

"I'm confused. The text just refers to laws that had to be given prior to this and the last sentence says they must be upheld forever. The new covenant that it's referring to seems to be a promise that G-d is binding the Jews to, that they must uphold what was given to them in the past."

"Very good" said Isaac. "You see, G-d repeatedly is making covenants with different generations. G-d gave us a set of laws. Now what holds the Jews to be the ones who are bound to follow those laws? It is the covenant that G-d has with the Jewish people. When a generation feels that it isn't bound by those laws, then that generation has, in effect, broken the covenant that the previous generation made. G-d then says that you, meaning those Jews of that generation, you have broken the covenant that was made by your ancestors because you thought the covenant to follow those laws only pertained to them. A new covenant will be made then, one that is between G-d and the current generation. This new covenant is a reaffirmation that the Jews are bound to those laws. Just like previous generations, from the ones that stood at Sinai, this one is also bound to those same laws.

"We can't change the laws that G-d instituted. According to this priest's argument, the New Testament proclaims that Jesus and his followers, on their own say so, based on the words of Jeremiah, declared a change in the laws. Jeremiah's words don't say that. A new covenant does not change the laws. If Jeremiah is the source of their justification for a new world order, then their argument falls flat. All of the quotes from the New Testament explaining a new set of laws is not based on Judaism at all, but are now independent declarations from someone who is setting up a religion that has nothing to do with Judaism. But the whole premise of the Christian religion is that Jesus is the Jewish Messiah. If his teachings, which are different from the standard Jewish teachings, have no prophetic vision authorizing them, Jesus must be a false Messiah. Jews cannot follow him."

"But isn't he from the line of King David?"

"Just because someone is from the line of King David doesn't make that person a Messiah. But let's look at the beliefs of the Christians. They believe in the Immaculate Conception, do they not?"

"Yes. They say that an angel put a seed into Mary, and she gave birth, even though she was a virgin."

"For now, let's not even dispute that, though I'll show you later that even that idea is easily disputed. So they say that the Father of Jesus was the angel."

"Actually", I corrected him, "they say that G-d put the seed in him through the use of the angel, so that G-d is his father."

"Okay. So what does that make Joseph, Mary's husband."

"Obviously, he's not the father. He's just the husband of Mary, who acts as a sort of foster father to Jesus."

"Now here's the first page of the New Testament. The object of the first page is to link Jesus to Judaism by saying that he is the Jewish Messiah. Now what does it say on the first page?"

Isaac handed me a book of the New Testament and asked me to open it to the first page. It was the book of Matthew. I began to read.

'1   The book of the generation of Jesus Christ, the son of David, the son of Abraham.

2   Abraham begat Isaac; and Isaac begat Jacob; and Jacob begat Judas and his brethren;

3   And Judas begat Phares and Zara of Thamar; and Phares begat Esrom; and Esrom begat Aram;

4   And Aram begat Aminadab; and Aminadab begat Naasson; and Naasson begat Salmon;

5   And Salmon begat Booz of Rachab; and Booz begat Obed of Ruth; and Obed begat Jesse;

6   And Jesse begat David the king; and David the king begat Solomon of her that had been the wife of Urias;

7   And Solomon begat Roboam; and Roboam begat Abia; and Abia begat Asa;

8   And Asa begat Josaphat; and Josaphat begat Joram; and Joram begat Ozias;

9   And Ozias begat Joatham; and Joatham begat Achaz; and Achaz begat Ezekias;

10 And Ezekias begat Manasses; and Manasses begat Amon; and Amon begat Josias;

11 And Josias begat Jechonias and his brethren, about the time they were carried away to Babylon:

12 And after they were brought to Babylon, Jechonias begat Salathiel; and Salathiel begat Zorobabel;

13 And Zorobabel begat Abiud; and Abiud begat Eliakim; and Eliakim begat Azor;

14 And Azor begat Sadoc; and Sadoc begat Achim; and Achim begat Eliud;

15 And Eliud begat Eleazar; and Eleazar begat Matthan; and Matthan begat Jacob;

16 And Jacob begat Joseph the husband of Mary, of whom was born Jesus, who is called Christ.

"Wait, there's something wrong." I said. "It follows the line of Jesus, but if the father of Jesus wasn't Joseph, then the line is broken, and Jesus can't be considered the Messiah, because he's not from the line of David."

"See? It doesn't make sense, does it? The confusion doesn't stop there. Let's take a look at Luke, Chapter 3, sentence 23 and 24. The lineage of Jesus is different." Isaac flipped the pages until he found the passage he was looking for and began to read.

23 And Jesus himself began to be about thirty years of age, being (as was supposed) the son of Joseph, which was the son of Heli,

24 Which was the son of Matthat, which was the son of Levi, which was the son of Melchi, which was the son of Janna, which was the son of Joseph,

"The text continues to give a completely different lineage of Jesus. If all the books of the gospels are divine, they should have only one lineage for Jesus, but instead, there are two. The only conclusion you can draw would be that the writer of one of the texts made a mistake. That would mean that the New Testament is not a book based on Divine information, but was composed by people who could err, just like us.

"After the New Testament was written, the Christians realized the error of Jesus not being from the line of David, so they claim that Mary is from the line of David. If you follow the Davidic dynasty, however, even in the New Testament, it always gives the male lineage, and not the female. Since the Messiah can only be descended from a male, their rebuttal falls flat as well."

"But you can't argue that Jesus' divine birth was foretold. That alone has to make him a figure that Jews should look up to."

"Here we have to again look at the source of that prophecy which is in Isaiah. For that we need a Bible written in the original Hebrew, as well as a King James translation." Isaac now pulled out both books and flipped through the pages of each, to the section that contained the prophecy of the Virgin Birth. "First, let's look at the King James translation." Isaac opened up the English bible to Chapter 7, verse 14. 'Therefore the Lord himself shall give you a sign; Behold, a virgin shall conceive, and bear a son, and shall call his name Immanuel.' Let's look at the Hebrew along with a Hebrew English dictionary. Can you read Hebrew?"

"I can recognize the letters, but that's about it." I said.

"That's good enough. Now let's look at the Hebrew. When it describes the woman, the Hebrew word used is almah. Let's look it up in the dictionary." He flipped the dictionary and pointed at the word. The letters were the same as in the Bible. The meaning was 'young woman'. "Now let's look up the word 'virgin' in the dictionary and see its Hebrew counterpart." I saw a different set of letters. "The word is pronounced betulah. Virgin is not mentioned in this prophecy at all. The correct translation is 'Behold, a young woman shall conceive and bear a son, and shall call his name Immanuel'."

I was dumbfounded. "You mean to say they made up their own meaning?"

"In a word, the answer to that would have to be yes. Just to show you that they knew the different meanings of both almah and betulah, let's look at other areas of the Bible which contain those Hebrew words and see how they were translated by the followers of the Church. First, in Leviticus Chapter 21, verse 3. 'And for his sister a virgin, that is nigh unto him, which hath had no husband; for her may he be defiled.' Now we look at the Hebrew. There's the word betulah. So they know that betulah means virgin. Now let's see if they translate almah in other areas also as virgin. If they do, then the translator was just deficient in Hebrew."

Isaac now flipped the pages of the King James Bible to Psalms 89:45, then to Isaiah 54:4, and lastly to First Book of Samuel, 17:56. The word almah was shown in different forms and it always was translated as something to do with youth. "Almah is the word for youth applied in a feminine tense. That's basic Hebrew which the translator apparently understood, but he chose to change the translation in the case of the sentence in the Isaiah passage to wrongly support the Christian claim that Isaiah spoke of a virgin birth. We can plainly see that Isaiah did not.

"In fact, if you read the full chapter 7, you'll see that the Jewish king, King Ahaz, was faced with certain defeat by three enemies: Syria, a country called Remaliah, and certain Jews under the leadership of the tribe of Ephraim. In response to that fear, G-d sent Isaiah to reassure the King, and told him that he had nothing to worry about. Isaiah was told to give the King a sign that this would be so. The King was told that a young woman, meaning the wife of the king, would bear a son. Before that child reaches the age where he can discern the difference between good and evil, which is the age of about thirteen, the troubles of the King would be over, which is what happened. You can read it in the King James version as well. It's a simple summary of events of that time period that has nothing to do with events that will happen 600 years later. Yet, this prophecy by Isaiah which gave a sign to King Ahaz, for the King's peace of mind, was distorted, and turned into a prophecy to foretell a virgin birth. Again, the Christians have attempted to use the Jewish Bible to support their contention that an extraordinary birth was predicted when nothing could be further from the truth."

I leaned back and looked at Isaac. "You're shattering their whole religion in just a few minutes", I said.

"Oh, there are a lot more damaging proofs than these. I really didn't even want to get into all of this now, but if you wouldn't mind, I'd like to shift for a second to Judaism. There are certain ideas I want you to understand before we go on.

"Before we really get involved in the negatives of Christianity, you should be aware of the positives of Judaism. A lifestyle change can't be taught by only telling someone what's incorrect about how they're now living. That only creates a vacuum which draws the person back into their negative lifestyle."

I didn't understand what he was getting at. "How do you mean?" I asked him.

"Let's look at a parent reprimanding a child. The child hangs around with a wild bunch of friends. Their acts may not even be that destructive, but they could have the type of characteristics that we don't want our children picking up on. Maybe we want our children to be kind to others, maybe we want our children to avoid speaking negatively about others, maybe we want our children to be involved in charity and help the elderly. Those wild friends, though, will push this parent's children on the opposite type of path."

"That makes sense", I said.

"What does a parent do if his child is with the wrong crowd? The parent sits with the child, and in an angry, demanding way, tells the child that he is forbidden to continue going with those friends. Or he says that the child is forbidden from going to the hangouts where those friends meet. Now the child has to refrain from those actions, but does it usually work? The child usually lapses into his former behavior and the parent can't figure out what to do.

"The problem is that you just can't take away from a child and expect him to fall into place. When you take something away, you must put something in its place. A child that's told to avoid a certain hangout because of the bad elements that frequent it must be given somewhere to go that would pique his interest in exchange. Little leagues, basketball practice, art. These are things that must be used to entice the child to a different lifestyle. When we take away what we perceive as negative, we must introduce something that we and the child would consider an acceptable positive."

He looked at me and paused to see if I was getting it, and he then continued. "What does this have to do with Christianity and Judaism? When we sat down, I told you that I wanted to first explain more things about Judaism and what it's all about. In effect, I was telling you that I wanted to introduce the positives about Judaism so that when you realized that Christianity wasn't right for you, you would already be aware of the positives of Judaism. My goal is not to knock down Christianity and walk away, thinking I did my job. I have to show you that the alternative, Judaism, is an attractive choice as a religion.

"People, in fact many Jews, look at Judaism as a series of prohibitions. For example, when everyone is going out on Friday night, the religious Jew says that he can't because of the Sabbath. On Saturday, again, it's a day when the world is out enjoying themselves with movies, amusement centers, or going places with the kids. For the Jew, those kinds of actions are prohibited. When it comes to eating out, Jews are again faced with a series of prohibitions as to what they can eat and where. We can't go to any restaurant since most establishments don't conform to kosher laws. Again, the Jewish lifestyle appears to be one of asceticism, which is not the least appealing to someone that has experienced the enjoyment of life from the non-Jewish perspective.

"There's a whole different way of looking at what's really happening. Let's start off by looking at the Sabbath. We have to examine it from the Jewish perspective on a number of different levels. Let's see how it relates to family structure. On Friday night, a man goes to synagogue, accompanied by his sons. They all sit together in prayer. In the home, the whole family sits at the table together and they first bless the entrance of the Sabbath, followed by the blessings before the meal, and then the meal itself. The meal is a time when they could discuss the portion of the Bible that is read for the week, or any other area within Judaism. They could talk about aspects of history, art, books, or articles on any part of the Bible. The parent uses this time to bond with his children. They review examples from the Bible, or from the stories of Rabbis and great men who lived before which shows the high moral ground which we, as human beings, must aspire to.

"Throughout this whole time, there are no distractions from cell phones, or television, or movies. We are able to give full attention to our children, since, isn't that what a child craves? Even in the time period during the walk to and from the synagogue, the child may open up to the parent about something troubling him. There is an accessibility of the parents which could never happen during the hustle and bustle of the work week.

"We end the meal by singing songs for the Sabbath, because, after all, it's a celebration. For us, it's one of the major holidays that exist in our religion and it comes once a week. The next day is also spent with the same atmosphere of thanks to G-d, and happiness. We also take time to learn more about what the Bible is teaching us by going to classes and delving into the words of the various Holy Books. From what you've told me, you greatly enjoyed the Bible classes that you had which were given by the priest. All people have a natural desire to know and understand the world around us, and that desire only has to be cultivated. For the small child, you make all of the learning enjoyable by rewarding him or her with prizes for answering correctly. As the child grows, he develops an interest in Judaism on his own, and begins to appreciate all that it has to offer. By the time that child becomes an adult, the love for his religion is part of him, and it's coupled with an understanding of what makes Judaism so desirable.

"A home which is centered in a religious atmosphere creates a much more stable atmosphere for the child. The parent gets to enjoy and interact with the children, and it makes it much easier for the child to grow up with a sense of security, that he belongs to a family and the family belongs to an even larger group."

"I'm curious," I said. "You said that the Sabbath was a celebration. You have to be celebrating something. Why do you celebrate in the way that you do, and why do you have to celebrate at all? You should be able to teach and bond with your children on any day of the week."

"That's a good question, Michael, and it has to do with our concept of the Sabbath and how it differs from the concept of Sabbath which is held by other religions.

"The Sabbath is known as our day of rest. The person outside of the Jewish faith who has an active work week, is usually mentally drained by the time the week is over. He would look on a Sabbath as the one day that's needed in order to recharge his batteries so that he can begin the next week anew.

"There was a Rabbi that I had referred to the other day, Rabbi Dovid Gottlieb, who gave a good explanation of what the day of rest actually is.[51] When we say our daily prayers, we have special prayers for each day of the week, but the Hebrew language doesn't have names for the days like we do in English. Sunday is called the first day of the week for the Sabbath. Wednesday is the fourth day of the week for the Sabbath, etc. Each day, then, is given a number of where it fits in, in relation to the Sabbath.

"In our prayers on Friday evening, one of the opening prayers has a line in it which states, "Last in action, and first in thought", and that line describes the Sabbath. Try to think of someone building a house. An architect makes a drawing of a house for approval by the client. The drawing shows what the completed house will look like, with all of the windows, types of brick, etc. When the house is being built, though, the first thing you do is dig and prepare the foundation, then the frame, then the plumbing and electrical wiring, and so on. The finishing touches to make it finally look like the approved drawing would be done at the final stage. It's the same with the Sabbath. When the world was created, the ultimate purpose of the creation can be summed up by looking at the final thing that was created, and that was the Sabbath."

I started to interrupt Isaac, but he asked me to let him finish. I leaned back and he continued.

"This is where I'd like to clear up the idea of the prohibition of working on the Sabbath. What is prohibited? If someone is going to lift their sofa to move it to another area of the room, you would think that the lifting would fall under the category of prohibited work. It doesn't. Yet the minimum effort that it takes to draw a picture is prohibited. Why?

"If you read the Hebrew Bible, it uses two words for work. One is avodah. The other is melacha. When describing the Biblical prohibition of work, the Bible uses the latter word to limit the meaning of the first. Melacha, then, is a type of work, and it has to do with craftsmanship. The prohibition takes on a whole new meaning. It isn't work by itself which is prohibited, but work which has to do with creating something that wasn't there before. Writing, sewing, painting, and building are examples of this.

"The Bible states that G-d created the Sabbath, then He rested. The fourth of the Ten Commandments says[52] "Remember the Sabbath day, to keep it holy. Six days shalt thou labour, and do all thy work: But the seventh day is the Sabbath of the LORD thy God: in it thou shalt not do any work, thou, nor thy son, nor thy daughter, thy manservant, nor thy maidservant, nor thy cattle, nor thy stranger that is within thy gates: For in six days the LORD made heaven and earth, the sea, and all that in them is, and rested the seventh day: wherefore the LORD blessed the Sabbath day, and hallowed it."

"G-d told the Jewish people that we are to be holy. Besides the moral and ethical definitions of holiness which were enumerated in the Bible, G-d commands the people to "Be holy for I am holy."[53] Since G-d sanctified the Sabbath as a holy day, we must emulate His actions. To do this, we acknowledge that it is a holy day by ceasing from all acts that have to do with creating. That would constitute almost all of the prohibitions for the Sabbath. In a sense, we put in our minds that all of our efforts in whatever it is that we were doing have now been completed. We don't have to concern ourselves with making money, or fixing things, or anything else of that sort. The Sabbath is the ultimate blessing where we put ourselves completely in the hands of G-d, and declare that all of our needs have been taken care of.

"The celebration that we undertake through the meals that we eat on this day, and the songs that we sing, are a result of that recognition. In order to give respect to G-d for giving us the gift of this day, we take it upon ourselves to study other ways that we can comply with G-d's request for us to be holy. The acts of enjoying the day and learning these laws give us a sense of fulfillment to the point that we feel bad once the Sabbath day is over.

"So here's the difference between Jews and non Jews as it relates to the Sabbath. The non Jew looks at the Sabbath as a day that he can rest so that he can face the work week. We look at our work week as a time of preparation so that we can thoroughly enjoy the Sabbath. It's the complete opposite."

Isaac paused as I digested what he said. This was fascinating to me and was something I had never heard before. I couldn't help contrasting this with what I had been learning in Father Baldino's class about the Sabbath. Jesus wasn't too happy with the laws of the Sabbath. That's something that certainly stood out in the New Testament.

"Isaac", I began hesitantly. "I know that you mentioned that you wanted to focus on Judaism, but my mind keeps flipping to questions that I have from the things that I learned with Father Baldino. He's the priest that I told you about. Didn't Jesus have a point that some of the Sabbath laws were cruel and should be disregarded?"

Isaac sighed. "You keep trying to push me in a certain direction. The truth is that the answer has to do with the concept of holiness and the concept of holiness is very different from the Jewish perspective as compared to that of the Christians. In order to explain this to you, I really have to go one step at a time. We have to first see what being holy means to the Jews and why." He glanced at his watch and quickly looked up and said, "If you don't mind, let's just take a small break. I have to make a phone call and I'll be gone for a minute, but we'll get back into this as soon as I return."

Isaac got up and left the room, while motioning for me to help myself to some soda and bottled water that was on the table. When he walked out I started thinking about what he said. Isaac had a way of opening my eyes to things I had never even imagined. The idea of holiness is something you would take for granted. Being holy was, I guess, holy. How do you explain it? Was it being a person that was humble; was it modesty; or did it have to do with ethics and morality? Maybe it wasn't so straightforward.

While I waited, I glanced to different parts of the room. The room was a conference room, with the walls all filled with books. It looked like there were probably hundreds of books, mostly reference books on law from New York State and the Federal Government. On the wall to the side of where Isaac had been sitting were other types of books, books with Hebrew writing. They were all of various sizes and filled the six foot wide section which they were in. In one corner of that section, at the top, were what appeared to be travel books, all on Israel. I pulled one of them down and started flipping the pages, which contained full color pictures of ancient sites in Israel.

Isaac walked back just a few minutes after he had left. I hadn't noticed him at first, as his footsteps were silent on the carpet, and I was engrossed with the beauty contained in the photos in front of me. I was startled when I found Isaac just a few steps away from me, and looking at the book that I had opened. "It seems that you found the answer on your own", he said. I really didn't understand what he meant by that. When I asked him, he said, "I was referring to my question to you before on what the point of holiness was about. I walk out of the room and here you are looking at a book about Israel." From the puzzled look that must have been on my face, he realized that he was running ahead of me again. He motioned for me to take a seat and softly said, "Let me explain."

We both sat down, and he opened up the Hebrew English Bible again, turning the pages to Leviticus, chapter 18. "There are several chapters in this section of the Bible where a whole listing is presented of what constitutes holiness. They're all parts of the puzzle, but first we have to look at the individual pieces.

"Here, in this chapter, we find a listing of the various prohibited marital relationships. Most are accepted without thought in this day and age, because we've been raised in a society that views the Bible's teachings as morally correct.

For example, the chapter starts by objecting to a person having a relationship with his father, mother, sister, daughter in law, and grandchild. Those are all universally accepted in the world. There are other Biblical standards of morality that, unfortunately, the society of today would reject. The chapter relates that a man can't marry an aunt, whether the wife of an uncle or a sister of a parent. There's a prohibition of having a relationship with both a mother and daughter, and yes, the Bible does include homosexuality as a prohibited relationship. The point of these prohibitions is presented at the end of the chapter beginning with sentence 24.

24. Defile not yourselves in any of these things for in all these the nations are defiled which I cast out before you.
25. And the land is defiled, therefore do I visit the iniquity thereof upon it and the land itself vomiteth out her inhabitants.
26. You shall therefore keep my statutes and my judgments and shall not commit any of these abominations neither any of your own nation nor any stranger that sojourneth among you.
28. That the land not spue you out also when ye defile it, as it spued out the nations that were before you.

Isaac now looked up and asked, "Well, what do you make of the Bible's concluding remarks?" "It seems to be straightforward", I answered. "The Bible seems to be saying that it's necessary to follow these things to be accepted by the land of Israel. Follow these acts, and you're in. Don't follow them, and the land will reject you."

"Exactly", he remarked. "Now chapter 19 continues to list out additional things that we should do in order for us to be holy because, as it says in sentence two "You shall be holy, for I the Lord your G-d am holy." The listing happens to correspond to the Ten Commandments, but they're repeated in a different way with additional corollaries. Sentence 12 says that you shouldn't swear; the sentence before says not to steal; sentence 30 says to keep the Sabbaths, etc. The message is again that you must be holy. How? By also following the laws set forth in the Ten Commandments. Why? There are two reasons. We are G-d's people and must be holy in order to emulate G-d's actions, as it's written in the second sentence; and then to be worthy of the land, as it repeats again in sentence 22 'Ye shall therefore keep all my statutes and all my judgments, and do them; that the land whither I bring you to dwell therein spue you not out.'"

Isaac now spun his chair around so that he could face me. He spread his hands apart as if he were holding something in the air and continued. "Even the land has to be used according to a set of rules that we must maintain because of the sanctity of the land. Chapter 25, for example speaks of the need to allow the land to lie fallow every seventh year because that year "shall be a Sabbath of rest unto the land".

"The commandments then, follow an order. First, we are to be holy so that we can emulate G-d. Once we are holy according to G-d's rule, we are accepted into the land. Once in the land, we conform to the laws of holiness to maintain the land, and our ultimate result is that on the Sabbath, G-d will arrange for the land to support us and give us enough produce to sustain us without our having to till the soil. In short we are told that if we maintain our state of holiness for ourselves and the land, we will no longer be subject to the requirement of having to work for our daily bread, for on the Sabbath of years we will be provided for, just as we are on the Sabbath which falls once a week. In a sense, those "Sabbaths" provide us with a preview of what the world will be like after the coming of the true Messiah. The land will provide for our needs on its own so that we can be fully occupied in study."

"So, wait a minute", I said. "You're saying that the Jews are tied into the land of Israel. In effect, without Israel, the Jews can't achieve their purpose of being."

"I'm saying even more than that", Isaac said, now getting more animated. "Just like the people of Israel are tied into the land of Israel, the land of Israel is tied into the Jewish people."

I thought he was going a little too far with his last comment. "That's an odd thing to say. How can the land of Israel need something? How can the land need a certain nation to live on it?"

Isaac settled down a little and grew serious again. "We have to compare the Bible's prediction of what will happen after the time that G-d presented it to us, with what has actually happened over the last centuries. Look at this." He now flipped another few pages to the next chapter, chapter 26. "Here is a prediction of what will happen if we don't conform to the commandments which were given to us. It says[54] 'If you will not hearken unto me and will not do all these commandments. [55]And I will bring the land into desolation and your enemies that dwell therein shall be astonished at it. [56]And I will scatter you among the heathen.' But this section concludes by stating that ultimately, G-d will remember us and allow us to return.[57] 'But I will for their sakes remember the covenant of their ancestors.'

"From what you know of the history of the land of Israel, how does that measure up to this prophecy?"

I now caught on to what he was saying. "I see now. Everything you read about the land of Israel before the Jews returned to the land in the end of the 19th Century describes it as a wasteland. That's over the two thousand years when the land was controlled by people other than the Jews. As soon as the Jews began to return to the land, it was transformed from a desert wasteland to a thriving agricultural society. But it didn't happen until Israel was habited again by the Jewish people."

A shudder went through my back. It hit me that all my life I was told to support Israel and how Israel was important solely because it served as a refuge for the Jews in order to avoid a repetition of what happened during the Holocaust. The reality was so much more than that. There was a whole miracle that was staring me in the face, and should have been obvious even to the whole world, and yet was being dismissed as a normal event. I was developing more of a respect for my Jewish heritage in these few days that I could have ever imagined.

I suddenly remembered my question that I had asked Isaac earlier, before we got into what being holy meant to the Jewish nation. Was Jesus right in his belief that some of the laws of the Sabbath were excessive? I now repeated my question to Isaac, and he said "There's a very famous section in the first book of the New Testament, in the book attributed to Matthew, called the Sermon of the Mount. The sermon consists of the words that were spoken by Jesus to his disciples, and which laid out his general beliefs.

"Those beliefs conflict with the laws which the Jewish people are obligated to follow, besides the fact that the beliefs expressed in one section conflict with those he expressed in others. All it will take is a simple analysis of what was written for you, or anyone else, really, to see it."

As Isaac paused, he quickly glanced at his watch, and then looked at it a second time. That prompted me to look at my own watch, and I saw that it was already almost 7:10 PM. "I'm sorry", he said, "but I really didn't realize how fast the time passed. I'd love to stay with you longer but I have to leave." As he began to put away the books, he continued on. "There's a thought that I'd like to leave you with. You mentioned that Jesus didn't really agree with certain of the laws of the Sabbath. You're right, but in addition, there were many other laws that he didn't agree with." Isaac now slid the King James Bible out from the pile of books he was gathering. He quickly opened the book to Matthew, chapter 5, sentence 17, and had me read while he continued to clear up the table. "Go on", he said, "and bear in mind what you just told me about Jesus preaching against certain of the laws previously decreed by

G-d to be a necessary prerequisite in order to produce that state of holiness that G-d ordained for the Jewish people."

I picked up the book and began to read out loud. "Think not that I have come to abolish the Torah and the prophets; I have come not to abolish them but fulfill them. For truly I say to you, till heaven and earth pass away, not an iota, not a dot, will pass from the Torah until all is accomplished. Whoever then relaxes one of the least of these commandments and teaches men so, shall be called least in the kingdom of heaven; but he who does them and teaches them shall be called great in the kingdom of heaven." I closed the book and passed it to him. I was shocked. "How could Jesus say here that you must follow all of the Jewish laws when he also says that certain of the laws should be dropped? Or are you now going to tell me he doesn't actually disagree with the Jewish laws?"

"That will have to wait for our next meeting" Isaac said as he put away the final book.

"Tomorrow night?" I asked, while reluctantly accepting this delay as something that I should have expected.

"No. Tomorrow night is no good. You see, tomorrow is Friday and the evening will be the Sabbath." My disappointment must have shown, as he hesitated and then said, "If you're able to, why don't you stop by first thing in the morning. I can get here early, and I can meet you at about 8 AM. I feel bad that I'm always keeping you in suspense."

"There's no need on your part to apologize. In fact, you're been very generous with your time by sitting with me as you've been doing. Tomorrow morning would be fine. In fact, maybe tonight I'll try and read some of what we discussed so it stays fresh in my head."

We walked out together into the dark of the evening. He reminded me that this was now the fourth night of the holiday as he hailed a taxi to go to the west side. As I watched him drive off, I couldn't help thinking how proud I was that I was a Jew, while at the same time I was humbled by the thought of all the things that I still had to learn about Judaism.

21

It took me only a few minutes to catch a cab for myself. As I got in, it was with a newfound confidence that I didn't have before. I was beginning to feel that I had a common link with other Jews in the world. The doubts that I had just a few short hours ago as to whether I should follow the religion of my wife or that of my family had given way to a firm conviction as to the road I now had to take.

As much as I was confident, I was also a realist. Isaac had been able to present a convincing argument to defend his views on religion, but I knew that I couldn't present it to someone else in the same way as he had done for me. With each question that I had posed to him, he entertained no doubts as to what he believed, but his only hesitation was in how to present his answers in a way that would be understandable to me, someone who was totally lacking in any background whatsoever. Although I understood what he said as he said it, the details seemed to flitter out of my mind with each passing minute.

The closer I got to the hospital, the more my confidence lessened. It wasn't my former feeling of self doubt that wanted to return, but it was what I can only describe as anger. At first my anger was directed at my parents for withholding the information that was now being fed to me, which may have altered my decision to marry Susan. That lasted only a few seconds, as I thought of how much I cared for Susan and she for me. If her original feelings on religion were as empty as mine had been, none of our problems would have come up. We would have gone on, just believing in a G-d who created the world, and not much more. That would have been the legacy that we would have left for our children.

Then it hit me. Judaism was a system that wasn't set up for my pleasure. It wasn't a life that was to be based on a 'live for today' attitude. A thousand years ago, a Jew, my ancestor, sat and taught his child what was written in the

Bible. He taught his child what was right and wrong and how to make the most of the life that we've been given here on this earth. He not only taught his child to be kind, and just, and that there was a G-d above who controlled everything. That child was given a guidebook with examples, and rules, and a system that showed him what was good and to be embraced and what was not good and to be avoided.

What I was learning now with Isaac was from the same source of knowledge that was used to teach that Jewish child of a thousand years ago, and his descendent of five hundred years ago, and now it was being used to teach me. Maybe that was the secret of Jewish survival. What was actually surviving?[58] Was it the Jew himself? It couldn't be. A Jew was a person with a belief. A Jew was a mortal human being who lived and died like other human beings on this planet.

I remember when there was a fund raising for the state of Israel, and the speaker spoke of the exile which we Jews now find ourselves in. This wasn't the first exile that we experienced. Over the centuries, we have been forced to live under the domination of all different countries and have been exposed to all different cultures. The Persians were the mightiest people in the world of their time, but where are they now? They are but a passing page in history. The Greeks then ruled Israel. There is nothing left of the Greek culture of that time. Their way of life and the myriad gods that they prayed to were pushed aside by the Romans. The Romans then dominated the Jews and even they were pushed aside by external forces. None of those civilizations survived. Maybe the people of today can claim that they are descended from those people, but what those people stood for did not survive; their way of life did not; their moral standards and religious beliefs certainly did not.

Yes, I am descended from Jews of that time period and I am one of the last links in the chain of the generations that have been born since the time of Moses. What exactly has survived over all of those centuries? People live and die, but what has survived was their way of life. It was the way of life dictated by the Bible that has survived; it was the way of life that used the Bible as its blueprint for a civilization that has lasted for thousands of years.

But that wasn't all. The Jewish religion has not only survived, but its message was so powerful, that it changed the whole world. All of the previous religions around the world were based on the belief in a collection of gods which proved to be false. All of the moral teachings of the world which existed in times past have been proven to be deficient. What has now moved in their place? The beliefs established by the Jewish religion. The Jewish religion has now spawned many religions which are followed by the majority of the world, but it was the Jewish religion that started it all and the Jewish religion is still a powerful guiding force in the world of today.

What right did the reform Jewish movement have to declare traditional Judaism passé? Judaism has been working to guide the Jewish people for thousands of years, and very successfully. It was only because those Jews of the reform movement thought they could improve on the religion. The truth is, the Reform movement failed as a religion that could continue for generations in perpetuity. I remember reading how the people running Temple Emmanuel in Manhattan, which was founded about one hundred years ago, decided to track down the families of the founding members in order to use them as a centerpiece for their centennial celebration. When they tracked down the families, they only found maybe less than ten people. The rest had converted out of the religion. Was theirs a religion that survived? No, Reform Judaism has shown itself to be a dismal failure. Contrast that with traditional Judaism and its strong continual presence over the centuries. It was only the Judaism of the Bible that survived.

When I was in Isaac's office and I looked at the pictures of the holy sites in Israel, I was overtaken by the beauty. An archeologist, when looking at ancient Greek or Roman sites, examines them from the point of view of an outsider. The people of those eras have died out and their beliefs have died with them. But to the Jews, the holy sites in Israel have a real meaning even today. One of the pictures I looked at was of the Western Wall outside the original Temple in Jerusalem which is still revered by Jews today. It isn't history; for Jews, it's the here and now.

What suddenly scared me was the thought of what all my searching was leading up to. If I was really serious about this religion, then I would have to change everything about the way I've been living. No more eating out, no more trips on Saturday. How would I start? How could I start? Even though I knew in my heart that learning about Judaism was right, how could I do all of the things that religious Jews do? I had to avoid thinking about that right now. I just had to continue to take one day at a time.

The ride to the hospital had been quick. I hadn't even noticed the time that passed. We pulled up to the front glass doors, and I paid the fare. I put on my gloves and slipped out of the taxi. When the taxi pulled away I stood in front of the hospital and looked up at the sky before going in. The night was clear, and you could see the stars overhead, like little angels looking down at all of us going about our lives. I let the cold wind blow against my face a few more moments while I watched the stars twinkle overhead. I then took a deep breath and walked inside.

22

The moment I passed through the glass entrance doors my cell phone rang. I opened it up without even looking at the number, expecting the call to be from Susan. I was surprised when I heard a familiar male voice on the other end.

"Michael?" he asked. "Steven, is that you?" I replied in turn. My brother, Steven, had ended up going to medical school in Nashville, and was now working in a hospital down there doing his residency requirements. He would come up to New York occasionally, but it looked like, for now, he was making Nashville his home. Being six years apart, I can't say we were particularly close, but I had always been responsible for him while we were growing up, and I had felt more like a parent to him than a brother. We would speak to each other at least once a month, but he was typically the one to make the call and I was glad that he did. I would always get so wrapped up with things that I was doing, between work and family, that I neglected to keep in contact with anyone not immediately around me.

"Yes. I just spoke to mom and she told me what's been happening" he told me, "but she said that it looks like Eric is going to be alright."

I stood to the side of the entrance of the hospital while I answered him. "We've been pretty lucky, I guess. Eric ate some honey, and it caused him to get sick. The doctors say it was botulism. But we were able to get him to the hospital early enough, and the doctors feel that he can make a full recovery. In fact, I'm in the hospital lobby now, and I was just going up to check on him. Anyway, how is everything with you?"

"Everything is pretty good. In fact, I was going to be giving you a call anyway. I'll be coming up to New York on Saturday for a few days and I was hoping we could talk a little."

The way he said that, with his voice slowing down as he said that he wanted to talk, made me hesitate. Something was wrong, but this wasn't the place for me to get into it.

"What time is your flight? If you'd like, I can pick you up."

"I really don't want to put you out of your way. You'll probably be busy anyway, at the hospital with your son".

"Don't even think about it" I said. "Hey, maybe I could use you here to check up on these doctors and keep them on their toes." I smiled as I continued, " . . . as long as you don't hit me with too much of a consultation fee. I hear you big time doctors are used to big fees."

"Don't worry", he said, "you'll be the first to get the family discount." Steven then gave me his flight information. He would be coming in to La Guardia about 4:30, which wasn't so bad. From the way he sounded, I thought it would be good if he and I had some privacy when he first arrived.

"Thanks, Michael. I'll see you Saturday. Blow a kiss for me to Eric, and wish my best to Susan. And tell Jennie her favorite uncle is coming to see her."

I clicked off the phone to go upstairs but the sound of my brother's voice still rang in my head. There was nothing I could do or plan on doing for him until I knew what he was going through, but it felt good to think about helping someone else for a change. For the last few days I'd been immersed in my own troubles, but there was a whole world out there where every day, people suffered hardships. The idea that others were going through difficulties diminished the severity of my own problems.

I viewed my surroundings quite differently now. I smiled at the nurses at the front desk, and they, in turn smiled back. The echo of the sound of my steps as I walked down the hall now seemed like the most natural of sounds. The white walls that met my stare as I continued down the corridors now represented a curative power that I felt surging all around me, and which would heal my son. Considering how this whole ordeal with Eric had started out, everything was falling into place. It wasn't hard to convince myself that I had hit bottom, but I was now back on track.

By the time I got to Eric's floor, I found Susan already there with her father. After Susan had come back from the city with Jennie and passed to her parents in Brooklyn, they all came back to Manhattan to our apartment. My mother in law felt that it would be better to avoid bringing Jennie to the hospital again, especially after the tiring day that Jennie had, so she stayed in the apartment to take care of her. While my mother in law baby sat, my father in law came here with Susan to get an update on Eric's condition.

It was with Dr. Johnston that I happened to find the two of them. From the look on their faces, there seemed to be cause for concern. When I approached them, I called out to Susan. She quickly turned around and, when I got near, her left hand instinctively reached for the lower part of my right arm, and then her right hand took hold of the upper part, pulling me next to the side of her body.

"Michael", she began, "my father and I were watching Eric just a few minutes before you came, and he seemed to be asleep. My father was asking the doctor how long Eric would be sleeping out of the day. Well, the doctor . . ."

Dr. Johnston then interrupted Susan and asked her to allow him to explain. "Nothing is happening now that isn't expected. As we mentioned this morning, Eric had to be placed on a ventilator to assist him with his breathing. Your wife had asked if she could hold him for a few minutes, but I explained to her that he can't be disconnected from the machines. He needs the ventilator to keep breathing."

"But", I asked "are you saying that he can't survive at this point without the aid of the machines?"

"Your son's body is utilizing its full energy to fight the bacterium. This is normal. Part of that process is that your son can't utilize his muscles until the bacterium in his body subsides, including the muscles around his lungs. You can speak to him and touch him, but he can't react to you, not yet anyway. The news isn't as bad as you would think, because, over the long term, he should exhibit a full recovery. It's only a matter of time."

Susan was now grasping my arm ever tighter. I was glad that her father was here as well. He turned to Susan and said, "Honey, we have to look at the overall picture. Yes, this time period is not going to be easy for anyone, but Eric's on the road to recovery. He's going to be fine. The doctors are going to do their job and keep Eric under observation. Our job is to give Eric some tender loving care." His mood was extremely positive. It was so positive that I couldn't help wondering if he was acting this way just to fill his daughter with hope. He was a good father, I thought. He turned to the doctor and continued speaking. "Is there anything else that we should be aware of, doctor?" The doctor replied in the negative. My father in law then excused himself so that he could call Susan's mom from the waiting room and give her an update.

Susan and I thanked the doctor for his efforts. Dr. Johnston then asked us to try and get a full night's rest tonight. He said that he knew that we had been under intense pressure over the last few days, and that we had to take care of ourselves. It wouldn't do either of us any good if we got ourselves sick. We would be able to make daily visits to see Eric beginning tomorrow.

Susan had relaxed her grip on my arm and was now holding my hand. We decided to walk over to where Eric lay sleeping. We watched Eric's motionless body, which only moved slightly with each breath of air that was pumped into his body. Susan then said to me in a firm but low voice "I'm sorry, Michael. I'm sorry I snapped at you this morning. I know all of this is hard for you, too, but I know that we're doing the right thing."

It was nice to have the old Susan back again, and I relished this peace. In the back of my mind, though, I knew what her last remark was referring to and it was disturbing. I knew that the ease that I felt at this moment would be temporary, and that my wife's wishes would ultimately prove to be a source of conflict between us.

We stood there, next to each other for at least ten minutes, not saying a word, and just staring at our son. It made me think of the sunset from that first day that we met in Club Med. You could stare for hours and it wouldn't be enough. That's how beautiful my little baby looked right now. We finally moved when we heard Susan's father walking behind us.

"I spoke to your mother. She said that Jennie's been an angel. She drew some pictures and she's waiting up to show them to you. Mary says Jennie is going to be an artist one day. Everything seems to be going okay here. Why don't we go back to your apartment? We could pick up some take out food on the way, and have a quick bite with Mary and Jennie. We'll check in with the doctors in the morning."

Susan lingered for a few more moments, while staring at Eric. When we left the hospital, we drove back uptown in my father in law's car and, luckily, traffic was light. We arrived at our apartment pretty quickly and, once there, Jennie entertained us with her art work. After a short while, my in laws excused themselves, as they still had to get back to Brooklyn and it was already 10:30. Jennie fell fast asleep just seconds after her head hit the pillow. Susan was going to turn in also, but I wanted to see if I could find some of the passages that Isaac had shown me, and review them before I retired. I told Susan that I wanted to look something up before I went to sleep. She was curious, but didn't say anything. When she noticed that I had pulled out a bible, she smiled and then went into the bedroom.

I sat on the bergere chair, the same chair which I relinquished to Father Baldino last night. I opened up the Bible to Leviticus, and began reading from Chapter 18. As I skimmed over the sentences, I was taken by the moral truths contained there which we take for granted. If we consider certain of these truths as sacrosanct then who are we to reject the others? How can this society, with its moral teachings sourced in the Bible, and with the majority of the people as followers of either a Christian teaching or Jewish, pick and choose which sentences we should adopt and which we should not? If this was a book that was believed to be G-d's word by those religions, then all of the words in the Bible should be considered the moral base of the nation.

Interspersed throughout the passages were references to the land. Almost every chapter had a reference to the land of Israel, just like Isaac was saying.

Here, in Chapter 18, sentence 28, then again in Chapter 20, sentence 22. We were being told to do according to the words in the Bible so that we would merit to be in the land.

The end of Chapter 24, though, had a story about a child that profaned the name of G-d. In the middle of the lists of commandments which were set before it and after it, was the story of this child who had an Egyptian father and Jewish mother. I didn't understand why this was put in the middle of the laws. It seemed out of context. I decided to read on.

I was reaching the end of Leviticus. Chapter 26 began with G-d telling us to keep the commandments, and as a result, sentence 4 stated "Then I will give you rain in due season, and the land shall yield her increase, and the trees of the field shall yield their fruit." Again, here was the idea of G-d declaring to the nation of Israel 'do my commandments, then I will reward you through the land'. When I reached the 14th sentence, and began reading, I understood the answer of why the Jews have been persecuted throughout the last two thousand years. A listing of punishments is presented, after the warning in sentence 14, "But if ye not hearken unto me . . ." The rest of the chapter continues in its description of what will befall the Jewish people if they don't follow the Bible. At that time it was a prophecy; in this time, it reads more like a history book. How can we not believe?

I decided to look at the New Testament, to the area that Isaac had directed me. I looked at the index for the book of Mathew. It was the first book. I flipped the pages looking for the section of the Sermon of the Mount, and the book first opened on Chapter 10. I looked at the beginning of that chapter and read "(5) These twelve Jesus sent forth, and commanded them, saying, Go not into the way of the Gentiles, and into any city of the Samaritans enter ye not: (6) But go rather to the lost sheep of the house of Israel."

Who is being preached to here? Is it the nations of the world or the Jewish people? According to this, which is from the New Testament itself, these teachings are being directed to the Jewish people alone. Now, I thought, the Jewish people, the original target of the preaching of Jesus, turned down what he was teaching because they couldn't accept his message. His disciples then directed their attention to those outside of the Jewish nation. That's when the idea of the virgin birth must have started. The Jewish people would have been well versed in the Jewish Bible. They would have known that the Bible didn't have any references to a virgin birth, so it would not have made sense to claim it. According to Isaac, the idea of a virgin birth came later, but to what end? Why would the introduction of the idea of a virgin birth have been of benefit to the founders of Christianity?

Since Christianity was rejected by the Jews of Israel then the benefit had to be apparent if it was being presented to people outside of Israel.

I recalled the conversation that I had with David Greenblatt, when he explained how different the Jewish people were with the people of that era. The Jews believed in one G-d, while the rest of the world believed in many. So if the Jews did not accept Jesus in his time, and he wasn't accepted until many years later by the people who lived in other countries, then the idea of a virgin birth had to have been a benefit for people with a polytheistic belief.

Then it struck me. Hercules. The story of Hercules was an accepted legend of the ancient world. In fact, it was not an isolated type of story. Hercules was given god like stature by the people of that era. What elevated him was the story of his birth. His mother was a mortal who lived on this earth and his father was a god of Olympus. Hercules was then accepted as a god. That's what the people of that time period believed in. How else would you be able to tell the people of the surrounding nations to abolish their pagan gods than by substituting another god that would be acceptable to them? They would accept a person as one to be worshipped if his father was believed to be a god even though his mother was obviously a mortal woman. That would have to be how Jesus was elevated from the Messiah of Jewish belief who was an ordinary human being, to the god status of the Christian.

I was suddenly startled by the sound of someone walking in the room. Susan had been waiting up for me, and decided to see what I was reading. "I see you're looking at the Bible. Is there anything special that you're looking up?" she asked.

I didn't want to bring up what I had just been thinking so I avoided it by giving a generalization. "I was looking up some of what Jesus was preaching, and I was trying to understand more about him as a human being."

"But", she quickly said, "Jesus can't be categorized with men. He was the son of G-d. He was born on this earth without sin and died without sin. There was no other person on this earth like him."

"What would be the definition of sin?" I asked her. Something of what Isaac had earlier told me came into my head. I decided to see if I could logically review the New Testament from a Jewish perspective with her, sort of the way that Father Baldino had been explaining to me the background support of Christianity from his perspective. Maybe I would be able to introduce some doubt in her mind to make her more open to what Isaac had been telling me.

"Sin has to be what G-d has decreed to be sinful."

"That's what has me confused", I told Susan. "Jesus lived during the time in Jewish history when every Jew was subject to the law of the Jews. Would breaking a Jewish law at that time constitute sin?"

She was getting a little uneasy. She said, "A sin is something that breaks what G-d said. The Bible tells us what that was. If we live according to the Bible, then we can't have committed a sin."

"Well", I told her, "here's where I'm confused. There was something that Jesus said that I remember reading, and which I'm now trying to find. It has something to do with the Sermon on the Mount."

"Oh", she said. "That begins in Chapter 5 of Mathew." She took the book from my hands and opened it to the section I was looking for. When she handed the book back to me, I located the passage that Isaac had shown to me and read it to her. [59]"For truly I say to you, till heaven and earth pass away, not an iota, not a dot will pass from the Torah until all is accomplished. Whoever then relaxes one of the least of these commandments and teaches men so, shall be called least in the kingdom of heaven".

"So", I continued, "the basis for determining the definition of a sin should be the Torah, the Jewish Bible."

"According to this, yes" she said hesitantly.

"Then if Jesus is truly without sin, he would have followed his own words and kept all the laws in the Bible." She nodded in the affirmative to this and let me go on. "There was a section that we learned with Father Baldino where Jesus healed a blind man. Do you remember that?"

"Yes", she said. "That was in John, chapter 9."[60]

I turned to the chapter. "It says here that Jesus broke the Sabbath in order to cure the man, but that means that he sinned. In fact, even Father Baldino told us that elsewhere, Jesus ordered his disciples to pick grain on the Sabbath,[61] which was against Jewish law. If he broke the Sabbath several times and taught others to do so, which, according to the Sermon of the Mount was not permitted, he's a sinner by the standard established by his own words."[62]

Within seconds of my having said this, I could see the tension mount in her, and she got up and erupted. "Why are you twisting everything? He's the son of G-d. He makes the laws and says what a sin is and what it isn't. You can't call him a sinner." As she continued to berate me for my "blasphemous" remark, I thought to myself that my wife was saying how, even though Jesus sinned according to Jewish law to which he was subject, the church can't accept it because that would expose their god to be a common human being with common frailties.

But Susan's agitation made me realize this conversation with her wasn't working out as I planned and I decided to end it. There was no reasoning with her about this. I had to calm her down by repeatedly apologizing. I explained to her that "The other night, Father Baldino said that I would have questions. This is probably something that he can answer. I didn't mean to put you on the spot. I'm trying to understand all of this from an outsider's point of view, and I'm naturally going to have questions."

She was still ill at ease, but she was also tired. My reply seemed to calm her down somewhat, enough to forestall an argument, but she told me that I should never talk like that again, for any reason. "Look", I said, "maybe I should rephrase my questions and present them to Father Baldino on another day. Right now, we should probably call it a day and get to bed. This has been a rough day from the second we got up."

The hope that I entertained the other day of introducing Judaism to my wife as an alternative to Christianity had almost entirely vanished. Hers was a firm belief that was established within her from when she was a child. After seeing how her relationship with her mother had been rekindled, I understood that her belief was also reinforced because of an inner need for parental approval. She had become closer to her parents since the birth of our kids, and she was blindly adopting their beliefs as her beliefs. As long as my wife was close to her parents and her church I would never be able to convince her of any other lifestyle. As I shut the book and entered the bedroom, the inevitability of a clash between the two of us became all the more a reality.

23

I had thought that it would be difficult for me to fall asleep, but it only seemed like a few minutes from the time I put my head on my pillow to when I heard my alarm clock. I quickly showered and got dressed, and then, on my way to the kitchen, I walked into the living room where the light from the newly risen sun was just beginning to penetrate the window. The Bible that I was reviewing last night was still on the coffee table where I had left it, and I walked over to it and picked it up. I started opening it but decided against it and I put it away. I went into the kitchen and had some orange juice and a cookie then went back to the bedroom to wake Susan and tell her I was leaving. She gave me a kiss goodbye and asked me to set the alarm for 8:00. I went back into the living room and looked around to make sure that there was nothing that I had forgotten, and I left the apartment.

I took the subway and ended up getting off at my usual stop. When I got out of the station, though, I walked for a few blocks in the opposite direction of my office, toward where Isaac worked. It was still too early for most people to go to work, so the pace of the few people who were walking the streets was not as hurried as I knew it would be in another hour. I entered the empty lobby of his building and got into the elevator. There was something pleasant about getting on an elevator and being the only rider.

The elevator let out a low hum as it was pulled upwards, until it arrived at Isaac's floor with a slight bouncing movement. The doors slid open and I proceeded to Isaac's office. To my surprise, his receptionist was already in, and was expecting me. She buzzed Isaac, and, just like yesterday, he came out of the office with a brisk walk, to greet me. He had a smile on, as if he was meeting up with a friend who he hadn't seen in a long while. He held my hand in a firm grip and gave me a warm hello.

On the way to the conference room, he remarked how he was enjoying our little talks, and that he hoped that I was getting as much out of them as he was. It happened to work out well for him to meet me this morning, as things were a little quiet this week, anyway.

Although my first instincts were to tell Isaac of the events of last night, I decided not to relate any of it to him. It was enough right now to get whatever information from Isaac which I could. It was satisfying to me when I realized that Isaac was not only teaching me facts, but he was giving me enough information to allow me to reason things out for myself. It was becoming more and more obvious to me that Judaism had so much to offer, but, after last night, I wasn't sure that I could ever get Susan to see that. That was the only unknown in all that had been happening to me that I was afraid of. There was always that glimmer of hope, though, that things would turn out fine between us, and that gave me the courage to go on.

I just smiled at Isaac and opened up my mind to him, and then said, "I've been looking forward to it too, and it's really opening up my eyes to a lot."

"We ended off last night with your unanswered question. Do you remember it?"

With all that had been going on since I left Isaac last night, it slipped my mind, but it suddenly came back to me. "Yes, I remember. I was asking you if Jesus was right when he claimed that some of the laws of the Sabbath were excessive."

"That's right", said Isaac. "I touched on one of the many discrepancies within the teachings of Jesus because I want you to understand that his words are not pertinent when discussing Jewish law. What he believes or doesn't believe should not even be considered. The question should revolve around the idea as to whether or not all the laws dictated by the Bible regarding the Sabbath should be adhered to in this day and age.

"In order to answer that, I'd like to ask you a question. Did you ever buy an electronic device that required a manual? I know that when I got my cell phone, in order to make it work correctly, I had to attach it to a computer with a cable and download specific files from the computer in a specific order. Now what would happen if I decided not to follow those instructions and I left out some details?"

"Well", I said, "it's very likely that your cell phone won't work correctly."

"Right", he replied. "You chose the right wording. The cell phone MAY work, but if it does, it won't work correctly.

"The laws that we've been given are more than just something to make us holy. They're an instruction guide to a proper life. If we follow those laws as they've been given, then we're able to achieve the most that we can for our physical as well as our spiritual life."

What he said sounded plausible, but I needed a more concrete example of what Isaac was trying to explain. My face betrayed my feelings, because Isaac then continued, "I can see you're a little skeptical of this idea. Let's pick an example that you can relate to. I think you once said that you liked science?"

I nodded in the affirmative. I couldn't imagine where this was going.

"We'll look at electricity. Did you ever take a physics course in high school?" I nodded again, and he then asked me, "Did you ever hear of something called the left hand rule?"

I thought back to my high school days. "Yes", I said. "The left hand rule has to do with electricity. We know that there's a current that goes through a wire and it goes in a certain direction. There's also a magnetic field that goes around the wire. Years ago, before shielded wire was used, it was common for the field around electric wires to distort the picture on a television set if the wires got too close.

"The left hand rule describes the magnetic field around the wire. In school we were told to picture a ring that was slipped over the wire. The magnetic field circles around the wire along the path of the ring and travels either in a clockwise or counter clockwise direction. If you were to take your left hand and extend your thumb, sort of like what the Roman Emperors did when deciding if gladiators would live or die, your thumb would point in a certain direction, which signifies the direction of the electricity in a wire. The direction in which your fingers would be curling would be the direction of the magnetic field."

"Very good", Isaac said. "Now according to the rules of electricity, if you were to start a current, the field would be automatically produced."

"And", I broke in, "if you were to create a field around a wire, the electric current would be automatically produced, and its direction would be determined by the direction of the field around it. Just hold out your left hand, point your thumb in a certain direction, and curl your fingers to see whether the field is going clockwise or counter clockwise, based on the direction of where your thumb is pointing.

"So", I continued, "I guess I have the science part. But how does this relate to religion?"

"Here's the amazing thing. We have an idea that what happens in the spiritual world is affected by the material world and vice versa. We also know that when G-d created the world, it was according to a set of laws. Now, those laws that govern the physical world also apply to the spiritual dimension as well."

I was puzzled. "You're saying that there are certain things that were done by the Jews in following the commandments that would have led them to understand electricity?"

"I'll describe the action, and I'll let you be the judge. There's a certain holiday which comes right after Yom Kippur, called Succoth. It's sometimes referred to as Succos. One of the things that we do on that holiday is to say a blessing over four items: a fruit, called an etrog, and three different types of leaves which are bound together. I won't go into the details of those items, but it's what we do with those items that has relevance here.

"They weren't aware of channels on a radio or television several thousand years ago, but we now understand that you can tune in to a different station just by turning the tuner knob. Our tuner knobs in prayer sometimes have to do with the numerical value of words. The Hebrew word for mercy is hesed, and its numerical value is 72.[63] During the prayers, we hold those four items that I mentioned and shake them in four different parts of the prayer. It happens that we shake them 18 times in each of those four parts."

"Totaling 72", I quickly said.

"Right. What we're doing is calling on the mercy aspect of . . ." He hesitated while searching for the right word. "I guess you would call it G-d's spirit. Now that we tuned into the right channel, we place a Torah scroll in the center of the room and walk around it to bring down that aspect of mercy from above. Judging from what we know about electricity, do you know which direction we would walk around the table with the Torah scroll?"

I held out my left hand and pointed my thumb downward. My fingers curled in a counter clockwise direction. "If we're trying to bring the spirit down to us from heaven, you would have to circle the Torah scroll in a counter clockwise direction", I said.

"Here's the question that I'd like to ask you. If we are looking to bring G-d's spirit or glory down to earth, and we walked in a clockwise direction, would we achieve what we're trying to do?"

"No", I said. "Because according to the laws of physics which you say also apply to the spiritual, the glory couldn't come down, but you would be sending something up. But that's not what you want to do. I get it now. You're saying that you have to follow the instructions, whether those instructions are related to science or whether they're related to the laws of the Sabbath. Just because we believe that something is excessive doesn't mean we can leave it out, because all the items are necessary in order to achieve the desired result that we want."

"You catch on very quickly, Michael", Isaac said. "The laws of religion are, in a sense, not much different than the laws of science. A person examining the procedures within the religious curriculum may see a series of meaningless actions. In this case, without knowing about electricity, the whole set of actions we just discussed would seem to be a set of actions that have no rhyme or reason. Once we know the concept of electricity, this whole series of acts makes perfect sense."

"I have to tell you," I said, "learning about the religion is nothing like I would have imagined. You make it seem to be something that's real and not just a matter of faith. I think that if religion were taught this way, a lot of people that would not even consider religion would begin to look at it with more interest. Is there a lot of science mixed in with religion?"

"There doesn't have to be science per se, but the religion does reveal a set of rules that the world is governed by."

"What sort of rules?" I now asked. Isaac now had my full attention.

"Sometimes rules are general and sometimes specific," Isaac began. "We'll start with something specific.

"There are certain dietary restrictions that are based on some animals being acceptable to eat, and some not. Within the category of acceptable animals, there are certain parts of animals that are not acceptable. One of these is the meat that surrounds a certain vein, called in Hebrew, gid hanasheh.

"There's a well known episode in the Bible which speaks of Jacob fighting the angel of his brother Esau. It ends off with an admonition that we are not to eat of a certain section of the leg of an animal, the gid hanasheh, because Jacob was wounded in the leg by the angel.[64] Now this is a very perplexing line of reasoning. Jacob was wounded in the leg and had a limp, and because of this, Jews are not allowed to eat that similar part of an animal. Although we still accept this as a valid reason, there's another explanation for this practice that's based on another rule."

I sat up and gazed intensely at Isaac while I waited for his explanation. "When Jews learn the Bible, the stories and events have different levels of meaning. The simple meaning here is that we don't eat that part of the animal in commemoration of the miracle of Jacob confronting an angel in battle and surviving. We can dig a little deeper to determine more of what happened by the words that are used.

"When the angel of Esau is trying to kill Jacob, the Bible doesn't use the normal word that we would associate with killing. Instead, it uses the word, avak, which means to turn to dust. From this we understand that the angel wanted to totally destroy every trace of Jacob. So now a picture arises of how the events unfolded.

"It's now the middle of the night, and Jacob is alone. The angel confronts Jacob in order to completely destroy all trace of him. From the beginning of the battle, though, the angel knows that Jacob had a weak spot and it was in his leg. He could have injured Jacob in that particular spot on his leg, but that wouldn't cause Jacob's destruction so he doesn't bother striking him there at this point of their encounter.

"The night proceeded and the angel was still not able to destroy Jacob. The angel, for reasons I won't get into here, was required to depart before dawn. When daybreak was approaching and it saw that Jacob was too powerful, it realized that it could not destroy him. Rather than just depart without affecting Jacob at all, it decided to at least hurt Jacob in his vulnerable spot so the battle would not be a total loss. It decided to wound Jacob in the part of his body that had a natural weakness, a part of his body that the angel could have injured at the start."

"So" I now interrupted, "you're saying that the prohibition against eating the part of the leg of the animal was because we learned that there was something not holy about it, since the angel easily injured Jacob in the same part of his leg."

Isaac sat back. "At the rate you're going, you'll be the one to give the classes pretty soon."

I blushed, but I then asked Isaac what it was about that part of the leg that made the leg weak.

"For that answer" he said, "we turn to the Zohar, which is part of the mystical explanation of the Bible and it's there that we find the rule that governs this episode. According to the Bible, there are 365 muscles and sinews in the body in the same way that there are 365 days in the year. According to our tradition, one day of the year is reserved for Satan, which is the ninth day of the Hebrew month of Av. That's a day when great calamities happen to the Jewish people. Just as one day out of the 365 is under the control of Satan, there is also one part of the 365 muscles and sinews of the body that is under his control and in Hebrew, that part is called the gid hanasheh."

I said, "I guess that's in keeping with the idea of the Jews being a holy nation. Anything to do with something that's connected to something that's not holy is to be avoided."

"Right" Isaac said. "Much of what we do is explained in the Bible, you just have to know how to interpret what's written, and to do so, we examine the oral law or the Talmud, as well as some of the mystical writings like the Zohar. There are not only rules covering the acts which we can and cannot perform, but there are also guidelines that cover our belief system. There are fundamental ideas which could range from knowing that everything that G-d does is for the best, to the idea that even Satan is under the command of G-d and can only do his will, and even to the details of what the Messiah is all about."

At the mention of the Messiah, I perked up. I couldn't help thinking back on the insistence of the followers of Christianity that Jesus was the Messiah. I wondered if the Jewish general concept differed somewhat. I asked him to explain.

"There is no universally accepted opinion within the Jewish community as to the specifics of what will occur in the time period leading up to the advent of the Messiah. Each individual opinion expressed which comes from a leading figure within Torah Jewry is accepted as a possibility, although not the only possibility. G-d doesn't want us to know exactly when the Messiah will come because then people wouldn't want to undergo complete repentance until that date. That's why the texts that we have of the early time period of the Jewish faith are vague when discussing this.

"Even though certain specifics about the Messiah are still debated, there are general points that are accepted, and I'd like to explain two of these ideas.

"Before I do this, I just want to mention one more thing. The word messiah is translated as "my anointed" or it could be loosely taken to mean, "G-d's anointed". When Kings or High Priests were put in office, they were anointed with oil and were called messiahs. Even non-Jewish kings are referred to in the Bible as messiahs. King Cyrus, a non-Jew who was king during the Persian exile, is referred to as a messiah.[65] I mention this so that you understand for future reference, that the word is a general term, but in certain instances only, does it refer to The Messiah, who will lead the Jews at the end of days.

"The first idea I'd like to cover is that there are actually two messiahs, with each one having a different function." Isaac raised his hand to stop me from interrupting. "You see, this is another idea that's basic to our messianic belief. One of these messiahs is destined to be King of the Jews and will be of the Davidic royal line. The other is destined to come from wealth, and will use that position of wealth to defend the Jews in the final war predicted in scripture. The first messiah to come will be the Messiah who will come from wealth, referred to as the Messiah of the house of Joseph. Subsequent to that Messiah, the Messiah of the house of David will arise.

"The background of this is explained by the story of Jacob, and his brother, Esau. When these brothers were born to Isaac, Jacob was to function as the Davidic messiah and Esau as the other. Esau failed to control his evil desires, and sold the birthright to Jacob. The result of this was that, in a future generation, both messiahs were now to come from Jacob. Jacob, though, was always unsure if he would prove worthy of this responsibility. It wasn't until his son, Joseph was born, that he realized that G-d now confirmed his dual role, and that it would be through the soul of Joseph that the job of that second messiah was to be carried out. That's one of the reasons why that second messiah is called the messiah from the house of Joseph.

"The other idea is that every generation has its own set of potential messiahs. Numerous Jewish leaders have written this, among them, the Bartenura, known as the Rav,[66] and Rabbi Tzadok of Lublin. They wrote that in every generation there will arise someone who will be worthy of being the Davidic Messiah and he will be revealed if that generation merits it. Scripture has numerous examples of this. A Jewish king by the name of King Hizkiyahu was considered to be a potential Davidic messiah in his generation. The first Davidic messiah was Hur, who lived during the time of Moses. It's written that before the Jews committed the sin of the golden calf, the Jews of that generation were in a potential messianic period. Once they committed the sin of the calf however, those Jews no longer merited for the Davidic Messiah to arise in their time period. The Bible records that one person was immediately killed when the golden calf was fashioned, and that was Hur. It was explained that since his purpose in life was to be the Davidic Messiah, when the Jewish people sinned, his death followed.

"There is no one person that we're waiting for who will be the Messiah. If the person who was the potential Messiah of a particular generation dies without being able to achieve his purpose, then a new potential messiah will be born into the next generation, and so on. The whole messianic idea proposed by the followers of Christianity, that only one specific person is the Messiah and we all have to wait until he's resurrected, is an idea that's foreign to us."

When Isaac stopped, I took that as my cue to now comment. "Without the concept of the resurrection there is no point to the religion of Christianity. I guess what you said last time about Jesus breaking the Sabbath was just the tip of the iceberg of how Christianity and Judaism couldn't be more different."

"Really," Isaac said, "the confusing thing is that there are also many similarities, but that's what makes comparing the two religions a necessity. On one hand, much of what Jesus preaches is straight out of Jewish teaching. Jesus says that one should not only avoid swearing falsely, but he adds that one should not swear at all[67]; he says that one should not commit adultery, but adds that one should not look at a woman with lust[68]; his remark that you should 'do unto others as you would have them do unto you' is probably his most well known teaching. Jesus, though, did not originate any of these ideas. They were already incorporated into our texts before the New Testament was written.

"A large number of our laws were extended by Rabbinic authority to yield the same effect that Jesus wants to arrive at here but with a difference. In order to avoid the chaos of hundreds of individual splinter groups setting up their own laws, we have a system which states that the laws can be extended only by consensus of the majority of the Rabbis who head the Rabbinical court.[69] It was commonplace throughout Jewish history for religious laws to be extended in this manner. The Oral Torah that I told you about earlier defines both the laws given by G-d at Sinai, as well as the extensions to those laws which were agreed upon by the Rabbinic council. In a book called 'Ethics of the Fathers' references are made to those laws. In Chapter 3 of that book, Rabbi Akiva declared "The transmitted Oral Torah is a protected fence around the (written) Torah."

"As long as Jesus was repeating what was already agreed upon by the Rabbis, you don't have a problem. If you look at the comments of Jesus on swearing you'll find that the laws of the Oral Torah already advise against any type of swearing due to the great penalty for swearing falsely. You set up a protective fence, so to speak, to insure that the prohibition against swearing falsely is not violated. The Oral Torah also discusses how a woman should dress with modesty, so that certain thoughts would not enter a man's head if he was in the presence of women. Another precaution which helps a man avoid improper thoughts is that he shouldn't gaze upon a married woman who leaves her hair uncovered, because that's part of what makes a woman attractive. The idea of loving your neighbor is picked up almost verbatim from the Old Testament. In fact, the Bible is filled with references of the proper treatment of our fellow man so that we can avoid hurting another person's feelings.

"The differences between the religions, though, are many. You start out with similarities, but then distortions of the writings of the Old Testament are presented in order to bolster the message in the New. In his attempt to show that he's improving on the Bible's teachings, Jesus himself proceeds to misquote the Bible to make his message stronger. Within the text of the Sermon of the Mount in Mathew, it's recorded that he says "You have heard that it was said 'You shall love your neighbor and hate your enemy.' But I say to you, Love your enemies and pray for those who persecute you."[70] Someone who is ignorant of the Bible who hears this message would assume that the Bible actually advocates hating your enemy, but there is no source to back that up. Nowhere does the Bible state to hate your enemy.[71] He's falsely quoting scripture to make his comment on loving your neighbor stand out more.

"In numerous instances, he rejects the validity of the Jewish laws. He prefaced his speech of the Sermon of the Mount by saying that no one who changes any of the commandments in the Torah will be allowed into the kingdom of heaven. Once he has the attention of the crowd, however, he goes against his own words. He begins to scoff at the commandments, which all Jews must obey. He proceeds to proclaim that Jewish commandments could be broken by his say so, but by doing this, he severs the link that he originally wanted to establish between Judaism and his teachings. We discussed how he advocated that it was allowed to break the Sabbath, which goes against one of the Ten Commandments. When you read further into the sermon, you find that he shows disrespect for his mother in chapter 12[72], so that he broke another of the commandments. He doesn't stop there."

Isaac took the King James Bible and opened it to Mark, chapter 7, sentence 18. He read ""And he saith unto them, Are ye so without understanding also? Do ye not perceive, that whatsoever thing from without entereth into the man, it cannot defile him; 19 Because it entereth not into his heart, but into the belly, and goeth out into the draught, purging all meats?" Here he ridicules as meaningless the kosher laws as specified in the Bible by saying specifically that something not kosher that a person eats 'cannot defile him.'"

Isaac again flipped through some pages to chapter 6 of Mathew.[73] "And when you pray, you must not be like the hypocrites; for they love to stand and pray in the synagogues and at the street corners, that they may be seen by men . . . But when you pray, go into your room, and shut the door and pray to your Father who is in secret; and your Father who sees in secret will reward you." Here he says that all of the laws of prayers where we are required to pray in a group of at least ten men are also no longer valid.

"We have a system which allows for the process of the extension of religious laws through the power of the Rabbinic council. Once Jesus broke from this, he can no longer claim to be speaking for Judaism. Jesus had no authority as an individual to determine which laws should be followed and which should not. Yet he constantly did so and led others to do the same. There was a rebellion against Moses by the cousin of Moses, named Korah, and Korah tried to use logic to show that certain of the commandments were not reasonable.[74] He was subsequently killed by G-d. If you examine the arguments of Jesus, he tried to use the same type of logic that Korah did. Just as in the case of Korah, Jesus admittedly had no authority to do so, but his only argument was his own type of logic. If the followers of Christianity accept the Bible as true, they would have to admit that Korah was the first one to attempt to ridicule the commandments, but he was shown to be wrong by G-d. If that's so, how can they accept Jesus when he does the same? Knowing that this argument was a weak link in their original belief, the founders of the Christian religion subsequently declared that Jesus is considered to be G-d, and that gave him the right to change commandments. We already reviewed other proofs that show that he can't be G-d. It even says in Numbers, Chapter 23, and sentence 19 "G-d is not a mortal that he should lie, nor a man, that he should change his mind." The Bible says openly that G-d is not a man, and yet the Christians pray to him as though the man, Jesus, born of a woman, was really G-d. It's because we Jews believe in the Bible that we cannot believe in Jesus.

"For the followers of Jesus, there's a Catch-22 here. A Jew must accept whatever is contained in the Torah as true. All the predictions of the messianic period are included, as well as the commandments given to the Jews for eternity. It follows then, that for a Jew to believe in the Messiah he would have to believe in the truth of the rest of the Torah, because they go hand in hand. If, to accept Christianity, you have to reject parts of the Torah as invalid, then how would you be able to determine if the predictions concerning the Messiah are invalid as well? If you're choosing a Messiah for the world based on the Messiah of Judaism, then he must conform to what Judaism dictates. You can't pick and choose and say that the Jewish Messiah is the Messiah for the world, based on the Torah, and then reject those parts of the Torah that speak of the commandments.

"The Christians, however, have attempted to do exactly this. They invented a second coming, which is found nowhere in our religion, they changed the Sabbath from Saturday to Sunday among other things, and then proceeded to declare that our commandments can be dropped. To justify this, they changed the words of our Bible to support their claims, but that doesn't change the fact that the Bible has stayed consistently the same through the centuries. We know this because the Dead Sea scrolls which contain the words of the Bible, match the current Bible that we use today and those scrolls are dated 600 years before Jesus was born. Because changing the words would not be a valid proof, they had to declare that Jesus was G-d, and since G-d gave us the Torah, then, by their reasoning G-d is allowed to declare it null and void. This argument doesn't hold up. The problem is that G-d already declared that He is not a man, so that Jews could never accept Jesus as a G-d, and by extension, Jews cannot embrace the Christian religion which reveres him as one."

It all fits together, I thought. Only someone who's unaware of what Judaism is all about would be attracted to Christianity. I realized that there was another difference between Judaism and Christianity, and I now commented to Isaac, "As much as it's apparent to me now that their religion doesn't add up, I can still see how someone would find Christianity a lot easier for him to follow than Judaism. Judaism is seen as having a list of actions that must be performed in order for a person to be loved by G-d. Christianity says that you don't have to do anything for G-d to love you."

"The truth is", Isaac replied, "that you really don't have to do anything for G-d to love you in Judaism either. But religion is not just about getting G-d's love. Try to picture someone who goes to college for a degree in literature, for example. While others in the class are forced to work hard and study, this one student is in a privileged position. His father is a major contributor to the University. He doesn't have to go to class, he doesn't have to take tests, and he doesn't even have to be present in the school. After four years when diplomas are given out, the privileged student is also handed a diploma along with the rest of his classmates. Now I ask you, to whom is the diploma more meaningful? Is it to the privileged child who never had to make any effort or to the other students who spent their four years of college struggling to get good grades in their courses? The student who works hard for his diploma appreciates that end result because of the effort he had to expend.

"G-d's love works the same way. Just as everyone in the class received diplomas, we are all beneficiaries of G-d's love. In order for us to appreciate what that means, G-d gave us a way to return his love by giving us a set of obligations which will glorify G-d's greatness and will also cause us to feel worthy of the many blessings that G-d bestows on us."

Isaac's reply made me think about all the commandments that Jews are supposed to perform. All of my life I had mistakenly looked at Jews who were observant as if they were behind the times. While my appreciation of the Jewish religion grew with each meeting that I had with Isaac, my sense of shame grew with it. I was ashamed at my lack of the most fundamental knowledge of Judaism. I was ashamed that even though I knew that I felt a spiritual emptiness inside of me, I never chose to question what was out there. I was most ashamed of the fear that I now felt that I wouldn't be able to observe the commandments that I was being introduced to, because they might seem too overwhelming to someone who's always lived the lifestyle that I have. I wasn't even aware of what those commandments were. As best as I could, I expressed my feelings to Isaac.

"It's just human nature to believe that our fears will pull us down, but the truth is just the opposite. Your fears, Michael, and the embarrassment that you feel can actually help you succeed." Isaac settled back in his chair and his tone changed to that of a kind grandfather figure who's giving advice to his grandson. "There's a story that I heard that would fit in with what's bothering you right now. The story revolves around a public debate that took place between members of a Reform congregation and an Orthodox one. They were discussing the merits of Torah Judaism versus Reform.[75]

"In the course of the debate, the Reform Rabbi turned to the head of the Orthodox congregation, and asked him to rise. He then asked him, "Are you a Shabbat observer?" The man became red faced, and slowly stammered that he was not. The Reform Rabbi then turned to the other officers of the Orthodox congregation, and asked them the same question. In like fashion, they all sheepishly admitted that they were not fully observant. The Reform Rabbi then turned to the rest of the people present, and in triumphant fashion declared. "We see that the members of the Orthodox congregation do not observe the Shabbat. We of the Reform do not observe as well. There is no difference at all between our two groups, so why are we even having this debate of the merits of observing the commandments of the Bible?"

"The crowd was silent, as those in the Orthodox camp had no reply, and the Reform group felt that their Rabbi had presented an irrefutable argument. In the audience sat the late Ponavezer Rav, Rabbi Kahanaman. He decided to break the silence and intercede. He asked for permission to speak. He then asked the head of the Reform congregation to rise and asked him if he was a Shabbat observer. The man responded with laughter, saying, "Of course not." Rabbi Kahanaman then asked the same question to each person of the rest of their committee and each and every person responded similarly with the same laughter.

"Rabbi Kahanaman then turned to the crowd and said "This is the difference between the two groups. It is the sense of shame exhibited by the Orthodox group that was absent from the Reform." You see, Michael, without the shame and remorse, we could never find it within us to attempt to be better. That's why the shame that you feel is a signal that you have a desire to be more observant, and that's precisely why you'll succeed."

What Isaac was telling me was comforting, but I couldn't help feeling that there was something that I should be physically doing. "I like what you just said. I should turn my fears into an asset, rather than a liability", I replied. But I still felt that there was something missing. "I'm still wondering how I can start to do whatever must be done to keep the Sabbath, or conform to the kosher laws, or whatever a Jew is supposed to do that makes him different from those people of other faiths. When would I be able to start doing the commandments that Jews are supposed to perform?"

"Michael, you've already started. The review of the Jewish religion and the studying of portions of the Bible are also fulfilling a commandment of G-d to the Jewish people. The individual laws can be taught and followed later. Right now, though, because of what you're going through because of your son's illness and the conflict with your wife's family, it's probably best to continue with general ideas." He thought for a second and then continued. "Maybe there is one thing that you could do. Every morning we say a blessing to thank G-d for returning our souls to us. We consider our souls to be a gift that's on loan to us from G-d. As the soul that we've been given belongs to Him, He may, at any time, decide to keep it, either because the time allotted for us is up, or because we aren't using his gift in the right way. We thank G-d for giving us another day to do the good that He put us on this world to do."

Isaac rose from his chair and walked over to the section of the bookcase behind us on which he stored the Hebrew and Jewish related books. He quickly glanced through a section in the middle and pulled out a dark, hard covered book that was about the size of a paperback. He looked inside to make sure that its contents were what he had in mind, and then walked over to me with the book in hand.

"Here", he said as he sat next to me. "I think this book will be helpful for you. It's a Hebrew-English prayer book, but it also has the pronunciation of the Hebrew words written in English."

I was reluctant to take it, but he insisted. "Please", he said, "you can use it for as long as you like. We've got plenty of other prayer books here. In fact, you would be doing me a favor if you took it."

He flipped open the book to the beginning, and showed me the prayer that he wanted me to say. It was shorter than I expected. "I give thanks before You, living and everlasting King, that You have restored my soul to me with compassion: great is Your trustworthiness."[76] I stumbled when I repeated the Hebrew version, but Isaac was patient with me.

"The key idea to keep in mind", he said, "is not just to thank G-d for restoring our soul on this morning, but to remember that we have to do something each and every day to warrant His returning our soul for the many days to come." Isaac leaned back in his chair, and smiled as the fingers on his hand delicately closed the book. "I think we've covered a lot of ideas today. We can end our session here. If you'd like, you can give me a call and we can pick up on some other points next week. In the meantime, you can look through some of the other prayers that are in the book."

"Thanks", I told him as he slid the book towards me. "I never felt the need to have a prayer book in my house. We've got a Bible, but that's only because of the wishes of my wife."

My mentioning of the Bible made me think about last night. The passages that I read were still fresh in my mind, but I suddenly remembered the question that I had about the insertion of the story about the man who cursed. Following a moment of silence, Isaac had started to rise, but, as long as I was here anyway, I decided to ask him about it.

"Would you mind if I asked you one more thing? I didn't understand something when I was reading the Bible last night. I reviewed those passages that we went over, but something didn't make sense."

"By all means, please ask. I'll be glad to answer you if I could", he said as he sat back in the chair again.

"After we had spoken yesterday, I decided to review some of the sections in Leviticus that you had spoken about . . . you know, the ones that explained what had to be done in order to be holy. Those things that make a person holy are being listed out, almost as in a checklist. For no reason, the chapter inserts a discussion of a person who cursed G-d and we are then given a story of how this person received the death penalty for what he did.[77] Immediately after this, the Bible then picks up on continuing with its checklist. This whole story seems to be out of place. Why would there be a discussion of this sort in the middle of a checklist on what it takes to be holy?"

Isaac asked me to show him where I had found the section that I was referring to. I pulled the Bible and flipped through the chapters until I located it. He scanned it quickly and then put the book down and looked up.

"It's very interesting that you should catch this, Michael. Everything that's written in the Bible is there to teach us something. We have to remember that the Bible is not simply a piece of literature. It's not meant to be a captivating story that will keep us lying awake until we get to the next chapter. The Bible is a way for G-d to speak to us. Throughout the Bible, G-d is giving us a series of messages. When certain sentences seem out of place, it means that we don't understand those messages. That's when we analyze the words in order to determine what G-d wants us to learn."

Isaac leaned back in his chair while his hands instinctively began to form around that imaginary object in the air which he liked to play with.

"The chapters before this episode speak about what's required of the Jews for them to be holy so that they'll merit the land. In this chapter, chapter 24, we find the episode of the man who "blasphemed the name of the Lord", and it does seem out of place. In addition, because of the preceding verses, you would automatically assume that there would be no question that someone guilty of that offense would be put to death, and yet we're told that the Israelites put him into some type of detention until they could inquire as to what to do with him.

"Here's where the analysis comes into play." Isaac's hands now started to dance on his imaginary object. He was becoming completely enveloped in his subject. "There are a few things going on here, but we'll try to focus on the aspects related to your question. Let's see what the Bible has to say about this man who cursed. The man is not just described as an Israelite, but he's the son of an Egyptian man and Israelite woman.

"Based on what was written, we're able to piece together the events which occurred.[78] An argument arises between this man and an Israelite. The argument escalates until it reaches a point where the two men are furious at each other. In the heat of the moment, the son of the Egyptian curses in G-d's name. To give us an idea of how serious the curses were, the Bible describes them in certain language that is not found anywhere else except for one other place. That's in the episode found in the first book of Samuel when Goliath came out to mock and curse the Lord of the Jews, in the days just before Goliath fought with David.

"The Israelites are now faced with a problem. They've just learned through the use of the 'checklist' that's been presented to them, of what to do and what not to do in order to achieve a state of holiness. With regards to this case, they've learned that it's a sin to blaspheme in G-d's name, with the punishment being death. The laws that were given, however, all appeared to be directed towards the Jews.

"There are disputes by Rabbinic authorities as to whether or not the blasphemer was considered to be Jewish, but from the wording in the Bible, it appears that his status is unclear. The question that this episode brings out is this. Is the law regarding blaspheming, and the laws which we have been itemizing in the previous chapters, to be applied the same to a non Israelite, as to an Israelite?

"Until they could find out, they had to hold him in detention. The answer was not apparent to Moses either, which is further evidence of this man's questionable status. Moses had to seek out the verdict from G-d. The reply that came back declared that the "Stranger and native born alike, when he blasphemes, he shall be put to death."[79]

"So now the inclusion of this story makes sense. The description of what entails holiness which is recorded in the earlier chapters, is now contrasted with an example of someone who does not embody this ideal. For the sake of the community, this person, Jewish or not, can have no part in the community. His act of cursing shows disrespect for G-d that cannot be tolerated. The issue of whether the laws enumerated in the previous and subsequent 'checklists' also apply to non-Jews has been settled. The verdict from G-d is that this law applies to everyone, and not just to those who are of the Jewish faith.

The verdict, as we had learned earlier in the 'checklist', results in a penalty of death."

As he spoke, my mind kept hanging on his description of the man who was sentenced to death. He was the son of a Jew and a non-Jew, and his status within the Jewish community was questionable. I suppose that people usually interpret things from their own perspective. Because of that I felt that this section was speaking about me, and so it dawned on me that the Bible was really telling a story of what could happen when a person married someone from outside the faith.

To anyone who understood the commitment that a Jew must have toward Judaism, I had committed a sin. In my own way, I was a Hester Prynne[80] who was forced to wear a scarlet letter embroidered on my chest to proclaim my sin to the world, but in place of the scarlet letter "A", my sin was represented by my guilt. The ones to really suffer, though, were my children. I was setting them up to be cut off from the possibility that they would have anything to do with Judaism. I was responsible for their being partially in my world and partially in Susan's but in reality, they were in neither.

I now understood that the commitment to religion transcends personal wants for the sake of your community and nation. The Jewish nation to which I belonged was the only nation that was defined not by territory but by the obligations to G-d through a religion. That's why moving to the United States, or England, or Argentina, couldn't change your required role as a Jew. Marriage to a non-Jew couldn't change what you were. A Jew was always a Jew, and a Jew was always defined by his religion. It was ironic that this Biblical episode which struck me in some unknown way, was really a hidden warning against assimilation and intermarriage. It was a warning that was meant for me but that reached me too late.

Isaac didn't notice my reaction, or maybe I didn't show my reaction, I don't know. But he continued. "Michael, you just hit on another major difference between Judaism and Christianity. Many Christians are able to quote passages from the Bible by memory. But even though they've learned the words, do they really know what the Bible is saying?

"For a Jew, there is an obligation to acquire the Bible. That means that they must not only know the words, but they must have an understanding of the true message of the Bible. That can only be done by analysis like we've just done here. There's a story that was told that illustrates this.[81]

"There was a wealthy art collector who amassed a large quantity of precious art for display in his home. A guard was hired to watch over this collection. Each night, the guard would walk through the house, and, as he walked into each room, he would try to memorize the contents and their placement. After a few days, he made an inventory list so that he had a complete record of every precious item that the wealthy man owned. Each passing day sharpened his memory more and more as he committed that list to memory, so that by the end of a few months he knew the contents of the home better than the collector did himself.

"Visitors who asked where a certain piece of art was located would get an instant reply from this guard, who answered without hesitation. It was when these visitors decided to ask more in depth questions, however, that the extent of the guard's knowledge was found to be limited. Although he knew where every piece was located, when the guard was asked why the piece was valuable, he had no answer. When he was asked for the history of the piece, he had no answer. When he was asked why the piece was placed where it was, he again had no answer.

"For Jews, just to know the words of the Bible is not enough. We must delve into the seeming contradictions of the Bible until we understand that they're not contradictions at all, but the key to its true message. That's what acquiring the Bible really means.

"Don't feel that you haven't done enough, Michael. You've come a long way in the last few days. Just take one day at a time and everything will fall into place."

With that, we ended our session. He made sure that I took the prayer book with me. He waited while I put on my coat and gloves while we made small talk about the hospital, and then he walked me to the door. He shook my hand and wished me a 'Shabbat Shalom', a peaceful Sabbath, and I wished the same for him. I thanked him and turned, and walked down the corridor to the elevators outside of his office.

24

When I reached the lobby and got out of the elevator I pulled out my cell phone to call my office. When I opened up the phone, however, I saw that the phone had been turned off. I must have inadvertently shut the phone at some point, though I didn't know when I could have done that. I turned the phone back on and the screen went through a series of displays until the time of day appeared: 10:15 AM. I was surprised to find that over two hours had passed since I arrived here.

A few seconds later, the phone signaled that three new voice messages had been left. I stood to one side of the lobby of the building and began to retrieve them. The first message was from Susan. She was going to the hospital and wanted to see if I had passed by there yet. The second message was from Rose, the receptionist in my office, asking me to call back. The final message was again from Susan. She had tried calling my office to locate me but was told that I hadn't called in. She again asked me to call back, but this time in a much more worried tone.

I dialed Susan's cell phone, and got a recording. I explained that I must have turned my phone off this morning by accident, and had just turned it on. I said that I should be in the office in a few minutes and that I would try her again later once I got in. After I left the message, I realized she must be in the hospital and wasn't able to pick up. I next called my office and explained that I would be there very shortly.

The walk to my office took about ten minutes. During that time, while my right hand held the book I was given, my left hand pressed my scarf close to my neck, to keep me warm. The temperature was dropping and I could feel the air biting at the skin of my face.

When I arrived at my office I propped up the prayer book on my desk next to a picture of Susan and Jennie. The last thing that Isaac told me kept playing in my mind. Jews analyze the Bible, others just read it. It's within the contradictions within the Bible that we find its true message. I could begin to understand how some Jewish people can spend hours a day just studying the intricacies of the religion. Even that probably would not be enough. As I thought of this my eyes rested on the picture, and then shifted to the prayer book, and back again to the picture. I was beginning to accept that the two images could never go hand in hand.

I tried calling Susan again, but I still got the recording. I called the hospital and was told that there was no change in Eric's condition, which was good. They also said that Susan wasn't there so I decided to just wait for her call.

My father walked into the office just a few minutes after me. He passed my doorway and asked me if everything was alright. "It's difficult", I replied, "but the worst is probably over." He smiled a forced smile and left the office again, while, for the next few hours I allowed myself to be absorbed in concentration over some legal documents I had to tend to.

At 1:00 PM Susan called me on my cell phone. She said that she had been in the hospital when my message came through and that she had meant to call me back right after she checked on Eric. She had brought a children's book to the hospital and had read it aloud to him so that he would hear her voice. She told me that afterwards she just sat there in front of him while she allowed several of her fingers to rest in his little hand. He still wasn't responding, but she believed that he heard everything she said to him and that he felt her hand next to his. Her voice sounded weary, and I attributed it to the pain she felt for Eric.

I should have realized that something not quite right was going on because her manner suddenly changed and she now spoke as though she were reading from a script. "We need a break", she told me, "just some quiet time for ourselves." I told her that I couldn't agree with her more. It was then that she asked if she could pick me up from work. "We could drop by the hospital and then have a nice quiet dinner out," she added. I could detect a slight nervousness in her voice, but I dismissed it as something expected. I told her that dinner would be a great idea. She said she would be able to pick me up at about 5:30 PM.

For the rest of the afternoon I was trying to concentrate on my work, but my mind was filled with thoughts of my father, with his comments that none of this was my fault. What was he trying to tell me? Was he saying it was his fault? I knew that no matter how much I would ask he wouldn't reveal anything until he felt it was time for him to explain. Then I thought of Susan's parents, who never, until this week, showed me their feelings as to where they wanted my family's religious observance to go. It was amazing at how I went from almost accepting Christianity a little over a week ago to where I found myself now. I replayed in my mind how I came to meet Isaac, and I felt comfortable . . . no, not just comfortable, the right word is probably fortunate . . . that I had met him in such a way that he was willing to spend the time to explain things to me, and that I was willing to listen.

As the hour neared 5:00, the sky started to darken. The office sounds started to diminish as the personnel began to leave. The setting sun seemed to announce the end of the day, and as twilight came and went, and the night was embraced, it felt as though this was the close of a chapter in my life that would change my future destiny. I put my head down on the desk and closed my eyes for a few minutes. When I raised my head again, I looked forward. I extended my hand to the photo in front of me and gently touched the images that were almost looking back at me. I slid my hand slightly to the right and grasped the prayer book, and then stuffed it into my overcoat pocket.

My intercom then clicked. The receptionist was calling to announce Susan. She came a little earlier than expected, but I just left whatever papers I had been reviewing on my desk and walked out. It would have been nice if I could just as easily have gathered all of my problems and placed them in a little folder which could be stored in a little drawer in my desk. Reality was much less orderly. I wanted to have control, but I would soon understand how little control I did have.

We took a taxi to the hospital and, thankfully, we were told that everything was going fine. Susan had left the book in the hospital that she had earlier read to Eric. When we got to Eric's bedside, she pulled out the book and read some lines out loud and asked me to read some portions to him as well. She was right that Eric heard our voices. I felt it too. The strong confidence I had felt as I was reading the words in the book was fleeting, for when I looked up at Eric lying motionless in his crib, I felt that part of my heart was being torn from me. The assurances by the doctors and hospital staff that he would recover bolstered my spirits somewhat.

When we left the hospital, we hailed a taxi to go back to midtown Manhattan. Susan had made reservations in an Italian restaurant that we had been hearing about called Alto.[82] It was supposed to be an exceptional combination of delicious food and beautiful decor. The taxi drove up Madison Avenue which was still busy with people moving to and fro, and dropped us at the corner of 53rd Street. We were now in front of a modern granite building. Large store windows on both the Madison Avenue and the 53rd Street sides were bordered by a thin brass frame. Each window must have been about eight feet wide by six feet high, and each of the displays consisted of two mannequins which were dressed in colorful men's suits and shirts, with the balance of the background in white. The large amount of white in the displays made the clothing stand out and appear even more appealing than they would have otherwise been.

We walked along 53rd Street until we reached the end of the building. There was an alcove which led to the entrance of the restaurant. A stone wall on the left side of the alcove had water cascading down and collecting in a pool at the bottom. The colored lights which were beamed on the wall of water gave a contrast to the view of the New York winter that was only a couple of feet away. A few more steps brought us to the doorway which was covered by a deep awning on which the word ALTO was tastefully written in block letters. All of those elements contributed to the impression that the restaurant was a private sanctuary that was far removed from the world around it. I was beginning to feel that this was exactly what I needed.

We checked our coats in the front and were escorted to our seats. Rows and rows of wine bottles were visible behind a wall of shimmering blue glass. Running the full length of that wall was a plush banquette with a series of small tables arranged in front of it. On the other side of each table was a high backed chair which faced the banquette. The maitre'd glided across the room as he showed us to our tables. He motioned for Susan to ease into the banquette, and then pulled out the chair opposite Susan for me to sit. A waiter quickly passed our table, filling our glasses with water, while a second waiter asked us if we wanted something from the bar. I was rapidly entering another world.

We were both marveling at the atmosphere and the service. This was like a much needed mini vacation that drew both of us to a kinder place, without the worries that we had been subjected to this past week. Our waiter later appeared and began to advise us of the specials of the day. His Italian accent, along with his warm and friendly smile, made me feel as if I was whisked away to a land thousands of miles away. I didn't even focus on the dishes that he was describing, and instead, let my wife do the ordering for both of us.

The food now began coming. First, a basket of dark hot bread was placed before us from which slight wisps of steam rose up, carrying with it a nutty aroma. The taste did not disappoint. The warmth of the bread, coupled with the nuts baked into it, piqued our taste buds and filled our mouths with flavor. We had to push the basket away so that we would leave room for the rest of the meal. The mood made us think about vacations that we had taken in the past, which brought back a lot of good memories.

The appetizers came next. Square white plates were set in front of us. On each plate was an artful arrangement of seafood garnished with various greens, along with a cappuccino glass. Inside the glass was a dark broth which I didn't recognize. I hesitated and began to take in the aroma to guess what it was. Susan laughed. "My grandmother used to make something like this, so I couldn't resist. If it's anything like what I remember, it's heavenly."

I still hesitated and asked her if she wouldn't humor me first, and let me know what it was. The waiter was just passing by and asked if everything was satisfactory. "Everything is fine, but my husband was just asking me to explain what type of broth this is."

"This is a specialty of the chef", he beamed. "On the plate we have warmed lobster. The broth next to it is a perfect complement to it. This is a squid ink broth, which is warmed just so, and inside are plump mussels. It is a dish that we get many compliments on. Please, enjoy." And with that he moved over to assist those at another table.

At the mention of squid ink, I sat there motionless, while I stared at the liquid. Susan began to laugh and she then called my name softly and said, "Michael, there's nothing wrong with it. I hope you don't think that by eating it, you'll become dirty inside."

At that moment, something inside my head was triggered. What she told me was vaguely familiar and made me very uneasy. As I glanced again at the cup in front of me, I suddenly recalled something that Isaac had told me this morning. It was a quote from the New Testament.[83] "Do ye not perceive, that whatsoever thing from without entereth into the man, it cannot defile him. Because it entereth not into his heart, but into the belly." That's what Jesus said to ridicule the laws governing kosher foods. But kosher foods were part of the purity that Jews were obligated to pursue. Just this morning I was pressuring Isaac to give me something to do which would symbolize my acceptance of Judaism. Despite the fact that he didn't acquiesce to my wishes, at the point that I spoke to him I was sincere that I really wanted to act like a Jew. It dawned on me as to how much of a hypocrite I turned out to be since, after just a few hours, here I was. This was Friday night, the beginning of the Sabbath. I was walking around with a prayer book in my coat pocket while at the same time I was eating out in a restaurant and was being served lobster and squid broth. I froze while staring down at the plate.

"Michael" Susan called out. Her voice had lost its softness, and now became very firm. "What's wrong?" The way she asked me was not so much a question where she sought the answer. I felt like she wanted me to admit to her what she already knew.

"This may be a delicacy for you, but I don't know if I can eat this. I believe this is an acquired taste."

When I said that, I had to laugh, because it made me think of the time I was in Europe one summer in my college days. Susan started to smile along with me. "Michael", she called out when I continued to laugh, "What's so funny?"

"Oh, it's nothing", I said. "This just reminded me about something from a long time ago."

"As long as you're not laughing at me", she said as she involuntarily also broke out in laughter. "But now that you've got me going with you, you have to let me in on what you were thinking of."

"It's really nothing, but when I said that this was an acquired taste, I suddenly thought of something from my college days, when I went to Europe one summer with a bunch of friends. We were taking a train right outside of London and we were in one of those closed cabin cars. In the car with us were some Norwegian girls and a finely dressed British man. The girls had a small metal case that contained hard candy. I believe it was called Zouse. They offered some to us. One of my friends as well as the British gentleman took a piece. Within seconds of putting the candy into his mouth, my friend spit it out and his face took on a contorted appearance as he cried out "That's horrible." I turned to look at the British gentleman and you could see from his face that the taste was as my friend had described, but being British, and proper, he kept the candy in his mouth and remarked, "I must admit, it is an acquired taste."

"Okay, that was funny. I guess what you're really trying to tell me in your own way is that your Zouse, I mean, your appetizer is going to stay on the plate where it is. What am I going to do with you, Michael. Sometimes you can be such a child."

Susan now looked to the right and left and reached over to my plate and slid it over to hers. She had eaten part of her appetizer and was now putting some from my plate into hers. "What are you doing?" I asked her.

The truth is that I knew exactly what she was doing. She had always had a thing about not insulting a chef in a restaurant, and she took some of the food from my untouched plate and put it into hers, so that it looked like part of each was eaten. By the time the waiter came to pick up the dishes, she proudly told him how good it was and that we would have finished it, but we were saving room for the main meal.

"Who's the child now?" I said to her.

"Oh, stop", she said as she started laughing again. "I think Jennie got her aversion to trying new things from you. She's just like you when it comes to that."

"Oh", I said. "What do you mean?"

"Well" she explained, "last month you were away for a few days, so I took Jennie out to a seafood restaurant and I ordered oysters on the half shell. I showed her how to eat them, but she just stared at the one I gave her and finally said "This looks like funny looking jelly. I don't think I want it.""

For some reason, I told Susan, "Maybe that's the Jewish side of her that wants to stay kosher."

She got quiet when I said that. The waiter now came and put our salads in front of us; arugula for her and tri color for me. I started to eat and remarked how good it was but she stayed back in her seat and looked at me.

"Why did you say that?", she asked.

"Say what?"

"About Jennie eating kosher."

I started to get a little nervous. What was she getting at? Was she thinking that this was a Freudian slip? "I didn't mean anything by it. I guess I just said it."

"Michael, I'm going to be honest with you. I wanted to go out with you tonight to talk to you. I know that there's something wrong. You've been acting strangely since we agreed to the baptism. When I got up today, I was thinking about what you told me last night. It's been bothering me a lot. What you asked wasn't the type of question that someone would ask if they were trying to understand more about G-d. You're pulling away. I don't know what you're thinking, but you have to talk to me."

I wasn't sure how to approach this. How do I tell her that I wanted to embrace my religion more strongly while she was being drawn more towards her own? I asked her if I could be honest with her, and she told me to go on. I could see that she clenched her hand, as she wasn't sure of what I would say, and at that point, I wasn't either.

"Remember", I began," when you wanted me to have some attachment to Judaism? You made sure that I went to synagogue and you wanted me to keep up with knowing when the Jewish holidays would fall out? Well, whenever I would go to the synagogue, I would end up going alone. When you were going to Church, though, I would go with you to try and learn more about what you believed in. I even went to classes to learn more. What I'm trying to say is that I'm not sure that Christianity is the right path for me. Just as I made the effort to learn about your religion, maybe you should try and learn more about mine. Now that I think of it, maybe I said what I did because we should look a little bit more into what we want for the kids. Maybe we shouldn't jump into the decision of what path the two of us should take with our children, instead of just accepting Christianity as our mutual choice."

Now she was quiet. She was thinking, but by her reaction, she wasn't surprised. She now began to answer in a calm and composed way. "When we got married, Michael, you never had an attachment to anything. I grew to love you but I also felt bad for you that you had so much to give, and yet you had no religion. I was raised to know the truth. I don't have to go searching through other faiths. I know the path to salvation; I know that I must believe in my savior; I know that I must follow what my family has been following for centuries. Judaism was the first true religion. I don't dispute that. But there is a New Testament now that's replaced the teaching and the laws of the old. The Old Testament foretold it, and the New Testament revealed it. No, Michael, I don't have to learn about Judaism. I don't want my children to follow it. I need them to follow the true lord in the way that he commanded, and I can't change my feelings."

This seemed like an ultimatum, and one that she'd rehearsed. This wasn't just her talking, that I was sure of. Those comments I made to her last night bothered her so much that she had to talk to someone about it. It's funny, I thought. She was being prompted on her end, while, in truth, I was being fed arguments from Isaac. She felt that she was being told what was right because her family had been doing the same thing for generations. I knew that I was being told what was right, because it was the only thing that made sense.

I didn't want to give up the hope that there was some way that I could reach her. "If I were to show you that your religion is not based on truth, would you be willing to listen to more of what I have to say."

Instead of replying to what I just said, she suddenly asked me, "Who is Isaac Cohen?"

That took me by surprise. I delayed for a moment, and must have blushed a little, but I caught myself and told her, "Isaac has a daughter in the hospital that's also ill. I met him through Dr. Birnbaum the first night that I stayed in the hospital overnight. I've been keeping in touch with him since then. He's sort of giving me encouragement as to how the doctors are treating Eric, and we've developed a friendship over the past few days." My voice wasn't as sure in my reply as I hoped, and I knew she was able to detect it. "How do you know about Isaac?"

She kept looking straight at me and continued with her direct answers. "Like I said before, I knew that there was something going on after we spoke last night. At first I thought it was the pressure of the baptism that was bothering you. You hadn't fully accepted it. But when I thought about how you questioned me, I knew that it was more than that. You were almost too smooth in how you were twisting things. It was difficult for me to sleep afterwards, and I kept waking up in the middle of the night. The third time I awoke it was still three in the morning, and I decided to get out of bed to get something to drink from the kitchen. When I passed the living room, I noticed your cell phone on the table, but I walked by and went to the kitchen."

"My cell phone?", I asked in surprise.

"Yes. When I left the kitchen I passed back through the living room. I couldn't help thinking about your phone. My curiosity got the better of me and . . .", she now lowered her head to avoid looking into my eyes, "and I had to pick it up."

She stopped for a second to collect her thoughts, and then continued, but this time, she spoke much more rapidly.

"When I looked at the phone, I wanted to see if there were any numbers that I either recognized or didn't recognize. Really, I wasn't looking for any specific thing, but I just hoped that I would find something to help me to understand more of what was going on. It's only because I love you, Michael, and I want the best for you.

"When I checked the call history, I saw that a certain number had appeared several times, and it belonged to an Isaac Cohen. I then checked the phonebook of the cell phone and found that you had marked down in the notes section, the word, "classes". I wrote down the number and put it away. I then clicked the "call end" button to change the screen, but I must have pressed too long and I guess I turned the phone off by accident."

"So that's why my phone was off this morning. It was you who turned it off." I had mixed feelings of anger and betrayal because of the way she checked my phone, but I realized that I wasn't too honest with her about what I had been doing either.

"I didn't mean to turn it off. And I'm sorry, Michael, that I even looked at it. I shouldn't have. I should have been more direct with you and just asked you, but I had this feeling that you were hiding something.

"After you left in the morning, I became very guilty and I was going to rip up the number, but I couldn't bring myself to do it. I finally resolved to call the number and see what answer I got at the other end. I dialed, and I found it was a law office. I quickly hung up. I thought that it must be something to do with your work, and that made me especially guilty. That comment that you entered next to his name, though, bothered me. What type of classes could you be going to with him? Then I even thought that maybe the classes you were referring to were being given by him."

When she said this, a weight seemed to be lifted off me, but I still decided to remain quiet and let her continue.

"I wasn't sure what to do at that point. I didn't know if I should find out more about who this person was, or if I should just confront you when you came home. I was getting so confused that I had to talk to someone. Being that Isaac Cohen was some type of attorney, I decided to call my father. At first, when I called, he thought that something had happened to Eric, but I told him it had to do with us, Michael. I told him that it seemed like you wanted to break your promise about the baptism, and that you were questioning whether Jesus was our savior. I guess I was getting excited on the phone, so my father calmed me down and told me to meet him at his office so we could talk."

Her voice started to break, and she stopped speaking and lowered her head. I instinctively reached across the table to her hand and held it, and she, in turn, squeezed my hand as well. She took a deep breath, looked up again, and slowly drew her hand away and continued speaking.

"By the time I got to my father, I found that my mother was there as well. I told them as best as I could of what you told me last night and then mentioned what I found out about Isaac Cohen. It turned out that my father knew who he was. There really weren't any details that he knew about him personally, except for the fact that he was an Orthodox Jew."

We were suddenly interrupted by the waiter who was asking if everything was alright. I told him everything was fine, and that we would be finished soon. He smiled and walked away. Susan continued. "Where was I? O, yes, I was at my father. Well, he didn't think the whole thing was such a big issue. He did say that if it did turn out that you were now leaning more toward Judaism, he was afraid that it would confuse the children. From the people that he would meet, he said he knew enough about Judaism to understand that you couldn't be a practicing Jew and accept Jesus at the same time. He said that I would be pulling the children one way while you would be pulling them in the opposite direction.

"He wanted me to talk to you first. You know my feelings, Michael. I don't want to demand, but I want to tell you that there is no other way for me. Eric must be protected, and the only way that he can be is for him to be baptized."

I remembered the conversation that I first had with Susan's father. He said exactly what he was telling Susan now. He had never changed and Susan probably never changed, but I had changed. That made me feel all the worse for what I was now doing, but I really had no choice. I couldn't embrace a religion that could be disproved so easily.

"I really don't understand why we even have to get into this now for our kids. When we got married, we both agreed that we wouldn't impose anything on them. We would raise them to know both and then when they got older, we would let them decide. Why can't we just keep to that?"

"I changed my mind, Michael. I really had no choice. Eric getting sick was a wake up call to me. It was like I was being warned not to fool around with what I teach my kids. Your family doesn't believe in Jesus, while Jesus is everything to us. My father was right. How can we teach them both and let them decide? Is it going to be their decision whether or not they follow him? It can't be their decision. They have to follow him. I can't leave it up to them."

I was now getting annoyed. What did that mean when she said that she changed her mind? "So, I don't know what you're telling me. Are you saying that I have to choose Christianity for them, and that anything to do with Judaism is out the window?"

"I really don't see why it should be such a problem. According to my father, Jews believe that the religion of the children go according to the mother, not the father. Even the Jewish religion considers them to be Christian."

"What are you talking about?" I must have raised my voice, because she looked at me and put her finger to her lips while saying "Shhhhhh" and then told me to talk lower. I repeated my remark to her in a calmer tone.

"Michael, I'm not trying to get you upset. I'm not even telling you to believe me now. You can check with your Isaac Cohen if you want, but the end result is that the children now are Christian. Being that they are Christian, I may as well raise them that way."

This was a blow. I had always been taught that when two people of different faiths get married, the children are half of each. You always hear it described that way. That song that they play on the radio by Adam Sandler this time of year, in which he sings of the different Jews that are in show business describes them that way. Harrison Ford is a quarter Jew; Goldie Hawn is half Jewish; Lenny Kravitz is half; Courtney Love is half. Even of the people in show business that I've read about, the description of their religious status is always part Jew. Michael Douglas, whose father is Kirk Douglas, a Russian Jew, calls himself part Jewish. Geraldo Rivera, whose mother was Jewish, is part Jew and he even had a Jewish wedding. No, Susan had to be wrong, but she was so sure. I decided to wait until I could ask Isaac. At least it would put this whole argument to rest for the time being.

"Susan, let's put this thing on hold right now." I looked around at the people who were eating at the tables next to us and I didn't want to take the chance of losing my composure again and making a scene. "I think I understand where you're coming from. I just wish I could explain to you why I'm questioning what you think."

She didn't want to continue speaking about this topic either. She started telling me how much she loved me, and started to remind me of little things that I did for her when we started going out together that she appreciated. She reminded me of how I would always open the car door for her when she entered; of how I never interrupted her when she was speaking, even though I had a completely different opinion; and how I always helped her with the dishes or housework if there was still something to be done when I got home. She said that I always tried to make her feel special and that's why she loved me so much.

She was appealing to my male ego, and it was working. We pushed aside that awkward topic and lapsed into a game of her revealing the qualities that she found in me that made her love me while I did the same about her.

The rest of the night proceeded in pretty much this same fashion. Both of us knew, however, that this topic was like a dormant volcano that suddenly developed a steady rumble and was ready to blow.

25

It became apparent to the two of us that there was no happy medium that we could look forward to. She seemed to have an unbreakable attachment to her religion. Any argument that had the capacity to shake her belief was, in her mind, the work of a Satan, who was attempting to get a foothold in her heart. After seeing her unwavering commitment to what she believed in, how could I feel less about the Judaism that seemed to be an answer to that spiritual vacuum that was within me? Neither of us could see a solution. There was no solution. Susan's father was right. A family had to choose either Judaism or Catholicism, but not both. The two could not coexist in the same home.

Despite everything that's happened over the past few days, I knew that Susan and I still shared a strong love for each other. I wanted her to see my world, but she shielded herself from it. I was faced with the prospect of losing someone with whom I had shared so much for so many years and it frightened me. For the rest of the night our conversation consisted of bits of small talk which skirted around the issues that were uppermost in our minds. As I watched her speak, I could tell that the same fear that I felt inside of me was bubbling up inside of her as well.

My thoughts kept focusing on my children. What she told me, about them being Christian by birth according to the laws of Judaism, hurt me terribly. But then I realized it didn't really matter. If our actions did lead to a separation, (it was hard for me to even think of the word, divorce), then I knew from most separations that the children would be raised by the mother, as Catholic. If we stayed together, then I would have to submit to her wishes, and, again, the children would be raised as Catholic. But they would still be my children and they would always be a part of my life. It was ironic, I thought. The fate of our children was pulling us apart, but if we parted, the fate of our children would always keep the two of us together.

As the evening wore on, we finally went to bed. Sleep was out of the question. I couldn't help but be aware of the movement and sounds of my surroundings that seemed to take turns in occupying my consciousness. Gusts of winter wind began to strike at my bedroom window, causing it to slightly rattle. The low drone of a plane that was flying overhead was now heard, but it quickly vanished into nothing as the plane flew off. Now it was the hum of my desk clock which began to grow louder in the midst of the silence that was around it, and it slowly turned into an hypnotic chant that was reducing my thoughts to a simple question: How could I have believed that this marriage to Susan would turn out to be that perfect relationship that I had hoped for when we had first met?

The steady background buzz was clearing my mind and helped me to understand that there is no such thing as a perfect relationship. To be with someone else and expect a fairy tale bliss is foolish. You have two different people, who are brought up by parents with different ideas and who come from different environments. Each person brings to the table their own likes and dislikes and nothing is ever smooth. This idea led me to another point.

Relationships require constant work. When you meet someone, you think that by being together for any number of months, you get to know how that person thinks. The truth is you're always learning about the person you're with, and you could go on learning over the course of a lifetime. You always have to be aware of those little signs that betray your wife or husband's reaction to things. Does he or she like the places you're going to; what kind of opinions do they have; what kind of people are they most comfortable with; what kind of things do they most like to do? Once you get past this idea, the next point I came up with becomes obvious.

Relationships require compromise, lots of compromise. When you're single, you only have to think about what you yourself want to do. I know that many people say, and I agree, that there's a major transition in your lifestyle when you go from being single to being married. From being in the position of controlling every aspect of your life's decisions, you now have to take another person's considerations into account. Though you think you've seen it all once you get through that stage, you've only just begun. When that first baby comes, you have to juggle not only your own lives, but you have to adjust to the demands of the child as well. It becomes all the more difficult if you enter a relationship with someone who comes from a different culture, because the compromises that you must work out are increased exponentially. Without being willing to put the considerations of your other family members in your decisions, you don't have a shot at a good marriage.

Susan and I were aware of all that. We knew things wouldn't be easy and we thought we would be able to plan for anything. So what went wrong? There was one more rule that I now had to add in. It was the cardinal rule of relationships and we each broke it. The rule was quite simple. It was "Don't expect the person that you're with to change". When you decide that you want to be with another person for what is hopefully the rest of your life, you become aware of some of his or her idiosyncrasies. It's hard to figure out which idiosyncrasies someone would be willing to give up, and which are a firm part of their lives. In a way, this rule defines the limits of compromise that are possible and the areas where no compromise can be worked out. As much as Susan liked me when we met, from her point of view, I had to be molded into something else. She thought of me as a lost soul who would be saved through her religion. She came into the marriage thinking, maybe subconsciously, that her religious practices would be accepted by me over the course of time. For my part, as much as I loved Susan, I saw her as the Jewess with the qualities that I couldn't find in any of the Jewish girls I had taken out before. She was everything that a good Jewish girl was supposed to be, but, for all her Jewish qualities, at the end of the day, she wasn't Jewish. We ignored the reality of who each of us really was.

These were my thoughts that night, as I tried to sleep. But those thoughts still coupled with a hope, though a rapidly diminishing one, that Susan and I could still live happily ever after.

The next morning didn't bring me much of a reprieve. We slept a little late, and Susan was clearing up the front of the house while I was getting dressed. As I walked out of the bedroom, Susan called out to me to come into the living room. From the way she spoke, I knew I wouldn't be greeted with a pleasant good morning. As I walked into the living room, I saw Susan standing with my overcoat draped over her left arm while she was holding something else in her right hand. As I got closer, I saw she was holding a book. It was the prayer book that I had taken from Isaac's office.

Rather than begin the conversation with excuses, I decided to state the obvious. "It's a Hebrew prayer book", I said, and then I waited for her response.

She stared at me while not moving from her position, and it took her a few moments to react. I had expected a blowout argument, but instead she put the book down on the table and turned to hang up my coat. I got more nervous from her not saying anything than I would have been from anything she would have said.

"Well?" I finally asked.

"Well, what?"

"Do you want to ask me something or tell me something?"

"I think I said all I had to say last night. You're a grown man, Michael. You can do whatever you want, but when it comes to the children, I have a say in their welfare, and I will not permit them to be led astray from the truth."

"Would it bother you if I left the book in the house?" I asked.

"No. We've always had a menorah in the house. It wouldn't be right to deny the children the knowledge that they have a Jewish father. I just don't want anything that negates the fact that Jesus is our Lord and that we must ultimately follow his teaching and pray for his return. That's the beginning and end of it."

With that, she turned from me and continued puttering around the house. To argue at this point would have been pointless. I decided it best to follow her lead and avoid a confrontation which would certainly not do anyone any good.

As she left the room, I walked over to where she had placed the book, picked it up and rubbed my fingers over the leather exterior. I then walked over to the bookcase, and started to place it in an open spot on one of the shelves, but realized I hadn't read the portion that Isaac had asked me to recite. Though I began to withdraw the book, I decided against it and put it back on the shelf. I was feeling anger that, even though I was trying to do the right thing, I still had to undergo these confrontations with my wife. I was not in a proper state of mind to thank G-d for anything at this moment. I released the book from my grip and backed away. I looked at the books on either side of the prayer book and it startled me. On one side was "The Resurrection" by Leo Tolstoy, and on the other was "The Last Days" by Joel Rosenberg. The hidden message in those titles spooked me a little and I quickly moved away from the bookcase and sat down.

Susan came in with Jennie and asked me if it would be a good idea for us to go to the Museum of Natural History for the day. We had never been to the new planetarium that was built there a few years back. I told her it would be a great idea.

While Susan was getting Jennie dressed, I sat with a magazine on my lap, but couldn't focus on it. I looked up at the big Xmas tree that was dominating my apartment. Accenting the background green color that pervaded its branches were the assorted colors of the decorations. There were gold and silver hanging balls and hanging figures of little angels, with colored pieces of tinsel intertwined throughout, and at the top of the tree was a gold star. Strings of small colored bulbs were draped over the outer sections of the tree.

You could picture the awe that would appear on Jennie's face when all the lights would be turned on and the tree would give off a glow of white, red and green. My little menorah was next to it, with its eight bulbs all lined in a row as if it were challenging the tree to a face off, to see who could attract the most attention. Its three bulbs which were already lit up were threatening the tree whose lights remained dormant. I laughed as I thought to myself that it would take a miracle for the menorah to be victorious.

I couldn't help looking back at the bookcase and zeroing in on my little prayer book. Flinging aside the magazine that was on my lap I walked over to the case and looked at the shelf. My eyes stared at the Tolstoy book next to it, and back to the prayer book. Yes, I thought. The title was probably describing me. It made me feel good to look for positive signs and this couldn't be a better one. That other book to the right, "The Last Days", was a sign I didn't want to think about right now. It was enough just getting through this day.

I pulled out the book, and took out the skullcap that had been inserted there by Isaac, and I put it on my head as Isaac had shown me. I opened the page and silently repeated the prayer of thanks, once in English and once with the Hebrew pronunciation. When I was done, a great feeling of satisfaction arose in my chest. I closed my eyes for a second and mouthed the words, "please G-d", without even thinking of anything specific. I then replaced the skullcap in the book and set the book carefully in its position.

An awkward feeling, the type that always follows when there's an unresolved argument, had now settled on both Susan and me. This wasn't the first argument that we had, but the cause of this argument just wouldn't go away. It was just going to be a few minutes until we would be leaving the apartment, but even in that short time period it was obvious that the two of us were avoiding conversation and even eye contact with each other. It was only because of Jennie's effervescent personality that we were able, for now at least, to push aside the wall that was developing between us. Jennie's excited prancing through the apartment which was followed by her non ending questions about snowflakes, helped to dissipate the tension that was in the air. By the time we watched Jennie stuff the front of her coat with a pillow so that she could try and bump into the wall without hitting her nose, our laughter caused the memory of our morning talk to recede into the background.

We bundled up for the winter air and left the apartment. Once outside the building, though, we were surprised to find an unusually warm day. While yesterday had been biting cold, this day was suffused with a warmth that made us feel like it was still early fall. The cloudless sky with its bright sunshine, along with a lack of wind made the 35 degree temperature feel at least twenty degrees warmer. I wanted to go back to our apartment to change our clothes, but Susan decided against it. She felt that we would probably be home after dark and she cautioned that the chill would return without the sun's warming rays.

We caught a cab, which took us cross-town to Fifth Avenue and Central Park. We then turned left and drove alongside the park, down Fifth Avenue. At the foot of the park, the taxi driver turned right onto Central Park South, in order to reach the west side of Manhattan. Just as we made the turn I caught a glimpse of one of the horse drawn carriages which catered to tourists in the area. I caught Susan glancing in that same direction, and, as if our movements and thoughts were synchronized, we both looked down at Jennie and then at each other. Even though no words passed between us, no words were necessary, as we knew what we would do next. I quickly asked the cab driver to stop the cab and let us off.

We walked along the avenue with Jennie between us. As we passed alongside a huge horse that was hitched to one of the carriages that we had seen from the cab, Jennie's face took on a look of incredulity as she gazed at its enormous size. Once we were in line with the rear of the animal Jennie's head turned so that she could continue looking at the horse. It was at that moment that she suddenly felt herself lifted up and onto the carriage. She now spun to me, speechless. I deposited her on the seat, while Susan said to her "Who'd like to go for a ride with this big beautiful horse?" As Susan and I followed up onto the carriage, Jennie let out a loud series of giggles and gave each of us a tight hug.

The carriage now glided down the street causing an invigorating breeze to blow softly unto our faces. While the steady beat of the horse's hooves on the road below us reverberated through the cool hollow air, the bells that were arranged along the bridle clanged like a chorus to the occasional neighing of the horse. As Jennie returned the smiles of the people we were passing, while calling out "I'm Cinderella!", I totally forgot the events of this morning and became absorbed in this idyllic love for my family that I never really wanted to lose hold of. With each expression of delight on Jennie's face, and the radiance that was beaming from Susan from the sight of our daughter's antics, I had a renewed hope that we would always be together just like we were at this moment. The reality of where my life was leading now lay covered up, so that for me, right now, that reality didn't exist.

The uplifting glow that had entered our bodies along with the rays of the bright sun seemed to attach itself to us as we went from one activity to another. After the buggy ride, we went straight to the Museum of Natural History and it was hard to decide who was the bigger kid, me or Jennie. Susan had apparently read up on the activities that were available, because we went straight to an exhibit called The Discovery Room.[84] It can best be described as a huge indoor playground. Jennie's love of animals was put to good use as she searched through a two story replica of a weird upside down looking tree that was called an African baobab. The tree was filled with specimens of birds, insects, small animals and reptiles which kept Jennie fascinated. Jennie got her first introduction to the world of dinosaurs at a recreation of a paleontology field site where we unearthed an Oviraptor nest. To one side of the room stood a Kwakiuti totem pole in an exhibit about various cultures around the world. There was another area that I began to take Jennie next which displayed pictures from land based and satellite mounted telescopes but our time in the room was now up, and Susan ended up pulling me and Jennie out to let others come in.

We next walked over to the Rose Center for Earth and Space which is in the planetarium portion of the Museum. It was humbling to stand in a tremendous glass walled room on the second floor lobby where an 87 foot tall globe stood in the center of the room. That globe, which was representative of the sun, was surrounded by a series of smaller globes which represented the planets. They were all fashioned in the same relative scale. Jupiter was 9 feet in diameter; Saturn was about the same, but with 17 foot rings while the Earth was shown to be only 10 inches across.

After a few more exhibits which were more to my liking than Susan's or Jennie's, we left the museum to get something to eat. With the sunshine still following us, we walked over to Columbus Avenue and stopped off for a quick bite. While we were waiting, I received a call on my cell phone from my brother. I had completely forgotten that he was flying in to New York today and that I was supposed to pick him up. He was calling me to let me know that his flight was cancelled because of a storm in Nashville. The next flight that he could take would not arrive until around 9:00 PM. That gave me enough time to enjoy the rest of the day with my family. When I explained to Susan that I forgot that I was to pick up Steven today, she started to tease me that from the way she had to take care of me in the Museum and my forgetting to pick up my brother, maybe I was regressing in age and she now had three children to take care of. "Or" she turned to Jennie and smiled as she continued, "maybe Jennie will take care of Daddy with me!" I couldn't resist soaking up the innocence of Jennie's laughter that followed.

After we ate, we took a walk along the avenue and stopped in to several of the stores. We went in and out of clothing stores, record stores (why they still call them record stores, I don't know, since most kids don't even know what a record looks like anymore) and ended the day in a Baskin and Robbins ice cream store, where, after every two bites, Jennie would call out the words, 'brain freeze' without even knowing what they meant, after some other kids in the store started saying them.

By the time we left Baskin and Robbins, the sun had set and, just as Susan had said, the winter chill was returning. We walked a little longer and then caught a cab to go back home. By the time we arrived at our building, Jennie's eyes were half closed. I carried Jennie in my arms when we got out of the cab while Susan carried up some bags of items she had bought. By the time we entered our apartment, Jennie was fast asleep. I took her into her bedroom where I lay her on the bed and took off her coat and shoes. I left her clothes on, though, but tucked her under the cover.

With an uplifted feeling at how nicely this day had turned out, I walked back into the living room. I saw that Susan had emptied the contents of the two shopping bags that she brought home unto the top of the dining table. There were some colorful clothes that she had picked up for Jennie and an outfit for Eric. To the side of the clothes lay a few CD's that she had bought. Curiously, I walked over to the table to take a look at them as it had been a while since we bought music. I really should not have been surprised by what I found when I read the jackets because the Susan that spoke to me in the morning was just another side of the Susan of this afternoon. After the enjoyment of this afternoon, though, it was hard to accept that the part of her that made me feel so uncomfortable would return to my life so soon. Maybe that's why it was with numbed emotion that I read the names of the songs on the first CD. "Pray"; "Yes, I Believe in G-d"; "Reborn". I stopped and picked up the next CD. ""Before the Throne of G-d Above"; "All My Praise"; "Raise Me Up". I tossed that CD to the side and picked up the last one. More songs about G-d. Susan was letting me know that she wasn't going to back down. She was letting me know that she would be in control of the type of home that we would have. It would be a home that was governed by the Bible,—her Bible.

I placed the CD's back on the table and told Susan that I was going to go through some of the books and magazines that we had accumulated to see what we no longer needed. I had to do something to pass the time, and this seemed like it would be the best thing that I could think of until the frustration in me died down. It turned out that I had the right idea, because the next few hours seemed to glide by quickly, and before I knew it, it was time to leave the apartment to pick up Steven. It was dark when I walked outside and along with nightfall came the return of the freezing temperatures of the last few days. As a result, there were very few people on the streets and there was very little traffic on the roads. For a New Yorker this was the kind of weather that signaled to you to stay home, and my natural aversion to the cold was not helping. I kept the heat set to high in the car all the way to the airport.

Once at the airport, I left the car in the short term parking lot and hurried over to the baggage claim section of the terminal. Steven would be passing through this area once he disembarked at the gate. My coat, hat and earmuffs stayed firmly affixed to my body, because, even though this area was indoors, the large exit doors nearby which were opening every so often, kept on letting in gusts from the outside.

I checked the video monitors that were positioned overhead for the flight arrival information. Steven's flight was scheduled to land about ten minutes early. Better for me, I thought. I hated waiting around in airports. After positioning myself under a stream of warm air that was being thrown off by a vent in the ceiling, I unbuttoned my coat and loosened my scarf. Lacking anything better to do, I continued to stare at the monitor, as if I were watching the final fifteen minutes of a mystery movie. When I realized what I was doing, I began to feel a little foolish until I noticed about a dozen other people staring at the video monitors along with me.

As I began to look around, my eyes were drawn to two young children who were standing with their mother. There was a girl who must have been about nine years old and who was dressed up in a dark peacoat, and wore a white knit hat with a little beanie on top. A matching scarf was draped loosely around her neck, and matching gloves were on her hands. One of her hands held onto her mother's hand while with the other, she was tugging at one of the buttons of her jacket to pass the time. The rosy color of her cheeks against the light color of the rest of her skin, contrasted with the darkness of her hair. In a way she reminded me of Jennie. The little boy must have been a few years younger and had a lot of energy, because he kept walking quickly around the mother and daughter with arms spread wide as if he were a plane getting ready to land. Except for his untied shoelaces, he was dressed like a child model from a Kids Gap commercial and exhibited that envious attitude of not having a care in the world. Even though I knew that I was staring, I couldn't help myself. It was only natural, I thought, for me to look at them, since they were almost like a glimpse into how my own kids would look like in the future.

It was only because I was looking at them that I was aware of what took place in those next few seconds. They were less than ten feet away from me when I heard the rumbling of a large luggage cart that was loaded up with suitcases and which was being hurriedly pushed by a young teenage boy. He was more focused on balancing the mound of luggage in front of him than looking at the path in front of the cart. As he advanced near the little boy who was now trying to race faster and faster around his mother, he didn't notice the little boy tripping over his feet and falling into the path of the cart.

The whole episode seemed to be happening in slow motion. Before the little boy even hit the ground, I could see his mother's face take on a horrified look as she spun to see the cart heading quickly toward her son. Maybe it was because these kids made me think of my own children that I was staring at those open shoelaces and was half expecting the scene in front of me, but without even thinking of what I was doing, my body reacted. At the same instant that the mother realized what was happening, I was already shooting out towards the little boy. It took just two large steps for me to reach him, and I just grabbed him by his jacket and lifted him up, out of the way of the cart which was just a fraction of a second away. Because of the way that I lifted him, my body was thrown off balance, and I felt myself starting to fall, but I was steadied from behind by someone who caught me. I wrapped my other arm around the boy to make sure I had a good grip on him as my own rescuer helped me to steady my own balance.

"Wow! I didn't think you still had it in you!" I spun my head around to look at where that familiar voice was coming from and I was shocked to find my shoulders being held by Steven. "I guess whoever says that once you pass thirty, it's downhill all the way never saw you in action." For a few moments I was too shocked to speak, and all I could do was just take in what was happening around me until I caught my breath. The mother reached out to her son and grabbed him out of my arms while chastising him at the same time. Some other people started to converge on me while they asked if I was alright. The mother of the child then thanked me while she clutched the little boy. My heart was still pounding and I had to take a deep breath in order to attempt a reply.

"Elly, you have to be careful!" she said to the little boy who she was holding tight against her body. "Thank you so much for what you did" she said to me. "My sister warned me that Elly is not so easy to watch." When I hesitated to reply, Steven took over. "You mean these aren't your kids?" "No", she said, "my brother and sister in law went away for a few days, and I've been taking care of their kids. I'm learning that being a parent is not such an easy job." Steven looked down to her left hand which was patting the boys back. I followed his gaze and noticed the absence of a ring.

At that point I sort of felt myself recede into the background as the two of them continued speaking. It turned out that her name was Sarah Berger and she also lived in the city. When she mentioned that her brother had to take a late flight because he had to wait for the end of the Sabbath, we realized she must be orthodox. Just by chance, I asked her if her brother's name was Morris.

"Why, yes. How did you know?"

"There was a Morris Berger that I was friendly with when I went to college at Baruch. If he's the same one that I knew, he would be about 34 years old now", I said.

You could see she was shocked. "Yes. That's how old my brother is. And he did go to Baruch."

"Talk about a coincidence" Steven said. "Who would have thought you would be saving your friend's son, after all these years."

There was something about the way Steven was talking and the eye contact between him and Sarah that made me feel that Steven welcomed this chance meeting. That line from the Fred Astaire movie, 'Chance is the fool's name for fate' popped into my head.

We ended up excusing ourselves, while she thanked us again, and we left the area to go to the car. Steven only had one carry on bag and didn't have to wait for luggage.

"When I came into the baggage area, I noticed you looking at the video monitor and figured I would surprise you", he began.

"I guess you could say that you did surprise me at that."

"I didn't mean to surprise you that way. I was actually thinking of just giving you a tap on the back", Steven said as he smiled.

"You looked like you were enjoying that little rendezvous we had back there. I thought you were going to ask her for her number."

"Oh", he said, "you mean Sarah's?"

"Am I missing something here? Yes, Sarah's. You know, that girl whose eyes you were staring into just a few seconds ago?"

"You would think that I would. But, right now, my life is too complicated. I really don't want another girl to have to think about." When he said this, his voice trailed off. He became quiet, and I thought it best to wait until we got into the car in order to continue our conversation.

When we were belted in the car and were on the road, I broke the silence. "Do you want to talk about it?" I was making sure to drive at just about the speed limit. I didn't want to rush home until I gave Steven a chance to tell me what was on his mind.

"You're probably the only one I could talk to", he slowly said. "I really need your advice. You went through this and you may know how I can handle it better than anyone."

Oh-oh, I thought to myself. I had a feeling of what he was getting at.

"You met a girl", I said, matter of factly.

"Yes", he replied.

"And you like her a lot", I continued.

"Yes."

"And she's not Jewish."

"Right."

I didn't say anything for a minute or so. I didn't think my parents were going to like this too much. They accepted Susan, but reluctantly. My mother didn't hold back the fact that she accepted Susan, but it was only because she was afraid of losing me.

"I know mom and dad aren't going to be too crazy about this. I don't know how to break it to them. I thought that, since your wife isn't Jewish, you may know what to say, to convince them that it's not so bad."

Oh boy, I thought. Did you come at the wrong time to ask me this.

"Do you want to tell me about her?" I asked.

"Well, she's from Nashville, and we really get along great. It's more than us just liking each other. We really have a good time with each other."

"How'd you meet her?"

"It's really a little crazy. I was hanging out one night with some of my friends at Friday's. You know, that restaurant, TGI Friday's? Well, one of my friends caught this girl looking at me. She was sitting with one of her girlfriends. My friend bet me that I wouldn't be able to pick her up and I took him up on it. Obviously, I won the bet, and that's how it started."

We continued talking and when we got into the city near my parent's apartment, I parked the car and we went into a Dunkin Donuts, where we sat and continued talking. He told me that her name was Christine and she happened to be from a religious Baptist family. Her parents weren't really crazy about their daughter going out with a Jew, but they weren't really fighting it so hard. Steven had this image of me and Susan as a perfect couple, and that sort of kept up his hope that he could have a good life with Christine. I had to burst his bubble.

I opened up to my brother of the events of my life over the past few years. I told him how there were similarities between Susan's background and what he told me of Christine; that a little while back I had thought of converting to Christianity but something held me back; that my wife and her family convinced me to agree to have Eric baptized. I told him of my discussion with David Greenblatt in Dad's office, and of my meetings with Isaac Cohen. I told him that, because of my marriage to Susan, I didn't have the option of openly learning more about Judaism, but I was stuck in a limbo. I told him that the most cutting thought was that my children would be deprived of a Jewish upbringing and there was nothing I could do about it.

This wasn't what Steven wanted to hear. Christine was different, he said. Maybe he could make it work even though I was having a rough time. I told him that I wasn't saying that Christine wasn't a good person. I wasn't saying anything remotely like that with Susan either. It's just that a Jew must do what he has to do in accordance with his faith and it isn't possible if he's not married to a Jew with the same understanding of their heritage. He had no idea what I was talking about. I didn't know what else I could tell him, and so I asked him not to say anything to our parents yet. I decided to see if I could involve Isaac in this. I was going to call him tomorrow anyway to ask him about what Susan said about my kids not being Jewish. He would probably be better at speaking to Steven right now and I asked Steven if he would accompany me to see him. Although Steven was reluctant at first, I explained that he was making a decision that would affect his whole life. Since he was looking for a way to make the proper decision he had to take the time to look as best as he could into what he would be giving up. Also, you really never know why things happen as they do. Tonight he met Sarah, and in really the oddest way. Maybe he was meant to meet Sarah or someone else for that matter and maybe what I was going through was a warning for his benefit. He finally agreed to go.

After dropping Steven off to my parents, I drove home. It was about 11:30 PM. I tiptoed into the apartment and all was quiet. I walked to my bedroom and saw the lamp next to Susan's side of the bed still on. Susan was asleep in her bed and propped up on a pillow with a book on her lap. I walked over and gave her a kiss, and she half opened her eyes and smiled. She said that she missed me tonight and asked me to come to bed. I answered her that I would just be a few seconds. I went back into the living room and put my coat away in the closet. I stopped by the window with the little menorah, and counted on my fingers. This was already night number 6. I turned on the additional bulbs and stared for a few seconds. My life was getting more difficult than ever but now I had my brother on my mind as well. No, I thought. Tomorrow was not going to be an easy day.

26

I awoke early, several hours before Susan. After getting dressed, I read the morning prayers from the book that Isaac had given me. I was still confused as to what to thank G-d for at this point, so I wished for my brother to make the right choices without any possibility of regret in the future.

After that, I looked around for something to do. I was already getting a headache from thinking about how I would handle this day so I ended up picking up the latest issue of Forbes magazine which just arrived in the mail. Articles about business would be a perfect diversion for me right now or at least, they should have been. As I flipped through the pages I felt that I was distancing myself from my previous thoughts, but I didn't count on the refusal of my subconscious to let go of my dilemma.

I had now turned to an article by the publisher, Rich Karlgaard.[85] He likes to delve into the psychology of what type of thinking would be indicative of a successful businessman. This article was written as an advice column for someone entering the business world; a set of "road rules" for the real world. Even though they were aimed at young college graduates, I found that they took on a whole different meaning for me.

He started by saying that everyone was created for a purpose. There is a spiritual purpose which he didn't want to get into, (and which made me think that I should) and there is also a purpose based on our talents in order for us to be productive.

The next rule was based on advice from Peter Drucker, who is a guru for anyone who reads books on business management. The advice stated that you should stop thinking about what you can achieve, and start thinking about what you can contribute.

The third road rule explained the importance of preparation. Money and talent move in the direction of freedom and opportunity. You have to be prepared in order to take advantage of the opportunity that exists all around us.

The last rule was perseverance. Don't give up if things don't work out the way you want. Keep plugging away to the goal that you envisioned for yourself. Very few people become successful without first being knocked around.

As I read and re-read the article, I very easily substituted the idea of religion for business and money. It all seemed so obvious. Even in the Catholic religion there's a belief that everyone is here for a reason. After sitting with Isaac, I knew that my purpose lay in following a "Jewish" way. This religion was the only one that claimed that G-d spoke to everyone in the nation. Isaac was right when he said that if this were not so, and the Bible made that claim, then when would a falsity like that take hold? It couldn't take hold in that generation, or the next generation or the third. In fact, you could never start a claim like that if it never happened. Since that's the case, then the laws given to the entire nation at that time must also have actually been given by G-d. The laws that a Jew must follow are his purpose in order to be Holy and deserve the bounty that is within the land of Israel. It's as simple as that.

Reading the second rule made me realize that because the Jews are a nation and have always been the recipients of the scorn of the people among whom they live, we developed that "all for one and one for all" mentality. It only stands to reason that by raising the image of the Jew in a general sense, you raise the standing of each individual Jew in whatever country he's living. The caveat is that you have to raise the standing in a way that focuses on the acts that a Jew does, which are required of a Jew according to the Bible. Otherwise, if a Jew performs an act of kindness, he is no different from someone else doing an act of kindness based on a personal judgment that it's the right thing to do. You can't take G-d out of the equation. It's G-d commanding the Jew to do the right thing through the medium of the Bible that makes him different from everyone else. And how can you do this unless you prepare properly by studying the Bible?

The last rule was perseverance. Perseverance is built into the makeup of every Jew. It's what has kept Jews going for thousands of years. Though we've been the subject of pogroms throughout the years, we still have held onto the Bible's teachings. Isaac was right. Jewish survival is not how Jewish men and women avoid being killed; it's the survival of the Jewish way of life, which is the way of life dictated by the Bible.

The more I began to accept these ideas the more I felt troubled at my predicament. I didn't know how I could become a more observant Jew while still being married to Susan. I had tried reasoning with her to at least be a little open to what Judaism was teaching but she was closed to the thought of doing that. Additionally, I felt bad for what Steven was going through, especially because I was his role model. I knew that my immediate concern should be for him; to focus on helping him and not think about what I should do for my own life at this point. He didn't have the complications that would result in a decision that I would make for my own situation. I have to concentrate on one thing at a time, and first, choose the thing that's easiest to do. Not to say that explaining my point of view to Steven would be easy, but at least he had a solution, while I really had none.

While in the midst of my thoughts, I heard a low voice call out "Daddy?" and then I heard the patter of Jennie's feet running on the carpet in the hallway. "I'm here, Jennie!" I said, as she ran toward me. She jumped on my lap and I hugged her. Something hurt inside as I thought about her and Eric. It was good for me that Steven came. Concentrate on one thing at a time, I thought, as I gave her a kiss on her forehead.

27

With Jennie still on my lap, I placed a call to the hospital to check on Eric's condition, and everything was still status quo. I next placed a call to Isaac, followed by a call to Steven. Isaac told me that I would be able to pass by him with my brother after 1 PM. When I called to let Steven know, Steven said that the timing would be fine, but he asked if we could first pass by the hospital to take a look at Eric.

When Susan got up, I asked her if she wouldn't mind if I spent the day with my brother, but first he wanted to pass by the hospital. If she'd like, I told her that we could all go there together, which she had wanted to do this morning anyway.

We got ready and went out to pick him up. We had given him a ring just before we left and he was waiting outside my parents' building when we arrived there. At the hospital he spoke to the doctors and asked questions I didn't really understand, but in the end Steven told me that the hospital staff was doing a great job.

Susan and Jennie ended up staying in the hospital after Steven and I left. Susan's parents had called, saying that they also wanted to visit Eric, and would meet Susan at the hospital. Susan had taken a new children's book with her to the hospital. She said that while she waited for her parents she and Jennie would read parts of that book to Eric.

Steven and I took a cab back uptown to where Isaac lived. During our conversation en route, it seemed that Steven wasn't as strong in his assertions about his affection for Christine as he was yesterday, although he still said outright that he didn't want to give her up. I knew that even if he decided to break off with her, it would be very hard for him to go back to Nashville with him knowing that she was there.

As we entered the lobby of Isaac's apartment and were announced by the doorman, Steven said that he felt nervous, like the first time he was going out on a date and was walking up to the girl's house to meet her parents. I laughed at that, as I remembered the pit in my stomach that I felt when I first met Susan's parents. I told him to give it a few minutes and he'll feel as though he's known Isaac all of his life.

We got out of the elevator, and I walked down the corridor ahead of Steven. He wasn't talking and, oddly enough, his nervousness made me calm. I rang the bell to the apartment and heard Isaac calling out that he was coming to the door. The door swung open and I was greeted by Isaac as his outstretched arm beckoned us to come in. As I proceeded to pass through the doorway, I turned to Steven and saw him hesitate, but he quickly followed me inside.

The apartment was spacious and was tastefully arranged with pieces that looked like French antiques. The seating in the living room was plush, and seemed to invite us to settle in and relax. I introduced Steven to Isaac and Isaac gave him his trademark handshake which was accompanied by a truly warm smile. He offered to get us something to drink and I could see Steven beginning to respond to Isaac's easygoing way.

"I didn't even know that you had a brother until this morning. I may not have realized it if I hadn't seen you together, but now that I see the two of you next to each other, I could see the family resemblance", Isaac said as he addressed me while looking at Steven. He now turned to my brother and said "It's a pleasure to meet you, Steven. Michael tells me that you're studying to be that most desirable profession for attracting young girls, a Jewish doctor." Isaac had turned to show us in the apartment as he said this and he didn't notice me flinching at what he said. I looked at Steven and I saw that he reacted as well.

I started to tell him a little about Steven, but I stopped short at relating what Steven had revealed to me last night.

"Steven happened to be visiting this weekend, and I couldn't let him go back without meeting you", I said. "I was explaining some of the things to him that you had told me, and he found it interesting also. I'm limited, though, in what I can answer him about religion and I was hoping that you could sort of help me out with questions that Steven has."

Both Isaac and I looked at Steven and we could see his face turn a little red. "I don't really know what kind of questions to ask", he said. "Maybe I'm just trying to understand the big picture. I mean what's so special about Judaism that isn't found in other religions?"

"Hmm", Isaac said. "That's a really broad question and not one that can be answered in a few words, but let's try to begin to tackle it. But, please, sit down first and relax." He motioned for me and Steven to sit in a large mohair sofa. Each of us sat at the ends on which were placed oversized rolled cushions. I could see from the way that Steven sat that his arm wrapped around the cushion almost as if it were a security blanket.

Isaac continued speaking. "Let's see now. Where do we start?" He sat there thinking for a few seconds until his eyebrows lifted up. "I don't think we could fully answer your question, but let's see if we can examine the similarities or differences in certain areas. Maybe you can help me with the answer, Steven. First, could you name the major religions in the Western world?"

"Well", Steven replied. "You have Christianity, Judaism, and I would have to say Islam."

"Christianity, Judaism and Islam" Isaac repeated. "These three religions have a lot in common, and they also have a lot of differences. Let's take a look at the things in common first." He continued looking at Steven. "Could you help me with some commonalities?"

"Well, for one, Judaism is centered on a belief in one G-d and the others share that belief. In fact, from what I know, the other religions have their sources in Judaism and build on it."

"You said something very interesting, Steven. The other religions build on Judaism. So I guess you mean they modify it somewhat."

"Yes. You could say that", Steven answered.

"Now I have a question for you." Isaac was now smiling and had raised his hands so that his fingers of one hand were tapping the fingers of his other hand. "Can you tell me what the modifications were in order to evaluate if they were actually improvements?"

"I don't know specifically, but each of those religions has attracted over a billion followers so they obviously have mass appeal. I'm not really aware of the specifics of those other religions but I would have to say that since the society in general is geared toward compassion and the importance of the rights of the individual, that those religions must exemplify those ideals."

"So you feel those religions bring out a greater compassion for the rights and livelihood of others in the world. But let's be more specific. Let's start with determining exactly what type of system existed before Judaism that Judaism improved on.

"For a nation to exist and the people to coexist, there must be a series of laws. That's a large part of what Judaism is about; laws that govern our actions. A preliminary question can be defined as this. Did the laws of Judaism appear to be better than the laws that existed beforehand?"

When Steven hesitated, I said, "I know that there were the laws of Hamurabi[86] that were followed by the nations when Israel first became a nation. The laws of Judaism really copy them."

"Did they?" Isaac got up and pulled a loose leaf binder from a bookshelf. "I have here a listing of some of law code of Hamurabi. The list itemizes various crimes, and the punishment to be meted out for those crimes."

Isaac read:

"Par. 22. If a man committed robbery and was caught, that man shall be put to death.

Par. 25. If a fire broke out in a man's house and another man who went to extinguish it cast his eye on the goods of the owner and appropriated the goods . . . that man shall be thrown into that fire.

Par. 209-210. If a man struck another man's daughter and caused her to have a miscarriage he shall pay ten shekels of silver for the fetus. If she died they shall put the daughter to death of the one who killed the other daughter.

Par. 211-212. If by a blow he caused a commoner's daughter to have a miscarriage, he shall pay five shekels of silver. If that woman died, he shall pay 30 shekels.

"When we continue to go through infractions, in one instance after another, the favored punishment is by death of some sort. The exception is when there is a nobleman harming a commoner. The law codes of Judaism were far different. Punishments resulted in a monetary penalty, except in certain cases which were actually very rare. The oft quoted phrase from the Jewish Bible of "an eye for an eye" is not to be interpreted literally, but actually means "the monetary value of an eye for an eye".[87]

"The lack of concern with taking a life as a punishment is directly opposite to the sacredness of life in Judaism. In our Talmud, which is the explanation of the written Bible, the question is raised of why Adam was created alone in the world. It would have been just as easy for G-d to have created a thousand men at the same time. Why was only one created? The reason is that we are taught from this that whoever saves a life, it's as if he saved a whole world.[88] It doesn't specify Jewish life. It specifies a life. Both the lives of Jew and Gentile are precious to G-d and therefore G-d really wants both Jew and non Jew to emulate that, but it starts with the Jews. That's a large part of why Judaism is an improvement over the previous system. By extension, since we all came from one person, all people are precious in the eyes of G-d and are considered equal before the law. The practice of slavery which formerly showed no concern for the life of the slave, took on a totally different meaning under Judaism, and the slave under the Jewish system was treated with great respect.[89] In general, the system of law under Judaism is very different from what came before. There are no class systems before the law. In Judaism, might does not make right."

"Okay", I said. "I guess I take it back. Judaism was a move forward, apart from advocating a monotheistic belief. So what makes it better than those other religions of today?"

"Before we go into that", Isaac continued, "I just want to bring up one more point. Judaism says that you don't have to be a Jew to follow G-d. The other religions don't have that tolerance. Christianity says that you must be a Christian and Islam says you must be a Moslem. For both of those religions, there is no other option.

"Let's take a look at Islam first through the writings of the Koran to see if it really is an improvement over the ideals propounded by Judaism." Isaac went to the bookshelf and pulled out a folder with some newspaper clippings. "Bear with me just one second. Ah! Here it is!" He pulled out a paper and started to read.[90]

"This is from the Koran (9:5) "When the sacred forbidden months for fighting are past, fight and kill disbelievers wherever you find them, take them captive, beleaguer them, and lie in wait and ambush them using every strategem of war." Here's another. "So, when you clash with the unbelieving Infidels in fighting Jihad in Allah's Cause, smite their necks until you overpower them, killing and wounding many of them. At length, when you have thoroughly subdued them, bind them firmly, making them captives . . . Thus are you commanded by Allah to continue carrying out Jihad against the unbelieving infidels until they submit to Islam."(Koran 47:4). How does that compare to the valuation of life that's promoted by Judaism?"

Steven now answered. "It seems to be a throwback to the Hamurabi laws. Either submit or die. Death doesn't seem to be something that's frowned upon. That's probably why you also mentioned how Judaism doesn't force someone to become a Jew but just demands that a person worship G-d."

"That's right. The sanctity of life which is an idea that is held up on such a high level in Judaism seems to be absent in Islam. On a familial level, there are the honor killings that are conducted against Moslem women by their families if they dishonor the family; killings that have been documented relatively recently throughout the world and even in cities in the United States.[91]

"Obviously, there's a lot more going on in their religion than just the area we're discussing, but based on the points I've raised, would you say that Islam presents itself as an improvement to Judaism?"

"I have to admit that you have a point", Steven said. "I remember reading about the honor killings that you mentioned. But Christianity doesn't have the same problems that you attribute to Islam. It seems to have been able to cope well with modern society."

"They also have the same line of thinking in their holy books as the Moslems when it comes to their method of handling non believers", Isaac began. "They, as well as the Moslems, have a long history of atrocity in the name of religion against each other and against the Jews."[92] As much as I felt that Isaac had backed up his prior arguments, I didn't think he could support this additional claim that killing was advocated in the New Testament, especially after all I'd learned from those classes on the New Testament that I had taken with Father Baldino.

"I can see that you don't agree with my statement, but just take a look at all the pogroms against the Jews throughout the centuries for our rejection of the Christian beliefs. Even the Holocaust was promoted because of the depiction in the Passion Plays of the Jew, which showed us to be a despicable group of people that caused the death of their Messiah. Their justification for their attacks against us didn't come out of the air. They're sourced in the New Testament which, according to them, is without fault. There's a quote that I've heard from the New Testament that goes[93] "All scripture is given by inspiration of G-d." In other words, all words written in the Old and New Testament reflect the will of G-d. So let's see what the Christian bible says about non believers.

"Though Jesus is known for his statement[94] "If someone smites you on one cheek, turn the other cheek" he also said[95] "Take my enemies, who would not have me rule over them, bring them here and kill them before me." As part of the sermon of the mount, in Matthew, Jesus is quoted as saying[96] "Think not that I have come to send peace to the world. I come not to send peace, but the sword." A comment in John was used during the Middle Ages as a justification to burn Jews alive who would not submit to forced conversions. It states[97] "He who does not abide in me is thrown away like a withered branch. Such withered branches are gathered together, cast into the fire and burned." This attitude against non believers appears throughout the New Testament, and is certainly a contradiction to the peace loving Jesus we are usually exposed to."

"I'm shocked by what you're telling me," Steven said. "I always thought that the New Testament portrayed Jesus as a totally loving and forgiving leader. If these quotes that you're giving me are true, then the heads of those religions should publicly declare their disagreement with those passages, especially after knowing the horrors that those passages led to," Steven said.

"That's why I go back to my original question as to whether these newer religions were improvements over Judaism. We can't hide from the fact that many Moslems perform acts of cruelty in the name of their religion, and that acts of anti Semitism are still performed by Christians against the Jews. Once we see the source for their actions, we understand that those actions were a direct result of what's written in their holy books. But I don't want to dwell on the relationship of Christians vs. non believers, or Moslems vs. non believers. There's another problem which I want to address that affects Christianity.

"The Christian religion took on the words of the Old Testament as the foundation for their New Testament, but they interpret the words literally, which is not the way they were always intended to be understood. That makes their position in the face of scientific discoveries problematic as well."

"I have to disagree with you" Steven said. "Both Judaism as well as Christianity have no credibility when it comes to science."

"You would think so, but instead of speaking in general terms, let's look at specifics. We'll start with a confrontation that faced the Christian religion in regards to science, and then we'll see how Judaism fares. Discoveries in astronomy make a perfect starting point." Isaac stopped for a second while he looked at my brother softly nodding his head and with a slight smile on his face. Isaac himself now started to smile. "From your expression" Isaac continued, "it's obvious that you know the direction I'm taking with this."

"You would have to be referring to Galileo. When he came up with the theory of the sun being the center of the universe he was taken to task by the Church and his theory was banned", Steven replied. He was enjoying the idea that he was taking an active part of the discussion. He also seemed to have developed a greater respect for Isaac's knowledge.

Isaac then went on, with a more detailed description of those events. "You're right in summary, but to be fair to the Church, we should understand what the Church was trying to stop."

Isaac leaned back, and began to explain.[98] "Galileo wasn't the first figure of the middle ages to propose the heliocentric theory. That same theory was proposed by Nicholas Copernicus over fifty years earlier. It was not previously perceived as a theological threat because it was just a supposition without any proof to back it up. The danger to the Church when Galileo promoted it came about because Galileo had shown from his mathematical computations that if the planets did orbit the sun, then his observation of the heavens concurred with that theory. In addition, Galileo's observation of sunspots which moved around the sun, proved that the sun rotated, and raised the strong probability that all heavenly spheres rotated. In short, the heliocentric theory was scientifically credible. To Galileo, who had no intention of attacking the Church, science was a way for G-d to allow man to examine the world around us, and man was supposed to analyze and question the workings of all things in nature. An apparent contradiction in the Bible was due to our errors in explaining what was written, and was not a fault of the Bible itself.

"Galileo was a highly religious man who didn't want to do anything contrary to the teachings of the Church. Over the many years in which he directed his telescope to the heavens, he realized that the Ptolemaic system of the universe, which is one with the earth at its center, was flawed. To the large number of wealthy and prestigious people in the country who were open to the pursuit of scientific discovery, Galileo was a hero. He responded to his admirers by writing and distributing books and giving lectures that espoused his beliefs.

"This presented the Church with a problem. It was Church policy that only the heads of the Church could define how to interpret the Bible. At this time Catholicism was experiencing massive defections to Martin Luther's Protestant Reformation because the Protestants, among other things, wanted to explain the Bible in a way contrary to the thinking of the Church. Without intending it, Galileo was reinforcing the ideology of the followers of Martin Luther that there was another alternative to what the Church leaders were dictating and the Church leaders could not allow this to happen. Galileo was reprimanded by the Pope in 1616 and was told to stop promoting the heliocentric theory as a viable alternative to the literal meaning of the words in the Bible.

"In 1623 a new Pope was elected, Pope Urban VIII. For Galileo, this was a signal that he could resurrect his ideas. You see, this Pope was a previous acquaintance of Galileo, and was an intellectual who embraced the discussion of scientific advances. Several years before, the Pope had sided with Galileo in a debate about floating celestial bodies. Galileo was admired by the Pope so much, that the Pope even wrote a poem of praise about Galileo's accomplishments. Galileo felt that this Pope would be more accepting of his ideas. Galileo had learned from his previous experience, though, and he knew that his ideas would have to be packaged as a theory only and could not appear to threaten the Church's understanding of the Bible.

"Over the next several years Galileo wrote a book called "The Dialogue" in which several characters would carry on a conversation, and they would debate the astronomical theories of both a sun centered, and an earth centered universe. The book was finally completed in 1629. Though the debate gave greater credibility to the theory of heliocentricity, Galileo ended the debate in the book by saying all evidence was inconclusive. Because Galileo knew that it was prudent that he not appear to go against the Church, he voluntarily submitted the book to censors under the Pope, as well as to censors in the city of Florence and allowed them to change anything in the book which they felt was against Christian theology. The book was declared to be in line with the teachings of the Church.

"Once the book was published however, readers understood from the presentation of the arguments how much more logical the heliocentric theory was. The Church was now in a difficult situation. A submission by the Church as to the possibility of the veracity of Galileo's ideas would allow other ideas of the Church to be questioned. The Protestant Reformation had already caused a serious loss of the Church's standing in Europe, and the Pope had to be seen as tough. Galileo was called to Rome, and his book was condemned as being contrary to the teachings of Christianity, and was subsequently banned. Galileo was forced to publicly admit that the ideas of a heliocentric universe were false. His book, The Dialogue" was placed on the index of Prohibited Books where it stayed until the Church allowed it to be removed in the year 1835."[99]

"His book was prohibited until 1835?" Steven asked.

"Yes. It wasn't until the 1890's that the pope of that time, I believe it was Pope Leo XIII, in order to reconcile the discrepancies brought out between the Bible and science, declared that the Bible didn't aim to teach science. From a Jewish perspective, though, when the Bible is studied using the explanations in the Talmud, the two are not in opposition."

When I saw Steven waiting for a reason why the Jewish understanding could accept a heliocentric theory, I interrupted. "I think you once explained that according to Jewish understanding, the writing in the Bible was according to the point of view of the person the Bible is discussing. From what we've already learned, I guess you can also say that Jews have the same idea of the Bible that Galileo had. We're flexible in our interpretation of the Bible as well."

"That's right, but our position is probably between that of the Church of that era and that time period's religious intellectuals. I don't want you to misunderstand me. Sometimes a strict interpretation works but in most cases, looking beyond the strict interpretation brings you closer to the actual intention of the words. We do not, however, allow for just any personal interpretation that a person reading the passage could come up with. We accept interpretations which are based on a logical Biblical analysis or which are based on prior declarations from accepted Biblical authorities who used a logical Biblical analysis. If you'll excuse me a second, there's something I can show you to help you understand this."

Isaac got up and left the room. He returned about a minute later with a thin magazine and a couple of books. "I showed you part of an article in this magazine once before, Michael, but there are some other parts that are interesting as well."

He handed me a magazine that featured an article by Rabbi Eli Mansour entitled "The Truth About Science".[100] It was opened to the article which excerpted a portion of the Zohar, which was written several thousand years ago. I recognized the portion that Isaac had previously shown to me and handed it to Steven for him to read aloud. "The whole world and its inhabitants revolve like a ball. Some live at the bottom and some at its top, and each ethnic group living on a different part of the sphere differs from its neighbors in color, physiognomy and the like, due to climatic changes. All manage to stand on the Earth, however, just as their neighbors in other lands. As a result of the spherical shape of the Earth, some people benefit from sunlight at the very same time that others lie in darkness. There is even a place in the world which is almost continually sunlit, visited by night for only a brief time. (Zohar Vayikrah 10a)."

"Wow! When was this written?" Steven asked.

"There's actually a dispute on that" Isaac said. "Some people say the Zohar was written about two thousand years ago, and others say about one thousand."

"You, know, I just realized something", I said. "You were just telling us about the discoveries that Galileo made in the early 1600's about his observation of sunspots which proved the sun revolved and that it was likely that the planets did so also. The Jewish writings displayed an awareness of astronomy that was impossible for them to have without the instruments that were available to men like Galileo who lived hundreds of years later."

"That's part of the reasoning behind our belief that the information in our Holy books has to be divine" said Isaac. "But there was another example of the knowledge of the Talmud that I wanted you to look at from this article. Rabbi Mansour points out how the constellation Pleiades, prior to the time of Galileo, was believed by the Western world to contain exactly eight stars. After Galileo examined that constellation, he determined that there were forty stars. It wasn't until the 1990's, when we had at our disposal the Hubble space telescope, that we discovered that there were hundreds of stars.

"Now we look at a passage that Rabbi Mansour brings out from the Talmud of about two thousand years ago. "Shemuel said: Why is the constellation (Pleiades) called Kimah? It is called Kimah because it contains 'about a hundred' (stars)." (In Hebrew 'ki' means about, and 'meah' means a hundred.)" In the 11th century, a recognized scholar known as Rashi explained this portion of the Talmud by saying that the one hundred refers to the core of the constellation. The total amount of stars is in the hundreds.

"So here it is again. It took until the end of the 20th century to confirm the information that Jews had at our disposal thousands of years ago."

From the look on Steven's face, I could tell that Isaac's words were definitely having an impact.

"What you're telling me is nothing short of amazing." Steven was sitting forward on the sofa and had released his hold on the rolled up cushion that was next to him. "I don't know why this information isn't publicized. I mean, if people knew what you're telling me now, then Judaism would be looked at with a lot more respect in the world. But you've whetted my appetite. Is there more in those books that you took out?"

"I don't really want to go too deeply into this right now" Isaac answered. "I only wanted to make you aware of science from a Jewish perspective."

Steven was now like a kid in a candy store. He couldn't get enough. I had felt like that when I first sat with Isaac. In fact I still feel that way. From looking at Steven's mannerisms, I could tell that there were a thousand questions that were circling in his mind, and he was trying to sift through them to come up with one important one. "You earlier said that you were going to contrast Biblical interpretation from the perspective of each of the religions." Steven now regained his composure and slid back into the sofa, while speaking in a more measured pace. "I'm curious. If the Bible says that the world is between five and six thousand years old, then how does the religion account for the age of the earth and the universe that we now know measures in the billions of years?"

"That's one of the most often heard questions which is used to debate the validity of the Bible. The answer is found by looking beyond the literal meaning of the Bible. Jews naturally do this, while the Christians, who adopted our Bible without understanding how to unlock its secrets, do not do this.

"In a case like this, there are actually many possibilities. The beginning of creation in the first chapter of the Bible is really the most difficult chapter for us to understand in the whole book." Isaac stopped speaking while he flipped open one of the books he had brought to us. During the seconds of silence that ensued, my body remained frozen as my eyes stared at the book in front of him. He suddenly stopped at a certain page and resumed speaking.[101] "I just want to bring out a few lines from this book called Reality Revisited. It's by Rabbi Solomon Sassoon of England. He passed away several years back, but was well regarded as an extremely knowledgeable Torah scholar. He wrote " . . . the kabbalists (e.g. Rabbi Perez of Barcelona, ca. 1350 and Rabbi Moshe Cordovero, 1522-70) taught that long periods preceded biblical chronology." There are other kabbalistic writings which refer to worlds that existed before Adam was created. Jews were actively teaching how the first chapter of Genesis was more complicated than it seemed in a way that would have been heretical in the Christian world.

"This second book that I brought, elaborates into one of the Jewish theories of the age of the universe. The book called 'Immortality, Resurrection and the Age of the Universe' was written by Rabbi Aryeh Kaplan, who was another brilliant and prolific writer. Rabbi Kaplan brings out that in Judaism,[102] we have a law that states that we are permitted to work the land in Israel for six years, but in the seventh year, the land must lie fallow. The law goes on to say that after seven of these periods or 49 years, we reach an unusual time period. The 50th year becomes a year where any property that was sold throughout Israel (apart from property within a walled city) reverts back to the original owner. Just as that 50 year cycle consists of 7 cycles of 7 years each, there is a Kabbalistic book said to be written by Rabbi Nehunya ben haKanah of the first century that expands on that concept and states that there are 7 cycles of 7,000 years each, and we're in one of those cycles. (As to what will happen after the final 50,000th year, we're not sure.) Rabbi Kaplan explained that there were many Rabbis who supported the idea that we're in the seventh of the 7,000 year cycles and cited a number of Rabbinic works to defend the concept.

"That theory then places the world at 42,000 years old at the time of the creation recorded in Genesis. Rabbi Kaplan then discussed another Rabbi by the name of Rabbi Isaac of Akko who was a student of a Rabbi known as the Ramban, and was one of the foremost Kabbalists of his time. (1250-1350.) He also subscribed to the idea of the 7 cycles of 7,000 years each, but with a twist. He gave reasons as to why the time period before the creation of Adam must be measured not in human years, but in divine years. Through various sources, he next determined that a divine day of that era consisted of 1,000 earthly years. When fully computed, the age of the universe according to Rabbi Akko was roughly 15 billion years old, which is very close to what the scientists of today have concluded. It's all the more amazing when you consider that this was written about seven hundred years ago.

"Rabbi Kaplan goes on to explain where support for this theory is found, but he stresses that this is only one acceptable theory among many others. The point is that we look at much more than just the literal interpretation of the Bible when determining the message that G-d wants to send to us regarding his Holy writings and we are not bound by the strict wording that's found in the Bible. In fact, it's our duty to analyze the words to find the hidden meanings within them. From this you can begin to understand why we consider Bible study a lifelong endeavor. In fact, several lifetimes aren't even enough."

We waited for Isaac to continue, but he paused for a few seconds. He then slowly rose and said, "Please excuse me, but would you mind if I stopped to get something to drink? I seem to have developed a thirst from all of this talking that I've been doing." He then asked me and Steven what he could get us. "If it wouldn't be too much trouble, I'll have a Diet Coke" I said. Steven asked for a Seven Up.

When Isaac walked away I turned to Steven and asked him: "Well, what do you think?"

"It's funny," Steven began to say. "I used to think of the Bible as just a book of stories. You know, like a book of fairy tales. In a class that I had taken, the Professor spoke about all of the different civilizations that incorporated a story about the flood, and he explained that the Bible's version is just one of those stories. He portrayed the ancient Jews as a backward and scientifically ignorant society. I never realized that the Jews were so advanced in their understanding of the universe around them."

"Before this week, I had the same impression" I said. When I spoke, my eyes picked up the presence of Isaac's menorah that was set up on a table next to a window. "It's only been about a week, probably since the start of Hanukah, that I've been exposed to a deeper side of Judaism."

I kept looking at the menorah when Isaac returned. I noticed that instead of electric bulbs, as on my menorah, there were eight small glass jars which contained oil, each of which contained a floating oil wick.

"On the menorah in my house I have electric bulbs," I told Isaac. "When you think about the holiday as being about a miracle of oil, I guess it's more traditional to use oil in the menorah."

"You've been lighting an electric menorah this holiday?" He asked this without waiting for a reply. "The proper way is to use some sort of flame, either with candles or using oil and a wick as I've done here. An electric menorah isn't valid when saying the blessings." He got up and motioned for me and Steven to follow him to the window. "This is one of those actions that we must do a certain way. For example, not only do we have to use a flame, but we must light the candles starting from the far left and we proceed to light them one by one from left to right."

Isaac then explained to us the proper way to place the lights, and the blessings that had to be said. There was an optimum time in which to light the candles as well, and they had to stay lit a minimum number of minutes, which differed on the Sabbath. In fact, there were separate rules for the Sabbath lighting. To make it easier, Isaac ended up writing up an instruction sheet for me for tonight in which we would be lighting seven candles. He had an extra menorah that one of his children had made in school several years back, and he offered it to us along with some candles.

As he went to get a bag for us to put away the menorah and candles, I began to wonder how Isaac knew so much about Christian scripture. That he was able to quote passages from the Old Testament didn't come as too much of a surprise, but I couldn't figure out why a religious Jew would know details about other religions. When he returned to pack things up I apologetically ended up asking him.

"I suppose it is a little unusual at that" he said while gently placing the menorah into the bag. "It's nothing that's so complicated though. You know how when you're young, events have a way of deeply affecting you? Well, when I was a teenager, I was always secure in my attachment to my religion. Being Jewish was something that I never questioned. I had no reason to question. All of my friends were at more or less the same level of strictness that I was at. I enjoyed learning; I enjoyed going to synagogue for prayers; and I enjoyed the various Jewish holidays that took place throughout the year. All in all, I had a very deep and secure religious upbringing.

"When I was in college, I got a part time job in an accounting office, where I worked every afternoon. Because I was a Sabbath observer and had to leave early on Fridays, I got to know most of the other Orthodox people who were there. Among those people was a young girl that I became very friendly with. Six months later she got engaged, and left the company shortly after. Before she left, though, she asked the personnel manager if her sister, who was a year younger than her, could take over her position. After being interviewed, the younger sister was hired. I felt that I should sort of watch over her, and I ended up becoming friendly with her as well.

"From about a month into the job, this new girl's boyfriend started picking her up. I remembered that he was tall, with dark hair, and wore a knitted skullcap. I never spoke to him myself, as he always seemed to be in a hurry. For the next several months in which she worked there, her boyfriend was there like clockwork to pick her up and quickly take her away.

"Because it wasn't my business, I really didn't think anything of it, and so I was surprised when she suddenly quit without even telling me anything. A few days later, I was even more surprised when I received a phone call from her older sister asking me if I knew where she was. At this point, I was concerned and, although I didn't want to pry, I naturally asked her if there was something wrong.

"She didn't answer my question right away, but she asked me if her younger sister was getting picked up. Yes, I told her. She was picked up just about every day, as far as I knew. "Was it by a man with a skullcap, a knitted one?" she asked. "Why, yes" I said. "As far as I know, he's her boyfriend." She told me that I was right, that he was her boyfriend. "I don't understand", I told her. "What's the problem?"

"The problem" Isaac slowly said to us, as though he were reliving the feelings of that moment, "was that her boyfriend wasn't Jewish."

"It turned out that for months, the younger sister had been going out with this boy, and she prompted him as to what he should say whenever he picked her up from the house, so that her father would think that her boyfriend was Jewish. When her deception was discovered, she ran away, and told her older sister that she didn't want to live where she knew she wouldn't be welcomed. Several days later, the information came out that she was converting to the religion of her boyfriend.

"The girl's family tried talking calmly with her, then angrily, finally threatening her, all to no avail. She then refused to take calls from anyone from her family. Her older sister then asked me to get involved, and I had this feeling, because of my years in Yeshivah, that I could reach anyone. After all, it seemed so logical to me as to why a Jew should retain his or her faith. When I did speak to her, all of my arguments fell on deaf ears. In truth, I was totally unprepared to deal with something like this. I was like the politician that was so confident of winning in the election that he never bothered to campaign, so that the election resulted in a landslide win for his opponent.

"Since then, I always thought about what would have happened if I had been more prepared. After that I made up my mind to learn certain facts. I didn't want to just go out and debate people about religion. That's not my intention. It's when Jews are approached by missionaries or people from Jews for Jesus and don't know how to answer that I would step in and explain why there's no basis for a Jew to leave his religion and go to another religion. If the Christians or Moslems want to say that they've created a whole new religion which is centered around the belief in G-d and that religion abides by the seven laws of Noah which non Jews must follow, then I have no problem with that. It's when they try to convince Jews that the Jewish religion has been superseded that I feel compelled to step in and show them otherwise.

"My point is not to attack other religions. What I'm trying to do is convey to Jews who don't understand the beauty of the religion of their birth, that there is no alternative for them other than Judaism."

"But" Steven asked, "what if someone who's Jewish just wants to worship the way he wants? I mean, all of this information about science that you've been explaining to me is now common knowledge in our society, so it's easier to learn that from our scientists. What I'm trying to ask is, doesn't each person have the right to worship the way that they want, even if it isn't in the Jewish faith?"

"I look at it differently. We're taught that all Jews are responsible for each other. If I see my fellow Jew being led down a path that's not for him, then I have a responsibility to try and help him. We're living in a very unique point in time. We all must unite as one people, with a shared goal. We survived the Holocaust against our people; we've witnessed the creation of the State of Israel; and now, many Rabbis feel, we could be the generation that actually witnesses the Messianic age. Even though it isn't politically correct to say what I'm saying, when you examine history and compare it to the predictions made about the period referred to as the end of days, it becomes urgent that all Jews must now accept their obligations to follow the Jewish laws. If my actions can help even one person, I consider that a great accomplishment."

What he said about the Messianic age struck a nerve and I had to interrupt. "You're saying that Jews have to go back to practice their faith because you believe that a Messiah could be coming to us now" I asked him? In my mind's eye, I began to picture the image of the book, 'The Last Days'.

Isaac softly replied, "We should practice our religion because it's our obligation, but as a side issue, we should always feel that the Messiah is coming soon. I've already told you certain things about the coming of the Messiah, but there are certain predictions which make many people feel that the time is now upon us. When we learn about the Messiah, we know that he'll either come when we're worthy, or in his proper time. Because of all the Jewish people who've turned away from traditional Judaism, with many leaving the religion altogether, we don't have too much confidence that we'll be found worthy. We do know that he'll come at a certain time period, which coincides with the final war."

"I learned about some of that with Father Baldino" I said. "At the end of days there'll be a huge war where many people will get wiped out, and the ones that are left will believe in the Messiah who will come to lead the Jewish people and all those others who believed in him. I think it's referred to as the war of Armageddon."

"In general, you're right. But the Christian faith misses the reason for the war. G-d gave us commandments to follow and we repeatedly break those commandments. There's a process, though, for us to be forgiven, and part of that process is for us to go through that final war."

"I think I see what you're saying. It's because we don't do G-d's commandments that the war has to come," I replied. "I guess it's like a punishment to straighten us out."

Isaac quickly corrected me. "It shouldn't be looked upon as a punishment, but as a way for us to come out rehabilitated. Once we are rehabilitated, we are given a series of chances to do G-d's will and follow His commandments. That's what the age of the Messiah is all about. The war is a necessary part of this rehabilitation, but the details of the war are not what most people think. In the Hebrew books, that war is referred to as the war of Gog of the nation of Magog. According to the writings of many of our great Rabbis, we know who Gog is right now."[103]

"Hold it," Steven said nervously. "This whole prediction is not of something far into the future?"

Isaac laughed at my brother's reaction. "I see that I definitely have your attention now!" Isaac said with a chuckle. "Let's first see who the original Gog was."

Isaac now took a Bible and opened it near the front. "The Bible gives us the genealogy right here." Isaac got up and handed the open book to Steven. As Steven examined the page, Isaac turned to me and continued. "Right after the episode of the flood, the Bible lists the descendents of Shem, Ham and Yafet who were the three sons of Noah. We have a tradition that the world can be broken down into 70 nations which correspond to the 70 descendents of the sons of Noah." He leaned over to point to something in the book and motioned for me to take a look as well. "See? There's a chart right there that lists the 70 descendents. One of those 70 nations from the line of Yafet was Magog. The term Magog later developed into the name of the nation, and its leader was referred to as Gog. But who is the modern day counterpart of this nation called Magog?" Steven now handed the book back to Isaac, as Isaac returned to his chair. He gently put the Bible down on a small table next to him and continued.

"Several thousands years ago, among the great Rabbis of Israel, lived a man named Jonathan the son of Uzziel. He traced the lineages of each of the original seventy nations listed in the Bible, and for the nation of Magog he determined that the counterpart in his generation was one nation that consisted of 300 city states. The name of that nation was Germania. According to our sages, Germania was a group that was extremely warlike, and that if they ever united, they would strive to take over the world. The only thing that was holding them back was their lack of unity. Those Germanic tribes are the ancestors of the German nation of today."

"I remember learning that the Germanic tribes were around in the time of the Roman Empire, but I didn't know that they were such a warlike people even then" Steven said.

"Apparently, it's in their nature to love war. We know from history that many of the soldiers for hire in the 17th and 18th centuries came from the German states.[104] They were known to have an unprecedented love for battle. But now that we know who Magog is, we ask when the final war will take place? And what were the First and Second World Wars about? Were they just a prelude to a huge final battle?

"Let's go back to see what the Rabbis say about the final war. The description of the final war is frightening. According to our sages, the killing will be so widespread that only one or two people out of entire families will survive. It's a wonder that anyone will survive at all. It's because of that, that many Rabbis go on to say that the final war will not be one catastrophic battle. We know that a war is required, and we know that for whatever reason, many people must die. But there's the concept of mercy. G-d had mercy on us. The attribute of mercy still allows for the full level of hardship which will effect us but instead of coming down to us in one huge war, it will be broken down into several smaller wars so that the full impact of the final war will not be as destructive.

"A Rabbi known as the Malbim[105] taught that the final war of Gog will be broken down into three divisions. There are two instances in the book of Yechezkel (Ezekiel) where the final war is discussed, followed by one instance in the book of Zacharia. From this and other writings he concluded that the first two parts of the final war will take place close to each other in time, and the final part will take place some time afterward.

"There's an irony here that I want to bring out. We know that G-d wants to be kind to the Jews and wants to afford them an opportunity to repent in order to avoid the destruction of the wars. When we examine history, we can see that G-d set up a block to prevent the Germans from waging war, but they were aided in their quest by a Jew."

A thought flashed in my mind and I interrupted. "Isaac, is this similar to what you told me about the Spanish Inquisition, where a Jew who converted pushed the Spanish King into throwing the Jews out of the country?"

"I hadn't thought of that, but even though you could find similarities, the cases are not really the same. Let's go through the actual history and see what we find."

Isaac sat in his chair and raised his hands. As he started to speak, his fingers began to slowly dance in the air.[106] "In the early 1800's Germany was a series of regions, which wasn't unusual. Italy was also set up in a similar fashion. The individual regions of Germany were loosely united through their membership in the German Confederation of Frankfurt. Though there was much discussion as to whether or not the various regions should unite, there were always dissenters. One of the largest and most powerful regions of Germany was Prussia, and its king set up as its Minister-President a man by the name of Otto von Bismarck who set the goal for himself of uniting Germany. Before the unification was even complete, Bismarck entered into a war with Austria, which was a sister German state, and followed that with a war with France. (The Franco Prussian War of 1870). That victory led to the smaller German regions uniting with Prussia so that Germany finally achieved the unification that the Rabbis of 2,000 years before fearfully warned of.

"All during this time period in Germany, there was constant debate about the Jewish question.[107] Were Jews only a religious group? Did they want to infiltrate into the German culture? If they were allowed to prosper, would they control the German economy? In some years, the fears of the public took hold and the rights of Jews became extremely limited. In other years, their rights were expanded, giving them hope of greater freedom. After the unification of Germany, the Jews were free to move about and enter different areas of business and professions. A large number of them became members of the upper middle class. The Jews made great strides, but there were still areas where discrimination persisted. It was only a matter of time until the tide again began to turn, and the jealousy and fear of the Jew made the Jew unwelcome in many areas of society.

"By the early 1900's, the government of Germany was the most powerful country in all of Europe.[108] It was only fitting, they believed, that this power entitled them to be equal to the various colonial superpowers of that time period, but there was no more land left to conquer. Spain, Portugal, England, and France had already subjugated most of the non civilized countries throughout the world. A great frustration was felt within the German republic, and one would have thought that they would have used military force at that point to take over the colonies of others or even make war on other countries of Europe. There was a great obstacle that stood in their way, however, and they were forced to do nothing.

"Germany was a country with extremely poor soil. The 1800's brought with it the Industrial Revolution. Populations exploded and farming machines were able to increase agricultural output tremendously. The intense farming of the land that followed was not without its downside for it was depleting the soil of its nutrients. Agricultural output now began to decline, which brought on the strong possibility of a famine throughout Europe. In the 1840's it was discovered that by adding nitrogen to the soil in the form of nitrates, food output would increase again. Most of the world's nitrate deposits were in Chile, and all of Europe, including Germany, became dependent on the shipments of nitrate that were imported into Europe by ocean vessel.

"A second use of nitrates was discovered by Alfred Nobel; it was used specifically for explosives and weapons of war. Without a sufficient supply of nitrates a country would not be able to produce the weapons that it needed to wage war, especially if the war they waged was against an enemy that did have such access.

"Germany, then, had a double need for nitrates: first, as a fertilizer to feed its citizens, and second as a vital ingredient which would allow them to wage war. England had the strongest navy in the world and controlled the ocean lanes. If Germany were to wage war which lasted longer than six months, their supply lines of this vital ingredient would be choked by the British Navy, and they would ultimately be forced to surrender. The German nation was held in check.

"G-d now wanted to give the Jews one more chance before the destruction would begin. Would they repent and go back to their Judaism? The Germans and all of the nations of Europe, were exhibiting a renewed hatred to the Jew that increased in intensity the more Jews tried to assimilate in order for them to be accepted as an equal in European society. They ignored the hatred around them and tried ever harder to blend in with the local populace, while hiding their Jewish identity to the point that they themselves no longer recognized it. It was at this point that G-d had to allow the next phase to continue, but it proceeded through the actions of a single Jew.

"Enter the Jew. Fritz Haber. He had a great interest in chemistry and attempted to get into the University of Karlsruhe in Germany. He was faced with an attitude by the German public which had again shifted to a discriminatory one. As a Jew he would be barred from entering the University and pursuing his career, but he was given a choice: remain a Jew or enter the University, but not both. He never hesitated. He enrolled in the University with his Judaism a thing of the past. In the early 1900's he came up with a method to cheaply produce nitrates using atmospheric nitrogen and hydrogen. It was in 1912, with the help of a large German chemical company, BASF, that he was able to perfect the newly named Haber-Bosch Process so that it was viable for large scale production. In 1913, the first commercial nitrate production plant was erected in Germany, and by 1914, World War I began.

"At the conclusion of the war, a Rabbi known as the Chofetz Chaim,[109] who was one of the greatest Rabbis of his generation, wrote that the war that just ended was the first of the three wars of Gog. He said that based on scripture, the next war would take place within twenty to twenty five years.

"World War II did start when it was predicted. It was also a war whose specific aim became the destruction of the Jews. Millions of Jews were killed and their property confiscated. Jewish memorabilia was collected so that Hitler could later show the world the artifacts of the Jews after a future he envisioned where the Jews would be no more. Towards the end of the war when the shipment of supplies to the battlefront was of utmost importance, Hitler kept on diverting cattle cars to transport more Jews to be killed instead of using the cars to ship supplies for his army. His actions were without reason, until you realized that Hitler's hidden purpose of starting this war was to destroy the Jew.

"After the Germans lost this second war, it would only be a matter of time until they started the final one, so G-d put them on hold again. This time he did it through the Allies, who split Germany in two. It was no longer the united Germany that had wreaked havoc on the world for over 70 years.

"In the course of the years that Germany remained divided, there was apparently a divine plan that allowed for other events to take place. We know that one of the most important events was the establishment of the state of Israel. This set the stage for the prophecy that all Jews will move to Israel and that ultimately, all of the land, including what's termed as the West Bank, will be part of Israel under Jewish control.

"It was not until 1989 that the German nation was again allowed to unite. It was then that the Berlin wall came down following the collapse of Communism. It was at that time that the process of the war of Gog was allowed to proceed."

"So now" I began, a little nervously, "you're saying that the war of Gog, or really the final phase of the war, is back on track. What's the prediction for the date of that final phase?"

"We don't know" he said. "But we do know that there are other prophetic events which must play out, and which are playing out. As a result, many Biblical authorities feel that the final days are close at hand. That's not a bad thing, though, but we should do whatever we can to follow the religious commandments that we were given, because our proper actions will hopefully be our protection."

I thought to myself of how I started to say that prayer in the morning, and even of the instruction sheet that was now in my pocket, which was to guide me through the last day of lighting the Hanukah candles. I wanted to do more. When the history of the Jewish people is laid out the way that Isaac had been laying it out, the success of the Jews coincided with their adherence to the Biblical laws.

The Holocaust was preceded by the events of the 19th century. There were mass defections by Jews from their Judaism. The Reform movement took hold in the early part of the century and was an attempt to respond to the anti Semitism that was prevalent against the Jews of that era. The tactic was wrong. Reform Jews thought that by being similar to the nations around them, their Jewish ancestry would be forgotten and the oppression would stop, but just the opposite was true. The more the Jews blended into the society of their adopted country, the more oppressive became the laws against them. They should have gotten closer to their Judaism instead of fleeing from it. They had no pride in who they really were, and because of that, they became nobody.

It's frightening when you think about it. Reform Judaism really began in Germany, and it was the German nation that was destined to battle against the Jews. Our lack of conviction to accept the laws of the Bible was what made us despised to the people of that country. We were apologists, and did everything that could be done to prove that we were like them, when we should have been trying to be more like Jews.

Isaac had explained to us how the Bible was not contradictory to science, but I could tell from my brother's question that he was missing Isaac's point. The purpose of the Bible was not to teach us science. It's almost as though G-d is telling us that the Bible is filled with truth and the science portion that we're now confirming was inserted as proof that the rest of it is true. There's a wealth of knowledge that's just sitting there in front of us which the Bible is meant to convey. As Jews, we must follow its laws because, whether we understand them or not, we know that they are there for our benefit. More than ever I wanted to learn more about what Jews do to make them religious Jews.

The effect that Isaac's words had on me was not mirrored on my brother because he now asked Isaac "You said that the Jews would be the ones to get all of Israel. I don't understand the justice in what you're saying. I mean, I know that Jews feel that Israel belongs to them, but weren't the Palestinian Arabs there first? Isn't that why we're having a problem in deciding who gets what for all of these years? The country has been been called Palestine for thousands of years, and Palestinians were in the land before the Jews even came in. How does that get reconciled if we're talking about things ending up as they should when all is said and done?"

I didn't think Isaac was going to even address that issue. Our sitting down here on one winter evening wasn't going to result in a solution to a problem that's been plaguing the greatest minds in the world for over fifty years. But, he didn't skip a beat.

"You think that the Arabs, these so called Palestinian Arabs, have a greater right to the land than the Jews?" Isaac definitely became noticeably agitated as he said this, but then he regained his composure. "When I was in Israel a few years ago, I heard the same remark from Jews that were living there. I was actually shocked. They had no idea of the history of their own county. They believed the claims of the Arabs even though they are without substance, and because the claims have been repeated so often, you, and many other people throughout the world, believe them too."

Isaac got up and walked over to the window and looked out at the Manhattan landscape. After a few moments, he turned to us. While still standing, he began to speak, but in a way that made me aware that he had repeated his words many times before.

"Let's go back to simple logic, Steven. In the first book of the Old Testament, there's an account of Abraham traveling to a region within the borders of Israel.[110] The name of that region using the Hebrew pronunciation is the land of the Pelishtim. That Hebrew word is more closely related phonetically to the English word Palestinian, although it's usually translated as Phillistine, but it's the same thing.

"In the account, Abraham encounters their King, who realizes the greatness of Abraham, and makes a treaty with him. So we know that the Palestinian nation existed prior to the time period of Abraham." Isaac now turned to face us. "Is that an acceptable assumption to make?"

I straightened up in my seat and affirmed that it made perfect sense. "But isn't that what Steven is saying, that the Palestinians were there first?", I asked.

"One thing at a time," Isaac said. "Here's where the logic comes in. The Arabic nation is descended from Abraham, are they not? Specifically from his son Ishmael?"

It now hit me what he was getting at. "I get it now", I said. "If the nation of the Palestinians was around during the time of Abraham, and the Palestinian Arabs were descended from Ishmael, who came much later, then the original Palestinians who lived in the land were not the same nation as the current Palestinian Arabs. But" I now hesitated, "then what's the relationship between the Palestinian Arabs and the original Palestinians?"

Isaac now smiled as the confusion that was hitting both me and my brother was plainly displayed on our faces. He continued again, but in a more relaxed tone.

"The original Palestinian people were destined to be defeated and evicted just like the other Canaanite nations that inhabited the land, when the Jews returned to Israel after the death of Moses. Because of the peace treaty that Abraham had made with the Palestinian king, however, the Jews were barred from initiating a battle with them. After the (Pelishtim) Palestinians attacked the Jews during the time of Samson, the treaty was nullified, and the Palestinians were ultimately defeated by King David. Records of them remaining on that territory exist, but after the fall of the first Jewish Temple in 587 BCE, they were sent into exile along with the Jews of Israel, and they assimilated with the conquering countries so that all trace of their nation ended. The Palestinian nation referred to in the Bible then ceased to exist.

"We jump ahead to the Roman conquest of Israel. Well after the fall of the second Jewish Temple of 70 CE, there was a revolt by the Jews under the leadership of a man named Bar Kochba.[111] The Romans had a difficult time in putting down this rebellion, and once they did, they decided to change the name of the country as a psychological method of making the people feel less attached to it. They chose the new name from an ancient people that no longer existed. In 135 CE, the country was given the arbitrary name of Palestine.

"Throughout the centuries, the official name assigned to the land by the Romans remained, but to Jews, the land was always Israel. Though many were exiled, the Jews continued to live and thrive on the land for hundreds of years, until the rise of Mohammed. His followers massacred whole towns of Jews who wouldn't follow him, and the Jews were forcibly dispossessed of their land and property. The wealth of the Jews, including their ownership of the land, was now transferred to the invading Arabs. Despite this, you have to bear in mind that no nation other than the Jews claimed this land as their own.[112] It was always considered to be conquered territory of various Arab empires with no specific borders. The inhabitants, though, were referred to as either Palestinian Jews or Palestinian Arabs.

"By the mid 1800's, the land of Israel was mostly desert, with very few inhabitants. Mark Twain visited Israel in that time period and described it as a land where one can travel for miles without encountering a single human soul.[113] The land was desolate and devoid of people. There were small communities of Jews whose families had never left the land for thousands of years, while there were also Arab squatters who set up their own small communities. The bulk of the land, though, was owned by Syrian and Lebanese businessmen who did not work the land themselves and were absentee owners.[114]

"In the 1880's, there was a worldwide call for Jews to escape persecution in Europe and they began to return to Israel in masses.[115] As they started entering Israel, they bought large parcels of land back from the Syrians and Lebanese and established cities with thriving industries. The poor Arab laborers from the surrounding countries heard of the many jobs which were now available, and they streamed into the land. By 1917, because of the huge influx of Arabs who entered Israel over the previous twenty years, the country was overwhelmingly Arab.

"After 1948, with the establishment of the state of Israel, the Jews in the country renamed themselves. What were once Palestinian Jews were now Israeli Jews. The newspaper that was once the Palestine Post, was renamed the Jerusalem Post. In their refusal to recognize the state of Israel, the Arab insisted on being known as the Palestinian Arab. Because the world leaders have such a short memory, this turned out to be a public relations coup for the Arab. The world, including many Jews, now believed that by virtue of their name, that they were the original inhabitants of the land from before the time of Abraham.

"The truth of the matter is that the land of Israel was always looked at as the homeland of the Jews. Our prayers constantly refer to this, and we actually cry over our expulsion from the land from almost two thousand years ago. The world, though, looks at the Palestinian Arabs as its true inhabitants and they use as a proof that in 1917, there were more Arabs than Jews living in Israel. The reality, however, is that the vast majority of those Arabs immigrated within 30 years prior to that date.

"Do you see how facetious their argument becomes? In the United States, many immigrants came in during the 19th century. For example, Germans that established Germantown in the mid 1800's were residents of the land, but after they were here for 30 years, did they have a right to make that area their own country? Since when did residence in a land entitle a group to the right of nationhood? At most it could entitle that group to citizenship, but even that isn't the case in other areas of the world.

"When you look at a country like Japan, people consider it a model of democracy. But their level of democracy is a far cry from what we have here in the U.S.[116] They have a policy that only people of Japanese ancestry can vote and even that doesn't always hold. There were many Japanese who moved to Brazil before the Second World War and set up their own communities. Over the years that they were there, they married only other Japanese so that their line remained pure. Now that these people want to return to Japan, they are being refused citizenship because their Japanese culture has been tainted due to their exposure to a foreign culture. And yet, how many outcries of the member countries of the UN do you hear of this discrimination? There were none. In Israel, however, if a discussion is undertaken of removing the voting rights of the Arabs, who openly preach killing Jews, and cannot go to the army because it would pose a danger to the state, the members of the UN cry out in the Arab's defense."

Isaac stopped and began to smile. "Logic doesn't apply when the Jews are judged by the outside world" he said.

We were all silent. Steven and I needed some time to absorb the information that was being hurled at us. Isaac was right. The logic was there, but it was as though nobody cared to acknowledge it.

"The only thing that could help us is our own actions. We have to act more like Jews. Now do you understand why it hurts me when I see Jews casting off their Judaism without having any idea of what a beautiful gift from G-d it really is?

"This brings me to something that I wanted to ask you, Michael. The last time we spoke, you wanted to see if there were other things that you could do as a Jew. There actually is, and it has to do with the signs that G-d decreed that every male Jew must evince.

"Every male Jew is recognized in our religion by two signs. The first sign is that of a circumcision. In modern times, however, the medical community is suggesting that all babies be circumcised because of the health benefits associated with it. There is a second sign that's unique to the Jew, and is at least as important.

"When you had your Bar Mitzvah, you were probably given a set of phylacteries, or, as we call them, Tefillin, but you were told you no longer had to wear them after that day. The reality is that these Tefillin are the second sign of our acceptance of Judaism. I'd like you" and then Isaac looked at Steven also, "the both of you, to consider putting them on with the blessing. Sundown hasn't yet occurred, and there's still time for you to wear them today, before you leave." He waited a few moments for me to respond.

I was embarrassed by the fact that I hesitated, but I rose, and said that I would love to put them on. I smiled and turned to Steven, but he shook his head and said, "No thanks. Maybe another time, but not now." Isaac then left the room and returned with a small pouch. He zipped it open and pulled out two black boxes that were covered with leather straps. Because it had been so long since I had worn a set, he had to explain what each piece was and how to put each one on. I unwrapped the leather from the first one and slipped my arm through a leather loop. The box it was tied to rested on my upper arm and Isaac then had me say the blessing. I then completed tying the strap around my arm and hand. Isaac helped me place the second box on my forehead, pulled the straps attached to that box to the back of my neck, and then allowed the ends of the straps to drop in front of my shirt. After I finished putting them on, I have to admit that I felt differently and the feeling remained even after I removed them. As I buttoned my shirt cuffs afterward, I turned to my brother and said, "It couldn't hurt, and you're here anyway." He looked at me and we both started laughing while he said, "I guess I did come to you for advice, so I may as well."

After Steven took them off, Isaac apologized that he had to cut our visit short as he had someplace to go. We all rose while I thanked Isaac for his time and hospitality. As we were all starting to put our coats on, Steven's cell phone rang. It was our father. Steven's face became pale as he said, "Okay, Dad, we'll come over now," and then he slowly turned off the phone.

"What happened?" I asked. "Is there something wrong?"

"Dad wants to speak to me" he said. "He just received a phone call from Christine."

28

I wasn't quite sure how to deal with this new development, but it couldn't be avoided. I was hoping to help my brother through this without involving either of my parents but apparently, this was not to be.

While I was growing up, my father's role was always the disciplinarian while my mother was the confidant. Even after my father and I began to work together, he never really got involved in my personal life. I was his business partner, and to his credit, he always treated me as an equal, but the personal heart to heart talks were never there. It was as though he had isolated himself from that part of parenting. It was only in this past week that he suddenly began to change course when he saw what I was going through and seemed to want to show that he was there for me. It was because of that, that I saw his phone call as an extension of that new side of him, in which there was a desire to get close to his children.

Steven still saw the old Jonathan Klein. To Steven, he was the one who would lay down the law in our house. Being the younger of the two of us, he was the more coddled, and he would usually get my mother to secretly drop whatever punishment my father decreed on him. Maybe it was partly because of that, and partly because Steven wanted to feel he was now an adult and able to make his own decisions, that he resented my father's involvement. I knew enough about human nature to know that right now my brother would lean towards any decision that was opposite of what my father would counsel.

We caught a cab and went straight to my father. When we rang the bell to the apartment, my father answered the door himself. My mother would usually play cards most Sundays while my father took advantage of the time to read books or magazines that he hadn't gotten to earlier in the week, and this was the case today. His stern expression masked the emotion that I knew he was feeling within. It was his eyes, though, that revealed part anger and part hurt. He motioned for us to enter and then turned and walked ahead without uttering a word. I saw that Steven's eyes had narrowed. He was preparing for a confrontation.

But the confrontation didn't come.

Instead, my father told us to sit down. "Before we can discuss anything", he said. "There's something that I have to tell you."

His expression was calm and soft. It was quite the opposite of what we both expected. Steven certainly wasn't prepared for it, and it was apparent that Steven quickly began to relax. He was not to be put on trial for his actions. We soon realized that my father was about to put himself on trial, with us as the judge and jury.

"Whenever I would tell you about your family," my father began, "I always limited the history to the life of your grandfather. Beyond that, all that you know is that we originally emigrated from Germany. But I think that now is the time to fill in the blanks, and once I'm done, I'm going to have to ask for your forgiveness."

Neither I nor my brother made a sound. It was so out of character for my father to speak like this that we just sat there staring, while trying hard to maintain our silence.

My father pulled an armchair in front of where we were sitting. He sat and didn't say anything for about a half minute or so. During this time, he was staring at the floor in front of us. I felt each second slowly pass. His right forefinger then began tapping on the arm of the chair while he took the time to put his thoughts together. He stopped tapping and finally looked up. He then quietly resumed speaking.

"It's true that our family originally came from Germany in the 1870's. Your grandfather, my father, had a golden touch for business, and built up a sizable estate. Judaism was never a priority for him. In short, he practiced his Judaism in a way that put his business and social position first, so that his religion was an afterthought. I was raised in the same way. But what you know is only a small part of the story.

"For that, I have to tell you of my own grandfather and his family. We have to go back to when my grandfather was born in Germany, in 1873.

"Though people generally think of German Jews as members of the Reform movement, because that's where it started, my family was Orthodox. Germany was not an easy place in which to live, and if you were Orthodox and showed outward signs of your Judaism, you were met with physical acts of anti Semitism. Despite that, my great grandfather was able to build up a sizable business manufacturing buttons." My father smiled when he saw our surprised reaction. "Remember that zippers were not manufactured until twenty years later. Where today all men's pants have zippers, then they had buttons; women's dresses also had buttons; everything which today is adorned with zippers had to have buttons, from pillow cushions, to coats, to all manners of clothing.

"It was in early 1873 that a financial panic resulted in the collapse of the Viennese stock market and continued throughout Europe.[117] It was into that situation that my grandfather was born, and the financial collapse caused the closing of my great grandfather's company as well. Between the financial difficulties, and the religious oppression that was running rampant in the country, he took it as a sign that they should start fresh in a new land. Everything that happened was really for the best, my great grandfather said. He looked at the birth of his son as a good omen, and a sign that they should start a new life. Along with thousands of his countrymen, he chose the United States as the place where they would go.

"Because of his knowledge of the works of artists of the past, my great grandfather would broker the sales of these works from his European contacts to wealthy Americans. He developed a reputation for honesty that made his business prosper. He maintained his strict adherence to the Judaic laws and passed on both his business and his beliefs to my grandfather.

"My father, you see, actually came from an Orthodox Jewish home, but fate would bring him great success, and with it, a desire to be equal to the non Jews of New York who were the elite of the society of his day.

"Because my grandfather would constantly rub shoulders with the wealthy, my father began to look upon that world as one which he would make it his life's goal to enter. Each time my grandfather would take my father with him to meet a wealthy patron of the arts, the aptitude and manners of my father would impress those clients, so that they would share with him certain information as to investments which turned out to be most fortuitous. In short order, my father became wealthy himself and he felt it was his ticket to be accepted into the world he so coveted from a young age. To do so, however, he would have to cast off his observance of the Jewish religious laws. The Sabbath was no longer precious to him, since Friday night was a night for socializing at parties and plays. His observance of the Kosher laws would have to be cast off as well, since, how could he attend these functions if he couldn't partake of the foods that the others in that social upper class were now eating? In short, his wealth brought with it a form of Judaism which had severed its roots. My grandfather watched this in horror. His family had left Germany to protect their ability to practice Judaism, and here was my father, voluntarily turning his back on what they held most sacred.

"It was into this household that I and my brothers were raised. Illness, however, did not respect one's money, and, by the time I entered high school, I became an only child. My father immersed himself in his work and both my parents filled the rest of their time furthering their societal aspirations and priming me to follow in their footsteps. The isolation from religion that my father planned for me was broken, however. By chance, I had a school assignment to interview a grandparent and, without telling my father, I began to visit my grandfather. It was from that point that we began to cultivate our relationship.

"Though I first looked at our meetings as the fulfillment of a project, they ended up opening my eyes to a whole new world. Over the three years that I visited him, I felt the love that he had for his faith. He told me of the struggles that Jews endured to hold onto their religion. He taught me by example of how lucky we should consider ourselves to be able to perform religious acts to the point that we couldn't help but do them with a smile. We both knew, however, that our meetings had to be kept secret, for if my father knew of what my grandfather was teaching me, I would be forbidden to speak to him again. That time finally came.

"I remember the anger my father felt towards my grandfather when he saw that his only child was being swayed from the plans my father had laid out for his son's future. He told my grandfather that he wanted a better life for me, a life where I would be accepted for what I was and not be burdened by our Judaism. I remember my grandfather saying to my father, "You speak of Judaism as if it's a suit of clothes that you can remove when you see fit, but you have it all wrong. Your Judaism is a part of you; it defines who you are. Do you imagine that by ignoring that fact, that you make your life better? It's just the opposite. Don't think that you're the first Jew who chose to turn his back on his heritage. Your actions have been done before with tragic consequences. Do you believe that you're being kind to the boy by teaching him to turn his back on his religion? Don't let the Jewish heritage of our family end with you."

"My father had no interest in what his father was trying to say. It was only because of the time that I spent with my grandfather that allowed me to understand my grandfather's fear. There was a story that my grandfather had told me of a well known public figure of his time that did turn away from his faith. I'm sure he had also told the story to my father. His words were meant as a warning. It was a warning that my father would ignore, but my grandfather hoped that I would not. In the end, though, I became my father's son."

My father paused with this remark. I stayed quiet, and when my father looked away for a moment, I turned to Steven. He was staring straight ahead and waiting for my father to continue.

"Did you ever hear of Emma Lazarus?"[118] my father then asked.

Neither I nor my brother could bring ourselves to break the rhythm of his voice. He ended up answering his own question.

"She's usually known for the poem that's inscribed in the base of the Statue of Liberty.

"Give me your tired, your poor,
Your huddled masses yearning to breathe free
The wretched refuse of your teeming shore,
Send these, the homeless, tempest-tossed to me:
I lift my lamp beside the golden door."

His recitation of those familiar lines jolted me into replying that I had heard them, and I had also read that she, a Jew, was the writer.

"That's right", he said. "And I, like you right now, would have been satisfied with that knowledge and I would have felt no need to find out more. But my grandfather offered to give me more, and I found that I had more in common with her life than I could have imagined.

"Her famous poem, called The New Colossus, was written in response to the plight of the many European Jews who were flocking to the United States to escape religious persecution. Throughout the latter part of her short life, she wrote numerous articles and plays which highlighted the plight of the European Jews, and she became actively involved in helping them settle in the United States. She even wrote of the need for a Jewish homeland in what was then called Palestine more than ten years before Theodore Herzl founded the Zionist movement.

"But I see the question on your faces. What does she have to do with my father and grandfather? It's with her father's story that you'll understand.

"Emma's parents were Moses and Esther Lazarus. They were Sephardic Jews who were able to trace their lineage to the first Jews who came to North America following the Spanish and then the Portuguese inquisitions. Moses became wealthy in the sugar trade, and his wealth made him eager to have his family integrated within the Christian society. He went in the same circles as the Vanderbilts and Astors, and even joined with them in establishing elite private clubs. Just as my father had done years later, he turned away from observing the religious laws to achieve his societal ambitions. The price he paid was being ostracized from his own father and relatives for turning away from his religious observance.

"Although Emma grew up with all Christian friends, she knew that the friendships masked a deep seated prejudice which she could not dispel. She often wrote of it in her articles. She reacted to the prejudice by attaching herself to Jewish causes. Growing up without a religious background, though, affected her siblings in a different way.

"Religious acts are like an anchor, and when you remove those acts from your lifestyle, you remove the very thing that binds you to the Jewish people. I remember that grandpa had tears in his eyes as he told me that Annie, Emma's sister, became an Anglo-Catholic convert. Her separation from the religion of her ancestors became so complete that, when she became literary executor of Emma's estate after Emma's death, she refused to grant permission to reprint Emma's Jewish poems.

"This was the future that was being offered to me. My grandfather had looked me straight in the eye and told me that if I were to follow the path of my father I would be choosing a future where either my children or their children might end up as Annie Lazarus. Our Judaism that could now be traced back for thousands of years would die with me.

"As much as his statement impacted my thinking, I was still a teenager with selfish needs and desires. My father had always told me of the many business deals that he was able to close on Saturdays that would not have been possible otherwise. To me, then, it was a choice of money or religion. The thought of doing without the things that my father gave me in order to follow Judaism did not sit well with me. I was too entrenched in the world I grew up in. When I told my grandfather that material success didn't mix with religious observance, he told me that material success did not come from our own brilliance, but was a reward because of the actions of our parents and grandparents. He sat me down and showed me a passage from Psalms. He had me memorize it in the Hebrew and it's one of the few things that I even remember today. The words were: 'Naar hayisi, gam zakanti, velo ra-eeti tzadik ne-ezav, vezar-o mevakesh lachem. Kol hayom chonen u-malveh, vezar-o livrachah.'[119] It means 'I've been young and now I'm old and I've not seen the righteous forsaken nor have his offspring been in need of bread. G-d is ever merciful (because of the righteous) and His seed will be blessed.' According to my grandfather, my father's wealth and business acumen was a reward for the righteous actions of those who came before him, but my father didn't see it that way and only believed in himself.

"When I entered the University and became involved with friends, it was very easy for me to forget my grandfather's warning. His death a few years later made me think about the time we spent together. As the years passed, in the absence of his guidance, I allowed myself to be molded into the person my father envisioned.

"After your mother and I married, the thought of my grandfather's warning weighed over my head, but I convinced myself that I would not be another Moses Lazarus. I didn't really have a good religious foundation, because the time with my grandfather only gave me a cursory knowledge of Judaism, but I did see how much the religion meant to him. I was sure that a belief that was so precious to him had to be worth holding on to. Although I was too entrenched in my lifestyle to do the religious acts, I took enough of my grandfather's teachings to make sure I always associated with other Jews and become involved in Jewish causes. But you both have proved to me that my grandfather was right. It wasn't enough."

He turned his head to the side, so that he avoided looking directly at us when he said this. Both my brother and I decided to remain quiet. Even if we wanted to say something right now, there was nothing that we could think of that would be appropriate.

He looked at me this time, and continued. "When you got married to Susan, I didn't want to accept that your actions were already predicted years ago. To do so would have placed the blame squarely on me, and that's something I didn't want to acknowledge. When you sat with me and told me of what you've been going through recently, I had to finally admit to myself that it was because of my mistake." He now turned to Steven. "When I received the phone call today from your girlfriend, I knew I had to tell you all of this. I had to tell the both of you why this is happening. What I fear is that you don't care, but I'm hoping that it's not too late."

With that, he asked Steven about his relationship with this new girl. As Steven spoke, you could see how intently my father listened. I knew that we were now at the threshold of a new beginning. Even though the days ahead would be difficult, our family now had a common goal and we would help each other reach that goal.

I thought of my father's grandfather and his admonition to my father. "Don't let the Jewish heritage of our family end with you." Now I knew that it wouldn't.

EPILOGUE

Steven ended up opening up to my father and spoke without interruption for over an hour. It's funny. When my brother came to me for advice, I tried using logic to convince him that he was wrong. It was my father, though, who really convinced Steven, but not by showing him pros and cons. All he had to do was be there for him. My father treated Steven like the adult that he'd grown up to be, and allowed Steven to decide on a course of action for himself.

Although Steven knew he had to break up with Christine, he admitted that actually going through with it would not be so easy. Besides the fact that it would be a difficult thing for her to accept, Steven acknowledged that it would be hard for him as well. He agreed with me when I told him that, for him, being in Nashville and being with Christine were linked in his brain somehow. Once Steven returned to school, he knew it would feel natural to lapse into his previous routine of being with her. My brother and I weren't sure of what he should do. It was my father who then came up with a suggestion. To even say that he suggested a course of action instead of just telling us what we should do showed how much he had changed.

My father offered to fly out to Nashville with Steven, but it was not to speak to Christine. Steven had said that Christine's family was religious. My father was sure that she would always feel that she could control the religious direction if the two of them were to get married, much as Susan had wanted to do in my case. The way to deal with this was not by dealing with her. My father would speak to her father and explain that if Christine were to marry Steven, she would have to accept the Jewish faith and convert. My father was hoping that her parents would never accept the notion of their daughter undergoing a conversion. This tactic would serve two purposes. First, it would push Christine's family to stop the relationship from their end. More importantly, Steven would see for himself that a marriage to Christine would have inevitably ended up with Christine pushing Steven to leave his own religion and follow hers. By seeing this, Steven would be able to have closure and move on.

Steven surprisingly agreed. His flight back to Tennessee would be departing in the morning. Knowing that this course of action couldn't be delayed, my father called the airline, and booked a seat on the same flight as Steven's. The next day, he flew in to Nashville with Steven and, at night, he gave me a call. He had met Christine's father in the evening and, sure enough, it was Christine's father who ended the relationship. My father didn't leave Nashville until the following morning, and Steven later told me that he was grateful that Dad was with him. That night the two of them were up until almost 3 in the morning. I would have thought that Steven would have been talking to my father about Christine, but that wasn't the case. Steven ended up asking all sorts of questions about my father's life when he was younger and my father got into a lot more detail with stories about his father and grandfather. Since that time, Steven and my father have made it a habit to speak to each other at least once a week.

My life continued to have its ups and downs. Over the next few weeks, Susan and I continued to be preoccupied with caring for Eric. Although Eric was forced to remain in the hospital until the end of January, he's since made a full recovery. It wasn't until the beginning of the fourth week after Eric's admission that he began to show signs of improvement. Susan and I got a call on that particular night that a nurse had noticed a slight movement in his leg. Neither of us was willing to wait until the next morning to see our son after receiving news like that. We immediately woke Jennie and rushed to the hospital to check up on him ourselves. Dr. Birnbaum happened to be on duty when we arrived, and he accompanied us himself to show us the improvement. Each day brought a dramatic change in our son's condition. By the end of that week Eric no longer needed the machines for life support. We were able to bring him home right after that. Just as the doctors had predicted, he gained complete control of his movements, and we never saw any signs of after effects. The tension between me and Susan which was suppressed during the time Eric was in the hospital seemed to come back with a vengeance once we brought Eric home. I have to admit that it was mostly a result of my own actions.

After my father went to Nashville with my brother, I ended up calling Isaac to let him know why I had brought my brother to him in the first place, and how things had turned out. The words that I had thought silently when Steven opened up to me, Isaac said aloud. "Maybe part of the reason why you had to go through what you did was to protect your brother from going down that same path." But after he voiced it, I thought to myself, why couldn't someone have stopped me before I got married? Then, I immediately answered my own question; my children wouldn't have been born. The truth is that no matter what I was going through, I couldn't imagine a world without them. For whatever reason, they were now forced to pay the price for my actions, and I had to accept it.

In the course of my conversation with Isaac, I related to him what my father had told me and he was fascinated at how my father attached past events to the current. He was obviously very impressed, and he asked me if he could meet my father when he returned from his trip with Steven.

When my father got back, he told me he wanted to resume the studies that he had begun years ago with his grandfather. I then told him of Isaac and related some of the things that he explained to me this week. Before I had a chance to tell him that Isaac wanted to meet him, my father asked me if he could meet Isaac. Needless to say, when the two of them did meet, they got along remarkably well and they've been good friends ever since.

Isaac ended up recommending a couple of different Orthodox Ashkenaz synagogues near my father's home that my father could choose from as a congregation for him to join. Accompanied by Isaac, my father sat with the various Rabbis and he explained his religious background as well as my own. My father chose one Rabbi that he felt comfortable with. According to the Rabbi, I would be permitted to go to synagogue and pray with the congregation despite my marriage to a non-Jew. There were two items, though, which made my situation problematic. The first was that the synagogue by laws prohibited a Jew who was married to a non-Jew from being an actual member. That seemed to be something that I could live with. The Rabbi, however, explained that if it was my intention to be a fully practicing Jew, it would be impossible for me to be married to someone outside of the Jewish faith. There were laws that pertained to the home that the woman was obligated to perform,[120] like immersing herself in a mikvah once a month; lighting candles for the Sabbath; and keeping the many Kosher laws when buying and preparing foods. These were all things that a non-Jew would not even be aware of. As much as I knew that he was right, I still loved Susan, and more than anything, I was afraid of how a divorce would impact my children. I didn't want to contemplate how I would handle taking a step like that just yet.

Rather than dwell on what I couldn't yet do, I put my energies into what I could do and I got into the habit of meeting my father every morning to go to the synagogue for prayers. I never told Susan where I was going, as I knew that her reaction would not be positive, so I made it a point to always sidetrack any conversation that touched on religion. It so happened that about a month after Eric was back at home, I had left the synagogue and, instead of going directly to work, I went back home. I had left an important folder in my apartment, and it was necessary for me to pick it up. For some reason I had neglected to remove my skullcap that I had worn during prayers, and it was still on my head as I walked into the living room to pick up my papers.

I remember Susan looking up at me when I walked into the room, surprised at first as to why I was returning home. When she turned to face me she just froze. At that point I had no idea why and asked her, quite innocently, if anything was wrong. She just continued to stare at me and didn't say anything, but the color had left her face. I don't know why, but I instinctively reached up to my head and felt the skullcap. I felt my own face turn a deep crimson as I took off the head covering and nonchalantly put it in my pocket.

The damage was done, however, and this time, there was no going back. Sometimes I think about that day and wonder if I returned to the house on purpose. Was I pushing to end my marriage? Was I thinking of what the Rabbi had told me in the synagogue; that I could never be an accepted Orthodox Jew as long as I had a non Jewish wife? Whether it was a Freudian slip, or an absent minded mistake, it no longer mattered. The damage was done. Susan issued an ultimatum to me on the spot, but I couldn't go back to the way things were. I was now forced to undergo the divorce that I had always tried to avoid.

The initial hurt and anger that each of us felt lasted for about a week, but once we got over that, Susan and I accepted that divorce was inevitable. Despite our feelings for each other, we were on different paths. There really was no way that we could make this work. It was strange because we really did love each other in so many ways, but we were faced with something where compromise was impossible for either of us. Because we didn't want to hurt each other, Susan and I tried to make the whole process as easy as possible. Once we accepted that our marriage was over, we actually got along much better. We knew that this separation could drag on for years, so in order to avoid that, we made a decision to work out what each of us wanted out of the divorce by ourselves. By not including our parents in the divorce negotiations, we were quickly able to come up with an agreement that both of us could live with. The sticky part could have been how our kids would be raised, but I made an agreement that I hope was for the best, even though it pains me each time I think of it.

In Judaism, the religion of a child depends on the religion of the mother. I found that Susan was right when she explained that to me. Despite the fact that Eric had a circumcision, Eric was not Jewish. Jennie was not Jewish. My kids could not be accepted in the synagogue to which I began to go. I had to be a realist. To insist that we each educate our children in our own respective religions would only confuse them. Either they were Jewish or not, and according to Jewish law, they were not.[121] Once I came to terms with that fact, there was only one choice. It was best for them that I not interfere with that part of their education, and so, their religious training would be under my wife's guidance.

I always wonder if what I did at the time was the right thing to do. It's very common for divorces to be damaging to the children and that's something that Susan and I wanted to avoid more than anything else. If we fought I took a chance that I would be an enemy to my wife and she would be an enemy to me. It's hard enough for kids to see their parents apart. I didn't want to compound the issue by each of us trying to pull the children to our respective religions, especially since they wouldn't be accepted in my religion anyway. Although this was the best solution that we could think of, we knew that it would still be confusing for the kids when they saw one parent performing certain religious acts and the other parent conducting a completely different set of acts. But I'm leaving something out.

To make this whole memory easier for me, I tried to think of the negotiations with Susan as a business deal, with me sitting on one side of the table and her on the other. I pictured us going over the points of contention and then coming to an agreement, shaking hands and walking away. But it wasn't really like that. I was lucky in a way, because Susan and I didn't fight. We avoided performing a re-enactment of Kramer vs. Kramer[122], but what's lucky in one sense is unlucky in another. As I sat across from Susan to decide how we should spend the rest of our lives apart, I'm not ashamed to admit that many tears flowed from my eyes and when I looked at her face and considered we wouldn't be together, there was a weight on my chest that made breathing difficult. There were frequent moments when I considered reconciling, thinking that she was worth anything, even if I were to sacrifice my religion.

We're brought up in a society where it's felt that love conquers all. Movies portray nothing standing in the way of true love. Neither social status, religion nor the color of one's skin poses an impediment if two people really care for each other. In real life, in England, we've seen a successor to the throne of England abdicate the crown in order to marry the woman he loved.[123] Love is the ultimate happy ending.

But when I imagine myself back with Susan, despite my tears, and my labored breathing, something jars me. I realize that I'm willing to give up my beliefs, but did she love me enough to give up hers? The answer made me try to be strong and stoic, but the reality is that my tears still flowed and the weight remained on my chest.

The whole divorce process took place over the course of three months. You would have thought that this was a down period for me, but the down period was still ahead. Susan got engaged.

After a divorce comes an emptiness, especially when there are children involved. Where once you would share duties around the house; where once you would help each other take care of the kids; where once you would have someone to share stories with at night, you find that you no longer have that someone else. When it's your ex who fills that emptiness first, a wave of jealousy and self doubt rises within you. As much as you try, you can never muster up that feeling of happiness for that other person because you're weighed down by what appears to be the bleakness of your own circumstances.

It turned out that the man she was engaged to had been a friend of hers when they were teenagers. He was the son of one of her father's partners. He had liked her from way back, but since he was only a year older than her, and he knew he would be in school for several years more, he didn't want to pursue the relationship. He had hoped that she would still be single when he felt that he was ready. My marriage to Susan killed those plans, but only temporarily, it seems.

When I was first going through these feelings, my father told me of something his grandfather related to him. It was a story about King Solomon, who was supposedly the wisest man who ever lived. He always wore a particular ring, and on it was inscribed the phrase "This too shall pass." When things were good so that King Solomon would feel haughty, he would look at the ring and his haughtiness would vanish. When things were going badly, he would again look at the ring, and his hope in the future would be restored. That's something that each of us should learn to do.

It was after that, that I looked at Susan's life in a different light. I took the time to get to know her fiancé, and after they were married, it didn't bother me as much to know that he was with my kids. He was a good person, and everyone deserved to have a proper life. Mine would come soon enough.

I learned something from Susan. Sometimes you're so busy looking for that special someone in far off places that you don't bother looking in your own backyard. Susan was lucky. There was someone standing very close to her who was interested in her. She had never thought to notice him until after the divorce. She now has someone who has the same background, and they share the religious values that I know are a big part of Susan's life. Once I saw past my own emotions I was able to feel happiness for Susan, and I think that's what helped me to get married again as well.

I often think of the unusual way that me and my wife, Sarah, got together. After Steven and I bumped into her in the airport, I got a call from her brother Morris, and we ended up renewing our friendship. Occasionally Sarah happened to be around, but I never thought of her as anyone other than my friend's sister. Morris helped me deal with my divorce, and it was really him who pointed out that Susan was able to find someone who was closer to home, and that maybe I should do the same. I didn't realize it at the time, but he had in mind for me to take out his sister, but he didn't want to push. Just before Susan's marriage I ended up taking out Sarah, and I found her to be a very comfortable person to be around. It wasn't love at first sight, although she is a very pretty girl, but there was something about her personality that allowed me to just be myself. The best thing was that I didn't have to worry about covering up my past, and by the third date I knew that I could be with her forever. Someone once said that he knew he was in love, not because of how special his girlfriend was, but because of how special she made him feel when he was with her. That's how it is with me and Sarah.

It's now been two years since Eric's sickness, almost two years to the day. Tonight happens to be the first night of Hanukah, and as I had set up the Hanukah menorahs earlier today, I thought of how much I changed in such a short time. Back then, I was counted among the Jews who wanted to be part of the American culture, and as a result, I was an American who happened to be Jewish instead of a Jew who happened to be American. In fact, even being a Jew was not something that I would broadcast, and if not for my last name, it would never even come up.

My brother in law, Morris, brought out a very interesting point when he explained what this holiday was all about. During the time when the miracle of the oil first happened, the Greeks were the dominant culture of the world. At that time, many Jews chose to abandon their Judaism and join the Greek culture. Oddly enough, they did it for the same reason that so many Jews today identify with the American secular culture instead of their own heritage.

Jews of today are identified with the atrocities of the Holocaust. In the years before that, we were expelled from Spain, Portugal, France and England. Over the centuries, we suffered through the hundreds of pogroms directed at us throughout Russia, Europe and the Middle East. In other words, from the perspective of both the Jew and non Jew, the Jew is always portrayed as the eternal victim.

Though Jews tried to fight off whoever their oppressors were at the time, they were never strong enough. Jews are then faced with a difficult problem. How do we shirk off that label of victim so that we can feel equal to the citizens of our adopted countries? Rather than having pride in being Jewish, millions of Jews have chosen to remove themselves from the religious practices that define them as Jews so they can blend into the general population. But all we're doing is re-living the unsuccessful pattern set by the Jews of over two thousand years ago. They too joined the popular culture of their own day in order to distance themselves from the label of 'Jewish victim' that was also attached to the Jews of that time period. We don't realize that it's only when we accept that label that we allow ourselves to be defined by it. We have to break from that way of thinking. It is this holiday that shows us that hiding our Judaism is not the answer. The Jews of that time period rose up and were not ashamed to say that they were different. The Hanukah lights remind us of what they did, and they tell us that the only lifestyle for us is to again act as the people of the book by returning to our religious roots with pride.

The Hanukah lights remind us of how we were able to discard our image of being the victim and become the people that G-d wants us to be. When we light the candles and think of what they signify we are made aware that a Jew must never dwell on the portions of our history where we were the beleaguered Jew, but on the fact that we were and continue to be a light unto the world with our moral and religious teachings. Leo Tolstoy once wrote:[124]

"What is a Jew, who never allowed himself to be led astray by all the earthly possessions which his oppressors and persecutors constantly offered him in order that he should change his faith and forsake his own Jewish religion?

"The Jew is that sacred being who has brought down from heaven the everlasting fire and has illuminated with it the entire world. He is the religious source, spring and fountain out of which all the rest of the peoples have drawn their beliefs and their religions. . . . Such a nation cannot be destroyed. The Jew is as everlasting as eternity itself."

This was the story of my own Hanukah miracle. I've finally come to appreciate the Jewish heritage that my great grandfather offered to my father so many years ago.

ENDNOTES

1   This refers to the story of the Hebrew sage Hillel which is explained in the Talmud in the section of Masechet Shabbat 31a. According to the story, a man came to the Hebrew sage named Shamai, and asked him to teach him the Bible while the man stood on one foot. Shamai threw the man out. The man then went to Hillel and asked the same question to which Hillel replied "Do not do onto others as you would not want done to yourself. The rest is just commentary. Go and learn it." The Bible consists of the written Bible which is the five books of Moses, and the various other writings, and the explanation to the Bible called the Talmud. The reference to the man standing on one foot referred to the man asking to learn the Bible without referring to the Talmud. In Judaism, we need both to fully understand the true meaning of the written text.

2   Don't Know Much About History by Kenneth C. Davis. Chapter 3: Growth of a Nation: What three letter word is not in the Constitution?

3   See The Lunar Men by Jenny Uglow

4   See Don't Know Much About History by Kenneth C. Davis. Chapter 3: Growth of a Nation: What three letter word is not in the Constitution?. In speaking about Jefferson and religion, Mr. Davis writes "Jefferson had also once produced an edited version of the Gospels (still available in book form as The Jefferson Bible) in which he highlighted the moral and ethical teachings of Jesus while editing out any reference to his divinity of miracles."

5   Fait acomplis: French expression meaning an action that is already completed.

6   The Jewish festival of Hanukah takes place on the 25th of the Hebrew month of Kislev. As the Hebrew calendar is arranged according to the solar year as well as the lunar month, the corresponding date in the Gregorian calendar changes each year but usually takes place some time in December. Because of the proximity of the Xmas holiday to that of Hanukah, there is a practice by some non-Orthodox Jews to combine the holidays and set up a tree which they call a Hanukah Bush.

7   The menorah is a type of candleholder which holds eight candles, one for each night of the holiday of Hanukah, as well as one separate candle which is lit each night of the holiday. The menorah that we use is symbolic of the Menorah made of solid gold which was used in the two Holy Temples which existed in Jerusalem.

8   Matzah is a type of unleavened bread that is used during the holiday of Passover.

9   High Holidays refers to the holidays of Rosh Hashana which translates as "the beginning of the Hebrew year", as well as the holiday of Yom Kippur which is known as the Day of Atonement. They are sacred days which determine the events of the coming year for each person in the world.

10   See Eccesiastes. Chapter 1, sentence 9. "and there is no new thing under the sun".

11   Reference is to the soliloquy of Hamlet in Shakespeare's play of the same name. See chapter 3.1 "To be, or not to be: that is the question: Whether 'tis nobler in the mind to suffer The slings and arrows of outrageous fortune, Or to take arms against a sea of troubles, And by opposing end them?"

12   See the Book of Job, one of the 24 books that make up the whole Jewish written Bible, which begins with the five books of Moses (Genesis through Deuteronomy)

13   Adapted from an interview of John Eldridge by James Dobson of the radio program, Focus on the Family. The later remarks of Father Baldino which are spoken in his office are also taken from the remarks by Mr. Eldridge in that same interview.

14   Refer to the Sephardic Institute Newsletter on the portion of the Bible known in Hebrew as Mishpatim, specifically Exodus, Chapter 21. The topic of the newsletter is entitled "Innovations in Law and Contrast to the Preceding". It is explained there that the Code of Hammurabi was the leading Mesopotamian law collection of the second Millennium B.C.E. It was established by the king of Babylon in the 18th century B.C.E. and was said to contain approximately 320 paragraphs of various laws. These laws predate the giving of the Bible to Moses by about five hundred years.

15   Tefillin are religious articles worn during morning prayers with the exception of the prayers of the Sabbath and certain Jewish holidays.

16   Rabbi Yehuda Loevy ben Bezalel became the chief Rabbi of Prague in the year 1572 and was known as the Maharal of Prague. He was born in the year 1513 and passed away in the year 1609.

17   See the Yeshivat Har Etzion lecture series on the holiday of Hanukah called Understanding Aggada: The Miracle of Hanukah part 7

18   Don't Know Much About History by Kenneth C. Davis. Chapter 2: What was the shot heard round the world/ Milestones in the American Revolution.

19   A Revolutionary War Hanukah Story by Evelyn Solomon Haies. Jewish Press. December 14, 2001.

20   Based on an actual medical case as described in Discover Magazine of August 1998. P. 42.

21   Based on an actual medical case as described in Discover Magazine of August 2004. P.30

22   "Hanukah—The Real Story" by Rabbi Ariel Bar Tzadok. December 20, 2000. See *www.koshertorah.com*

23   The earlier pronunciation of the name of the leader of the Macabees was written as Matisyahu. The spelling here is Matityahu. The Jews who originate from Europe have a different pronunciation of the Hebrew language as compared to the Jews who were already in various countries of the Middle East. The former spelling is according to the speaking patterns of the European Jews (also referred to as Ashkenaz Jews) and the latter spelling is according to the speaking patterns of the Jews in the Middle East. (Also known as Sephardic Jews.) David Greenblatt is an Ashkenaz Jew, while Isaac is a Sephardic Jew.

24   The Story of Hanukah by Rabbi Shalom Klass. Jewish Press. November 22, 2002.

25   Columbus Cracks an Egg by Stephen Jay Gould. Natural History Magazine. December 1992. Page 4.

26   Foiled—Hitler's Jewish Olympian—The Helene Mayer Story by Milly Mogulof.

27   Foiled—Hitler's Jewish Olympian—The Helene Mayer Story by Milly Mogulof. "The Early Years in Offenbach". Page 27.

28   Foiled—Hitler's Jewish Olympian—The Helene Mayer Story by Milly Mogulof. "Helene and the Games". Pages 155-6.

29   The Gay Divorcee (1934) With Fred Astaire, Ginger Rogers, and Edward Everett Horton.

30   Genesis. Chapter 21, sentences 9-13.

31   "The Truth About Science" by Rabbi Eli Mansour. Community Magazine. October 2003. Page 18.

32   A Short History of Nearly Everything. By Bill Bryson. Part III: A New Age Dawns—Einstein's Universe. "The most challenging and nonintuitive of all the concepts in the general theory of relativity is the idea that time is part of space. . . . According to Einstein, time is variable and ever changing. It even has shape. It is bound up—"Inextricably interconnected" in Stephen Hawking's expression—with the three dimensions of space in a curious dimension known as spacetime."

33   The Sex Lives of Scales by Benjamin Normark. Natural History Magazine. September 2004. P. 38

34   The Reality of Miracles by Rabbi Dovid Gottlieb. The ideas in this argument are presented in an audio tape of an actual classroom lecture given by Rabbi Gottlieb of Or Sameach in Jerusalem. The lecture was aired on a radio program called "A Taste of Torah". The article in Natural History Magazine, which came later, just happens to support his argument.

35 Rabbi Avigdor Miller. Audio tape #26 on Christianity.

36 Certain laws cannot be changed at all, but there are laws that could be changed temporarily due to special circumstances. In order to do so, however, the Sanhedrin, which is the 71 member ruling religious body, had to make a ruling to that effect. No single person, no matter how holy, had the power to modify a law on his own.

37 The Perils of Pauline was a serial that was shown in the movies during the time of the silent films. At the end of each segment, the main character, Pauline, was left in a life threatening situation from which there appeared to be no escape. Moviegoers would have to wait until the next episode to see how she would be saved.

38 The actual quote in John is as follows: John 16:13 "Howbeit when he, the Spirit of truth, is come, he will guide you into all truth: for he shall not speak of himself; but whatsoever he shall hear, that shall he speak: and he will show you things to come."

39 Jeremiah Chapter 31, sentence 31.

40 John 3, sentence 3. "Jesus answered and said unto him, Verily, verily, I say unto thee, Except a man be born again, he cannot see the kingdom of God."

41 Mathew. Chapter 19, sentence 14. "But Jesus said, Suffer little children, and forbid them not, to come unto me: for of such is the kingdom of heaven."

42 Colossians. Chapter 2, sentence 11-12. "In whom also ye are circumcised with the circumcision made without hands, in putting off the body of the sins of the flesh by the circumcision of Christ: Buried with him in baptism, wherein also ye are risen with him through the faith of the operation of God, who hath raised him from the dead."

43 Peter hinted to the idea of Limbo of the Fathers in Acts. Chapter 3, sentence 20-24. "And he shall send Jesus Christ, which before was preached unto you: Whom the heaven must receive until the times of restitution of all things, which God hath spoken by the mouth of all his holy prophets since the world began. For Moses truly said unto the fathers, A prophet shall the Lord your God raise up unto you of your brethren, like unto me; him shall ye hear in all things whatsoever he shall say unto you. And it shall come to pass, that every soul, which will not hear that prophet, shall be destroyed from among the people. Yea, and all the prophets from Samuel and those that follow after, as many as have spoken, have likewise foretold of these days." Based on this and other passages, the Church created the phrase called the Limbo of the Fathers during the Middle Ages. The actual phrase does not appear in the Biblical text itself. According to the Random House Dictionary, "There are two forms of **limbo.** One is called **limbus patrum** 'limbo of the fathers'. It is the place where the righteous of the Old Testament, who had died before Christ's coming, dwelt until Christ "descended into hell" and released them to heavenly bliss. This was known in the Middle Ages as "the harrowing

of hell" ("harrowing" in the sense of 'plundering', related to "harry") and was believed to have taken place after Christ's crucifixion and before his ascension. The harrowing of hell was a popular theme in medieval literature and art. The other **limbo** is called **limbus infantium** 'limbo of the children' and is the place where unbaptized infants dwell forever. They cannot enter heaven because they have not been freed of original sin through baptism, but they have no other sin so they are not condemned to hell. There have been considerable differences of opinion for many centuries concerning the nature of this **limbo**—some theologians have declared it to be a happy place while others have said there must be an element of sadness because the denial of entrance to heaven is, by definition, a punishment."

[44] Jon Stewart interviewed on Larry King Live

[45] Leviticus. Chapter 25, sentence 35-41,55. Also Deuteronomy. Chapter 15, sentence 12-14.

[46] Sephardic Institute Newsletter. Parashat Mishpatim Part II Concerning Slavery. Discussion of the attitude that Jews are to have regarding slavery. A quote from the Talmud is given: "The Sages remark "Whosoever purchases a Hebrew slave is as if he purchased a master for himself."" (Babylonian Talmud Qid. 20a) When the issue of a non Israelite slave is brought up, a quote is brought from the book of Job to show how a slave must be treated as a fellow human being. "Did I ever reject the just cause of my man-servant or my maid-servant when they contended with me? What then would I do when G-d rises up, when He calls me to account what would I answer him? Is not He who made me in the stomach made him; did not One form us both in the womb?" (Job Chapter 31, sentence 13-15)

[47] Deuteronomy. Chapter 20, sentence 19

[48] Leviticus. Chapter 19, sentence 10

[49] Resurrection by Leo Tolstoy. Book III, Chapter IV

[50] A mezuzah is a rectangle box that is affixed to the right side of a door frame and which contains a scroll on which is written certain sections from the Bible.

[51] Shabbos, Day of Rest by Rabbi Dovid Gottlieb. The concepts of the holiness and uniqueness of the Sabbath which are contained in this section are presented in an audio tape of an actual classroom lecture given by Rabbi Gottlieb of Or Sameach in Jerusalem. This lecture was aired on a radio program called "A Taste of Torah".

[52] Exodus. Chapter 20, sentence 8-11.

[53] Leviticus. Chapter 19, sentence 2. "Speak unto all the congregation of the children of Israel, and say unto them, Ye shall be holy: for I the LORD your God am holy."

[54] Leviticus. Chapter 26, sentence 14.

[55] Leviticus. Chapter 26, sentence 32.

[56] Leviticus. Chapter 26, sentence 33.

[57] Leviticus. Chapter 26, sentence 45.

[58] The Phenomenon of Jewish Survival by Rabbi Dovid Gottlieb. Some of the concepts of the meaning of Jewish survival which are contained in this section are presented in an audio tape of an actual classroom lecture given by Rabbi Gottlieb of Or Sameach in Jerusalem. This lecture was aired on a radio program called "A Taste of Torah".

[59] Matthew. Chapter 5, sentence 18-19.

[60] John. Chapter 9, sentence 1-16.

[61] Matthew. Chapter 12, sentence 1-2

[62] A Rabbi Talks with Jesus by Jacob Neusner. P.62-63. Mr. Neusner questions the right of Jesus to advise his disciples to break the Sabbath. He quotes Matthew, Chapter 12, sentence 9-12 in which Jesus is questioned as to why he advised others to break the Sabbath, and the reply of Jesus in sentence 12 was "So it is lawful to do good on the Sabbath". Mr. Neusner brings out the point that " . . . that statement is simply beside the point; the Sabbath is not about doing good or not doing good; the issue of the Sabbath is holiness, and in the Torah, to be holy is to be like G-d."

[63] The Hebrew alphabet can also be used to signify numbers. The word hesed in Hebrew is spelled with three Hebrew letters. The letter pronounced as Het, which is also the number 8; the letter pronounced as Samech, which is also the number 60; and the letter pronounced as Daled, which is also the number 4. The total is 72.

[64] Genesis. Chapter 32, sentence 32. "Therefore the children of Israel eat not of the sinew which shrank, which is upon the hollow of the thigh, unto this day: because he touched the hollow of Jacob's thigh in the sinew that shrank."

[65] Rabbi Avigdor Miller. Audio tape #26 on Christianity.

[66] Rav Bartenura and Rav Tzadok of Lublin are quoted in a book which is published in Hebrew called Otzrot Aharit Hayamim. The seventh chapter reviews details of The Messiah and the comments of both Rav Batenura and Rav Tzadok are quoted related to this topic.

[67] Matthew. Chapter 5, sentence 33-34.

[68] Matthew. Chapter 5, sentence 27-28.

[69] 71 member council known as the Sanhedrin.

[70] Matthew. Chapter 5, sentence 43-44, 48.

[71] A Rabbi Talks with Jesus by Jacob Neusner. P.27. According to Mr. Neusner, the passage in the New Testament "cites a saying not to be found in the Torah, which contains no commandment to hate one's enemies . . . . Anyone who knows the Torah will wonder where we are supposed to have heard that commandment which G-d did not command Moses to tell us."

[72] Matthew. Chapter 12, sentence 46-50. "While he yet talked to the people, behold, his mother and his brethren stood without, desiring to speak with him. Then one

said unto him, Behold, thy mother and thy brethren stand without, desiring to speak with thee. But he answered and said unto him that told him, Who is my mother? and who are my brethren? And he stretched forth his hand toward his disciples, and said, Behold my mother and my brethren! For whosoever shall do the will of my Father which is in heaven, the same is my brother, and sister, and mother."

73   Matthew. Chapter 6, sentence 5-6.

74   A Kingdom of Priests and a Holy Nation by Rav Yair Kahn. Distributed through Yeshiva Har Etzion. Korah claimed that the entire Jewish nation were a kingdom of priests, and therefore "there was no need for a separate priestly class. Although (the Jews) did not challenge Moshe's authority, they nonetheless identified with Korah's argument." It made sense to them to question why they should be barred from the sacrificial services because of the way Korah raised the question, but, Rav Kahn explains, "this barrier was not unilaterally imposed upon (the Jews) by G-d. It was erected with the implicit consent of the people." When taken in context, the logic of Korah was a twisted logic that did not make sense if fully thought out. Being in the presence of the Almighty on a constant basis is extremely demanding and "Behavior which under usual circumstances is acceptable, becomes intolerable within the context of the sanctuary. Normal human reactions of anger and grief must be suppressed. Emotional outbursts are unacceptable." When the arguments of Jesus were first heard, on the surface, they seem reasonable, but when they are examined from the point of view of the religion as a whole, they immediately fall short.

75   Aram Soba Newsletter. Commentary on Leviticus, Chapter 16, sentence 30. This story is given with a reference to the source as "Vedibarta Bam".

76   The first prayer of the grouping of the prayers said in the morning, is the prayer cited here. It is also referred to by the first few words of the prayer in the original Hebrew. (The Modeh Ani).

77   Leviticus. Chapter 24, sentence 10-16.

78   The Law of the Blasphemer by Rav Amnon Bazak distributed through Yeshivat Har Etzion. A commentary on the section of the Bible referred to as Emor.

79   Leviticus. Chapter 24, sentence 16.

80   The Scarlet Letter by Nathaniel Hawthorne. Hester Prynne was a main character in the story who lived during the Puritan era in the United States. She bore a child through an adulterous affair and was forced to wear the letter "A" embroidered on the front of her dress.

81   Quoted from a lecture by Rabbi Raymond Beyda.

82   All descriptions of the restaurant Alto are based on a review in the website, *http://newyork.citysearch.com*.

[83] Mark. Chapter 7, sentence 18-19.

[84] American Museum of Natural History. The Discovery Room is an actual exhibit in the Museum. The description shown here is based on the information presented in the Museum's web site.

[85] Real World Advice for the Young by Richard Karlgaard. Forbes. April 11, 2005. Page 41.

[86] Refer to the Sephardic Institute Newsletter on the portion of the Bible known in Hebrew as Mishpatim, specifically Exodus, Chapter 21. The topic of the newsletter is entitled "Innovations in Law and Contrast to the Preceding". Certain sections of the actual code are presented, which are copied in this section.

[87] Refer to the Jewish Talmud. Baba Qama 8:1. Also see a commentary in the Sephardic Institute Newsletter on the portion of the Bible in Exodus known as Mishpatim. "Parashat Mishpatim Part III on 'An Eye For An Eye'".

[88] In the section of the Talmud known as the Mishnah, in Masechet Sanhedrin, Chapter 4, part 5 (Perek 4, Mishnah 5), it states in our modern versions that "Therefore, Man was created as a single person so that it will be known that anyone who takes the life of a single person from the nation of Israel, it's as if he destroyed a whole world." The comparison, though, doesn't make sense, because the simile should include all mankind, and not only individual people from the nation of Israel. In the Library of the Hungarian Academy of Sciences, Budapest, there exists one of the earliest versions of this section. The word "Israel" is not shown. The original intent by the writers of the Mishnah, then, was that taking the life of any person, whether he or she is from the nation of Israel or not, is the equivalent of destroying a world.

[89] Sephardic Institute Newsletter. Parashat Mishpatim Part II Concerning Slavery. Discussion of the attitude that Jews are to have regarding slavery.

[90] What Bush Said—And What He Left Out by Robert Miller. Jewish Press. October 14, 2005. Page 7.

[91] The War for Civilization by Phyllis Chesler. Jewish Press. November 4, 2005. Page 7

[92] Infidels: A History of the Conflict Between Christendom and Islam by Andrew Wheatcroft. Throughout the book, atrocities are listed which were done by both Muslim and Christian alike during their wars between each other. In addition, see also Genghis Khan and the Making of the Modern World by Jack Weatherford. He presents atrocities performed by both religions against each other, and by each religion against the Jews. See Page 246-7. During the period in which the Bubonic Plague was spreading throughout Europe, Jews were massacred as they had been throughout the centuries. "In Europe, the Christians once again turned on the Jews . . . . On Valentine's Day in 1349, the authorities of Strasbourg herded two thousand Jews to the cemetery outside of the city to begin a mass burning . . . . City after city picked up the practice of publicly burning Jews to thwart the epidemic . . . . between

November 1348 and September 1349, all the Jews between Cologne and Austria had been burned."

[93] Second Timothy. Chapter 3, sentence 16.

[94] Luke. Chapter 6, sentence 29.

[95] Luke. Chapter 19, sentence 27.

[96] Matthew. Chapter 10, sentence 34.

[97] John. Chapter 15, sentence 16.

[98] Galileo's Daughter by Dave Sobel. Chapter One. A reconstruction of the events surrounding Galileo's life based on surviving letters written to Galileo by his daughter.

[99] Galileo's Daughter by Dave Sobel. Section of Appendix entitled "In Galileo's Time" giving a timeline of the events in Galileo's life.

[100] "The Truth About Science" by Rabbi Eli Mansour. Community Magazine. October 2003. Page 18.

[101] As quoted in the Sephardic Institute Newletter on Genesis. Part 1, page 4.

[102] Immortality, Resurrection and the Age of the Universe—A Kabbalistic View by Rabbi Aryeh Kaplan. Chapter 1.

[103] The End of Days by Rabbi Sammy Sitt. An audio lecture on the Biblical information on the Messianic Age and the various interpretations of that information by Biblical scholars.

[104] Hessian soldiers.

[105] The name, Malbim, stands for Rabbi Meir Leibush ben Yechiel Michel. He wrote many commentaries on the Bible and lived 1809-1879.

[106] Otto von Bismarck, His Life and Legacy. As explained in Wikipedia.

[107] Foiled—Hitler's Jewish Olympian—The Helene Mayer Story by Milly Mogulof. Chapter on The Jewish Legacy. Page 21.

[108] The Nitrogen Bomb by David E. and Marshall Jon Fisher. Discover Magazine. April 2001.

[109] The Chofetz Chaim is the Rabbi known as Rabbi Yisroel Meir HaCohen of Radin, Poland. He lived from 1838-1933 and was considered one of the greatest Rabbis of his generation. He was most known for his book on the laws of proper speech (avoiding speaking ill of others) and used as the preface for his book the sentences in Psalms, chapter 34, sentence 13-14: "Who is the man who wants life and loves many days that he may see good? Keep your tongue from evil and lips from speaking deceit." The Hebrew for "who wants life" is translated as chofetz chaim, and after his book on proper speech was published Rabbi Yisroel Meir HaCohen was known as the Chofetz Chaim.

[110] Genesis. Chapter 21, sentences 22-34. Treaty between Abraham and Abimelech, King of the Philistines.

111 From Time Immemorial by Joan Peters. Page 139. Based on an excerpt from the historian, Bernard Lewis.

112 Most Favored Nation Status by Rabbi Eli Mansour. Community Magazine. July-August 2004. An excerpt is presented from Professor Sir John William Dawson from over one hundred years ago. "Until today, no people have succeeded in establishing national dominion in the land of Israel. The mixed multitude of itinerant tribes that managed to settle there did so on lease, as temporary residents. It seems that they await the return of the permanent residents of the land."

113 Most Favored Nation Status by Rabbi Eli Mansour. Community Magazine. July-August 2004. An excerpt from the writings of Mark Twain after his trip to Israel of 1867. "We never saw a human being on the whole route . . . . There was hardly a tree or a shrub anywhere. Even the olive and the cactus, those fast friends of a worthless soil, had almost deserted the country. No landscape exists that is more tiresome to the eye than that which bounds the approaches to Jerusalem . . . . It is a hopeless, dreary, heart-broken land."

114 The information presented here and in the next few paragraphs was taken from an interview conducted on NPR radio by Brian Lehrer. Two sides of the Jewish Arab conflict in Israel were being presented. For the Jewish side, there was a Professor Wasserstein, and for the Arab point of view, there was a Professor Sayid. The information taken is solely from Professor Sayid.

115 Refer to the JWA.org website. History of Emma Lazarus. A description of the time period in which she lived is presented.

116 Jewish Statemanship by Professor Paul Eidelberg. Japan and Democracy. Jewish Press. October 21, 2005.

117 Meet You in Hell by Les Standiford. Part One, Chapter 5.

118 JWA.org. History of Emma Lazarus.

119 Psalms. Chapter 37, sentence 25-26.

120 According to the laws of family purity, a woman must immerse herself at a certain time, according to her menstrual cycle. It is approximately once per month. There are laws which dictate the exact time, etc. Once a woman does this she is permitted to have relations with her husband. Another act which falls mainly on the woman to perform is the lighting of the Sabbath candles. Two candles are lit just before the onset of the Sabbath, and prayers are recited. There are procedures to be learned and followed in this instance as well.

121 (As quoted from the weekly article called The Rambam Yomi by Rabbi Abraham Stone in the Jewish Press.) According to the Laws of Prohibited Relations by Rabbi Moshe ben Maimon (Maimonides) in Chapter 12:7 "This sin—of having relations with a non-Jewish woman although it is not punishable by death at the hands of the Beth Din (Rabbinical court)—should not be taken lightly, since it causes a loss

which is not found in all other prohibited relations with a Jewish woman. For a son born from the latter relations is his son in all respects and is considered a Jew, although he is a mamzer (illicit child). Whereas a son born from a non-Jewish woman is not his son, as it is written (Deueronomy 7:4) 'For he will turn away your son from Me'—that is, he removes him from following Hashem." Based on the Talmud: Tractate Yevamot 21a.

[122] Kramer vs Kramer. (1979) A well known movie starring Meryl Streep and Dustin Hoffman, in which they play two parents, who both happen to be attorneys getting a divorce and who are involved in a custody battle.

[123] According to Brittania.com/history/monarchs, Edward VIII, eldest son of George V and Mary of Teck, was born June 23, 1894. He married an American divorcee, Wallis Simpson, abdicating the throne on December 10, 1936, after reigning for only eleven months. The couple failed to produce children; Edward died in 1972.

[124] Most Favored Nation Status by Rabbi Eli Mansour. Community Magazine. July-August 2004.

Printed in the United States
106531LV00008B/162/A